KU-287-896

On a rainy night in Steedman Street, near the Elephant and Castle, a figure lay motionless on the pavement – the first victim of the Walworth strangler. For some reason the murderer was obsessed with fair hair and every time a lock of hair was taken.

Constable Harry Bradshaw, tramping the streets of London looking for clues, found himself becoming deeply involved with the Wilson family – involved to the extent of sending them anonymous parcels of food – and trying to find out more about their new lodger. For Maggie Wilson, the gutsy young widow trying to hold her family together, thought the new lodger seemed very nice indeed, even if he did have some very funny ways. Harry Bradshaw didn't like him at all – especially when he considered Maggie had fair hair.

THE LODGER

Mary Jane Staples

CORGI BOOKS

THE LODGER

A CORGI BOOK 0 552 13730 8

First publication in Great Britain

PRINTING HISTORY
Corgi edition published 1991

This book is set in 10/11pt Plantin
by Busby The Printers Ltd, Exeter

Corgi Books are published by Transworld Publishers Ltd,
61–63 Uxbridge Road, Ealing, London W5 5SA, in Australia by
Transworld Publishers (Australia) Pty. Ltd, 15–23 Helles
Avenue, Moorebank, NSW 2170, and in New Zealand by Transworld
Publishers (N.Z.) Ltd, Cnr Moselle and Waipareira Avenues,
Henderson, Auckland.

Printed and bound in Great Britain by
Cox & Wyman Ltd, Reading, Berks

CHAPTER ONE

Miss Russell, the history teacher at West Square School for Girls, put another question to her class concerning the unfortunate monarch, Charles I.

'What was the date of his execution? Yes, Ellen?'

'It was in the winter, Miss Russell,' said Ellen Noakes.

'Can't we do better than that? Can you, Trary?'

Trary Wilson, refreshingly engaging, said, 'January thirty, 1649, Miss Russell.' Miss Russell smiled. Trary Wilson was bright in every way.

'Quite right, Trary. Can anyone tell me what followed his execution?'

'The Commonwealth, miss!' cried a dozen girls.

'And what did that do for the country?'

'It let Parliament rule instead of the King,' said Agnes Moore.

'Blessed bliss that was, I don't think,' said Trary.

'Would you like to stand up and enlarge on that remark?' invited Miss Russell, and Trary came willingly to her feet in her old school frock.

'Well, Miss Russell, I think – '

'She's off,' said Agnes Moore, but most of the girls sat up in happy anticipation. Most were Trary's champions, even if she was awfully poor.

'No interruptions, if you don't mind,' said Miss Russell, fifty-four years old and highly practised in the art of maintaining order. 'Proceed, Trary.'

'Well, Miss Russell, first I think Oliver Cromwell had a blessed cheek signin' the order for the King's execution after what he'd done himself, rampagin' up and down the country – '

'Pardon?' said Miss Russell. 'What was that word?'

'Rampagin', Miss Russell,' said Trary, born in 1894 and very ready on this April day in 1908 to show that the years in between had not been wasted. 'Well, that's what it was, I think, all his persecutin' of people who weren't Puritan, breakin' up religious images, damaging castles, puttin' the King's Cavaliers to the sword, and then cuttin' the King's head off. And he didn't really let Parliament rule, everyone had to do what he said. He stopped people dancing and singing, and havin' country fairs and puttin' up maypoles. He told them they'd all got to live in misery because God didn't like people goin' about smiling, specially on a Sunday.'

The girls giggled. Trary Wilson was a riot once she got going.

Keeping her face straight, Miss Russell asked, 'Did he tell them that, Trary?'

'Oh, I'm pleased you asked, Miss Russell, and don't you think Oliver Cromwell accusin' the King of being an absolute monarch was like the pot callin' the kettle black?'

'Yes, we might argue that, Trary, but you haven't answered my question.'

'What question was that, Miss Russell?'

'Did Oliver Cromwell tell the people they'd all got to live in misery?'

'Well, Miss Russell,' said Trary, 'I don't think he actu'lly told them, I don't think he knocked on their doors and said it, I think he let it be known.'

'Let it be known? Yes, I see.' Miss Russell's gravity masked her appreciation of Trary's entertainment value.

'Yes, you can let things be known if you're a king or a Lord Protector, Miss Russell. I'm sure the people didn't like livin' gloomy lives, I think it made them rotten ratty.' Trary paused for thought. 'Well, imagine no dancing or singing, and not being able to do a knees-up, and 'aving to read the Bible all day every Sunday.' Trary dropped an unusual aitch.

'All day every Sunday?' enquired Miss Russell, entranced.

'Oh, as good as, don't you think so, Miss Russell? I think the Bible's very religious, and that bits of it ought to be read during Scripture lessons, but not all day every Sunday.'

'Is there anything more you'd like to say?' asked Miss Russell.

'Well, only that I don't think it was right the King's head being cut off in front of all the people in White'all.' Another aitch went absent. Trary, conscious of her slip, frowned at herself. 'The King couldn't have liked that very much, it was a cryin' shame, really, because he was a husband an' father as well as a monarch. That's all, Miss Russell.' Trary sat down.

'Well, class?' said Miss Russell, and the girls clapped.

'Oh, you are a laugh, Trary,' said Jane Atkins, seated next to her.

'I didn't say anything funny,' declared Trary.

'We'll begin our next history lesson by discussing some of the points raised by Trary,' said Miss Russell, at which point the bell signalling the end of classes was heard. 'Over the weekend, think about everything she said. Now, kindly tidy your desks. Then you may leave, and without treading on each other.'

The girls made short work of tidying up, after which there was the usual rush for the door, which brought a rebuke from Miss Russell. She detained Trary, but waited for the classroom to clear before she spoke, except that Trary spoke first.

'Did I say something wrong, Miss Russell?'

'On the contrary, you were very good. Perhaps you over-simplified one or two things, but that's better than making too much of a meal of them.' Miss Russell eyed the thirteen-year-old girl kindly. 'Is everything all right at home?'

'Yes, thank you.' Trary answered politely. She just couldn't confess how awfully hard-up her mum was, and how she and her sisters were suffering hungry days.

7

'Well, look, if you don't mind getting home a little late, would you do an errand for me? I meant to do a little shopping after school, but there's a teachers' meeting, and the grocers down the road may be shut by the time it's over. Would you go and shop for me? I've made a little list of the things I need, and I'll give you my shopping bag, and threepence for going, of course.'

'Thruppence?' said Trary. That kind of errand was usually done for a ha'penny or a penny, and either coin was always gratefully received. 'That's an awful lot, Miss Russell, for an errand just down the road.'

'You'll be doing me a great favour,' said Miss Russell. It was one way of giving a little something to a girl who could look obvious poverty in the eye and challenge it to do its worst. For her part, Trary recognized kindness, but hoped her shabby frock didn't make her look as if the workhouse was looming for her and her family.

She did the errand at the grocers in St George's Road. The half-crown Miss Russell had provided her with felt a rich coin. It purchased tea, sugar, dried fruit, barley, rice, Scott's Porage Oats and two nutmegs, and still brought a little change from the till. She took the shopping back to the school. Miss Russell was at the teachers' meeting, and Trary left the items on her desk in the classroom, together with the change. On the desk was a little note of thanks from Miss Russell, and a silver threepenny bit.

Then, in her old straw boater and her rather limp-looking school frock, Trary made her way home to Charleston Street, close to St John's Church, Walworth. She began to think how to spend the threepence to the very best advantage. Three pounds of potatoes? No, you could get four pounds for threepence. Or half a loaf of bread and a pennyworth of cheese? Or a pound and a half of tomatoes? Or some sliced brawn? Or, if the Maypole Dairy had any cracked eggs left, six for the threepence? Eggs, yes. Mum could scramble them and serve them on toast for tea. Mum was ever so worried about being hard-up. Eggs would be best, or baked potatoes with salt and marge. Did they have any marge in the larder? Even if they did, baked potatoes would take a long time and use up such a lot of gas. Yes, eggs were favourite, if she could get six cracked ones.

She went to the Maypole in the Walworth Road, not far from home. Just inside the doorway stood the basket where cracked eggs were usually placed. But there were only three. She spoke to Mr Cummings, a nice man who served behind the long white marble counter. Did they have only three cracked eggs? She wanted six. Mr Cummings disappeared. He returned with four eggs in a small basket.

'Here we are, Trary, all fresh-cracked,' he said.

'Oh, you didn't just go an' crack them, did you?' she asked, glancing at the manager, who was talking to a customer at the far end of the counter.

'Well, no, that wouldn't be right, would it?' said Mr Cummings. He put the four eggs in a brown paper bag, went to the doorway basket and added the eggs there to the bag. Trary said she'd only got thruppence for six, he'd given her seven. Mr Cummings took the threepenny bit with a smile and a wink. 'Well, we don't want one cracked egg sittin' here all night, Trary. By the way, regards to your mum, and tell her our marge is down to a bargain price.'

'Thanks ever so much, Mr Cummings.' Trary took the bag of eggs. A couple were a little wet, but the cracks weren't ruinous. Holding the bag with care, she left the shop. As she did so, a young woman passed by. Such a nice little hat sat on hair which was as fair and bright as sunshine. A man coming the other way cast dazzled eyes at her. Blindly, he blundered into Trary, who almost dropped the bag of eggs. As it was, one plopped out and fell, breaking on the pavement. The man stopped, startled and apologetic. He wore a gas-company uniform, and beneath his peaked cap his blue eyes regarded her ruefully.

'Sorry, girlie, wasn't looking where I was going, now see what I've done.'

'It's all right,' said Trary, although she sorrowed for the lost egg.

'Don't move, stay there, won't be a tick, stay there now,' he said, and hurried into the Maypole. He was out again quite quickly. With a smile, he gave Trary another bag, a white one, containing three eggs.

'Oh, but I only bought cracked ones,' said Trary, 'and I only lost one, and you're giving me three new ones.'

'It's to make up for my clumsiness, you might've lost the lot,' he said.

'Oh, that's awf'lly kind,' she said. He smiled and went on his way, and she carried all nine eggs home to her hard-up mum and three sisters. Served scrambled on toast they were a golden feast, and Trary was voted best girl in the family.

A little after nine o'clock that evening, sixteen-year-old Bobby Reeves of East Street, Walworth, was on the outskirts of Dulwich. His wily father was about forty yards ahead of him, treading the pavements quietly. Bobby, a tall and long-legged boy, kept close to the front hedges of houses, tracking his dad with caution. Occasionally, Mr Reeves cast a casual look back, but Bobby was never more than an indistinguishable part of the darkness, and he knew, in any case, that his old man wasn't looking out for him. Street lamps weren't too much of a problem, they were far apart, and the light they shed was blurred by the damp and misty night air.

In Dulwich proper, the houses were large. Curtains or blinds masked the lamps of drawing-rooms. Ahead, Bobby noted the looming bulk of a three-storeyed mansion that looked in complete darkness. It sat back from a bend in the road. A figure materialized out of the shadow of a high brick wall fronting the residence. Jagged chunks of glass set in mortar along the top of the wall were cruelly deterring. Bobby saw his dad pass closed wrought-iron gates and meet the man who had appeared. A big tall bloke, he began a whispered conversation with Mr Reeves. Bobby, at a halt, watched them. He saw the big man pick something up and throw it over the wall. It hung down, covering the thick barrier of broken glass. Bobby guessed what it was, a long strip of tough coconut-fibre matting, probably about a yard wide. The neighbourhood was in total quiet, and his dad and the big tall man were going to climb that brick wall by way of the protective matting.

Tucked into the thick growth of a boxwood hedge, Bobby brought a scout whistle to his lips and blew two loud blasts. The sounds were as resonant as those of a police whistle. At once his father and the big man were away, running for their lives, and he watched them disappear into darkness around the bend.

'Dad, you need talkin' to,' he said, and was away himself, returning the way he had come before people came out of these big houses to investigate the reason for the whistle blasts.

His mother was up and waiting for him when he arrived home, by which time the April night had turned rainy. His two sisters were in bed.

'Well, were you right, Bobby?' asked Mrs Reeves.

'Wish I hadn't been, but I was,' said Bobby. 'I thought he was up to something when he said he might be 'ome a bit late tonight. I thought I'd best go after him an' see exactly what. He 'ad that look.'

'I didn't notice no look,' said Mrs Reeves, a plump and equable woman.

'No, well, you've got kind eyes, Ma, they don't notice funny looks. It was dad's holy look, the one that makes 'im seem as if he's thinkin' about all things bright an' beautiful. He's clever, yer know, he got off the tram at Brockwell Park an' walked to Dulwich from there.'

'What was clever about that?' asked Mrs Reeves, showing worry.

'It was so that no tram conductor could say a man who looked like dad took a ride to Dulwich on a partic'lar night

11

at a partic'lar time. I'm sorry to inform you, Ma, that we've got problems, an' that someone's got to talk to dad. Loudly. He won't like it comin' from me, so you'd better do it.'

'Bobby, you 'aven't said what 'e got up to.'

'He met a bloke at a house in Dulwich that looked as if no-one was at 'ome,' said Bobby. 'They were goin' to climb over the front wall. I blew the whistle on them, and they both bolted, reckonin' the rozzers had spotted 'em.'

'Oh, lor',' sighed Mrs Reeves, 'I suppose I'd better talk to 'im when 'e gets back.'

'Loudly,' said Bobby.

'I can't shout at 'im, it'll wake yer sisters up.'

'I don't mean that kind of loud, Ma, I don't mean hollerin'. I mean make sure that what you say gives 'im a headache.'

'You got to remember 'e's had a lot of 'ard luck.'

'He'll have more if he starts doin' Dulwich over,' said Bobby. 'He'll get nicked for sure. Last time it was on suspicion of receivin', and he ought to 'ave been grateful Constable Bradshaw put a word in for him. Next time it'll be for liftin' the swag himself. I've got to be candid, Ma, I've got to tell you I'm not in favour of us havin' to go about with people knowin' the head of our fam'ly's doin' time in the Scrubs. We've got grandad's fam'ly name to protect, we don't want 'im turnin' in his grave, and I also don't want to start my promisin' future by havin' to call meself Smith. I'll wait up with you till dad gets in, and back you up when you start readin' the Riot Act.'

'Bobby, I don't know nothing about the Riot Act,' said Mrs Reeves.

'Now, Ma, it's no good you bein' soft on him all the time, you can make up a riot act of your own. Use the right kind of words, with a poker in your mitt. That's a riot act.'

'Oh, lor',' said Mrs Reeves, 'I suppose I'd better show a bit of vexation.'

'And the poker,' said Bobby.

12

'Bobby, I couldn't take no poker to your dad. 'E's got 'is faults, I know, but 'e's always been a lovin' father.'

'Trouble is, Ma, that kind of lovin' could land us all in the workhouse. Now if he 'appened to be a lovin' and *workin'* father, we could hold our heads up a bit. If it wasn't for you an' your stall, we'd be in the workhouse already. So you talk to 'im, you give 'is ears a rollickin', Ma.'

'I suppose I'd better,' said Mrs Reeves.

By eleven o'clock, however, Mr Reeves was still not home.

In Steedman Street, near the Elephant and Castle, a blank-looking bedroom window became yellowly transparent as a gas mantle was lighted. A woman moved to the window to close the curtains. She checked, and her hands stayed still. It was just a minute or so past eleven on this rainy Friday night. A street lamp cast drizzly light. Just beyond it she glimpsed a bending figure, and something else, a huddled shape on the pavement. The figure began to straighten up. Agitated, she pulled the window up, the frame rattling. She saw a man. It *was* a man. He jerked fully upright, something in his hand. Putting her head out of the window, the woman screamed. The man, tall and broad-shouldered, turned and shot away, running fast and silently in his rubber-soled footwear. She screamed again. He vanished into the drizzle.

A police constable, on his late-night beat, broke into a sprint from the Walworth Road end of the street. When he came up to what lay huddled on the wet pavement just outside the circle of light, he switched on his police lamp.

'Christ,' he breathed, and blew his whistle.

It was all in the rushed early editions of the evening papers the next day, the details of a horrible murder, the victim a young woman, and what a middle-aged woman had seen from her bedroom window. A tall and bulky man in a flat cap and dark mackintosh bending over the poor woman.

13

She had seen him straighten up, something in his hand. That something was thought by the police to be a strand of the murdered woman's hair. The murderer was well away before an alerted constable arrived on the scene. The papers, of course, made it sound as if Jack the Ripper had crossed the river in his old age to go to work in South London.

Inspector Greaves of Scotland Yard took charge of the case. He assigned a certain part of the investigation, house-to-house enquiries, to Detective-Sergeant Nicholas Chamberlain and Detective-Constable Frank Chapman.

CHAPTER TWO

Saturday morning.

Mr Reeves had received the talking-to from his wife, but had escaped being injured by the poker. He professed himself iggerant of the charge. It was then put to him that Bobby had followed him all the way to Dulwich and seen everything. Mr Reeves, aghast at such perfidy, said he could hardly believe his own flesh-and-blood could do a thing like that. He was innocent, just out for a walk round Dulwich way, and didn't know the geezer who stopped him outside a house. The bloke happened to be the upstanding gent who owned the house, and he'd locked himself out accidental. He begged Mr Reeves to help him get over the wall. A likely story, said Mrs Reeves, considering you both disappeared quick when Bobby blew his whistle. Mr Reeves nearly fell over at hearing the full extent of his son's perfidy, but he recovered to point out you couldn't trust coppers, and how was he to know it wasn't no copper? The upstanding gent was likewise untrusting of flatfeet. Mrs Reeves said she still didn't like the sound of it. Mr Reeves said it was circumstantial, that's all, that a bloke could be as innocent as he was, but still look guilty on account of circumstances. What kept him out so late, anyway? Well, the upstanding gent needed a reviver, so they went to a pub and forgot about the time. Oh, all right, said Mrs Reeves, and Bobby resigned himself to the obvious, that his mum would never read a real riot act to his dad.

'Jack the Ripper? Talk sense, Frank,' said Detective-Sergeant Nicholas Chamberlain in the morning light.

'Just pointin' out,' said Detective-Constable Frank Chapman, a taciturn man.

'Pointing out what?'

'What the papers mentioned. Jack the Ripper.'

'The papers like gore,' said Nicholas, 'but there's not a drop of blood anywhere, not even under her fingernails. That means she had no chance to scratch or claw. I'd say he took her from behind. Charteris is certain positive he used a cord.' Charteris was the police surgeon in question. 'She was strangled, you know that, not chopped up. And the killer's peculiar.'

'Bloody right,' said Chapman. 'Sawed off a lock of her hair. Beats me. Queer, that sort of thing is.'

'She was strangled from behind, she lost a lock of her hair, and was found without any handbag. That might mean she was robbed as well as strangled. It definitely means we don't know who the hell she is. But she was quite young, and as there's no wedding ring her closest relations have to be her parents. The old man's waiting for them to come forward, since she didn't get home last night.'

'Livin' with her parents, was she?' asked Chapman.

'Good question,' said Nicholas, 'but don't pat yourself on the back, it's already been asked. Whoever she was living with has got to come forward.' He and Chapman entered the Walworth Road, and turned south. 'You know what sawing off a lock of her hair means, don't you?'

'I know. Lunatic asylums. And who's gone missin'.'

'More than that,' said Nicholas, walking briskly. 'The house-to-house enquiries need to include specific questions about lodgers. Some lodgers are odd types.'

'Someone's lodger, is it?' Chapman was wasting not a word. 'Who said?'

'Wake up, Frank.' Nicholas eyed the streams of horse-drawn traffic. A Saturday morning street cleaner stood growling about it. 'No-one's said. I discussed the possibility with the Inspector.'

'Lodger, eh? That a bee in the old man's bonnet, is it?'

'Not in his. Mine.'

'Could take weeks,' said Chapman. 'Lodgers all over the place here.'

'Well, we've got a decent description,' said Nicholas. 'Good build, flat cap, dark mackintosh, fast runner.'

'That's something,' said Chapman.

'How much of something?'

'The bleeder's not as old as the Ripper would be.'

'Forget the Ripper,' said Nicholas. 'Think about that young woman, doing no harm to anyone. In cases like this, I suffer prejudices.'

'Rule number one, sarge. No prejudices.'

'Rule number a hundred and one, Frank. Allow for exceptions. I'm very prejudiced against murderers of women. Women have a rough enough time as it is. But don't worry, I won't be wearing a label. But I will be wanting a lot of work out of you. Tell your wife.'

'You tell her,' said Chapman. 'Your bonnet. Your bee.'

'Just a feeling,' said Nicholas, 'that's all. Come on, let's get busy, with the help of the uniformed branch. The old man's covering north of the Elephant and Castle, we're covering south of it.'

By eleven o'clock that morning, the weather had improved and the day was bright with April sunshine. Police Constable Harry Bradshaw, notebook in his hand, was knocking on doors in Charleston Street, Walworth. The little terraced houses with their bay windows, railed gates and scrubbed doorsteps, looked presentable in the main. All the same, many net or lace curtains once white were now ivory or even yellow with age. That meant money was hard to come by. The people of Walworth had their priorities. Clean curtains, yes. New curtains, seldom.

Constable Bradshaw, along with several colleagues from Rodney Road police station, was after particulars of lodgers, as well as information on all resident males who were tall, well-built and owned mackintoshes. Scotland Yard, for

17

some reason, wanted keen attention paid to lodgers. Detective-Sergeant Chamberlain had been insistent on that, while not overlooking the possibility that some woman's husband or son could be suspect. Well, there were a number of odd fish among the lodgers of Walworth, such as those who kept to themselves and lived hermit-like lives in the upstairs back.

Harry, thirty-five and coming up for promotion, he hoped, knocked at number fourteen Charleston Street. It opened a little, just a little, after a few moments. A face appeared, a small face, topped by curling brown hair in need of a brush and comb. Blue eyes, slightly smudged, peered warily up at him. They took in his uniform and the authority of his helmet.

'Mornin', young lady,' he said cheerfully, 'is your mother in?'

'Dunno,' said small face.

'Would you mind findin' out?' His weathered features broke into an encouraging smile.

'What for?'

'I'd like to speak to her.'

'She ain't in,' said small face.

'Sure? What about your father, he's at work, I suppose?'

'We ain't got no farver.'

'I'm sorry. You sure your mum's not in?'

'She can't pay yer anyfink.'

'I'm not goin' to ask her to. What's your name?'

'Daisy.'

'Daisy what?' asked Harry.

'Dunno.' Small face was adamant about giving little away. Above her head another face appeared, also with smudged blue eyes and untidy curling hair, except that the hair was yellow.

'Who's 'e?' demanded second face. 'What's 'e want?'

'Our mum,' said Daisy.

' 'E's a copper, 'e can't 'ave 'er.' Second face was also adamant. 'What d'yer want 'er for, mister?'

18

Harry knew the score. No father, very little money coming in, and the kids standing shoulder to shoulder to prevent creditors getting a foot inside the door. A policeman to them was on the side of the creditors.

'I'd just like to talk to her,' he said.

'She don't 'ave no money,' said second face.

Harry smiled and said, 'I'm not from the landlord.'

'What yer come knockin' for, then?'

'What's your name?' Harry was willing to be patient, and he was pretty sure their mother was in. 'It's Tulip, I bet.'

'Tulip?' Second face looked indignant. 'I'm Lily, I am.'

'Here, who's 'e?' Of all things, a third face appeared, also from behind the partly opened door, and also with smudged blue eyes. Her tangled hair was auburn. 'Crikey, 'e's a copper.'

' 'E won't go away,' said Daisy.

' 'E just keeps standin' there,' said Lily.

Third face, above the others, looked defiantly up at Harry.

'You're not comin' in our house,' she said, 'we ain't done nothing.'

Harry smiled again. Three young girls who might have been pathetic figures of poverty were bravely challenging instead. There were kids all over Walworth, some a burden to striving parents, some cherishable.

'Let's see,' he said, 'she's Daisy, she's Lily, so you must be Buttercup.'

'Buttercup?' Third face looked outraged. 'Ugh.'

' 'E's barmy,' whispered Daisy to Lily.

'We best get Trary to see 'im orf,' whispered Lily.

'I'm Meg,' said third face.

'That's nice,' said Harry. 'Well, Meg, can I talk to your mother?'

'She ain't in,' said Meg.

'She's gone away,' said Daisy.

'To Australia,' said Lily. 'On a tram,' she added.

'It's a long way to go, even on a tram,' said Harry and

19

then had a stab at the crux of the matter. 'Is there a lodger lookin' after you?' Lodgers proliferated in Walworth. They helped with the rent.

'He ain't 'ere,' said Meg.

'Gone away,' said Lily.

'We don't want 'im back, niever,' said Daisy.

Footsteps sounded in the passage.

'Who you talkin' to, you monkeys?' A hand pulled the door farther open. Another girl appeared. She wore a clean but aged pinafore dress. Her dark brown hair was in no need of a brush or comb, it was dressed in two pigtails. The complexions of the younger girls were pale. Hers was creamy. It had withstood all the assaults of winter murk and summer dust. Her deep brown eyes were quite brilliant, even if they too were slightly ringed. Harry felt he might have seen her before, and probably had during his daily beats. She was one of the phenomena of Walworth, where some girls did blossom into loveliness despite fog, smoke and hardship. She stared at Harry and his uniform.

'Oh, lor',' she said, and wrinkled her nose and looked wry.

'It's nothing to worry about,' said Harry. He had to persist now because of the mention of a lodger, a lodger who had gone away and wasn't wanted back. Why not? 'If I could have a word with your mother?'

'Has that rotten Mr Monks put the law on Mum?' asked Trary in disgust.

Harry's mouth tightened a little. Mr Ronald Monks was the local moneylender, a far harder and more grasping character than any of the obliging pawnbrokers. It was Harry's ambition to catch Monks overstepping the law.

'I don't work for Mr Monks, Miss . . ?'

'I'm Trary.'

'I like that,' said Harry. 'Daisy, Lily, Meg and Trary.'

Trary smiled. He looked a nice copper, a nice man, with eyes a clear and manly grey.

'Trary?' A woman's voice sounded from the kitchen.

'What's goin' on out there? What're those mischiefs up to?'

Harry, smiling, said, 'I think that's your mother, just come back from Australia. Could I talk to her? Word of honour, I'm not goin' to ask her for money.'

Trary looked at him. All Walworth knew about the murder. Trary was intelligent enough to put two and two together. But, of course, it didn't really concern them, not if he was going round asking questions about 'the man'. There were no men in their house, no father, no husband, no lodger. She could tell him that and save him wasting his time.

'I'll see,' she said, and opened the door fully. There they were, the three younger ones, seven-year-old Daisy, nine-year-old Lily, and eleven-year-old Meg. They all wore long grey frocks that reached to their patched boots. But the frocks were clean, and so were the faces. It was only their hair that needed attention. Harry thought their stomachs might be in need too.

'You ain't goin' to put our mum in prison, are yer, please?' begged Lily.

'Cross my heart, Lily,' said Harry, and Trary didn't know any policeman she'd liked so much at first sight. In her fourteenth year, Trary was the bright light of the family.

'You can step into our parlour, if you like, and I'll tell mum,' she said. But her mother appeared in the passage then. She wore an apron. Her light brown hair was pinned up, although little wisps had escaped, wisps that had a faint glint of gold to them. Her attractive looks were slightly marred by the small shadows and little hollows consistent with hard times. The high neck of her dress clasped her smooth throat, and her hazel eyes might have been her finest feature in their largeness if they hadn't been ringed by dusty blue. She was thirty-three, and had a woman's worry that the poverty trap would age her well before her time. The worry surfaced as she saw a policeman on her doorstep.

21

'Oh, don't say the landlord's sent you, not on a Saturday,' she said.

'I don't do errands for landlords,' said Harry. He knew his sergeant would have told him to hurry it up ages ago. But there were occasions when one wasn't inclined to. 'If I could have a few words with you, Mrs . . . ?'

'I'm Mrs Maggie Wilson. You'd best come through to the kitchen, I expect I'm in trouble with the law.'

'You're not, Mrs Wilson.'

She brightened visibly with relief.

'Well, come through, all the same,' she said. 'I only got back from the market a little while ago, and the kettle's on. I mean, would you like a cup?'

'Well,' said Harry, 'I – '

'Yes, you must give him a cup, Mum,' said Trary, 'and I'll take the kids in the parlour an' keep them out of your way.'

' 'E's not goin' to put our mum in the police station, is 'e?' asked Daisy anxiously.

'As if he would, a nice policeman like him,' said Trary.

'Are you nice?' asked Maggie of the man in blue, a faint smile on her lips.

' 'Orrible ragamuffin when I was a kid,' said Harry, 'but I'm a bit better now. I hope.'

'Come in,' said Maggie, and led the way to the kitchen. He noted it was clean and tidy, but there was no fire going in the range, and nor was it laid. No wood or coal, he thought. He wondered about the larder. The shopping bag on the square table didn't seem to contain much. Scarcity of food wasn't uncommon in Southwark. Life was a hand-to-mouth existence for many families, and one's sympathies had to be general, but he couldn't help feeling a particular sympathy for this woman with no husband and four daughters. He supposed Daisy hadn't been telling a fib when she said she'd got no father.

Maggie quickly made the pot of tea. Harry placed his helmet on a chair and advised her he was making enquiries

22

in connection with a certain incident. Maggie caught on at once and said she supposed it was the murder. She'd seen no newspapers, she couldn't afford one, but the cockney grapevine had spread the news hours ago, and the East Street market had buzzed with it.

'You're lookin' for the man that done it? Well, I . . .' She showed a faint smile again. 'Well, I don't have any man in this house.' She poured the tea and handed Harry a cup. He thanked her. 'There hasn't been any man here since me 'usband went.'

'Your husband left you, Mrs Wilson?'

'Yes, in his coffin,' said Maggie. 'Five years ago.'

'I'm sorry. Hasn't there been a lodger?'

'A lodger, yes.' Maggie sipped her tea. 'A man, no. I shut the door on the 'orrible creature two days ago.'

That gave Harry food for thought. 'Mind tellin' me why you did that, Mrs Wilson?'

'He was oily, disgustin', and he hadn't paid no rent for weeks. He got to be . . .' Maggie frowned in distaste, 'well, unpleasant.'

'Very unpleasant?' Harry put his tea down and picked up his notebook. 'Did he frighten you?'

'No, he didn't.' A little spark flashed in her eyes. 'Take more than his kind to frighten me. Objectionable, that's what he was. He 'ad his eye on Trary as well as me. What with that, and not payin' no rent for weeks, out he went. I put all his stuff out on the doorstep and locked the door on 'im.'

'What was his name, Mrs Wilson, and could you describe him?'

Maggie, eyeing the tall, masculine constable, shook her head at him.

'Oh, he won't be the one you want,' she said. 'He was a little fat man, with fat fingers and a fat oily smirk, like he was always pleased with 'imself. I was told in the market the police were after a tall and well-built man, not a little fat one. Still, I'll give you 'is name. Wally Hooper. But I

23

don't know where he is now.' Maggie frowned again. 'Oh, Lord, but just suppose it was 'im, just suppose me an' the girls had had that kind of man in the house?'

'We'll find him, Mrs Wilson, and check on him. I'd like to find him myself and have the pleasure of – ' Harry coughed. He had prejudices too. Maggie's faint smile reappeared.

'You wouldn't do that on my account, would you?' she asked.

'Wouldn't do what?' asked Harry cautiously.

'Kick 'is backside for me,' said Maggie forthrightly.

'Against the regulations,' said Harry solemnly. He had dark brown hair the same colour as Trary's, she noticed. 'Well, thanks very much, Mrs Wilson, sorry I've had to bother you.'

'It's not been a bother,' said Maggie. 'You've been kind, specially in not saying anything in front of the younger girls. Little girls get nightmares all too easy.'

'I hope yours don't,' he said.

Maggie sighed. Born in Peckham, she was in service to a family in Norbury from the age of fourteen. At eighteen, she met Joe Wilson, who worked for the railways and lived in Walworth. Joe was a laughing man, a joke a minute. At nineteen, she married him, and they set up home here in Charleston Street. Two months later, her parents and her sister emigrated to Australia, selling everything they owned to sail all the way Down-Under in the hope of prospering. Maggie stayed to enjoy married life with Joe. Trary was born in 1894, Meg in 1897, Lily in 1899 and Daisy in late 1900. Joe hadn't minded a bit that they were all girls, he spoiled them as much as he could on his limited wages. But five years ago a shunting accident had cost him his life. The railways paid her a pension as his widow, but it wasn't very much. She had to struggle. She got temporary jobs now and again, and a year ago the local laundry took her on for four hours a day. She also took a lodger, four months ago. That was the one who was oily and disgusting, a fat

24

drunk who thought he was God's gift to a widow. He got behind with his rent of five bob a week, he got weeks behind with it. To make matters worse, the laundry said there wasn't enough work for her and laid her off, six weeks ago. She tried all she could to get some back rent out of the lodger, and he said he'd pay her all of ten bob if she'd be nice to him. She got rid of him, although she was badly in debt, specially with Mr Monks, who'd loaned her a few pounds. She owed him more every week, it seemed, and she was behind with the rent. The girls were having to go short on food and decent clothes, and the workhouse was beginning to stare her in the face. She meant to fight that with every fibre of her being. The one relative she wouldn't have been too proud to turn to for help was Uncle Henry, a favourite of hers, but he was in South Africa. And down there in Australia, her mum and dad and sister weren't any better off yet than they'd been in England.

She came to. The policeman was saying something about her girls being little angels. She noted how stalwart he was and not unlike Joe in his looks. Without any man of her own, her future prospects made her silently wince. Somehow, she had to get a new lodger, and a decent one this time.

'Angels still need feedin', you know,' she said, and Harry felt her tired little smile covered a multitude of worries. He knew he ought to go on his way, but he still lingered.

'Look, I know it's none of my business,' he said, 'but have you got yourself into a bad fix with that moneylender?'

'Some moneylender,' said Maggie, 'chronic bloodsucker more like.'

'And you've not got much comin' in?' Harry remembered the years when his parents had had to struggle.

'I've got a small pension from the railways,' said Maggie, 'and I did have a bit of a job round at the laundry, but they laid me off six weeks ago. I need another job and a decent lodger. But I don't want to burden you with me worries, everyone's got their share, and I manage to get parish relief now and again.'

'Well, I wish you luck,' said Harry. 'Thanks for the tea and for being so helpful.'

'Me? What've I done?'

'Answered my questions. Goodbye, Mrs Wilson.'

Going through the passage with him to see him out, Maggie asked, 'Were you really a little 'orror as a boy?'

'Perishin' little 'andful I was, missus,' said Harry, mimicking himself as a boy. ' 'Orrible 'eadache to me suffering mum.' Reaching the front door, he put his helmet on. The parlour door opened and three faces appeared. 'So long, girls,' he said.

' 'As he been nice to yer, Mum?' asked Meg.

'Of course he has,' said Maggie.

Impulsively, Harry dug a hand into his pocket and drew out three pennies. He gave the girls one each. They looked up at him in astonished bliss.

'Oh, yer swell, mister,' said Meg.

Trary appeared, and Harry felt that if trees could grow in Brooklyn, the reputed wasteland of New York, flowers could certainly blossom in Walworth, the smoky heartland of cockney South London.

'Trary, 'e's give us a penny each,' said Daisy excitedly.

Trary gave the tall policeman another long look. She liked him even more. He'd be just right for her mum.

'You're not too old for one?' said Harry, well aware his sergeant would give his ears a rollicking if he knew how much time he'd spent at this one house. He found another penny. Trary accepted it without any awkwardness, her smile flowering.

'Oh, how graciously kind, thank you,' she said, and Maggie smiled. Her eldest daughter had already developed her own kind of words.

'So long now,' said Harry. 'So long, Mrs Wilson, many thanks.'

26

'Nice to meet you, it's been a pleasure,' said Maggie, and closed the door.

'Mum, what a lovely man,' said Trary.

'He's kind,' said Maggie.

'Mum, we're goin' out now to spend what 'e give us,' said Lily.

'That you're not,' said Maggie, 'not till you've all 'ad your hair combed. I've got time now.'

'Oh, blow,' said Meg.

'Never mind oh blow,' said Maggie, 'and what that kind policeman thought of the three of you all lookin' like mops that's been out in the wind, I daren't hardly think. Oh, I didn't get 'is name, did any of you?'

'I'll run and ask him,' said Trary. Her real name was Mary, but her dad had called her Contrary. Contrary quickly became Trary, and Trary had stuck. Even her teachers called her that.

'You'll do no such thing,' said Maggie. She knew what was instinctive with Trary. The girl still missed her dad, and was always looking for a father figure.

'But, Mum, he liked you.'

'He didn't say so.'

'Well, no, he wouldn't, would he? Not when he's only just had the pleasure of meetin' you. But I think you could see he liked you.' Trary longed for her hard-up mum to meet a really nice man, a man who would take her worries off her, worries she'd never had when their dad was alive. She thought the policeman was just right. Of course, he might be married, the nicest men always were. Oh, what a gloom and doom thought, that he already had a wife. She'd have to find out. He looked a real man compared to that lodger. Trary had hated him. He'd actually tried to pull her clothes up once, when her mum was out. She'd given him such a kick that it brought tears to his eyes.

'Mum, I'll do the kids' hair,' she said.

'Thanks, love,' said Maggie.

'Who's a kid? I'm not,' said Meg. 'That's Daisy.'

27

'No, it ain't,' protested Daisy. 'I'm a little girl, I am, and nice too.'

'Well, all of you be nice and let Trary tidy your mops,' said Maggie, 'while I see about doin' some toasted cheese on toasted bread for your dinner.' She gritted her teeth that it could only be cheese on toast. They all needed some really good meals. The girls were getting thin. She'd simply got to find a job. And a new lodger. She'd put a card in the newsagent's window yesterday, saying she had a room to let, but no-one had applied yet. The thought of the workhouse loomed again. She shuddered. Then she set her mouth firmly. No, she'd never give in, never. She'd see on Monday what she could get out of parish relief. Perhaps a couple of loaves, some marge, a tin of syrup and some sugar. She'd never let her girls starve, never. She'd put her soul in pawn first.

In pawn, it would be redeemable.

CHAPTER THREE

Harry, back at the police station in Rodney Road, submitted his notes on the streets he had covered so far. He had no leads to offer. There had been lodgers at some addresses, but they'd all been put in the clear by their landladies. And husbands or sons who might have fitted the bill had all been at home at eleven o'clock last night, according to wives and mothers. However, Harry did make a special mention of a certain Wally Hooper, the lodger of a Mrs Maggie Wilson of fourteen Charleston Street up to two days ago, when she'd thrown him out because he hadn't paid his rent for weeks and because he'd made unpleasant advances.

'That makes him a suspect, does it?' asked the sergeant.

'It makes him a bit of no good, sarge,' said Harry. 'Nasty little fat man.'

'Scotland Yard don't happen to be lookin' for any little fat man.'

'Didn't like the sound of him myself,' said Harry. 'And you never know, on a dark rainy night, a little fat man in a mackintosh might look twice as big to a scared witness.'

'Now don't come clever with me, Harry, I'm gettin' all I want of that from the CID. Still, all right, I'll pass the word. Wally Hooper? All right, we don't want the Yard remindin' us it's our duty not to overlook anything, not even little fat men.'

'With hot fat hands,' said Harry.

He snatched a quick meal at the station, then returned to the job of knocking on doors. He first went back to houses where occupants had been out during the morning. It took him to Charleston Street again, to number four.

A Mrs Buller answered his knock. She informed him she'd been out till half-past twelve, that her husband had been at work and that he'd been at home all Friday evening. No, she didn't have any lodger.

'Thanks, sorry to have bothered you,' said Harry.

'Wait a tick, I did 'ave someone call about half-hour ago, askin' if I had a room to let, which I don't. But it so 'appens a friend of mine's in the way of wanting a lodger. I told 'im to go and see her. Mrs Carter, fifteen King and Queen Street.'

'Ah,' said Harry. A man looking for lodgings. The CID would want to know about him. A man looking for lodgings might be a man who'd decided it would be safer to leave existing lodgings. 'Could I have a description, Mrs Buller?'

'Tall, he was, dressed nice and 'ealthy-lookin'. Grey suit and boater. About thirty, I'd say. Why, what's 'e done?'

'We're just makin' enquiries, Mrs Buller.'

'Here, I've just thought, you said – oh, gawd 'elp us, it's about the murder last night, isn't it?' Mrs Buller turned faint. 'It wasn't 'im, was it? Oh, when I think, me standin' here talkin' to 'im and near to bein' done in on me own doorstep, it's givin' me the 'orrors, and I never had the 'orrors in all me previous life. I don't know what things are comin' to when – oh, I just thought some more, what about me friend Mrs Carter? Lord 'elp us, she might be lyin' stricken dead and chopped up, and her a poor young widow all these years, after them Boers killed her husband in the war.' Mrs Buller paled with agitation, while Harry thought there had to be something better to his day than troubled widows. 'You've got to go round to her 'ouse straight away. Oh, when I think it was me that told the murderer to go and call on her about lodgings.'

'Don't give yourself those kind of worries, Mrs Buller,' said Harry soothingly. 'I'll check.'

'You better 'ad, and quick,' said Mrs Buller. 'I'm 'ardly able to stand upright, it'll be the death of me if Mrs Carter's been done for.'

'Don't worry, I'm on my way,' said Harry.

He made for King and Queen Street, going up through Turquand Street. A woman in a huge hat, short coat and voluminous skirts, noted his quick stride and spoke to him as he passed.

'Goin' after the bleeder, are yer, constable? Well, give 'im one in the eye for me before you 'ang 'im.'

That was the way of it when a woman was murdered, a steaming need to see the murderer swing.

Crossing Browning Street, Harry saw Detective-Sergeant Chamberlain from Scotland Yard talking to his colleague, Detective-Constable Chapman. He spoke to them. Nicholas listened with interest to the information given by Mrs Buller. There had been no real leads so far, no member of the uniformed branch had come up with anything promising. But a tall, healthy-looking man in search of lodgings? Nicholas's reaction to that was the same as Harry's had been.

'Right, constable, thanks.'

'Leave it to you, then?' said Harry, who liked Sergeant Chamberlain.

'I'll see to it. Fifteen King and Queen Street? We're on top of it. Right.' Nicholas spoke to Chapman. 'Let's take a look.'

Mrs Emma Carter, answering a knock on the door of her little flat-fronted house in King and Queen Street, gazed in surprise at the two men in plain clothes. One was tall and homely, with a mouth that looked ready to break into a smile, and the other, shorter, was as lean as a whippet, with a businesslike air. The tall one spoke.

'Mrs Carter?'

'Yes?' said Emma.

Nicholas experienced unusual relief in finding that this neatly-dressed, pleasant-looking woman was visibly unhurt and intact, even though he had not really expected a possible suspect to walk here from Charleston Street with

31

murder on his mind. A second killing so soon after the first was very unlikely. It was never like that, particularly with homicidal maniacs. There was always a more deliberate pattern. All the same, the fact that the unusual had remained the unusual, did give him a feeling of relief. Mrs Carter was quietly attractive and feminine, the kind of woman the most hardened policeman would hate to find violently murdered.

'I'm Detective-Sergeant Chamberlain, Mrs Carter, and my colleague is Detective-Constable Chapman. We're from Scotland Yard.'

Emma, twenty-eight years old, said in a composed way, 'And you've come to see me? What about?'

'It concerns a certain man who may have called on you earlier today,' said Nicholas, and made a mental note that her braided hair was as fair as that of the murdered woman.

'A certain man?' Emma regarded him with curiosity. 'Perhaps you'd better come in,' she said, 'or the whole street will be gawping.'

Saturday afternoon street kids, coming from the market or going towards it, had stopped to stare and nudge each other. Walworth kids could always recognize strangers, and two strangers at a woman's door made them very nosy. The Scotland Yard men stepped in, removing their hats, and found themselves in the living-room. The front doors of all these little flat-fronted houses opened straight onto living-rooms. Emma's was a reflection of her neat and pleasant look, although a bright note was struck by colourful chintzes. Married at eighteen to a long-legged soldier of a cavalry regiment, she was widowed at twenty when he fell to sharp-shooting Boer irregulars. Since then she had existed on a war widow's pension, augmented during the last few years by a morning job behind the counter of a department in Hurlocks, the drapers near the Elephant and Castle.

'Sorry to bother you,' said Nicholas.

'Is it going to be a bother, sergeant?' she asked, closing the door.

'Not too much, I hope,' said Nicholas, while Chapman glanced around in instinctive professional observation of the room. 'Mrs Carter, do you know a Mrs Buller of Charleston Street?'

'Yes, I know her.'

'We understand that a man called on her today to ask if she had a room to let. She told him no, but recommended him to call on you. Do you have a room to let, Mrs Carter?'

My, what a very polite policeman, thought Emma.

'Oh, that,' she said, and smiled. 'Actually, I don't. I did mention to Mrs Buller recently that I thought my morning job at Hurlocks might be coming to an end, and that if it did I'd have to think about taking a lodger. So many people in Walworth do. But it was really said as a joke. I'm not the kind of person to welcome a lodger, especially not in a house as small as this. I'd always prefer to scrape along on my own. I've been widowed much longer than married. I lost my husband in the Boer War.'

'That was damn bad luck,' said Nicholas. 'It always is for a woman, it leaves her very vulnerable.'

'I've managed to manage,' said Emma.

'So it seems,' said Nicholas, thinking the atmosphere quietly charming and very different from that of noisy cockney homes. 'Could you tell me if the man recommended by Mrs Buller did call on you?'

'He hasn't called this afternoon. He may have done before I arrived home from my morning job at Hurlocks, the drapers. I finish at one o'clock. I did some shopping on my way home today and didn't get in until two. So I suppose the enquiring gentleman could have called while I was out. He lost nothing by not finding me at home, as I couldn't have helped him. Why are you asking questions about him?'

'Oh, it's part of the routine process of an investigation,' said Nicholas.

'He's a suspect?' said Emma, looking interested. The matter had created agitation in Mrs Buller. Emma took it

33

very coolly. 'I think I understand now. That poor woman last night.'

'Yes,' said Nicholas, and found himself thinking about fair hair and the fact that the victim had had a strand sawn off. There was a bizarre note to that. A plain murder was always bad enough, a bizarre factor added uneasiness to one's sense of outrage. One could become uneasy about Mrs Carter's brightly fair hair. The man looking for lodgings, how would he have reacted to the colour of her hair? Nicholas dismissed the thought. He was being absurd. 'Have I alarmed you, Mrs Carter?' Nicholas did not know it, of course, but Constable Harry Bradshaw had done his best not to alarm another widow in the area.

Emma, no more the kind of woman to reach for smelling-salts than Maggie, said, 'Alarmed? Should I be?'

Nicholas could have said he'd had thoughts about her fair hair and the man looking for lodgings. But he knew he might just as well worry about every woman in Southwark with fair hair.

'Doesn't it alarm you that a possible suspect may be in this neighbourhood?' he asked.

'I'd be alarmed if I thought he was looking for me,' said Emma, 'but from what you've told me so far I gather he's only looking for lodgings. What do you want me to do if he does arrive at my door?'

Nicholas liked her coolness, and the way her mind was obviously working. The man might be finding it difficult to rent a room. Women who had one to let would now be on their guard against strangers. That might bring the suspect to the recommended address. If he had called already and received no answer to his knock, that wouldn't necessarily put him off calling again. It was a shot in the dark to make a suspect of him, and not a very good shot. The murderer was hardly likely to be openly parading himself in a search for lodgings. If he was not sitting quietly under cover, he'd be acting as he did every day, wherever he lived. Nevertheless, Nicholas felt he could take no chances.

'Open the door to him, Mrs Carter, but only if it's daylight. Tell him yes, you do have a room to let, but that you've got visitors. Ask him to come back in an hour.'

'I see,' said Emma, 'and I'm to gallop to Rodney Road police station as soon as he's gone?'

'If there's a horse available and you can ride,' said Nicholas with due gravity, 'but if not, you can take your time by walking. It's not far.'

Heavens, thought Emma, a polite policeman with a sense of humour? How unexpected.

'I'll walk,' she said.

'It'll be the thing to do,' said Nicholas, 'to report to the station. On no account let him in. He may be completely innocent, but I'd rather you didn't take chances.' He glanced at Chapman. 'Frank, go and ask Mrs Carter's immediate neighbours if they spotted anyone knocking on her door earlier.'

'Makes sense,' said the terse detective-constable.

'Might I suggest you go first to the house immediately opposite?' said Emma. 'Mrs Duncalfe lives there. She's an elderly lady, but doesn't miss very much from her upstairs window.'

'Right, Mrs Carter,' said Chapman. Emma opened the front door for him. He gave her a nod as he went out. She closed the door.

'Your colleague doesn't say very much,' she said to Nicholas.

'He likes police work, but doesn't go much on conversation,' said Nicholas. 'Look, we've a decent description of the man seen running away from the victim. He was tall, with a good build, and was wearing a flat cap and a dark mackintosh. The man described by Mrs Buller was a tall healthy character in a grey suit and straw boater. But the difference in clothes doesn't eliminate him, of course.'

'Well, the murderer isn't likely to be walking about in what he wore last night, is he?' said Emma. She became serious. 'Murder's a hideous crime, sergeant, and the man

35

responsible should forfeit his own life. I'm quite willing to do what I can to help.'

'You're not Walworth-born, are you?' asked Nicholas with interest.

'I live here and like it here,' said Emma. 'I like the people. My husband was born in Brixton, I was a shop assistant in Reading.'

'I don't know Reading,' said Nicholas, 'does it produce good shop assistants?'

'I've no idea.' Emma laughed. 'I simply hope I'm a passable one myself. I also hope I'm a passable citizen, and that I won't let the law down if that certain man does knock on my door.'

'Perhaps I'm worrying over nothing,' said Nicholas, finding her charming to talk to. But women on the whole did talk more easily than men. Cockney women loved a chat with anyone whose ears came within range of their extrovert tongues.

'Dear me, you don't call a murder nothing, do you?' said Emma.

'Not by a long shot, Mrs Carter. Any murder is top of the worrying list. I meant I might be worrying unnecessarily about this man who's looking for lodgings. I hope you won't be troubled, but if you are – '

'I'll do as agreed,' said Emma. 'I must say you're a very pleasant change.'

'From what?'

'From most policemen.'

'Why'd you say that?' asked Nicholas.

'I'm a suffragette.'

'Oh, Lord,' said Nicholas.

'You don't approve, of course.'

'It's difficult work for the police.'

'Arresting women?' smiled Emma.

'It embarrasses some members of the force.'

'Really?' Emma looked sceptical. 'I've seen embarrassed suffragettes, sergeant, I've not seen any embarrassed policemen. Not that I've been arrested myself. I give Mrs Pankhurst my support and devotion, and I march with her followers, but I'm not a militant. I feel we must win the people over, not upset them. Aren't the English a peculiar lot? We're never satisfied with any of our governments, but we don't like militants breaking our laws. Mrs Pankhurst, however, is convinced it's the only way women will get the vote.'

'I'm sitting on the fence,' said Nicholas. 'Best thing for a copper to do.'

Chapman knocked on the front door at that point, and Emma let him in.

'Right, yes,' he said.

'Yes what?' asked Nicholas.

'Mrs Duncalfe. Saw a man in a grey suit and boater knock on Mrs Carter's door. About twenty past one. Knocked a couple of times. Then went away.'

'That's a fact?' said Nicholas.

'Tall bloke. Good shoulders.'

'We'll get his description circulated,' said Nicholas. 'Meanwhile, will he or won't he come back here?'

'I know what to do if he does,' said Emma, who thought the interview had gone on long enough in view of the fact that she had some baking to do.

'Might be genuine,' said Chapman brusquely.

'He probably is,' said Nicholas, 'but under the circumstances, let's treat him as guilty until he's proved innocent.'

'I thought in law it was supposed to be the other way about,' said Emma.

'It is, when he gets to court,' said Nicholas. 'Well, thanks for your help, Mrs Carter.'

'Goodbye, sergeant,' said Emma. 'If we do meet again, I suppose it'll be in connection with this man?'

'Yes, it will,' said Nicholas, 'so take care.'

'Of course.' Emma opened the door and let them out. Chapman gave her a nod, Nicholas gave her a homely smile.

She watched them go on their way to Browning Street, then she closed her door.

'Superior sort,' said Chapman.

'She's a lady, Frank, not a superior sort.'

'Got a red herring here. That's my opinion.'

'It's a question, you muttonhead, of not taking chances,' said Nicholas.

'If you say so.'

'Let's get to the station,' said Nicholas. They had work to do, studying afternoon reports brought in by the uniformed men. And they would have to follow up any leads. Nicholas also had to persuade Detective-Inspector Greaves to let him concentrate on Walworth. He had a feeling about Walworth, but a feeling wasn't something that always satisfied the Inspector. A feeling had nothing to do with method or professionalism.

Mrs Carter. A suffragette? Nicholas showed a little grin as he made for Rodney Road in company with the laconic Chapman. Not every suffragette looked as quiet and as peaceful as Mrs Carter.

He wondered if Inspector Greaves had yet discovered the identity of the victim. At the station, there was no message to that effect, only some half-leads contained in reports handed in by constables on the house-to-house routine.

CHAPTER FOUR

Constable Harry Bradshaw came off duty at six o'clock. He'd had a long day, since seven in the morning, and he'd just been told to report in tomorrow, Sunday. Well, the overtime pay would be welcome, even if he did feel a day off wouldn't have come amiss.

He walked to the East Street market, which was always open well into the evening on Saturdays. He made his way to a greengrocery stall, one run by Ma Earnshaw, who prided herself on the superior quality of her fruit and vegetables.

'Watcher, Ma,' he said, 'pound of Granny Smiths.'

'Well, if it ain't the arm of the law,' said Ma. 'Sorry about yer dear old mum, 'Arry, but I 'eard yer give 'er a fine funeral, includin' six black 'orses.'

'She wanted to go in style,' said Harry. His mother hadn't accepted ten years of widowhood at all well, especially as it had seen the departure of her two daughters and her eldest son in marriage. Harry looked at one time as if he might follow them. The prospect of being alone kept making her fall ill, which in turn made Harry postpone his proposal to a certain young lady. The young lady gave him up in the end, which Mrs Bradshaw thought a blessing. It was only right that one of her children should stay home to look after her. But in the end she grumbled herself into a decline and took to her bed. She did not last long after that. Harry felt guilty at her funeral, and it was a week before he realized he was free. 'On second thoughts, Ma, make that two pounds of Granny Smiths, there's a good old girl.'

' 'Ere, I ain't old yet,' said Ma Earnshaw, just past forty

and running to overflowing plumpness. 'Nor ain't I 'ad the pleasure of servin' you recent.'

'Well, treat me proud,' said Harry, 'and I'll come round more often.' Ma Earnshaw weighed and bagged the polished green apples. 'Now five pounds of your best cookers,' said Harry. A couple of young market scroungers appeared as if by magic out of the crowd. Shabby, with patched shorts, darned jerseys, and socks down to their ankles, they were typical of their kind. They conducted their activities at elusive speed, darting under a fruit stall to grab rejects dropped into a crate and scarpering off before the stall-holder had even noticed them. These two materialized with their eyes already sizing up Ma Earnshaw's involvement with her customer. Then they saw the customer's blue-bottle uniform. They disappeared into nowhere in a split second. Harry grinned.

'Got a shoppin' bag for the cookers?' asked Ma.

'Got a box?' countered Harry. He bent down and pulled an empty wooden crate out from under the stall. 'Good on yer, Ma, this'll do.'

'You got thievin' 'ands for a copper, 'Arry, that's me best crate.'

'Well, I like you for lettin' me have it,' said Harry. She emptied the cookers into it. Harry was a popular bobby, and straight as they could come. 'I also want a dozen bananas, a dozen oranges, two pounds of dates, a couple of lettuce, two pounds of tomatoes and six pounds of potatoes. Oh, and give me three pounds of those wallopin' onions.'

'You feedin' an orphanage?' asked Ma.

'Just stockin' up,' said Harry.

She supplied him with the best she had, putting everything into the crate. He paid her and carried the crate away. He did a little more shopping, then searched the crowds for an obliging young confederate. He spotted just the right face, cheerful, cheeky, talkative and well-known to him. Bobby Reeves, the sixteen-year-old son of Mrs

Gertie Reeves, who ran a second-hand clothes stall. Cap on the back of his head, blue jersey belted around his waist, trouser cuffs a little frayed, Bobby showed a ready grin to the world.

'Here, Bobby, can you do me a favour?'

'You bet,' said Bobby, as they met on the less crowded pavement. 'Well, we're both Bobbies, like, don't yer reckon, guv? And you were kindly obligin' to me dad, that time he minded a sack for some geezer out of the goodness of 'is jam tart. You come along an' give him a talkin' to, and he only got – '

'Yes, he got off with a warning.' Harry smiled. Bobby had what was known as the gift of the gab. 'Listen, I'll give you tuppence if you'll take this box of stuff to a house in Charleston Street. It's from the Salvation Army.' Harry had chalked the words on the side of the crate. 'It's for a Mrs Wilson, number fourteen. Hand it in. Say it's with the compliments of the Salvation Army. It's a bit heavy.' He deposited the load into Bobby's arms. The boy, tall, slim and strong, embraced it and held it to his chest. He whistled at its weight.

'Might I ask yer to place it on me bonnet, guv, which is superior to me chest, which might get splinters in it.'

'Good idea,' said Harry, and lifted the crate onto Bobby's capped head. Bobby balanced it and held it in the fashion of a young costermonger, with one hand. Experienced costermongers used no hands. Harry put two pennies into the boy's trouser pocket. 'Much obliged, Bobby.'

'Me too, for the copper coins, guv. Here, have yer been after that bloke that done in – '

'We'll catch him,' said Harry. 'Off you go.'

'I'm on me way,' said Bobby, and off he went, the crate balanced, his walk brisk and confident. That was a lad who would get on, thought Harry.

Maggie was getting supper, doing fried potatoes with bacon scraps bought cheap from the grocers when the front door knocker was hammered. Trary answered it. A boy with a wooden box on his capped head gave her a grin and a look. Then another look. Then an admiring whistle.

'Crikey,' he said, 'where'd you come from?'

Haughty brown eyes took on the challenge of cheeky blue eyes.

'I happen to live here,' said Trary loftily. 'Might I enquire what you think you're lookin' at?' She had the gift of the gab too, and a girl's gift of the gab at that.

'I dunno,' said Bobby, 'not 'aving had the pleasure before. All right, what's yer monicker?'

'Excuse me, I'm sure,' said Trary, 'but I do not tell my name to cheeky boys with boxes on their heads. And kindly don't bash our door in when you come knockin'. My mum don't like our door bashed in.'

'Me hand slipped,' said Bobby, 'and this here box is only on me head because I wasn't able to get it into me pocket. It's a bit big, y'see.'

'Think I'm daft, do you?' asked Trary.

'Hope not,' said Bobby, 'be a cryin' shame if a girl as pretty as you was daft. Tell yer what, would yer like to come up the park with me Sunday? That's tomorrow. I'll call for you after me dinner.'

'You'll be lucky,' said Trary. 'Comin' round here, bashin' our door, givin' me grinnin' looks and askin' me up the park, you got more sauce than a tramful of monkeys, you have.'

'Well, I like that,' protested Bobby, the crate swaying a little. 'Is it my fault you're pretty?'

'It's not mine,' said Trary. 'I happen to be the 'andiwork of God.'

'Crikey, was it you said that?' asked Bobby in admiration.

'Yes, it was. And I don't go up the park with anyone I don't know. You might be an escaped convict, I've heard about escaped convicts goin' round knockin' on doors. Kindly don't knock on ours any more. What d'you want, anyway?'

'I come bearin' gifts,' said Bobby.

'What?' asked Trary, coveting that phrase for her own use.

'In this here box,' said Bobby, 'which I'm willin' to carry indoors for you, if yer ma's name is Mrs Wilson. It's come with the compliments of the Salvation Army from a friend of mine, and I've got to tell you it's startin' to push my head in.'

'Good thing too,' said Trary, always able to play a notable part in a boy-versus-girl dialogue. 'Boys like you shouldn't have no heads, then they wouldn't be so cheeky.' She gazed in suspicion at the crate. 'What d'you mean, Salvation Army? What's in it?'

'Paper bags, mostly,' said Bobby, 'and they're all full up. But I dunno what with, me friend didn't tell me. I've brought 'em because I've got a kind 'eart.' Bobby paused. 'An' because me friend give me tuppence,' he conceded.

Trary, mystified, said, 'Look, you better not be havin' my mum on. Or me, either, or you'll get a punch in the eye.'

'Blimey,' said Bobby, admiration climbing, 'I like you.'

Haughtily, Trary said, 'Just wait there, boy, and I'll see what my mum says.'

'All right,' said Bobby, 'but I'd be obliged if yer wouldn't take too long. This lot's goin' to push me under yer door-step in a minute.'

'Oh, dear, what a shame,' said Trary, and made for the kitchen. She stopped and turned. 'Who did you say sent you?'

'A blue-bottle friend of mine.'

'Who's he?'

'A copper, of course, name of Mr Bradshaw.'

'Mr Bradshaw?' Trary's bright eyes gleamed. 'Oh, d'you mean the tall and nice one, with a kind smile?'

'Don't ask me,' said Bobby, 'he's just a copper. Decent bloke, though.'

'Well, don't just stand there,' said Trary, 'bring the box

in. Why didn't you say about the policeman? I don't know,
I'm sure, but it's aggravatin' that boys can't talk a bit of
sense sometimes.'

Bobby stepped in, steadying the crate with both hands.
He followed Trary into the kitchen. Around the table sat
Daisy, Lily and Meg. In the scullery, Maggie was busy at
the frying-pan. The girls stared at the cheerful-looking boy
with a large wooden box on his head.

'Who's 'e?' asked Daisy.

' 'E's got a box on 'is 'ead,' said Lily.

'We never 'ad a boy with a box on his 'ead in here
before,' said Meg.

'Mum, come and look,' called Trary. 'You can put it
down, boy.'

Bobby lowered the crate to the floor. Maggie appeared,
a frying fork in her hand, her apron on.

'What's this?' she asked.

'It's a boy,' said Trary, 'he's brought a box with things
in it.'

'With the compliments of the Salvation Army,' said
Bobby, 'if you're Mrs Wilson.'

'Yes, I'm Mrs Wilson,' said Maggie, liking his looks and
his cheerfulness. 'But I don't know no-one in the Salvation
Army.'

'The kind policeman sent 'im, Mum,' said Trary, gazing
into the crate. 'You know, the one that called this mornin'.
Well, that's what I think.'

'I'll unload it for yer,' said Bobby, and began placing
bags on the table under the fascinated eyes of the family.
Unbagged cooking apples were uncovered. Maggie stared
at the bags. Trary investigated one. It contained Osborne
biscuits. Another contained sugar, another, two half-pound
packets of tea. Two tins of condensed milk came to light.
So did fruit and vegetables. There was also a bag of flour
and a pound of bacon. Maggie stared in utter astonishment,
emotions welling.

'Mum, it's a Salvation Army food parcel, I've heard of

them,' said Trary. 'Wasn't it lovely of that policeman to speak to them for us?'

Maggie and her girls simply couldn't take their eyes off what looked like a miraculous mountain of food. Oranges shone, and a whole twelve bananas made a cluster of bright yellow. Maggie looked at Bobby. He was looking at Trary, a boyishly cheeky grin on his face. Trary was looking at the laden table, her face glowing. Her sisters were breathless.

'What's your name?' asked Maggie.

'Bobby, Mrs Wilson, Bobby Reeves.'

'And you collected these things from the Salvation Army?'

'Well, no, missus, Constable Bradshaw must have, I suppose. He just asked me to bring 'em. He's a friend of mine, well, he done me dad a good turn once, when me dad . . .' Bobby paused. 'Well, me dad suffered a turn of blissful ignorance once, and Constable Bradshaw kindly put a word in for 'im.'

'Blissful ignorance?' said Maggie.

'Well, there was some swag about once, which me dad didn't know was swag.' Well, that was what his dad had sworn before the magistrate. 'That's blissful ignorance, Mrs Wilson.' Bobby decided to paper over the cracks, and added, 'Not that me dad's simple, he's like me, he's just got a kind 'eart. Mrs Wilson, would you kindly excuse me sayin' I like your daughter and don't mind goin' up the park with 'er tomorrow afternoon?'

'Oh, I never met such a cheeky devil,' said Trary.

'Bobby, what was the policeman like?' asked Maggie. Bobby described him.

Trary, clapping her hands in delight, said, 'There, it was him, Mum, and we know his name now.'

'Just a minute,' said Maggie, and went and turned the gas very low under the frying-pan, in which there was a mound of crisping sliced potatoes and bacon pieces. She returned. 'Bobby, where did the policeman give you this box?'

'In the market, Mrs Wilson.'

'I see.' Maggie smiled, and it made Trary think that her mum was really awfully attractive. 'And 'is name is Bradshaw?'

'It's Harry Bradshaw, Mrs Wilson, and 'e's straight up for a copper.'

'Well, when you see him, ask him to let me know which Salvation Army address to write to, as I've got to send 'eartfelt thanks for all this food.'

'Yes, Mrs Wilson.'

'You make sure now.' Maggie had her own ideas about the source of the food. She supposed her pride ought to be hurt, but it wasn't. The gesture was typical of what could happen to a Walworth family down on its luck. Acts of generous neighbourliness did take place, and one was grateful, not proud. 'You tell Mr Bradshaw, won't you, that I've got to write someone a letter of thanks.'

'Soon as I see him,' promised Bobby.

'I must find you some pennies for bringing the box.'

'You don't 'ave to do that, Mrs Wilson, Mr Bradshaw's already given me tuppence,' said Bobby. 'It's been a pleasure meetin' you and your fam'ly. Shall I talk to Mr Wilson about takin' 'er up the park?'

'I'm a widow, Bobby,' said Maggie.

'Oh.' Bobby looked as if he'd come up against the sad wreck of the schooner *Hesperus*. 'I'm sorry, Mrs Wilson, I didn't know.'

'It was five years ago,' said Maggie, liking the boy, 'we're over it now.'

'Still, it's hard times, Mrs Wilson, I don't know when there's been more hard times. Well, never mind, you've got nice girls.'

'I'm nicest,' said Daisy.

'You're just littlest,' said Lily.

'I'm nearly twelve,' said Meg.

'I'm sixteen meself,' said Bobby, 'and I'll come tomorrow, shall I, Mrs Wilson, an' take your oldest daughter up the park? I don't mind she's not told me 'er name yet.'

46

'She's Trary,' said Lily.

'She's bossiest,' said Meg.

'Oh, I don't mind that,' said Bobby. 'I've got two sisters, as well as me mum an' dad, and they all say I'm the bossiest one of the fam'ly. So it won't worry me if Trary's the same as me.'

'I'd faint if I was,' said Trary.

'Can we give Bobby one of the apples, Mum?' asked Lily. 'And could we all 'ave one ourselves?'

'After your meal,' said Maggie, 'but you can give Bobby one now.'

'Could you make it a banana, Mrs Wilson?' asked Bobby. 'I'm partial to bananas. I'm not sayin' I don't like apples, but a banana's me fav'rite.'

'You can have both,' said Maggie.

'Well, no, I don't think I'll do that, Mrs Wilson, I'll just take a banana. As I've already got tuppence from Mr Bradshaw, I don't know I deserve an apple as well, it might make me feel I been overpaid for just bringing you the box.'

'Can't he talk?' said Trary, rolling her eyes. 'I never heard more talk from anyone. I suppose he can't help it, I suppose it runs in 'is fam'ly, I've heard things like talkin' do run in some fam'lies. Still, give him a banana, Lily.'

' 'Ere y'ar, Bobby,' said Lily, breaking one from the stalk and handing it to him.

'Swell,' he said. 'I'd best push off now, Mrs Wilson. It's been really nice gettin' to know everyone. Specially Trary. Ain't she pretty? What time shall I call for 'er tomorrow? I don't mind comin' round at three, say.'

'You'll be lucky,' said Trary.

'Hope so,' said Bobby breezily. 'See you tomorrow, then.'

'Not if I see you first,' said Trary.

'Well, we'll all see, Bobby,' said Maggie, 'you can come and knock.'

'I'll take her on the tram, of course,' he said, 'I won't make her walk. So long, then, Mrs Wilson.' He departed whistling.

Trary drew a breath. 'I don't believe it,' she said, 'I just don't believe it. I never heard more blessed cheek in all my life.'

'Is Trary blushin'?' asked Daisy of Lily.

'She's gone all pink,' said Lily.

'No, I haven't,' said Trary.

'I fink 'e's nice,' declared Daisy.

'All right, you go up the park with him, then,' said Trary. Maggie smiled. It wasn't often that her eldest daughter was out-talked. She'd gird herself up for the next encounter. 'Look at all these things, pets, just look at them.'

All her girls took a mouth-watering look.

'Mum, it's like Jesus and the five loaves,' said Trary, 'you'll have to write him a really nice note.'

'Crikey, to Jesus?' said Meg.

'No, soppy, to that kind policeman,' said Trary, 'I'm sure he gave mum a very special mention when he was talkin' to the Salvation Army. When you write the note, Mum, I'll take it to the police station. I'll take it after dinner tomorrow, in case that talkin' boy does come round. I'm not goin' up the park with him.'

'I'll dish up supper,' said Maggie, 'and we'll have some of the fruit for afters.' Oh, Lord, she thought, if everything was from him and not the Salvation Army, he must have felt her girls looked starving.

They enjoyed the fruit. They had a banana each, as well as an apple and an orange. Maggie felt almost emotional at the way her hungry girls relished what was a rapturous treat to them. And they were delighted when she finally dished out some of the dates. Her larder wasn't empty now. There had even been eggs, in a bag on top of the pile of stuff in the crate.

'Who'd like to put the kettle on for a pot of tea? We can use the condensed milk.'

'I'll do it,' said Trary, an active girl who liked being busy. She filled the old iron kettle at the scullery sink and put it on the gas ring. She felt ever so pleased for her mum, for the fact that Constable Bradshaw had been so nice to her.

The front door knocker sounded.

'I bet that's Trary's boy come back,' said Lily.

'Yes, 'e forgot to give 'er a kiss,' said Meg. 'I'll go and see.'

'No, I'll go,' said Trary, 'I want to do meself the kind pleasure of puttin' him in his place.'

Maggie smiled. Trary answered the knock. It wasn't that talking boy. In the fading evening light, a man stood on the step, a brown-faced man with broad shoulders, good looks and a large smile. He had a brown moustache and even white teeth, and was dressed in a light grey suit and a straw boater, jauntily tipped. He was carrying a carpet bag and a medium-sized trunk with brass edges.

'Hello, hello,' he said, 'what's this I see, Walworth's May Queen?'

'It's not May, it's April,' said Trary, not a girl to encourage familiarities, especially from strangers. 'What d'you want, please?'

'Does Mrs Wilson live here?'

'Why d'you ask?' Trary was cautious.

'Well, if she's got a room to let, which I believe she has, I'm just what her doctor ordered.'

'Beg your pardon?' said Trary.

'Give her my compliments, and tell her Mr Jerry Bates is requestin' to be her lodger.'

49

CHAPTER FIVE

Trary put her head round the kitchen door.

'Mum, could you come a minute?' she asked.

'Who is it?' asked Maggie.

'If you'd come a minute?' said Trary, and disappeared. Maggie got up. Trary was in the passage. The front door was closed. Trary beckoned and went into the parlour. Mystified, Maggie followed. 'Mum,' said Trary quietly, 'I didn't want the girls to hear, but a man's just called askin' about the room to let. He saw the card in the newsagent's window. I thought – well, he's tall and well-built, and everyone's supposed to be keepin' a lookout for strangers, specially men lookin' for lodgings.'

That was what had come to be on the minds of the people of Walworth following the house-to-house calls of the uniformed police. Trary and her mum hadn't discussed the murder, because of the younger girls, but it had been on their minds, as had the advisability of being wary of strangers.

'Trary?' Maggie saw the set look on her daughter's face. 'Lord, is that what you're thinkin', he might be the one that – oh, is he still there?'

'No, I told him you were out, that you wouldn't be back till late. I told him he could call again in the mornin'. He said it would be a pleasure, he said he'd be here at half-past nine. Well, you see, Mum, if it is him, I think the police ought to be here waitin' for him, don't you? I think I ought to go round to the police station now, and tell them. Perhaps Mr Bradshaw might be there, I could talk to 'im, couldn't I?'

'Trary pet, you're a brave an' clever girl, that you are.'

Maggie eyed her eldest daughter with visible pride. Neither of them knew it, but what Trary had proposed coincided with what Emma and Detective-Sergeant Chamberlain had arranged under similar circumstances. Trary, quick-witted, had seen it was the best and most obvious thing to do. 'But I'll go, lovey.'

'No, don't you think it's best if you stay with the girls, Mum? I can describe the man, can't I? I mean, suppose he doesn't call back tomorrow mornin'? That might mean he went away suspicious about me saying you were out and tellin' him to come back in the mornin', and if he's suspicious that means he's got something on his mind, don't you think so? Mind, he was as cheerful as anything, and ever so fancy, and a bit saucy as well, he asked me if I was Walworth's May Queen.'

'Oh, 'e sounds a very cheerful gent, lovey, at your age I'd've liked to be asked if I was a May Queen,' said Maggie. 'Still, you did right, we can't be too careful.' She mused. 'I don't know I'm sure a man that's done a murder would walk around lookin' for lodgings the day after, though, specially not in the same neighbourhood. But all right, you go to the police station, then, and I'll stay with the girls. Oh, they're up to something.'

There were yells and squeals from the kitchen. Maggie didn't have too much trouble on the whole with her girls, but they had their moments of argument and quarrel. She returned to the kitchen to restore order, and Trary put her boater on and went to the Rodney Road police station. She was hoping to see Constable Bradshaw again. In the space of a day, Trary had decided that if he wasn't married he'd do very nicely for her mum.

He wasn't there. But she met none other than Inspector Greaves himself, the man in charge of the case. She also met Nicholas Chamberlain. She thought the detective-sergeant homely, friendly and manly. To Trary, manly was admirable. She thought Inspector Greaves grizzled and fatherly, if a little bit awesome. She was surprised how

51

encouraging he was, how carefully he listened to her, and she liked the smile Detective-Sergeant Chamberlain gave her. Inspector Greaves told her she was the most sensible girl he had ever met. Detective-Sergeant Chamberlain told her, after he had seen her home, that she was a peach of a girl.

He would be there himself in the morning, he said, with a colleague. He spoke to her mum. Maggie agreed to receive the man, whom Trary said was a Mr Bates, if he did come back. She'd receive him in her parlour. Nicholas would be in the street, with Chapman, and knock on the door five minutes after Mr Bates had arrived.

Maggie's parlour was comfortable enough with its solid, upholstered Victorian sofa and armchairs, but lacked any pictures or ornaments. There had been one lovely picture, a large one, of a storm at sea, a depiction of the Spanish Armada meeting its doom, which her husband had acquired just before they were married. But that was in pawn now, with the other pictures, all the ornaments and the nice pieces of china kept in the corner cabinet. There was a bare look to the walls, the mantelpiece and the hearth. The brass companion set, a wedding present, was in pawn too. So was the lovely brass fender. The pawnbroker had offered her money for the fender, and Maggie was presently thinking she'd have to go and accept his offer.

The cheerful, smiling Mr Jerry Bates wasn't put off by the obvious.

'It's a tidy house you've got, Mrs Wilson, I can see that. I've been places, yer know, and seen all kinds, and I always say if someone keeps a tidy house, you can lay to it you'll get a good bed with a decent mattress.'

'Well, I wouldn't offer no-one a bed that didn't have a decent mattress,' said Maggie, hiding her nervousness as she studied him. His boater was off, his brown hair thick and wavy, his moustache handsome, his wide eyes full of light and good fellowship, and he looked as if he'd spent lots of time in the sun.

52

'I can offer references,' said Mr Bates. 'I last had lodgings with a fam'ly in Dartford.'

'I'm sure,' said Maggie. She was having an awkward and nervous time. Mr Bates was different in every way from the oily, smirking Mr Hooper. He was very open and frank in his manner, and so cheerful. Just the kind of lodger she'd like. Oh, Lord, he couldn't be the man the police were after, he surely had to be just a man looking for lodgings. 'What fam'ly d'you 'ave yourself?' she asked.

'Just me old ma and pa, and they're in Australia, near Sydney. That's a place, I can tell yer, Australia.'

'Oh, my parents – ' Maggie was interrupted by a knock on her front door. Swallowing, she said, 'Excuse me a minute, Mr Bates.'

'Pleasure,' said Mr Bates.

Maggie knew who it was, of course. While she was out of the room, Mr Bates contemplated the ancient wallpaper and the absence of hanging pictures. There weren't many houses, even in Walworth, where the parlours contained not a single picture, not even one of a Highland stag at bay. Unless the occupants had pawned everything. Amid the murmurs of voices at the front door, Mr Bates counted the lighter patches, square or rectangular, on the wallpaper. Six. All with 'Uncle' now, of course. No ornaments, either. And the fire was empty of fuel, the hearth bare. This was a case of a woman with her back to the wall. She'd welcome a lodger. And maybe some charitable gestures.

The murmur of voices became louder. The parlour door opened and Maggie reappeared. There were two men with her.

'Oh, Mr Bates,' she said, 'these gentlemen's from the police, they're doin' the rounds of houses and makin' enquiries, like.'

'Morning, sir,' said Nicholas briskly, 'sorry to barge in, but the enquiries concern the – '

'Hold on, hold on,' said Mr Bates, coming to his feet, 'it's Sunday, yer know, and it's a bit much, disturbin' this lady and her neighbours on a Sunday mornin'.' His cockney accent had a twang to it. 'Don't think much of that meself.'

'It's a murder investigation, sir,' said Nicholas.

'Murder?' Mr Bates sobered up. 'That's different.'

'And most people are at home on a Sunday morning.'

'True,' said Mr Bates, 'I grant yer that, inspector.'

'I'm Detective-Sergeant Chamberlain, sir, and this is Detective-Constable Chapman. We understand from Mrs Wilson that she's a widow and has no lodger at the moment. Our enquiries, of course, concern – '

'Men,' said Mr Bates, and nodded. 'One man in partic'lar, eh? Well, I read about the murder. Nasty. Don't like that kind of cove meself.'

'Neither do we,' said Nicholas. 'However, Mrs Wilson did tell us you were here, asking about a room she has to let. Would you mind answering a few questions?'

'I get you, sergeant,' said Mr Bates cheerfully, 'so go ahead. I wouldn't want Mrs Wilson to think I'd got something to hide.'

Maggie already thought nothing of the kind. She already thought Mr Bates was quite genuine.

Nicholas was quizzing the man. Handsome devil. Fine build. Hearty. Healthy. Frank eyes. Friendly smile. All the same, there were men whose smile was like that on the face of a tiger before it sprang.

'Your name, sir?'

'Jerry Bates.'

'May I ask why you're looking for lodgings, Mr Bates?'

'Because I'm a travellin' bloke, a minin' engineer, just up from Australia.'

'You've just arrived?' enquired Nicholas.

'No, I've been back in the Old Country a few days, stayin' with a friend in his lodgings in Dartford.'

'Could you tell me where you were on Friday night, sir?'

'Same place, sergeant. Dartford.' Mr Bates smiled. 'I'm takin' no offence, I'm appreciative you've got yer duty to do. Ask anything you like.'

'You were in Dartford all Friday night?'

'I was. I left there about six on Saturday evening. You can confirm that with me friend, name of Rodney Foster. Twenty-one Essex Road, Dartford.'

'I see.' Nicholas mused. Chapman gloomed. Waste of time. 'Mr Bates, did you call on any other prospective landlady before you knocked on Mrs Wilson's door?' asked Nicholas.

'Didn't need to,' said Mr Bates. 'I know Walworth. I looked in a newsagent's window and saw Mrs Wilson's card advertisin' a room.'

'Well, the fact is, sir,' said Nicholas, 'a man answering your description did apply for a room at the house of one of Mrs Wilson's neighbours.'

'Well, you bring that neighbour here, sergeant. A lady, was it?' Mr Bates raised an eyebrow, and Nicholas nodded. 'She'll tell you it wasn't me. I came straight here yesterday evenin', here to Mrs Wilson's.'

It's a nothing, thought Nicholas. He saw that Chapman thought so too. And Mrs Wilson was fidgeting, a sign that she no longer liked the questioning. Well, it had had to be done.

'Many thanks, Mr Bates,' he said.

'I appreciate the process,' said Mr Bates, good humour undiminished.

'What process?' asked Nicholas.

'Elimination, yer know.' Mr Bates laughed. 'Except, of course, you could also say elimination's a hanging job.' He laughed again.

'Oh, Mr Bates,' protested Maggie, feeling uncomfortable about everything.

'Apologies, Mrs Wilson. Sometimes me sense of humour gets the better of me.'

'Sorry to have bothered you,' said Nicholas.

'Don't mention it, sergeant,' said Mr Bates. 'Murder's very nasty, and you've got to do your job. I'm still not takin' offence.'

'Sorry we interrupted your Sunday morning, Mrs Wilson,' said Nicholas.

'It's all right, Mr Bates and me both understand,' said Maggie, and saw them out. On the doorstep, she whispered, 'He's just not the one, is he?'

'I can't fault him,' said Nicholas. He noted the colour of Maggie's hair. Light brown, not golden, like the murdered woman's or Mrs Carter's. He shook himself. He was getting obsessive about women's hair.

'Look,' said Maggie, 'I'm sorry we wasted your time, but Trary an' me both thought . . . well, we thought it was right to tell you about 'im.'

'It was absolutely right,' said Nicholas, 'and it can't count as wasted time. Thanks for everything. Goodbye, Mrs Wilson.'

'Goodbye,' said Maggie, stepping out to watch them go. The sharp April sunlight caught her hair and tinted it with gold.

Walking down the street, Chapman said, 'Waste of time all right. If you ask me.'

'I don't need to ask. But let's just check a couple of things with Mrs Buller while we're here.'

Mrs Buller experienced a tingle of importance in having Scotland Yard men call. Nicholas asked what shade of grey was the suit of the man who enquired about lodgings yesterday. Dark grey, said Mrs Buller. Sure? Yes, said Mrs Buller, she didn't have eyes for nothing, she hoped.

Mr Bates's suit was light grey. The girl Trary Wilson had said so last night. And it was light grey this morning. Was the man a cockney with a twang? No, said Mrs Buller.

Nicholas and Chapman went on their way again, heading for the Yard.

'Ruddy useless lead,' said Chapman.

'It was only routine in the first place,' said Nicholas, 'just something to check on. It became an embarrassment for Mrs Wilson.'

'Hard luck. One thing, though.'

'What one thing?' asked Nicholas.

'Dartford. Why'd he leave it to come here?'

'Wake up, Frank. If he left Dartford to commit murder in Walworth, he'd have been back in Dartford an hour later.'

'Only asked,' gloomed Chapman.

'It could have been a good question if it had made sense,' said Nicholas, who had no qualms now about letting Mrs Wilson take Mr Bates in as a lodger.

'I'm only sorry it embarrassed you, Mrs Wilson,' said Mr Bates, 'but give 'em their due, they were rightly quick off the mark as soon as you told 'em you had yours truly in yer parlour. It's got to be faced, a stranger comin' after lodgings does put 'imself in line for being questioned. Under the circs.'

'You stood up to it very good,' said Maggie.

'If I hadn't been able to, I wouldn't have been here,' said Mr Bates amiably.

'Well, it couldn't be helped,' said Maggie, 'they just . . .' She resigned herself to a little lie. 'They just 'appened to be goin' the rounds of knockin' on doors. We needn't talk about it any more. You were saying about Australia when they arrived.'

'So I was.' Mr Bates seemed at home already. 'Yes, that's a place, take my word for it. All kangaroos. More kangaroos than people. Not much work, though, and the goldmines ain't what they're cracked up to be. I'm a minin' engineer, yer know, I'm here to see some City firms that give contracts to travelled engineers like me. That's why I'd like to take lodgings in Walworth. It's handy for the City. Would you like to state what you're askin' by way of rent?'

Maggie felt sensitively contrite that she'd brought the police to a man so obviously genuine. She also felt she'd been thrown a lifebelt that would save her from going under. She was prepared to accept the man was a bit of a joker, but lots of men were jokers, and a woman could deal easier with them than with creatures like that Hooper man.

She made up her mind to accept Mr Bates.

'Five shillings,' she said.

Mr Bates sat up.

'Five bob?' he said. 'Mrs Wilson, that's a giveaway costin'. Like to show me the room?'

'I'd be pleasured,' said Maggie, and led the way to the upstairs back room. Mr Bates, following her, noted the sway of her skirt, the glimpse of a petticoat hem and fine ankles. If Maggie was short of new clothes, if everything she had was past its best, she was very attached, in the way of many women, to wearing clean apparel. Monday washdays were long days of work for her. The upstairs back was, to Mr Bates, singularly clean-looking, the brass and iron bedstead shining, the bed itself covered with a patchwork overlay. There was a gas ring mounted on a metal stand on top of a four-feet mahogany cupboard that contained crockery and utensils. There were two upright chairs, a small table, a small wardrobe, and a basin and pitcher on a little marble-topped table. And there was still room to swing a cat.

'Well, well,' said Mr Bates, 'this looks like home from home to me. Five bob for all this, and a fireside as well? Can't be right, Mrs Wilson, it's a doddle at five bob. I've seen a few lodgings in my time, believe me, and my opinion is you're cheatin' yerself. Let's call it seven an' six, how's that?'

'Mr Bates, no-one in Walworth pays seven an' six for rentin' just one room,' said Maggie.

'And why's that, Mrs Wilson?' he asked, looking her in the eye. 'Because they can't afford it, so you ladies don't ask for it. Five bob's their limit. It's not mine, not for this kind of tidy comfort. I can afford seven an' six, it's worth seven an' six, so that's what I'll be pleased to pay. My motto is fair do's from the start.'

'Well, seven an' six is more than fair, I must say – '

'Done,' said Mr Bates heartily, 'and I hope it won't inconvenience you if I move in now. I brought me bags,

58

you'll have noticed. Well, I had rosy hopes, this address suitin' me just fine.'

'All right, Mr Bates,' said Maggie, frankly pleased by his generosity and his acceptability. 'And it's not inconvenient for you to move in now.'

'You're on, Mrs Wilson, I'll go down and bring me bags up from yer parlour. No, wait, I like to show good faith.' He drew a leather wallet from the inside pocket of his jacket. He opened it. He looked at her, at her facial hollows and the slight rings around her eyes. 'How about if I pay you monthly in advance, not weekly?'

'You don't have to do that,' said Maggie. 'It's a lot, a month's rent, specially at seven an' six a week.'

'Well, for me first four weeks, let me pay that in advance. I like your kind treatment, an' more so considerin' you had to see me stand up to police questions. There, how's that?' He handed her a pound note and a ten-shilling note. It represented manna in the desert to Maggie. She could pay a bit to Mr Monks now, and a bit of her rent owings as well.

'That's nice of you, Mr Bates.'

'You've got children, I reckon,' he said.

'Yes, that's Trary and Daisy you can hear downstairs in the kitchen. My two other daughters, Lily an' Meg, are out playin' with friends.'

'You've got four girls? And you're a widow?' Mr Bates looked sober. 'It's a rough ride, I'll wager it is. Four girls to bring up.' He frowned at what life could do to some people. 'I've met a few hard luck cases in me time, I don't know I've met more hard luck than yours. If there's anything I can do while I'm here, just say the word, Mrs Wilson. A bit of repairin', or any jobs that don't come easy to a woman, you ask Jerry Bates. You won't find me un'elpful. I can handle tools and suchlike.'

'Yes, thanks,' said Maggie, 'but Trary's learned to be useful, an' so 'ave I. Well, I'll let you settle in, then you can meet my girls sometime.'

*

In his house in Westmoreland Road, Harry was tidying up the kitchen before going to the station. It should have been his day off, but the murder investigation meant compulsory overtime for several men, including himself. He was due at the station at ten-thirty, and would probably have to work through the day. Well, once he'd finished in the kitchen he'd be ready. He'd learned to cope domestically, especially during the times when his mother was too unwell to attend to things herself. To give her her due, she'd been a very good housekeeper, taking a pride in ironing his shirts and collars to perfection, and frequently cooking for him the kind of dishes he was fond of, like toad-in-the-hole, steak-and-kidney pudding, and rich meat stews with dumplings. He was eating in simpler fashion now that he had to do his own cooking. Couldn't beat a woman's touch, not in a kitchen.

He thought of the calls he'd made yesterday, and of the women he'd spoken to about lodgers or husbands or sons. He'd come across nothing that he could offer the CID as a promising lead. He'd met some lodgers, and been told about others. They all had alibis. That was routine work for the CID, checking every alibi. They hadn't taxed his own mind very much. They were in his notebook, but outside his province. What he remembered most about the long day was a woman who had four young daughters and no husband, who was in debt to her landlord and to a moneylender called Monks, a blight. He hoped she'd accepted the box of groceries as a gift from the Salvation Army. He should have told Bobby Reeves not to mention him. Perhaps the boy hadn't.

The girls were all in, having a cup of mid-morning cocoa. Lily and Meg, who'd been out, were given the news that they had a new lodger, a nice cheerful man.

'The uvver one wasn't nice,' said Lily.

'Ugh,' said Meg.

'Mum's got some rent,' said Daisy.

60

'Yes, I have,' said Maggie. She had money in her handbag, a whole thirty bob and one and sevenpence besides. And she'd be drawing her weekly pension from the Post Office on Wednesday. 'I'm goin' down the Lane now, we're goin' to have a nice joint of mutton from the market butcher. A shoulder.' A shoulder of mutton was the cheapest joint. It might have a lot of fat, but she'd serve it up as hot and crisp as she could. Her hungry girls would wolf it down, and the fat would be just what they needed, along with the meat. She'd got potatoes, they'd come with so many other things in that box, including onions. She'd make onion sauce to go with the mutton, and buy a fat cabbage. Her girls could have a real Sunday dinner for a change, a roast. There wasn't going to be time to make an apple pie. She'd make one tomorrow, a huge one. Today, she'd give the girls banana custard, something they all loved.

'I'll come down the Lane wiv yer, Mum,' said Lily.

'Me too,' said Meg. Everyone liked going down the Lane, as the East Street market was called.

'I'll take Daisy to church,' said Trary.

'Oh, bovver that,' said Daisy.

'Do you good,' said Trary.

'I dunno I want to be done good to,' said Daisy, 'not in church.'

'I'll iron my best frock, Mum,' said Trary, who had had a conversation with her mother about Mr Bates and the policemen. Mr Bates had proved to be an upright gent with a bit of a twinkle in his eye and a breezy cheerfulness. And he'd insisted on paying seven and six a week rent for his room, and handed over a month's payment in advance. Trary said she hoped he wasn't too good to be true, that after a month he'd start falling behind. Maggie said no, she was sure he wasn't like that. Trary wrinkled her nose, an indication that she hoped her mum didn't get to like their new lodger better than Constable Bradshaw. 'Yes, I'd best run the iron over it if I'm takin' Daisy to church. It's clean, but it needs a new ironing. I don't want Mrs Nosy Parker saying we can't even afford to iron our Sunday frocks.' By Mrs Nosy Parker she meant Mrs Phillips from next door.

'No, lovey, we don't want that,' said Maggie, and smiled. She felt Trary might be thinking more about the threat of Bobby Reeves calling for her than about church or Mrs Phillips.

'Mum, you ought to write that note to Mr Bradshaw before you go out,' said Trary, 'then I'll take it to the police station after Daisy and me come out of church.'

'I thought you 'ad this afternoon in mind,' said Maggie.

'Yes, so's you could dodge that nice boy,' said Meg.

'What nice boy?' asked Trary aloofly.

'The one that forgot to kiss yer when 'e left,' said Lily.

'Oh, that one,' said Trary. 'He's more like a talkin' parrot than a boy. I really wonder how he got out of his cage.'

'I'll write the note now,' said Maggie, and did.

Many people in Walworth were preparing to go to church. Caring crusaders like Sidney and Beatrice Webb, devoted to improving the lot of the poor, were sometimes amazed that people struggling to survive went regularly to church, where they were given sermons instead of something like a side of beef. Mrs Emma Carter, whose small pension and small wage helped her to keep her head above water, frequently attended Sunday morning service at St John's, although she disagreed with the Church of England's refusal to give its blessing to women's emancipation. This morning she was eschewing St John's in favour of composing a letter to the suffragettes' leader, Mrs Emmeline Pankhurst, about the escalation of extreme militancy, which Emma thought would alienate the whole country in the end, and do the cause of women's rights no good at all.

At Scotland Yard, Nicholas was studying a large-scale map of Southwark, together with a great many notes. His concentration was not what it should have been. Thoughts of Mrs Carter kept intruding. She hadn't reported to the police station yesterday, which meant she'd had no caller. But there was some man somewhere who'd been looking for lodgings. Not Mr Bates. Someone like him. A description had been issued, although Inspector Greaves had been heavily sarcastic about assumptions, guesswork and the time spent on Bates, a straw in the wind. Nicholas suggested they might come closer to the murderer once they discovered the identity of his victim. It was damned odd no-one had come forward to report her missing from wherever she lived.

CHAPTER SIX

Trary and Daisy were on their way to church. Trary's
Sunday frock, a summer one of rose pink, with puffed
sleeves, had been carefully ironed by Trary herself. Her
mum had bought it second-hand in the market last year,
and it just about passed with a push. Trary carried herself
along in defiant pride, her Sunday boater on the back of
her head. If there were some Walworth girls with frocks
still crisp with newness, there were few who could match
Trary's proud, springy walk. Little Daisy, in her one worthy
pinafore frock, trotted along beside her.

Behind them came Mr Bates, his walk as jaunty as he was
himself. Maggie had introduced him to her girls before she
went out. As Trary and Daisy entered the little paved
pathway to St John's Church at the end of Charleston
Street, Mr Bates veered towards Turquand Street, a letter
in his hand. 'Be good, girlies,' he called.

Trary put her nose in the air, and Daisy said, 'Crumbs,
what's 'e mean? You got to be good in church, you can't
enjoy yerself.'

'Oh, you can in a way,' said Trary, 'if you think of the
kind miracles Jesus performed, and the joyous multitudes.'
She was proud of 'joyous multitudes' and other expres-
sions of which she was capable. She liked talking, and she
liked hearing herself speak words of several syllables. That
boy yesterday, he just talked as if he was the only one who
could. He'd better not come round this afternoon and start
more of it, or give her any cheek, either.

Outside the church, teenaged boys swooped on her. Trary
was a stunner to them, a corker.

64

' 'Ere, gedorf,' protested Daisy, 'you're treadin' on me feet.'

'Well, you just buzz off, Daisy, we'll look after yer big sister.'

'I can look after myself, thank you, Henry Smithers,' said Trary.

'Cor, yer a fancy gel, you are, Trary.'

'Kindly stop smothering my little sister, you're all 'ooligans. *Hooligans*. Come on, Daisy, let's go in.'

'See yer up the park 's afternoon, Trary?'

'They don't let hooligans in,' said Trary, and took Daisy into the church, collecting some girl friends on the way.

The service to Daisy meant you had to sit, kneel, stand, sing, pray and listen. It wasn't half as good as following a Salvation Army band down the Walworth Road. Trary, however, liked church and loved singing the hymns. And there were moments when she could sit in reverent hope that heaven would be kind to her mum and send her a nice man in place of the one heaven had taken away. That was what the vicar had said at dad's funeral, that a good man had been taken up to heaven.

At the end of the service, after Daisy had fidgeted all through the sermon, she and Trary were out of the church quickly, to avoid getting mixed up with boys again. Trary, coming up to fourteen, didn't have any special boy, mainly because she didn't know any boy she could have a decent talk with. They were all as soppy as daft kids. And some had shiny faces, as if they'd just stuffed themselves, which wasn't exactly appealing to any girl who'd gone hungry with her family for days on end.

'Come on, Daisy, we'll take mum's note to the police station now.'

'Crikey, I ain't never been in a police station,' said Daisy.

'Nor me,' said Trary, 'but I don't suppose we'll get put in prison, specially after we've just come out of church and more specially that we're not wrongdoers. It's not far.'

Daisy trotted gamely along with her bobbing, spring-heeled sister, their boaters yellow in the April sunshine. They went up through Wadding Street, where kids were running in and out of each other's houses amid the fearsome yells of distracted parents. Older male kids called after Trary.

'Oi, gel, 'ow's yer farver down in the Old Kent Road?'

''Ere, 'ow's yer muvver more like, bet she likes yer, don't she?'

''Oo's that wiv yer, yer funny talkin' doll?'

'Take no notice, Daisy,' said Trary.

'Oh, lor',' said Daisy, 'I fink me tape's broke, I fink me drawers is fallin' down.'

'You Daisy,' said Trary in horror, 'don't you dare let 'em fall down, not in this street.'

'It ain't my fault I fink me tape's broke,' said Daisy, right hand clutching at her middle.

'Oh, you blessed girl, you hold them up till we get to the police station.'

'A' right,' said Daisy, putting her faith in the understanding of a kind and fatherly copper.

The desk sergeant looked up as an attractive girl, accompanied by a small girl, walked in.

'Hello, hello?' he said, coming to the counter.

'Good mornin', sir,' said Trary.

'And good morning to you, miss, can I help you?' The sergeant looked fatherly. Walworth kids had a hard time, even if some of them were holy terrors.

'Well, I don't actu'lly need help,' said Trary. Daisy wriggled.

'What's up with the little 'un?' asked the sergeant.

'Nuffink,' said Daisy, a bit pink.

'Excuse me, sir,' said Trary, 'but I've got a letter for Constable Bradshaw – oh, that's 'im.' She dropped an aitch in her glad surprise as Harry appeared. She waved to him. 'Mr Bradshaw, my mum's written you a note, can I give it to you?'

'I'm comin' through,' said Harry, recognizing her.

Putting on his helmet, he reached the counter, lifted the flap and joined Trary.

'Could I whisper first?' she asked.

'Permission granted,' said Harry, and lent her his ear.

'Could I take Daisy somewhere private?'

'Private?'

'She's havin' a bothersome time with her underneath clothes,' whispered Trary.

'Sounds like a calamity in the offing,' said Harry. 'Bring her this way, Trary. Excuse me a moment, sarge.'

'Permission granted,' said the sergeant solemnly.

In an interview room, with Harry waiting outside the closed door, Daisy revealed the bothersome.

'Oh, you fusspot,' said Trary, 'the tape's not broken, you've just tied it lazy. It's too loose.'

'Well, I only said I fink it's broke,' protested Daisy. 'I didn't say it was, I only said I fink.'

Trary undid the tape and re-tied it.

'You're a monkey, you are,' she said, 'givin' me fits in Wadding Street with all them boys about. Come on.'

Outside, she gave Harry her mother's thank-you note. He read it in the corridor. It said she was very grateful for what the Salvation Army had sent. It was an unexpected blessing, especially as she didn't know anyone in the Salvation Army. It was like a miracle, them getting to know about her, and if it wasn't that, then she could only think someone had been very kind, which was just as nice as a Salvation Army miracle.

Smiling to himself, Harry put the note away and left the station with Trary and Daisy. They had to go one way, he another. He had other addresses to check on. Never mind it's Sunday, his sergeant had said, it's a murder enquiry, so get on with it.

'Tell your mother thanks for the note, Trary.'

'Oh, I'll be pleasured to, Mr Bradshaw,' said Trary in her most gracious fashion. Smiling up at him, she added, 'Mum really was most awf'lly touched and kept saying how kind you were, and that your wife was so lucky to have a nice husband like you.'

'I didn't 'ear 'er say – ' Daisy's voice was stopped from operating further. Trary's hand was over her mouth.

'I'm not married,' said Harry.

'Well, upon my soul, aren't you?' exclaimed Trary. 'You do surprise me, Mr Bradshaw.' What a happy piece of news, she thought. 'Oh, you should see our larder now, I don't know when we've ever had so much in it, wasn't it a blessin' you gettin' the Salvation Army to be so good to us? I'm not sure, but I think mum said there's always a cup of tea for you anytime you're passin'.'

'I didn't 'ear – ' Again Daisy's voice was cut short.

'Well, we won't keep you, Mr Bradshaw,' said Trary, 'I'm sure you've got lots of duty to do, and I'd better take Daisy home in case she has more bother. Goodbye, it's been a pleasure, we all hope to see you again soon.'

'So long, Trary,' said Harry, 'so long, Daisy.' He watched them go on their way. The girl was adorable, her mother a fighter.

Going down Wadding Street, still alive with boisterous kids, Daisy said, 'I didn't 'ear mum say about 'im 'aving a lucky wife and about cups of tea.'

'Oh, Daisy, don't you know mothers can't always say what they're thinkin'?' said Trary. 'Specially if they're thinkin' private.'

'Oh, lor', I fink it's really broke this time,' said Daisy.

'What? Oh, not here, you little 'orror.'

'I only said I fink.'

'I'll cut your head off,' said Trary.

Daisy giggled. A boy called after Trary.

'Oi, darlin', want to play muvvers an' farvers?'

Trary, nose in the air, journeyed haughtily on, Daisy skipping along beside her and still giggling.

Maggie, feeling life was kinder, served up a lovely dinner of roast mutton, roast potatoes, lush green cabbage and thick onion sauce. Everyone ate with hungry relish. Halfway through, Mr Bates knocked on the kitchen door and put his cheerful face in.

'Hello, that looks good,' he said. 'Smells even better. No, I don't want to interrupt, Mrs Wilson, I've 'ad a bite to eat meself, but if I might step in and deposit an item or two?' He stepped in. The family watched him place four large bars of wrapped milk chocolate on top of the old sewing-machine, a must in every Walworth home. 'For your girlies, Mrs Wilson. Just a small gesture of appreciation, just a small something, yer know.'

'Crikey,' gasped Lily. Chocolate was a luxury sweet.

'Crumbs,' breathed Daisy in bliss.

'Mr Bates, you shouldn't,' said Maggie.

'Think nothing of it,' said Mr Bates cordially. 'Well, I've got some Sunday papers, and am retirin' to me comfortable quarters to put me feet up an' take a look at what's news and what's been made up. You carry on.' He disappeared.

'He's got a kind heart,' said Maggie.

'Mum, Constable Bradshaw liked your note ever so much,' said Trary.

'Yes, you already said so, love. Twice.' Maggie smiled, then pondered. 'I wonder if we ought to ask 'im to join us for tea.'

'Mr Bradshaw?' said Trary.

'No, Mr Bates. Just to show 'im a bit of welcome. Not to make a habit of it, though. Makin' that kind of habit with a lodger could turn into a rod for our backs. I thought just for tea this afternoon.'

Trary wasn't in favour. Her sisters were.

Daisy, Lily and Meg went out after dinner. Trary helped her mum with the washing-up. At five to three, there was a commanding knock on the front door. Trary, in deep suspicion of who it was, answered the summons.

'Well, here I am, I've come round,' said Bobby, 'and am

I glad, I'll say. You must be the best-lookin' little girl in Walworth. I was tellin' – '

'Just a minute, whoever you are,' said Trary, 'what d'you mean, little girl? I'm gone five feet and nearly fourteen, so kindly don't come round here callin' me little.'

'I'm five eight meself,' said Bobby blithely, 'and I was tellin' my dad he ought to see the girl I'm goin' up the park with. I see you've got a nice Sunday frock on. Ain't it pretty, Trary? Shall I come in an' say hello to yer mum?'

'You can go and jump off a bridge, that's what you can do,' said Trary, and shut the door on him. She waited for the cheeky devil to knock again, but no knock came. She re-opened the door. He was leaning on the gate, cap on the back of his head, his knitted brown jersey and brown trousers obviously his Sunday best. 'Haven't you gone?' she asked accusingly.

'I don't mind waitin' till you're ready,' said Bobby, 'then we can walk to the tram stop. It'll be nice in the park, the sun's shinin'. I'll look after you, Trary, and you can tell me about yerself now we're friends.'

'I'm not goin' to any park with you,' she said.

'Why not?'

'Because with all your sauce an' blessed cheek, you're a talkin' hooligan,' said Trary. 'You don't think my mum would let me go out with a talkin' hooligan, do you? My mum's partic'lar, and so am I.'

Maggie appeared then. She hadn't been able to resist finding out what was going on. Things had suddenly got better for her family, and everyone was more perky. And Trary looked very alive and challenging.

'Hello, Bobby, you've come callin' for Trary, then?'

'Yes, how d'yer do, Mrs Wilson, I did promise I'd come, and I don't like not keepin' a promise. Besides which, I didn't want to disappoint Trary. Don't she look a treat in 'er Sunday frock? You don't mind me takin' her for a tram ride to Ruskin Park?'

'No, I don't mind,' said Maggie.

'He'll be lucky,' said Trary, 'I never heard a more cheeky devil.'

'I'll bring her back, Mrs Wilson.'

'I'm goin' to have a fit in a minute,' said Trary.

'I'd like you to bring 'er back, Bobby, of course,' said Maggie, finding it hard not to smile.

'Mind, if she wanted to, she could come and 'ave Sunday tea with us afterwards,' said Bobby. 'I told me mum she was a nice-behaved girl.'

'Oh, thank you, I'm sure,' said Trary, 'but when you get home with a black eye and a broken leg, you can tell your mum that the nice-behaved girl done it.' She frowned. 'Did it,' she said.

'Well, go an' put your hat on, love,' said Maggie. 'It'll be nice for you, a tram ride and a walk in the park.'

'All right, you boy,' said Trary, 'I'll come to the park, then, but I'm not walkin' to the tram stop with you. We've got lookin' neighbours, and I don't want them lookin' at me walkin' with you, they'll think I've come down in the world. You walk first and I'll follow. I don't mind gettin' on the tram with you, as long as there's no-one about. And would you mind stoppin' your grinnin'? When you're not talkin', you're grinnin', and sometimes you're talkin' and grinnin' together. Well, now I'll go an' put my boater on. You can start walkin'.'

Maggie laughed. Trary was giving Bobby such a hard time that it had to mean the beginning of a special kind of friendship. Trary had her own way of dealing with unwanted boys. She just put her nose in the air, spoke a few well-chosen words, and left them wondering if their proper place was in the Zoo. Bobby looked as if he was going to be different. All her well-chosen words bounced off him, and her nose in the air only made his grin widen. You could tell he was taken with her, and the fact that she couldn't put him off was a challenge to her. Maggie was sorry she was going to miss the rest of their afternoon's conversation.

'I got you, Trary,' said Bobby, 'I'm off to the tram stop, then. So long, Mrs Wilson, I'll see she gets 'ome safe and don't do any wandering about, seein' she's only young.' And he strolled off whistling.

'You just can't believe his sauce,' said Trary. Maggie smiled. 'Still, I suppose I'd best do what I said and follow him, or he'll come back and talk us to death through our letter-box.'

'Oh, I expect you could 'old your own, pet,' said Maggie, feeling sure she knew why Trary had ironed her Sunday frock.

CHAPTER SEVEN

Emma, just about to make herself a cup of tea, alerted to a knock on her front door. King and Queen Street was enjoying Sunday afternoon quiet. The closure of the nearby market at midday was always the beginning of the quietest hours of the week. Some children went to Sunday school, others went to the nearest park, and the rest called a truce. Hard-working parents put their feet up and enjoyed a blissful forty winks.

Emma came out of her kitchen and ascended the little staircase to her bedroom at the front of her house. Silently she slid the window up. She put her head out just as the knock was repeated. On the pavement, at her door, was yesterday's plainclothes policeman, Detective-Sergeant Chamberlain.

'Hello there,' she called.

Nicholas looked up. He saw the sunshine gilding her braided hair, and he saw the smile on her face.

'Good afternoon, Mrs Carter.'

'Good afternoon, Sergeant Chamberlain. I'll come down.' Emma closed the window and appeared at her door a few moments later. 'Come in,' she said.

'This isn't really an official call.'

'On a quiet Sunday afternoon? I should hope not.'

'I happened to be passing,' said Nicholas.

'Really?' said Emma, her cream brocade dress giving her a touch of elegance, something not too common in Walworth, where ladies' attire was practical blouses, homely shawls and coarse skirts in the main. In the summer, however, girls flaunted their bows, their sashes and their bright hair ribbons. 'Well, Sergeant Chamberlain, perhaps you could now happen to step inside, before my neighbours spot you again and think I'm capitulating.'

Taking his Homburg hat off, Nicholas stepped in. Most plainclothes policemen wore Bowlers. Nicholas went along with Inspector Greaves in favouring a Homburg.

'Capitulating?' he said. 'I think you're ahead of me.'

'Am I?' said Emma. 'I'm sure Sherlock Holmes would make the right deduction.'

'I think my Inspector sees me as a Dr Watson, not a Sherlock Holmes.'

'Well, I rather like Dr Watson,' said Emma, 'he's more lovable than Mr Holmes. Mr Holmes would look down his fine nose at women's rights. Dr Watson would lend his sympathy and support. Where was I?' Emma knew precisely where she was. She was teasing the opposition. 'Oh, yes, capitulating. I meant, of course, that I didn't want my neighbours to think I'd gone over to the enemy by inviting one of them to Sunday tea. If Mrs Pankhurst got to hear, she'd have me shot at dawn.'

'She's formidable enough to give the order,' said Nicholas. 'I listened to her once, in the line of duty.'

'You're in favour of votes for women?' asked Emma.

'I've an open mind.'

'That means you sit on the fence,' said Emma. 'That's almost cowardly, you know.'

'I do know. I'm more at home chasing crooks.'

'Don't you think you come down a little heavily on suffragettes?'

'Only when you're naughty,' said Nicholas, and she made a little face at him. 'Anyway, as I was passing, I thought I'd knock and see how things were with you.'

'That's very kind,' said Emma, 'but what things?'

'Oh, visits or enquiries from strangers.'

Emma gave him a look of curiosity.

'That doesn't really make sense to me,' she said. 'The stranger in question, the man recommended by Mrs Buller, has obviously found lodgings now. You seem to think he's still interested in me. Why?'

'Ask me another,' said Nicholas.

Emma laughed.

'Well, since you're here, worrying unnecessarily, would you like a cup of tea?' she asked. 'I was about to make one for myself. I usually do at this time on a Sunday.' It was almost three o'clock.

'I won't say no.'

'Find a place for your hat, then. Anywhere will do. Then please sit down and I'll make the pot.' Emma departed to her kitchen. Nicholas placed his hat on a chair and sat down. He thought the room very pleasant. She might be a suffragette, but she had a very feminine touch. In his book, only a woman could turn a house into a home and place her special mark on it. Men had a different purpose in life. He thought of his wife, a Lancashire girl who had been in service in London, and how she had made a home of the flat in which they started their married life. A sweet girl, she had died in childbirth six years ago, when she was only twenty and he twenty-five. He had lost them both, wife and child. It had made him feel how much harder and more difficult life was for women, and how vulnerable they were, despite their own kind of strengths. He understood the aims of the suffragettes, but their aggression dismayed him. They spoiled for him his image of women, or perhaps the image of what he wanted them to be. He liked them to be like Molly, who had blessed his life all too briefly.

Emma brought a laden tray in. She placed it on a small table and sat down opposite Nicholas. He thought her quite different from Molly. Molly had been bubbly. Mrs Carter was composed. Pouring the tea, she asked if he took sugar.

'No sugar, Mrs Carter, thanks,' he said, and she passed the cup and saucer to him.

'A home-made biscuit?'

'Home-made?'

'From a recipe of Mrs Beeton's, called farmhouse biscuits.'

75

'I'll try one,' he said, and she offered the biscuits from a tin. He took one. He tried it. It was crisp and good. He said so. She accepted the compliment with a modest smile.

'Are you worried about me?' she asked.

'I've no real reason to be,' he said, and finished the biscuit. Its appealing flavour lingered. 'I suppose it's to do with your hair, it's identical in colour to the victim's. You read, did you, that the murderer cut off a strand?'

'Yes. Poor woman. But you're being ridiculous, aren't you, sergeant? I'm presuming, of course, that you think the monster is going to make a nasty habit of going for women with fair hair.'

'It's a feeling I have,' said Nicholas, 'and it's not doing me any good.' She offered the biscuit tin again. He shook his head. 'No more, thanks.'

'That's not very flattering,' said Emma.

'They're very good, believe me,' he said, and sipped the excellent tea.

'I add a little honey to the recipe,' said Emma. 'If I had some capital, I'd start my own little biscuit factory. Are you always a worrying policeman?'

'Not always, no.'

'I thought all policemen were hardened and objective men,' said Emma.

'We do get hardened, Mrs Carter.'

'I can understand that, but it's not very fair of you to take it out on inoffensive and long-suffering women.'

That little arrow, aimed with directness but no malice, made Nicholas smile.

'Long-suffering, yes, I'll agree with that,' he said, 'but inoffensive? Did you actually say that?'

'Of course I said it. Compared to crooks and footpads and ruffians, the suffragettes are very inoffensive.'

'The cup of tea was very welcome, and the biscuit first-class,' said Nicholas, 'so I'll forgive you for trying to flannel me.'

'Flannel?' said Emma crisply. 'Nothing of the kind. And

76

I refuse to be forgiven. Have you ever seen your uniformed men in action against us?'

'I've stood on the sidelines.'

'And what have you observed from the sidelines?'

'Nothing very creditable.'

'How nice of you to make such an honest admission,' said Emma.

'I meant on the part of both sides,' said Nicholas.

'Oh, dear, now you've spoiled yourself. Don't you sympathize with the anger that drives my sister suffragettes into acts of provocation?'

'I'm not keen on aggressive women, Mrs Carter.'

'You prefer us meek?' said Emma.

'No, not at all.'

'Obedient?'

'I don't picture them like that.'

'Sweet and uncomplaining, then?' said Emma gravely.

'No, like you,' said Nicholas.

'Like me?' Emma looked astonished. 'But I'm a terrible person, finicky, fastidious and fault-finding.'

'Good Lord, all that?' he said.

She laughed.

'But I can say I'm a pacific suffragette myself.'

'I'm relieved,' said Nicholas.

'Nevertheless, Sergeant Chamberlain, I want the vote and mean to have it.'

'Yes, why not?' he said. A little grin appeared. 'But what would a terrible person like you do with your vote?'

'My word, you really are surprising for a policeman,' she said. 'You're actually quite entertaining. Are you in charge of this murder investigation?'

'No, Inspector Greaves is. I'm one of two detective-sergeants assigned to help. Mrs Carter, thanks for being so hospitable. I'll get out of your way now.' He rose. Emma rose with him.

'There's no need to worry about me, or about strangers calling on me,' she said.

'You're right, of course. Anyway, I think you can handle a situation, Mrs Carter, I think you're a resolute woman.'

'Dear me,' said Emma, 'is that a compliment?'

'Just my impression,' said Nicholas. He picked up his hat and opened the door. 'Goodbye, Mrs Carter, and good luck.'

'Goodbye, sergeant.'

He stepped out. She stood at the open door. A burly man in a tight-fitting Sunday suit passed by, a small boy with him and holding his hand. A woman was following, also in her Sunday clothes, a bulky-skirted brown dress and a large round black straw hat adorned with bunches of rosy cherries. Behind her two young girls straggled. She turned.

'If you two little perishers don't come on,' she called, 'I'll 'and yer over to a policeman.' She stopped to address Nicholas. 'You seen any coppers about what'll take charge of me two monkeys?' she asked loudly and for the benefit of her straggling daughters.

'Try the Zoo, madam,' said Nicholas, 'they've got cages there for monkeys.'

'There y'ar, you 'ear that?' shouted the woman to the girls. 'It'll be the monkeys' cage for yer if me an' yer dad don't get yer to yer Aunt Ivy's on time.'

The little girls hurried up and went on with their mother. Nicholas crossed the street. He turned and gave Emma a little salute. She smiled, then closed the door on the April sunshine, gathered up the tea things and thought about the pleasure that awaited her in the contents of the current issue of the *Strand Magazine*. The contents included the latest adventure of Sherlock Holmes and Dr Watson. Yes, perhaps Sergeant Chamberlain was more like Dr Watson than Holmes. That would not be surprising. Most men were not really as sharp-minded as Holmes.

'What was I saying?' asked Bobby.

'How should I know?' asked Trary, walking the paths

78

of Ruskin Park with her new acquaintance. 'I mean, you've said most things twice over. I can't think why I've come out with someone who talks as much as you do, then can't remember what it's about. You ought to go to a doctor about it, I've heard some doctors can help boys like you. It's best to have a complaint like that seen to while you're still young, it can't be cured once you're grown up, no-one can help you then.'

'I wasn't plannin' on goin' to any doctor,' said Bobby, watching boys getting off with girls, 'I didn't know I'd got a complaint.'

'Course you have,' said Trary, 'I never met any boy who's got a complaint more chronic than yours. Bless my soul . . .' She paused. She liked that phrase. So she said it again. 'Bless my soul, you might never get cured, even if you do see a doctor, you might go on talkin' for ever and ever. No-one'll ever marry you, ladies don't like marryin' talkin' machines.'

'Funny you talkin' about marryin',' said Bobby. 'Well, I've never thought about it meself yet, well, not till . . .'

'When I get married,' said Trary, 'it'll be to a nice jolly man, like my dad was, someone who won't mind if I do a bit of talkin' myself.'

'Well, I like that,' said Bobby, 'you been – '

'I wish you wouldn't keep interruptin',' said Trary, 'I can't hardly 'ear myself think.'

Bobby grinned. What a girl. He'd never met anyone like her. All the airs and graces too, like he'd read about in books. And she was three years younger than he was. Cheeky. He grinned again. The park was overflowing with sunshine, with boys and girls, and with strolling men and women. The white Sunday frocks of the girls fluttered, their long hair or pigtails hanging down their backs, and flowers dancing in their straw hats. Park-keepers in their regulation brown suits and brown bowlers watched to make sure rowdy boys didn't chase squealing girls over the grass. Signs said, 'Please Keep Off The Grass'. Old people sat on benches, looking at young Walworth ladies promenading with their young men.

'Would you like a sit-down, me lady?' asked Bobby generously.

'Kind of you to ask, I'm sure,' said Trary, conscious that the soles of her button-up Sunday shoes were threadbare.

'There's seats, there,' said Bobby, and they walked towards an empty bench. Two sturdy boys loomed up and stood in the way, eyes on Trary. The sunshine enriched her remarkably creamy skin, and the tilt of her boater gave her a piquant look.

' 'Ello, girlie, 'oo's you, then?' asked one boy.

'Yus, 'oo's yer muvver?' asked the other.

'None of your business,' said Trary, putting her nose in the air.

'Push off,' said Bobby.

' 'Ello, 'ello, did someone say somefink, Charlie?' asked the first boy.

'Dunno,' said the second boy, 'I wasn't listening.'

'I fink it was streaky 'ere. Where'd 'e come from? Did you see where 'e come from, Charlie?'

'Fell orf a barrer somewhere, I shouldn't wonder,' said Charlie.

'There y'ar,' said the first boy to Bobby, 'yer fell orf a barrer. So just 'oppit.'

'Sorry,' said Bobby, and trod on his foot. He exhaled painfully. 'Now push off,' said Bobby.

'Oh, yer bleeder,' said the injured party, 'yer near crippled me. Did yer see that, Charlie, did yer see what 'e done?'

'Trod on yer,' said Charlie.

' 'Oo's goin' to nobble 'im first?'

'You 'ave first go,' said Charlie, 'I'll look after me young pearly queen.' He grinned at Trary. 'Come on, I'll take yer for a lemonade.' He put a hand on her arm.

'Oh, sorry,' said Trary, and trod on his foot.

'Cor, strike a light,' he gasped, 'yer done me big toe in.'

'Could've been yer nose,' said Bobby, 'me girl's a terror. So am I. So push off. Go an' do yer Sunday knittin'.'

'Listen, I got a good mind – '

'Buzz off.' Bobby had a glint in his eye. Two girls fluttered by.

'It ain't bleedin' civilized 'ere,' said Charlie, 'let's get after the decent stuff.' He limped off with his friend.

'I don't know, some boys,' said Trary, seating herself on the bench and giving her threadbare soles a rest. Bobby sat down beside her.

'Good on yer, Trary, good bit of work you did,' he said. 'I'm proud of you. I don't know I ever met – '

'Excuse me, I'm sure,' said Trary, smoothing her frock over her knees, 'but what d'you mean by tellin' those hooligans I was your girl? Blessed cheek, I still don't hardly know you, I've just come to the park with you, that's all. And I only come because I didn't want to be talked at through our letter-box all day.'

'Well, Trary, I don't know I've ever talked at anyone through a letter-box – '

'Excuse me again, I'm sure,' said Trary, 'but I don't remember sayin' you could call me Trary. I'm Miss Wilson to you, I'll thank you to know.'

'I can't call you that, you're not grown up yet,' said Bobby. 'Mind, that don't mean I don't want you for me girl. D'you know, I never – '

'Here we go round the mulberry bush,' said Trary.

'Yes, I never had a girl before,' said Bobby, 'not a reg'lar one, not till I met you. I'm glad I waited till I was old – well, fairly old – before makin' up me mind, or I might be goin' out with someone not 'alf as crackin' as you. When you're younger, like I was once, you can get victimized by yer own impetuosity.'

'Impetu – impetuosity?' Trary went green with jealousy that she'd never used that word herself, and that he'd come out with it just like that.

'When you're younger you don't stop to think like you

do when you're older,' said Bobby. 'Imagine if I'd already
'ad a girl when I met you, I wouldn't 'alf have felt sick.
I feel fine, actu'lly. We can go out Saturdays an' Sundays,
you an' me, I could treat you to tram rides, I've got a bit
of money saved up. Of course, you're too young for us to
be kissin' friends, but when you're a bit older – '

'Listen to him,' breathed Trary, addressing the park in
general and no-one in particular. 'I never heard anything
more aggravatin'. What d'you mean, kissin' friends? You'll
be lucky. I'm kissin' age now, I am, but not with you. I'm
partic'lar, I'll have you know. Besides which, if you think
I'm goin' out with a talkin' gasbag, you can think again.
Of course, I can't stop you comin' round and bashin' on
our door and hollering through our letter-box, but that
don't mean I'm goin' on tram rides with you.'

'Crikey,' said Bobby in admiration, 'you can't 'alf speak
your piece, Trary. You're better at it than me mum. I keep
tellin' her, she ought to speak a real piece to me dad, he
needs – well, never mind that, the fact is I like you more
all the time. I don't know I can wait till next Saturday to
take you out, I'll probably call for yer one evenin' in the
week. Say Wednesday.'

'Well, I don't know,' said Trary, exhilarated, 'you don't
'appen to have won medals for your sauce, I suppose?'

'I won a bottle of port for me mum in a Christmas raffle
once,' said Bobby, 'but I didn't get any medals. Is your
fam'ly poor, Trary?'

'Mum don't have much comin' in,' confessed Trary.

'We don't have a lot, either,' said Bobby, 'it's mostly
from me mum's old clothes stall. But I'm not goin' to be
poor all me life, I can tell you. I don't mind bein' poor for
a bit, but not for ever. So I went up to Fleet Street last
week to ask in newspaper offices about bein' apprenticed
to learnin' a newspaper trade.'

'Which one?' asked Trary.

'Printin',' said Bobby, 'newspaper printin'. Constable
Bradshaw, a friend of mine, put me up to it.'

'Yes, isn't he kind?' said Trary, already fond of Harry.

'He told me newspaper printin' is where the good wages are. Go up and show your face, he said, and ask about bein' taken on as an apprentice. They might chuck you out, he said, but they won't do a hanging job on you. Well, I went in everywhere. I didn't exactly get chucked out, but they all said not this year, Mr Reeves.'

'I bet they didn't call you that,' said Trary.

'Yes, they did,' said Bobby, 'they have to talk polite to you in case you don't buy their paper. Next day I saw Mr Bradshaw and told 'im no luck. He asked did I go to the *Daily Mail*, which was a thrivin' paper, he said. I said I didn't see any *Daily Mail* offices in Fleet Street, so he told me where it was and to try me luck there. He said to ask for Lord Northcliffe.'

'Who?' asked Trary.

'Yes, ask for Lord Northcliffe, he said. So I went up and went in, and I said could I see Lord Northcliffe. I said please, of course. The bloke at the desk asked was I a friend of 'is Lordship, and I said not yet I wasn't, but I would be if he'd give me a job as a printin' apprentice. The bloke gave me a funny look and asked what my name was. I told 'im and he took me to see another bloke down in some basement. I asked was he Lord Northcliffe, and he said no, he was Harold Briggs and hoped I wouldn't mind about that. Well, he 'ad a talk with the first bloke, and Mr Briggs kept laughin'. Then he asked me questions about meself an' me fam'ly, then he wrote things down on paper an' told me all right, they'd take me on. He said men like me was few and far between – '

'Men? Men?' said Trary. 'I bet he didn't say men, I bet he said talkin' gasbags.'

'Well, he didn't say men exactly, but he did say I was to be a teaboy and runner first off, and learn in between, and I was to start on the last Monday in July. I'm not gettin' much wages, not at first, just seven bob a week, but he said I could count on favourable prospects. So what d'you think, Trary?'

'Crikey, favourable prospects?' Trary looked at him with new eyes. 'Would you like a piece of chocolate?' She took the wrapped bar, the present from Mr Bates, out of her little handbag. Bobby gazed at it. 'Our new lodger gave us all a bar each,' she said.

'You got a new lodger?' said Bobby. 'That's a help for yer mum. Is he a bit of all right?'

'He better be,' said Trary. Undoing the wrapping, she broke off a piece of the chocolate bar and gave it to Bobby.

'All this?' he said.

'Look, it don't mean I'm your girl,' she said.

'No, but a big piece like this does mean you're gettin' fond of me,' said the irrepressible Bobby.

'Oh, you daft lump,' said Trary. She was young, not yet fourteen, but the suggestion that this cheeky ha'porth thought he could start courting her was more comical than embarrassing. Because of the death of her dad, Trary, as her mum's eldest daughter, had had to be a support as well as a blessing to her. She had an outlook and a resilience that equated her with maturer daughters of hard-pressed mothers. But she was still young in years, and knew it was laughable to have a boy talking as if they could go courting. Even so, it was laughable in an enjoyable way.

Bobby looked at her, a grin on his face.

The sunlight was dancing in her eyes.

CHAPTER EIGHT

When Trary arrived home, the kitchen table was laid for tea, and her mum was ready to put the kettle on. Trary noticed shrimps, a whole heap of them, in a basin.

'You didn't go to tea with Bobby and 'is fam'ly, then?' asked Maggie, whose harassed look had eased considerably.

'That boy, he never stops talkin',' said Trary. 'And no, I didn't go home with him, not knowing him all that much.' Trary did actually like to take her time making new friends and establishing new relationships. 'But d'you know, he had the sauce to say I was his girl.'

'Did 'e kiss yer?' asked Daisy.

'I don't allow unknown boys to kiss me,' said Trary haughtily.

'She's blushin' again,' said Meg.

'Crumbs, 'e must've give 'er six kisses,' said Lily.

'Did yer like it, Trary?' asked Daisy.

'What a life for a girl,' said Trary, 'first I go up the park with a daft boy, now I've got to have tea with me daft sisters. Mum, all those shrimps, can we afford it?'

'Mr Bates treated us,' said Maggie, 'he bought them from the muffin man. He's comin' down to 'ave tea with us. Well, just this once, I thought we ought to ask him.' Maggie had thought that as it was his first day, and as it was Sunday, and as he'd shown himself genuine and generous, it was right to be a bit hospitable and give him a bit of a welcome.

Trary wrinkled her nose. Their new lodger might be handsome and friendly, but all Trary's instincts pointed her at Constable Bradshaw, not Mr Bates. She hoped it wasn't going to prove too difficult, bringing her mum and Mr

Bradshaw together. She'd have to think carefully about her next step. Mr Bradshaw would make a lovely new dad. Trary weaved hopes and wishes.

'Well, well,' said the jovial Mr Bates, as he sat down with the family. Maggie had baked a cake, having bought some dried fruit during her morning's shopping. There was also a large plateful of bread and margarine and a pot of jam, as well as the shrimps for a starter. 'What a spread, girlies, eh? Home from home, yer know, as far as I'm concerned.' Extrovert, tanned and manly, he was larger than life to Lily and Daisy, his handsome moustache and boisterous healthiness making him look like someone from another world. He had them giggling as he talked about how the shrimps reminded him of his days as a boy, when he dug for cockles at Southend. 'You don't find cockles in Australia, not like you do at Southend. Soon as the tide runs out, there they are, showin' just their eyes in the wet sand and winkin' at you. Shrimps, well, you can find shrimps anywhere, but not cockles. Thanks, Mrs Wilson, I don't mind if I do, but let the girls 'elp themselves first. Little ladies before large grown-ups, eh, Meg?' He passed the basin of shrimps to Meg on his left.

On his right, Daisy said, 'Mister, I'm most little.'

'So you are, Daisy, so you are. All right, you're next, then.'

Trary looked disgusted. Their new lodger was taking over. Her mum didn't seem to mind, and her sisters were already treating him like an uncle. There he was, teasing them, winking at them, and making them giggle. But Trary had to admit he did have a way with them. He was jolly, like their dad had been, and she had to further admit he was a lot better than their previous lodger.

Daisy and Lily were fascinated that he'd been to Australia. Meg said it was as far away from England as a country could be. Mr Bates said it wasn't as far away as all that. You only had to dig a hole deep enough in your back yard and you'd come out right in the middle of Australia. And probably the first thing you'd see would be a kangaroo. Had they ever seen a kangaroo?

'I seen pictures in books,' said Lily.

'We all 'ave,' said Meg.

'But we ain't never seen a real one,' said Daisy.

'I expect they've got some at the Zoo,' said Maggie, fully aware that Mr Bates was like a tonic to her girls.

'We ain't been there,' said Lily.

'Not to the Zoo?' said Mr Bates. 'Well, that's a shame. Mind, I don't suppose they've got kangaroos there like they 'ave in Australia. In Australia, you fall over them. You can have a nasty accident fallin' over a kangaroo. And do they jump, you bet they do. In Australia, yer know, they don't say "oh crikey", they say "jumpin' kangaroos".'

'I meant to say before, it's a funny thing you 'aving been to Australia, Mr Bates,' remarked Maggie, 'because that's where me sister and parents are, and in Sydney too. I suppose you didn't come across them, did you?'

Mr Bates, looking highly intrigued, said, 'I might have, I've met quite a few people Down-Under. What's their name?'

'My dad's Alfred Palmer, my mum's Margaret Palmer,' said Maggie. 'My sister's Joyce, and she's married now, to an Australian called Mick Kennedy.'

Mr Bates searched his memory.

'Palmer, Palmer,' he mused. 'And Kennedy, you said? Well, no, I can't say those names ring a bell, Mrs Wilson. Mind, I wasn't in Sydney a lot, I spent most time up-country, bein' a minin' engineer. I suppose you could do with havin' your parents back here, 'elping you to bring up yer girls. All the same, no-one could say they're not a credit to you. And I meant what I said this morning, that if I can give you any needful 'elp at times, you just say the word.'

'We all give mum help all the time,' said Trary.

'I'm sure you do,' said Mr Bates admiringly. 'Well, now

I'm ready for a slice of yer home-made cake, Mrs Wilson, it looks a work of art. That's what arrives out of some kitchen ovens, works of art.'

Undoubtedly, he was an entertainment, but when the tea was over he didn't outstay his welcome. He spoke his thanks to Maggie, told the girls they were the pick of Walworth, and then said he'd take a stroll round his old haunts of South London. He left the house ten minutes later.

Maggie settled down for a quiet evening of darning. The younger girls played ludo, and Trary did some homework. When Daisy, Lily and Meg eventually went up to bed, Trary made what sounded like an irrelevant remark.

'I've been thinkin' it's a shame, really.'

'What is?' asked Maggie.

'That nice policeman,' said Trary.

'Mr Bradshaw? What about 'im, love?'

'Livin' all alone, a kind man like that.'

'All alone?' said Maggie.

'Well, not havin' a wife,' said Trary.

'Oh?' said Maggie.

'They say men go to early graves when they don't have wives to look after them. Wouldn't it be tragic, Mum, if Mr Bradshaw passed away early through not havin' a lovin' wife?'

'He didn't look to me as if he was going to pass away that early, love,' said Maggie.

'Oh, you can't tell by a man's looks, Mum, specially a man like Mr Bradshaw, who has to show a brave face to the world on account of bein' a policeman. He could be ill inside, havin' to live alone.'

'Dearie me, that is sad,' said Maggie, trying not to smile.

'Yes, he can't be happy about it,' said Trary. 'Oh, by the way, that boy's goin' to work in printin', for a newspaper.'

'What boy?' asked Maggie. 'Oh, Bobby Reeves, you mean?'

'Is that his name? I can't remember it myself,' said Trary.

Maggie smiled. She felt life had suddenly got better for her family. Nice things had happened.

Except there was still Mr Monks.

Daisy, Lily and Meg went off to St John's Church School the next morning, Trary to West Square School for Girls, where she could make the most of what it could offer if she stayed until she was sixteen. She had told her mum she ought to leave at fourteen and try to get a job, but Maggie said no, they'd manage somehow.

With the house reduced to quiet, Maggie bagged up Monday's washing. There was no fuel either for the kitchen range or the scullery copper. But with money in her purse, she could afford to take her laundry to the local Bagwash, which charged a shilling for twenty-eight pounds. And she could order some coal on her way back.

A knock on the kitchen door was followed by Mr Bates putting his head in. Maggie conceded he was a vigorously good-looking man, his tanned face and breezy smile very welcome after the fat, pasty face and oily smirk of Mr Hooper.

'Morning,' he said, 'any odd jobs required to be performed, lady?'

'Odd jobs?' said Maggie.

'Like knockin' in a nail or two, or mendin' a chair leg?'

Maggie smiled. 'It's good of you, Mr Bates, but I don't 'ave any broken chair legs today.'

'Are you goin' out?' enquired Mr Bates. Maggie had her well-worn velvet toque hat on.

'Yes, I'm takin' me Monday laundry to the bagwash, I've run out of anything to light the copper with.'

'I'll take it,' said Mr Bates, 'I was goin' out meself, in any case. I'd count it a pleasure, yer know. You don't want to carry a heavy bag like that when I can perform.'

'But don't you have to go on business to the City?' asked Maggie.

'Not today,' said Mr Bates. 'You place that bag in me

arms, Mrs Wilson, and I'll give it a quick walk to the old bagwash. Believe me, even if I ain't had the privilege of bein' a husband yet, I know a woman's work is never done. I'll lay odds you've got a houseful of work to get on with, so you let me – ' He was interrupted by a sharp rat-a-tat on the front door. Maggie winced.

'Oh, that's Mr Monks,' she exclaimed in a rush. Mr Monks always announced his arrival with a peremptory rat-a-tat.

'Who's Mr Monks?' asked Mr Bates, noting her worried expression.

Maggie hesitated, then said, 'A moneylender. I went an' borrowed three pounds from 'im several weeks ago, only I've not been able to . . . oh, it's me own 'eadache, I don't want to bother you with it.'

'The gent's one of those, is he?' said Mr Bates. 'Says you owe 'im a lot more than you borrowed, does he? Mrs Wilson, you leave him to me.' The rat-a-tat was repeated on an even sharper note.

'Mr Bates, I can pay him a bit off now.'

'I know, but a bit won't do much good with a bloke like him, I've met 'is kind before. Don't you worry, Mrs Wilson, I'll see to the geezer.'

Mr Bates answered the door. A plump, heavy-jowled man in a dark suit and black bowler hat showed himself. He gave Mr Bates an enquiring look. Mr Bates responded with a steely smile.

'Your name Monks?' he asked.

'What's it to you? Where's Mrs Wilson?'

'Nursin' a headache.'

'Well,' said Mr Monks, showing a row of irregular and disbelieving teeth, 'you tell 'er to bring 'erself and 'er headache to the door.'

'Don't give me orders, Monks, just state yer business,' said Mr Bates.

'My business ain't your business, it's hers, it don't concern a third party.' Mr Monks, a heavy man, was used to dealing with people who tried to stick their noses in.

'I'm not a third party,' said Mr Bates, 'I'm a referee.'

'Don't waste my time,' said Mr Monks, 'I'm not in the mood.'

'That's your 'ard luck. Say what you want from Mrs Wilson or bugger off.'

'You keep this up, whoever you are,' said Mr Monks, 'and I'll get awkward.'

'Don't try it on me,' said Mr Bates, taller and with harder muscle than the plump moneylender. 'You loaned Mrs Wilson a few quid, right?'

'Legal transaction, signed an' sealed, and 'ow much 'as she paid off? I'll tell yer, not a bleedin' farthing.'

'I'm cryin' me eyes out for yer,' said Mr Bates. 'So how much does she owe yer now?'

'None of yer business,' said Mr Monks, then discovered he didn't like the ferocious gleam in his opponent's eye. 'Well, all right, I ain't got time to stand 'ere all day. I'll tell yer, even if it is breakin' confidence with a client.' He took a well-thumbed notebook from his pocket and leafed through it. ' 'Ere it is. Fifteen quid and seven-six.'

That amount was a fortune to many people in Walworth.

'You bugger,' said Mr Bates, 'you loaned her three quid a few weeks ago, an' she now owes yer over fifteen?'

'It's arrived at correct on account of she ain't made any repayments. And listen, that loan was lent gen'rously, considering it was on unsecured credit.'

'Don't come it with me, ratface,' said Mr Bates, 'you're not gettin' fifteen quid-plus out of Mrs Wilson, or how would you like me to break your neck?'

'The law's on my side,' said Mr Monks, 'it's a legal transaction I've got goin' with Mrs Wilson.'

'Six quid,' said Mr Bates.

'Eh?'

'It's more than you'd get if she had to sell what she's got left in this house. I'll lay you sniffed around when you made the loan. Well, it's all sold, except some beds an'

91

chairs. It might pay for some cat's meat, nothing else. Well?'

'Six quid?' The heavy jowls doubled in umbrage. 'That ain't even – '

'It's all you're goin' to get. I trust,' said Mr Bates with sarcasm, 'that a hundred per cent profit in several weeks ain't goin' to ruin you.'

Mr Monks looked very disagreeable about it.

'Mrs Wilson's got 'erself a fancy cove, has she?' he said nastily.

'See that?' Mr Bates presented a hard, balled fist for inspection. 'That's been around, like I have, cully, and it's done a mite of injury. Like a mite yourself, would you?'

'No more than you'd like a dose of Dartmoor for inflictin' grievous bodily 'arm,' said Mr Monks.

'Talk sense.' The cheerful new lodger was having an aggressive mood. 'You need a witness, and there ain't goin' to be one. So use yer common.'

'All right, wait a minute, wait a minute,' said Mr Monks. 'Make it seven-ten and I'll call it square.'

'I said six. That's the limit, you greedy sod. Sign a discharge.'

Mr Monks gave in. He was still onto a good thing, and he knew it.

Maggie, who had heard most of the doorstep conversation, stared at Mr Bates when he returned to the kitchen and placed a piece of paper on the table.

'That shows you're settled up with Shylock,' he said.

'You gave 'im six pounds,' she breathed.

'Well, I'm fortunately in funds, Mrs Wilson. My kind of engineering pays a bit 'andsome sometimes.'

'But now I owe you instead of Mr Monks.'

'Well, there's no hurry to pay me back,' said Mr Bates, good-humoured again. 'You've been up against all that hard luck, but hard luck don't last for ever. You can pay me a bit now and again when you're in funds yerself.'

'Lord, I don't know what to say,' said Maggie. There

was enormous relief at having Mr Monks off her back, but embarrassment at being beholden to a man she'd only met yesterday. 'I'm that uncomf'table about it.'

'Think nothing of it, Mrs Wilson,' said Mr Bates, his breezy smile arriving. 'If I can't do a good turn to a woman that's givin' me good lodgings and 'ospitality, then I'm not much of a friend. You look at it like that, Mrs Wilson, that I'm a friend. Right, now give me that bag of laundry and I'll see to it.'

He took the bag, leaving Maggie with the feeling that she'd been gently steamrollered. He whistled on his way to the laundry.

CHAPTER NINE

At Rodney Road police station, Nicholas's first port of call that morning, he was waiting for Inspector Greaves, having notified him by telephone that the identity of the murdered woman was known. Her landlady had turned up at the station to volunteer the information. When Inspector Greaves arrived, a story unfolded.

Mrs Barker, the landlady, had spent from Friday to Sunday night at her sister's home in Leigh-on-Sea. When she got back to her own home in the New Kent Road and found her lodger not there, she simply assumed she'd gone out for the evening. This morning, however, finding her still missing and her bed not slept in, she put two and two together by thinking about that description in the newspaper. She had a terrible moment of realization. The poor young woman's name was Mabel Shipman, her age twenty-six. Unmarried. She didn't have a job, but she always payed her rent prompt. She behaved nice and went out most evenings. Up West mostly, she always said, where she could always get a few hours work behind a bar, especially theatre bars. She often didn't get home till midnight. No, she didn't have any gentlemen callers, ever. She dressed nice and respectable, and didn't paint her face. What she was doing in Steedman Street on Friday night, Mrs Barker couldn't say, as it wasn't on her way home from up West, was it?

As for friends, the landlady had only ever met one, Linda Jennings, who often visited Miss Shipman on Sundays. She lived in Heygate Street, off Walworth Road. You could hear the two of them laughing and joking a lot. Miss Jennings dressed respectable too.

What about Miss Shipman's family? No, the landlady didn't know any of Miss Shipman's family. Miss Shipman only ever said her parents were dead, and that was why she was on her own. Didn't she have a steady young man? Mrs Barker said not that she knew of. There just didn't seem any gentlemen in her life.

Having repeated herself at length, Mrs Barker was asked by Inspector Greaves if she would go with a detective-sergeant and formally identify the body. Mrs Barker said she wasn't very keen on looking at dead people, specially ones dead by murder, but if it was her duty, well, she'd go. That left Inspector Greaves to point out to Nicholas that Miss Shipman's close friend, Linda Jennings, hadn't come forward, although the Saturday and Sunday newspapers had all carried descriptions of the victim, and her clothing. Perhaps Miss Jennings, like the landlady, had been away for the weekend. Perhaps.

'And perhaps Miss Shipman didn't go up West on Friday night,' said Nicholas. 'Perhaps she never went up as often as Mrs Barker thought.'

'Prostitute?' said the Inspector.

'Possible. No job, but out late most nights and paid the rent promptly.'

The Inspector pondered. A burly man, born in Bermondsey, he had come up from the ranks and was a policeman of experience and method.

'Not on the streets, no,' he said, 'or she'd have been known to the uniformed branch, and probably had convictions.'

'Could she have made appointments, sir?' asked Nicholas.

'Could have. Some do.'

'She didn't use her lodgings, that's obvious,' said Nicholas. 'Assuming she met men in respectable surroundings in the West End, we could also assume she arranged to visit them at convenient addresses. There'd have been no problems with bachelors living alone, and any well-off married men might have had the use of town flats.'

'What you're pointin' at, my son, is a needle in a 'aystack,' said the Inspector testily.

'Yes, looks like it,' agreed Nicholas, 'but what else have we got at the moment?'

'Guesses.'

'But we might not be wrong in suspecting the man might be someone's lodger, one who could have admitted Miss Shipman without his landlady twigging. In any event, the number one suspect has got to be the man she was with on Friday night.'

The Inspector's bushy brows drew together. 'Hold up,' he said, 'that's not a fact. She might just as easy been jumped on by a stranger.'

'I'm offering it as a reasonable conclusion,' said Nicholas.

'Up in the air, sergeant, up in the air. But let's see. You're saying that after she spent the evening with him, the bugger was so 'ighly appreciative that he followed her and strangled her? Then pinched her handbag?'

'Sounds fairly reasonable to me, inspector,' said Nicholas.

'I'm not against it.' Inspector Greaves pondered again. 'Listen, my lad, if that theory's got something to it, then there's a notebook that wants findin'.'

'That's right on the button,' said Nicholas, 'a notebook containing the names and addresses of certain men.'

'Penny's dropped, has it? It could mean she was on the game definite. Get busy, I've got to see the Assistant Commissioner myself.'

Nicholas took Chapman with him. They gave Mrs Barker time to get home from the morgue before knocking on her door. She let them in and allowed them to make a thorough search of the murdered woman's room, the woman she had identified at the morgue. They turned the room inside-out, although Nicholas didn't think she would have kept the notebook hidden. She was far more likely to have carried it in her handbag. All the same, he and Chapman searched every possible place, including coat and jacket pockets. Her clothes, he noticed, were of very good quality. The exercise was fruitless. There was no notebook, nor letters of any kind. Perhaps there wasn't a notebook, perhaps everything was in her head, or perhaps he and the Inspector had reached the wrong conclusions. If they hadn't, he felt her handbag was the natural repository. And it led to another reasonable conclusion.

'Frank,' he said, 'if we're right, if she was with a client on Friday evening, a peculiar type of man, he'd have had all the time he wanted to think about how much of a sick thrill it would be to strangle her and cut off a lock of her hair as a souvenir.'

'Ruddy sick,' said Chapman.

'And suppose he knew, or found out, that she had a note-book containing names and addresses, his among them?'

'NBG,' said Chapman. 'He'd've had it off her before she left.'

'Wake up, muttonhead,' said Nicholas. 'A lodger, or a married man, with ideas of murdering her, would have let her leave, then get after her. Right, he catches her up, whips a cord around her neck from behind, strangles her in quick time, cuts off a lock of her hair in a sick frenzy and makes off with that plus her handbag. He wastes no time seaching for the notebook, he does the obvious, he pinches her handbag. How's that?'

'Sounds all right,' said Chapman.

'Don't fall over yourself, will you?'

'What you after, then? Certificate?'

'With your amount of chat, you're wasted in the force,' said Nicholas. 'Get yourself into a debating society. But not yet. First, let's take ourselves to Heygate Street and find out if Miss Shipman's friend, Linda Jennings, is at home.'

She was. A lively young woman in her mid-twenties, and attractively plump, Linda Jennings at this particular moment in her life was a grieving human being, her natural bubbliness very subdued. She'd only realized this morning that it was her best friend who'd been murdered, she said.

'I'm not swallowing that,' said Nicholas.

'But I tell yer – ' Linda bit her lip. Her eyes looked swollen. 'Oh, all right, I knew it was 'er soon as I read all about it in Saturday's *Evening News*.'

'Oh, you did, did yer?' said Chapman.

'Why didn't you come forward?' asked Nicholas.

'What good could I 'ave been to 'er then? She was dead, done in, poor girl. Let 'er rest in peace nameless, I thought. She wouldn't 'ave minded, she wouldn't 'ave wanted questions asked about 'er, and nor did I want to answer 'em. All the same, I been thinkin' about the swine that done it an' maybe gettin' away with it. That's been makin' me burn, I can tell yer. I'm only glad you told me Mrs Barker identified 'er. It would've cut me to bits meself, seein' her dead an' murdered.'

'Yes, I'm sorry,' said Nicholas. 'You're not married, Miss Jennings?'

She was not married. She had two rooms in this house, and she worked for a bookie. She picked up the bets for him from punters on street corners. Chapman said she could get run in for that.

'You wouldn't do that to me now, would you?' she said.

'Watch yourself,' said Chapman. 'Someone might.'

'Why are you living in lodgings?' asked Nicholas.

'Because me fam'ly 'ome's in the East End,' said Linda, 'and it 'appens to suit me better livin' in Walworth. Me fam'ly wouldn't be partial to me bein' a bookie's runner, not seein' I'm female.'

'I think you're telling me fairy stories,' said Nicholas, but quite gently.

'Me?' Linda looked very upset. 'I been cryin' me eyes out all weekend. Oh, that bleeder, doin' Mabel in like that, when she never did no 'arm to anyone 'erself. If yer don't catch 'im and 'ang 'im, I'll go sick to me own grave when me time comes. I feel I wouldn't care if it was now. Mabel was a lovely girl, but lost 'er parents one after the other when she was twenty, and then 'er fiancé as well, when 'e fell off some high scaffolding up Brixton way. She 'ad to make 'er own way then. An' look what life's done to 'er now.'

Nicholas's mouth tightened, and he felt the unprofessional rise of white-hot anger at the man who had murdered Mabel Shipman. If she'd gone on the game out of bitterness, that was regrettable but her own business. It did not give any man the right to murder her.

'Life doesn't give some people much of a chance, Miss Jennings,' he said, and Linda gave him a long look.

'You got feelings, mister?' she said. 'I never 'eard coppers got as much as ord'n'ry people.'

'Coppers get hardened by people who aren't ordinary,' said Nicholas. 'Tell me about Miss Shipman's men friends.'

Linda stiffened and she cast agitated glances around her little living-room. Nicholas thought it cosy and homely. She obviously made what she could of it, and there were several quite pretty ornaments. It was sadly clear, of course, why she lived away from her family in the East End.

'What men friends?' she asked.

'Now come on,' said Chapman.

'I don't know about any men friends, I just know I was 'er best friend.'

'Then you probably know how she made her living,' said Nicholas. 'She had no regular job, so how did she make do?' There was a smile of encouragement on his face, a smile that was welcome to Linda.

'Well, she did bits of work.'

'What sort?' asked Chapman.

'What a question,' she said. 'I mean, I don't know 'ow you can ask questions like that when there's a bloke out there who done 'er in and ain't been caught yet.'

'Yes, I'm sorry,' said Nicholas, 'but don't you see, Miss Jennings, if we don't ask questions, or if people won't answer them, we'll never catch him. I've an idea you could be a great help, and I promise we'll do what we can to keep everything confidential except that which might relate directly to the one man concerned.'

99

'What d'yer mean, everything?' asked Linda nervously.

'Well, to start with, we'll forget you said you're a bookie's runner. We'll put you down as assistant to a course bookie. Then there's the question of exactly how Miss Shipman kept body and soul together, paid her rent promptly and bought very good clothes. I'm afraid bits of work won't add up.'

'I don't see why,' said Linda defensively.

'And then there was her notebook,' said Nicholas.

'Oh, gawd 'elp 'er soul, poor love,' breathed Linda.

'It's really all there, you know,' said Nicholas, 'why she could pay the rent promptly, why she could buy good clothes, and why she was out late most evenings.'

'Oh, yer bugger,' said Linda, mentally pain-racked. 'I forgot about 'er notebook.'

Chapman's mouth twitched. His sergeant had pulled a fast one and got away with it.

'The point is,' said Nicholas, 'the man responsible may be in that notebook. You might be able to lead us to him. For instance, did you know where she was going on Friday evening, and if she had a certain man in mind?'

Linda wrapped her arms around her body, hugging herself as if she was cold. 'No, honest, Mabel never told me anytime where she was goin', an' she never mentioned names, either. We . . . she met gentlemen in theatre bars mostly, she always knew how to get into a theatre bar at the interval, without 'aving a ticket for the show. Well, yer can do it easy when yer know 'ow, and if yer dressed nice. She always dressed to look like a real lady. Quiet clothes, like, not loud an' flashy. Some gentlemen would start talkin' to us – I mean Mabel – ' Linda faltered. She hadn't expected the police. She was unprepared, and her normally facile tongue was letting her down. She was a shocked and wounded young woman grieving for another young woman, her best friend, whose name she wanted to protect but couldn't now, because of the notebook.

Nicholas felt for her. Chapman spoke.

'We know,' he said.

'What d'yer know?' she asked.

'We know what you mean.' Chapman was not unkind.

'Yes, all right,' said Linda resignedly, 'I did go with 'er. Sometimes. The gentlemen we'd met in the bar would meet us when they come out of the theatre an' take us to supper. Mabel could act so posh, really put on the style.' Linda's mouth quivered. Chapman was taking notes, licking the point of his pencil. Nicholas made a gesture, which Chapman correctly interpreted as a suggestion not to be too hard on this young woman. 'She wouldn't ever bring any of 'em back to 'er lodgings, she said that would muck up the ideas her gents 'ad that she was genuine posh. She said it was more excitin' to them to think she wasn't ord'n'ry or common. She'd make an appointment to visit them somewhere of an evenin'. Listen, I did say I was only with 'er sometimes, to keep 'er company, like. Only he's writin' things down.'

'Linda,' said Nicholas, 'we want the man responsible, we don't want you.'

'Well, I did go an' meet one or two of the gentlemen meself, but – ' Linda floundered to a stop.

'Don't put that down, Frank,' said Nicholas, 'she's not herself, she's forgettin' she just works for a bookie.'

Linda cast him a look of gratitude.

'Could yer keep it like that?' she begged. 'Only me mum an' dad – oh, gawd, if you catch the rotten sod would I 'ave to go to court? I'd get me name in the papers.'

'Only as Miss Shipman's friend,' said Nicholas. 'We don't want to know about any gents you might have brought back here, you only need tell us about Miss Shipman and her acquaintances. You'd have to tell the court from the witness box, Linda, so stick to what you'll say then. You talked a lot with her when you were with her some Sundays, didn't you?'

'Well, yes.'

'Good. I'm hoping you can remember if she said anything

101

about a man who didn't live too far away from her, a man she might have met in the West End but who wasn't her usual kind of gentleman.'

'She just talked about all of them in a jokin' way,' said Linda.

'What about the times you were with her and had supper with her and the gentlemen you'd met?' asked Nicholas.

'They was just faces,' said Linda. 'No-one asked for names. Well, Mabel always said she was Clarice, and I'd say I was Bubbles. Mabel said that suited me. She'd always speak private to the gents that fancied 'er. I know she 'ad fun with 'em when she – well, you know. She'd got fed up with life chuckin' bricks at 'er, she said she was goin' to 'ave a short life and a merry one. Oh, the poor girl, it was short, wasn't it? But she was savin' up, all the same, for 'er old age, she 'ad money in the Post Office.'

'Didn't see one,' said Chapman.

'One what?'

'Post Office Savings book. Not in her room.'

'No, well, I got it,' said Linda.

'Why?' asked Nicholas.

'Because she asked me to keep it for 'er, she didn't mind me knowin' about 'er savings, an' she trusted me. She didn't want to lose it or get it pinched, she knew too much about 'ard luck.'

'We'll have to have it, I'm afraid,' said Nicholas.

'I suppose so. Only there was another reason why she give it to me to mind for 'er. She said . . .' Linda was wet-eyed, 'she said if anything 'appened to 'er, it was mine, that if I 'ad it here I wouldn't 'ave to fight no solicitor for it. There's a note in it, yer see. It says that, it says if anything mortal 'appens to 'er, the savings is mine. I didn't want 'er to do that, I said it might be unlucky – and it was. Oh, that poor love, real 'ard luck was always just be'ind 'er, wasn't it?'

'You'll get the book back if that piece of paper is signed and dated,' said Nicholas.

'Well, it is,' said Linda, 'but I'd rather 'ave her walkin' in through that door than that book.'

'Listen, Linda,' said Nicholas, 'when she talked about her friends, her gentlemen friends, in a joking way, what sort of things did she say?'

'Oh, yer keepin' on at me, ain't yer?' said Linda. 'Look, I can't remember 'er sayin' anything about where any of 'em lived, if that's what yer after, only I do know she 'ad the notebook. Well, you've got it now, you've got all the names in it, an' the addresses too. So you can call on all of 'em till you get to the bleeder who done it.'

'Yes, but you could still cut the field down a bit, there could be a pointer in some of the things she said.'

'Oh, she said things like there was one that liked 'er to dress up as a French maid, she said that was real fun. An' she said one of 'em always 'ad a new black corset and black silk stockings ready for 'er to wear, she said 'e was a lovely man, ever so saucy but ever so kind. I remember she talked about another one who liked to sit an' watch 'er dress an' undress. Oh, and another one that told 'er she'd got lovely hair an' liked 'er to undo it and let it 'ang down 'er front – well, over her – well, 'er bare bosom. We'd both be laughin' all the time about – '

'Hold on,' said Nicholas. 'Think about the man who liked her hair, Linda, and exactly what she said about him. Didn't you read that the murderer cut off a strand?'

'Oh, 'oly Jesus, so 'e did,' gasped Linda, turning pale. 'I didn't think about it, I just thought 'e ought to 'ave 'is hands cut off before you 'anged 'im. And Mabel only said what I just told yer, that was all.'

'That he said her hair was lovely and liked her to undo it to cover her bosom?'

'I can't remember she said anything else, not anything special. I wish there was something. She'd just go from one gent to another, quick like, but I think she was careful about not givin' any of 'em away, even to me.'

'Protective, was she?' asked Chapman.

'What of?'

'Her bread and butter?' said Chapman.

'That ain't a nice thing to say,' said Linda.

'It wasn't meant in that way,' said Nicholas. 'Linda, you've been a tremendous help, you've given us our best lead yet.' He gave her a smile. She was in need of a belief, a belief that life wasn't wholly rotten. He could imagine how tough it had been for her, growing up in the teeming streets of the East End, with its smoking chimneys, its factories and its sweatshops. She was on the game, he didn't doubt, but not as a street-walker. She had copied her best friend, Mabel Shipman, and opted for discretion. Perhaps she had a notebook too. And she probably had a heart of gold. 'Many thanks for all your help, Linda, you're a peach of a girl.'

'No, I ain't,' said Linda sadly, 'you know I ain't, only if you could keep it from me mum an' dad?'

'We'll do our very best,' said Nicholas, 'there's more to life than respectability. Now, can you let me have that Post Office Savings book?'

She went to her bedroom and returned with the book. Nicholas checked it. There were regular deposits and only one withdrawal, not long after Miss Shipman had opened the account, two years ago. Currently, it was in credit to the amount of two hundred and nine pounds. The written bequest, on a small sheet of writing paper, was inside the book. It was well put together and quite clear, and it was signed and dated. In the event of her death, her savings were to pass to her friend, Miss Linda Jennings of Heygate Street, Walworth.

'I'd sooner 'ave Mabel than 'er savings,' said Linda, 'she was a lovely friend, honest she was.'

'It's a rough world,' said Nicholas. 'Meanwhile, we'll need to see you again. Good luck.'

'Good luck?' Linda was bitter. 'You bein' funny?'

'No, Linda, I'm not. So long for the moment.'

Leaving the house, Chapman said, 'Poor tart.'

'I'd like it if we could go easy on her,' said Nicholas.

'Mister?'

They turned. Linda was at the open door. Nicholas retraced his steps.

'There's something else?' he said.

'I don't know if it's important, but it's just come to me,' she said. 'You think you can't remember, then you do. It's about 'er hair. It looked like real gold sometimes, yer know. Well, 'e told 'er that women with hair that colour was like afternoon glory.'

'Afternoon glory? Not morning glory?'

' 'E said afternoon. Mabel an' me laughed about it. 'E said it was like 'aving the afternoon sun in 'is eyes. I don't know why I didn't remember it till now. Is it any 'elp, any more 'elp, I mean?'

'It's a great help,' said Nicholas. The April breeze plucked at her own hair, her unpinned black hair, and tossed it around her pale face. Her lace-fronted blouse with its high collar clasping her neck, and her long skirt, were garments of respectability. He wondered how far down the road of no return she was. 'Wouldn't you like a steady, decently paid job?' he asked.

'Is that a joke?' she asked.

'I know a few course bookies, one of them might do me a favour. I mean a big bookie, with a reputation, not a street-corner character.'

' 'Ere, you're a copper, not a bishop,' said Linda.

'Well, never mind,' said Nicholas.

'No, wait,' said Linda, as Chapman began to wander back. 'Ask me again next time you see me. I suppose I got to sign a statement, ain't I? Only right now . . .'

'Understood,' said Nicholas, 'see you again sometime.' He went on his way with Chapman. 'Frank, our number one bugger told Miss Shipman that her hair was like afternoon glory, that it made him feel he had the afternoon sun in his eyes.'

'That's the trouble,' said Chapman.

'How's that?'

'Off his bleedin' chump,' said Chapman.

'We've got a lead,' said Nicholas, 'and it's pointing us at Walworth, at a house visited by Miss Shipman on Friday night, I'm damn certain. She was walking home from it, by way of Steedman Street. Walking. So it couldn't have been too far from Steedman Street. He has to be a man living on his own or a lodger who can admit a visitor unnoticed. Miss Shipman would have arrived in the dark and probably spent an hour or so with him. We're committed to knocking on more doors.' Nicholas felt then that he could justify knocking again on Mrs Emma Carter's door.

'What about the statement?' asked Chapman.

'From Linda Jennings?'

'Who else? Number one witness, she is. At Rodney Road or the Yard?'

'Rodney Road,' said Nicholas. 'I'll like to keep her out of the old man's way.'

'You got a hope,' said Chapman.

CHAPTER TEN

'Mister! 'Alf a mo'!'

It was after three o'clock, and Harry was on his way to the station, having at last made contact with the occupant of a house in Penrose Street. There was no lodger, but there was a woman who'd said yes, of course her husband was out on Friday night, he was out every bleeding night, and he'd be out for good if he didn't start staying in a bit. Harry wormed a description out of her, and he was now taking back what he thought might be a slight lead. Bobby Reeves hurried up to him. A horse-drawn corporation water-cart trundled by, the nag's head nodding sleepily, the cart's rush of water cleaning the gutter.

'What can I do for you, Bobby?'

'Nice you asked, Mr Bradshaw, but I'm all right, thanks. It's just I promised Mrs Wilson to give you 'er thanks for that Salvation Army stuff. Pleased 'er, it did, no end.'

'Yes, I had a note from her,' said Harry.

'She's got a new lodger,' said Bobby. Not born yesterday, he thought he ought to mention it, what with the police enquiries that were going on.

'Yes, he's all right, Bobby,' said Harry, who knew Mr Bates had been cleared by the Yard.

'I thought I'd go an' meet Trary out of school,' said Bobby. 'I thought I'd walk 'er home. She's a bit young, y'know, best if I go an' meet her.'

'Good idea,' said Harry, cottoning on to the obvious, that Bobby had fallen for Maggie Wilson's eldest daughter.

'Yes, I'll do that,' said Bobby. 'Me mum's finished

107

with me services for the day, the market's not too busy Mondays. So long, Mr Bradshaw.'

'So long, Bobby.'

'Trary?' Miss Russell, meeting the girl in the corridor at the end of the day's classes, stopped to talk to her.

'Yes, Miss Russell?'

'Nothing important,' smiled Miss Russell, 'just that you've been very lively today. Are things better at home?'

'Oh, yes,' said Trary, looking a little like a boatered Alice in Wonderland in her short-skirted school dress. It showed her slender calves and black cotton yarn stockings. 'Much better, thank you, Miss Russell.'

'That's good. You've been slightly woebegone lately.'

Oh, what an interesting word, thought Trary.

'Yes, mum's been very woebegone, Miss Russell,' she said. 'I haven't liked to mention it. I might have, only I don't have impetuosity like I used to.'

'Pardon?' said Miss Russell.

'I had it when I was younger, I give more thought to things now before speakin',' said Trary. 'Yes, everything's a lot better at home for mum. I'll be in 'istory class tomorrow, Miss Russell, I've thought of more things to say about if it was good or bad, Oliver Cromwell executin' King Charles I. I mean good or bad for the people.'

'I'll look forward to it,' said Miss Russell. 'In fact, I can hardly wait. Off you go then, Trary.'

Trary made for the school gate, along with scores of other girls. Outside, some girls were mingling with pupils from the adjacent boys' school. A tall boy, cap on the back of his head, threaded his way through the throng and approached Trary.

'What a relief,' he said, 'thought you'd got yourself lost.'

Trary put on her haughty look.

'Excuse me, I'm sure,' she said, 'but do I know you?'

'Thought you'd say that,' said Bobby, his grin appearing, 'but I still thought I'd better come an' walk you 'ome.'

'Blessed sauce,' said Trary. 'I can walk myself home, thank you.'

'Trary, who's he?' Jane Atkins, a flirtatious friend, pushed her question in while gazing at Bobby's good looks.

'Don't ask me,' said Trary, 'I just happened to meet him when he had a box on his head.'

Jane giggled. 'Oh, come on, Trary, what's his name?' she asked.

'I'm Dick Turpin,' said Bobby, 'but I can't stop, I'm walkin' Trary 'ome. It's my good turn for the day.'

'Talkin' me home more like,' said Trary, but she went with him. 'Dick Turpin, that's a laugh. How can anyone be Dick Turpin when he's been dead for years? Anyway, whoever you are, what d'you mean by comin' to my school and draggin' me off home with you?'

'Well, it's best someone walks you 'ome, Trary,' said Bobby. They turned into St George's Road and proceeded towards the Elephant and Castle. Apart from the open-topped trams, horse-drawn traffic predominated. A huge dray, laden with barrels of beer and pulled by two enormous shire horses, barged its way through lighter traffic, a small delivery van giving it a very wide berth. 'Not anybody, of course,' continued Bobby. 'Me. I'll do it as much as I can. Not this week, though, except today, I'll be busy 'elping mum right up to evenin' times. I'll try and start bein' regular next week. A young girl like you ought to have someone see you get home safe. Not anybody, of course. Me.'

'That's twice you've said that – oh, of course, now I know who you are, you're that talkin' boy. I think your name's Nobby or Robbie or something. Well, I hope I'm not goin' to suffer all the way home. Some of us like to do a bit of talkin' ourselves, you know, you can go dumb if you're not allowed to or someone won't let you.'

'I'm glad that won't 'appen to you, Trary, I like – '

'Have you ever thought you might turn into an actual talkin' machine that's got to be oiled at least once a week?'

109

asked Trary, her satchel swinging to her springy walk. 'You'll probably take to drink and oil yourself like that. It wouldn't surprise me if you ended up like a drunk talkin' machine.'

'Actu'lly,' said Bobby, 'I've got too much respect for me future than to pour drink into meself. A fat lot of use I'd be to meself if – '

'Now you're arguin',' said Trary. 'You don't think I want to walk home with a talkin' *and* arguin' boy, do you? That sort of thing can turn a girl woebegone.'

'Woe what?' Bobby asked the question admiringly.

'Yes, you may well ask,' said Trary. 'It's doom and gloom, if you must know.'

A West Square boy passed them, turning his head to wink at her.

'Trying to make me jealous, Trary?' he said.

'Oh, you awake today, Charlie Figgins?' she said.

'Now then, cheeky,' he said, and went on.

'Friend of yours?' asked Bobby.

'I happen to have lots of friends,' said Trary. 'I'm already well sought after, if you must know.'

'Sought after for what?' asked Bobby.

'Bobby Reeves, are you arguin' again?'

'No, askin',' said Bobby. 'I don't like not askin' when I don't know something. If you don't know something, it's best to find out what it is, or you stay ignorant. I don't like stayin' ignorant, specially about what you're sought after for. I mean, if it's something interestin', I might want to do some soughtin' after meself.'

'Soughtin' after? You can't say soughtin' after, you daft boy, there's no such thing. You mean seekin' after.'

'Yes, what?'

'What d'you mean, what?' Trary, on top of her form, was scoffing as they approached the busy junction of the Elephant and Castle, where the trams clanged and rattled over intersecting lines. 'What's what?'

'How do I know if you don't say?' Bobby's grin was

broad. What a girl. Best he'd ever met. And big brown eyes as well. 'I keep askin', don't I, what it is your friends are seekin' after.'

'I don't like to sound vain,' said Trary, 'but it 'appens to be my growin' beauty, which I'm keepin' to myself. So just remember I don't do kissin' or cuddlin' or holdin' hands.'

They entered the subway that would take them to the Walworth Road. Descending the steps, Bobby said, 'Well, I like yer growin' beauty, Trary, I noticed it as soon as we met, but as I also like yer for bein' nice, I won't do any kissin' or cuddlin' with you till you ask.'

'Till I what?' Trary emitted a scornful laugh. Its echo travelled lightly around the tunnel. 'You've got a hope, Bobby Reeves, who wants to be kissed an' cuddled by a cheeky devil like you? And you haven't said what you mean by comin' to meet me when you weren't asked to.'

'Well, I thought I ought,' said Bobby, 'an' Constable Bradshaw said what a good idea.'

'Oh, did he really?' Trary sounded as if a good idea from Constable Bradshaw was a good idea for everybody. 'Isn't he a nice man?' They ascended the steps to the Walworth Road, and the sunlight brightened her shabby boater as they emerged from the subway. 'Were you talkin' to him about me?'

'Well, I did tell 'im that you only bein' a young girl, I'd best go and walk you safely 'ome,' said Bobby, dodging a large oncoming fat man. The pavement was crowded at this point, and the voluminous skirts of women, almost sweeping the ground, took up as much room as swaying, moving tents. 'Mr Bradshaw offered me 'is opinion that it was a good idea. We didn't like to think of you gettin' lost.'

'Lost? Lost? Me? Comin' home from school? You've got bats in the belfry, Bobby Reeves, d'you know that? And what a blessed cheek, givin' Mr Bradshaw the idea I'm daft enough to get lost walkin' home. D'you want a punch in the eye?'

111

'Well, to be honest, Trary, no, I don't, specially not in front of people. Besides, it wouldn't look nice, would it, a young girl goin' in for punchin'.'

Oh, I'll have hysterics in a minute, thought Trary, but no, I'm not going to have them in front of him. 'I'll have you know I'm nearly fourteen,' she said, 'an' that I help mum with cookin' and bakin', and make pastry as well.'

'Can you do all that, Trary?' Bobby's admiration grew. 'That's it, then, I know I'll never get to meet a girl I'd want to marry more than you.'

'You what?' Trary bobbed around a stout party, female, and sprang into step again with her talking boy. 'Did you say marry?'

'I don't mean now, we're not old enough.'

'Crikey, what a blessed relief,' said Trary, 'and what a nerve.'

'Well, a man's got to think about 'is future,' said Bobby, 'and about who's goin' to be 'is future wife. You can't not think about it.' A couple of ragamuffin kids scooted by, each clutching a currant bun. From a little way back, an irate woman assistant yelled at them from a baker's shop.

'Oh, yer little pinchin' perishers, come back!'

But the kids, running pell-mell, disappeared.

'They're hungry, that's what,' said Trary. 'You were sayin', Bobby Reeves?'

'Yes, you can't not think about a future wife,' said Bobby. 'You got to consider it serious. If you don't, you end up lookin' in a mirror, and all that's starin' at you is wrinkles and a bald loaf of bread. Yes, and a lonely jam tart as well.'

'Oh, you Bobby!' Trary shrieked with laughter. Passing people looked and smiled. 'You'll make me die a death, you will.'

'It's not funny,' said Bobby, but he was grinning, all the same. 'It won't make me laugh if I end up with just wrinkles, no hair and no-one to cook pastry for me.'

Trary shrieked again. The driver of a horse-drawn van

cracked his whip playfully at her and called, 'Good lively young 'un you are, gel.' Trary waved.

'There,' said Bobby, 'didn't I say you were only young?'

'It's not my fault you're daft,' said Trary, 'an' could you kindly spare me more talkin'? Did Mr Bradshaw mention my mum?'

'He said he 'ad a nice note from her.'

'Did he? D'you think my mum's nice?'

'Not 'alf,' said Bobby, 'if I was old enough and you were still too young, I wouldn't mind marryin' her instead. She's got nice looks and a nice figure.'

'Oh, you're cheekier all the time,' said Trary. 'Boys your age shouldn't talk about my mum's figure. D'you really think it's nice, though?'

'Well, I like bosoms,' said Bobby. 'I think every woman should 'ave one, which they 'ave, mostly. I can hardly wait till you're a woman, Trary. My ma's a woman, y'know, and we're all proud of 'er bosom. Then there's me Aunt Ada, hers is renowned, accordin' to me dad.'

'Oh, I don't know I'll ever get home alive,' gasped Trary, as they passed the handsome town hall. 'I never heard any boy take such liberties.'

'I'm only talkin' about what's natural,' said Bobby. 'Bosoms are natural. Well, on women they are. When you're a woman – '

'Don't you dare,' breathed Trary, who had never enjoyed herself so much with any boy, 'don't you dare say it, Bobby Reeves, or I'll push you under a tram.' They turned into Larcom Street. 'It's private.'

'It wouldn't feel private to me, bein' pushed under a tram in public,' said Bobby.

'I mean talkin' to a girl about – well, it's private.' Trary, whose girlish bosom was budding nicely, was actually pink. 'Mr Bradshaw wouldn't talk private.'

'He might to yer mum,' said Bobby, 'considerin' she's got lovely mince pies as well.'

'Yes, I think so too,' said Trary.

A surging bunch of street kids, out of school, stopped to watch the approach of her and Bobby. Some of them began a singing yell of doggerel:

> Walkin' up the garden, wiv 'er Charlie darlin',
> 'E's a lad, she's a gel, they ain't got a farvin'.
> Upsadaisy, yer a lady, kiss us in yer parlour,
> If yer don't, we'll run an' tell, we'll run an' tell
> yer farver!

Trary's nose went high in the air, and she passed the kids as aloofly as a duchess. Bobby grinned at them.

In Charleston Street, Maggie was out at her gate, looking all ways, Daisy with her. Seeing Trary and Bobby, she smiled.

'Hello, Bobby, did you just meet Trary comin' home from school?'

'Walked 'er all the way, Mrs Wilson. It's best for her at her age. I'll – '

'Here we go,' said Trary.

'Yes, I'll do it as much as I can from next week, Mrs Wilson,' said Bobby. 'I help me mum with her stall, that's me job at present, and I can get time off most afternoons, except this week, when I'll be out pickin' up loads of new seconds for her.'

'Is Trary goin' to 'ave Bobby as 'er nice boy, Mum?' asked Daisy.

'He'll be lucky,' said Trary. 'What you doin' out here, Mum?'

'Well, I'm a bit bothered, love,' said Maggie, the sun bringing little golden glints to her hair. 'Mr Bates took our laundry to the Bagwash this mornin', and I 'aven't seen him since.'

'Well!' said Trary.

'Crikey, yer new lodger's nicked yer washin', Mrs Wilson?' said Bobby. 'I'm not standin' for that. You're me most likeable lady friend. I know Trary's me girl, but that

114

don't mean I don't 'ave a fond likin' for you. I'll go and find Constable Bradshaw.'

' 'E's comin',' said Daisy.

'Mr Bradshaw?' said Trary gladly, and turned. But the man striding along the street towards them was Mr Bates. His smile was one of pleasure as he spotted what looked like a reception committee. He arrived at the gate, a large parcel under his arm, another in his hand, held by its string.

'Mr Bates, what 'appened?' asked Maggie.

'Met some old friends from old haunts, yer know,' he said. 'Might I now deliver your clean laundry?'

'But that's not bagwash stuff in those parcels,' said Maggie.

'Ah well, the fact is, Mrs Wilson, I took the liberty of havin' it all laundered. You just say if it's too much of a liberty, only knowin' you've got yer hands full most of the time, I thought let the laundry take care of everything for once, eh?'

Maggie looked uncertain. Trary looked unresponsive. Bobby studied the new lodger. Well, he thought, he's a handsome bloke for Mrs Wilson to have around, but I don't reckon Trary's blissful about it.

Maggie said, 'Mr Bates, that can't be my laundered washin', you only took it this mornin' and they don't do full laundering the same day.'

'I found a silver coin that wasn't doin' anything special except sitting in me pocket,' said Mr Bates, 'and crossed a palm with it. Hello, is that young Daisy down there? And Trary up 'ere? And is this yer young man, Trary?'

'That's Bobby Reeves, a fam'ly friend,' said Maggie. 'Mr Bates, now I owe you for a full laundry on top of – oh, lor', it's kind of you but you shouldn't do it.'

'It's best you don't, Mr Bates,' said Trary.

'Couldn't help meself,' said Mr Bates, 'and I'd be pleased if you'd just regard it as a token of rightful thanks for Sunday tea yesterday, Mrs Wilson. Let me cart it in for

115

you.' He carried the parcels into the house, whistling.

Maggie looked at Trary. 'His 'eart's in the right place, love.'

'Yes, but we don't want to be beholden to wherever his heart is,' said Trary.

'Well, I'll push off,' said Bobby, 'and I'll start lookin' after you next week, Trary.'

'Honestly, Mum, that boy,' said Trary, 'you can hardly believe what he's talkin' about most of the time, and nor can't you understand what he's saying the rest of the time. Imagine him tellin' me I'm too young to come home from school on me own. I never met anyone dafter, not in all my life.'

'I heard all that,' said Bobby.

'Oh, you still here?' said Trary.

'I'll be all right in a minute, Mrs Wilson,' said Bobby. 'I'll be on me way then, but right now I'm just faint with admiration for Trary's talk. You've got a one and only oldest daughter, Mrs Wilson, did yer know that?'

'Just about,' smiled Maggie. 'You're a funny young man, Bobby.'

'Yes, I mean to look after yer little girl Trary, Mrs Wilson, I'm the right age, thankfully.'

Trary, hand over her mouth, rushed indoors.

During the following days, Mr Bates proved himself much more welcome as a lodger than the odious Mr Hooper. He had, by sheer force of personality, divorced Maggie from the worrying clutches of Mr Monks. He accepted that he should not, however, have taken it upon himself to deal with her Monday washing in the way he had. He placed a restraint on his expansiveness and his readiness to dig into his pocket on her account. His breezy friendliness did not diminish, nor his willingness to be a help, but by becoming less intrusive he became a much more acceptable presence in the house. Maggie liked to be friendly, she did not like being embarrassed. Nor was she a simpleton. She

116

knew that many of Walworth's widows needed lodgers to help with the income, and she knew too that some lodgers were only too pleased to pay an increased rent for certain extra comforts that they persuaded the handsomer widows to provide. If her mirror frequently told her the hollows in her face needed to fill out a little, it also told her she had not yet become unattractive. And she could still take pride in her figure. Not that Mr Bates, an obvious man of the world, was already making advances. He remained a cheerful man who showed admiration for the way she had fought hardship, and with that admiration was perceptible respect. His admiration did not displease her. But she was not the kind of woman to encourage an affair, not as the mother of four growing girls, and not in any case. Maggie believed in marriage or nothing.

Daisy, Lily and Meg responded to their new lodger. Trary remained cool, and it pleased her that he was out most of each day, in the City, and not at home making up to her mum. She wished Mr Bradshaw would call, just to ask her mum how she was.

Another study of the street map convinced Nicholas that Mabel Shipman, assumed to have visited a client on Friday night, had done so in a house off the west side of Walworth Road, and not too far from Steedman Street, the scene of the murder. Had her appointment taken her farther abroad, she would have travelled by tram back to the Elephant and Castle to reach her lodgings in the New Kent Road. And had the house been in any of the streets east of the Walworth Road, she would have gone nowhere near Steedman Street on her return to her lodgings. No, that house had to be in one of the streets on the west side.

He and Chapman spent days knocking on doors. The uniformed branch helped in the matter of knocking on those doors that remained closed to Chamberlain and Chapman because all occupants were out at the time. Nothing positive had happened yet.

Linda Jennings did not escape Inspector Greaves, who ordered Nicholas not to complete any statement for her signature for the time being. He gave Linda a nervous time. He was the complete, searching professional, with a ponderously methodical approach. Yet he got no more from her than Nicholas had. He turned fatherly and asked for her co-operation. Linda in return asked for protection if ever she had to appear in the witness box, for the sake of her mum and dad. Inspector Greaves promised he would speak to the defence counsel in the event of the man being caught and tried. Linda accordingly agreed to accompany him and a detective-sergeant to West End theatres at night, to look during intervals at the faces of men in the bars, and to point out any whom she knew as gentlemen friends of Mabel Shipman. But she did, of course, ask why he didn't make use of Mabel's notebook and its addresses. Inspector Greaves cast complications over that tactic, and proceeded to follow his own line, with Linda's help. During the course of four successive evenings, Linda alighted on only one known man, a man thoroughly disgusted at being questioned and able to supply a cast-iron alibi.

It was Friday. Trary answered a knock on the door. She had just got home from school. Constable Bradshaw smiled at her from the doorstep.

'Oh, Mr Bradshaw, sir, 'ow nice to see you,' she said, dropping an aitch.

'Much nicer to see you,' said Harry.

'You're just sayin' that,' said Trary. 'D'you want to see mum?'

'Well, I just thought I'd come and ask how you all were, Trary. How's your new lodger?'

'Oh, him,' said Trary.

'Something wrong with him?' asked Harry, instinctively the policeman.

'Well, not really, I suppose, he's better than our previous

118

lodger. You're goin' to come in an' say hello to mum, aren't you? She just happens to have the kettle on.'

'I'm on duty,' said Harry, 'but as it's traditional, a cup of tea for a passin' copper, I'll step in.'

They were all in the kitchen, the girls and Maggie, and about to have the cup of tea Maggie always provided when they came home from school. The girls were delighted to see Harry, and Daisy offered to stand on her head for him. She'd accomplished that trick recently. Maggie, pleased that Harry had stepped in, informed Daisy that she wasn't to perform any of those larks with a visitor present. Daisy looked mystified.

'But I'm best of all the girls in our class,' she said, 'and I'm only little.'

'Mum means she don't want you showin' yer drawers,' said Lily.

'But they won't come down,' protested Daisy.

'You can't show yer drawers when mister's 'ere,' said Lily.

Harry coughed. 'Everything all right, Mrs Wilson, apart from Daisy wantin' to stand on her head?'

'I'll give 'er stand on her head,' said Maggie.

'Crikey,' said Daisy, 'I ain't even done it yet.'

'Sugar in your tea, Mr Bradshaw?' said Maggie, smiling.

'If it's – '

'Oh, we've got some now,' said Maggie, 'due to the kind Salvation Army or someone.'

'Oh, yes,' said Trary, 'and that boy Bobby Reeves, who brought it all in a box on his head, did you know what a terrible talkin' boy he is? He came and walked me home from school last Monday, and I never had a more tryin' time in all my life.'

' 'E kisses 'er,' said Lily, hands around her cup, head bent to it.

'That's ever so tryin', gettin' kisses,' said Meg.

'He's got a hope,' said Trary.

'She blushes,' said Meg.

'I am not in the habit of blushin',' said Trary, her well-known aloof air raising a smile in Maggie.

'I like kisses,' said Lily, 'only I ain't 'ad none yet. Except from me mum.'

'Trary, is kissin' wiv a boy nice?' asked Daisy.

'I don't do kissin' with daft boys,' said Trary.

Daisy cast a glance at Harry. He winked. She giggled. She whispered to Lily. Lily looked at Harry, then whispered back.

'I know what you two are sayin',' said Maggie. 'They've got their eye on you, Mr Bradshaw.'

'Do policemen kiss, mister?' asked Meg.

'Not each other,' said Harry, at which Daisy and Lily spilled giggles into their cups.

The girls talked, mainly to Harry, and Trary thought it was nice how he talked back to them, making himself at home with everyone in a different way from Mr Bates, who was, well, sort of overpowering. No-one asked him if the police had caught the man who had murdered a young woman. Maggie never talked about it to her girls, and so her younger girls never even thought about it.

Harry stayed only a short time. He was far too sensible to linger, and he was on duty, in any case. Maggie said it had been nice of him to call to see how they all were, and she thanked him again for the Salvation Army gift, doing so in a way that suggested she knew who the real donor was. But she didn't say come again, which was a grievous blow to Trary.

Frank Chapman, tired out after a long day's stint, went home at eight o'clock. Nicholas walked to King and Queen Street in the fading light of the evening. He knew Walworth well, and its teeming streets, the playgrounds of lively boys and girls, and of young scallywags and ragamuffins. They were becoming a jumble in his mind, those streets. How many doors were he and Chapman going to knock on before they found the right one? A thousand?

Two thousand? He was here in Walworth somewhere, the man who had taken Mabel Shipman's life and her handbag. Nicholas was positive about that, his feeling was deep-rooted.

Browning Street had been swept, so had King and Queen Street, the gutters washed by the ever-active water-carts. A man in his shirt sleeves was painting the window frames of his house. The people as well as the corporation fought a constant battle to defy the soot of Walworth. London as a whole deserved some invention that would put an end to the effects of soot.

Nicholas permitted himself the ghost of a smile and turned a blind eye to the antics of two urchins playing 'Knocking Down Ginger'. That was a game loved by all Walworth urchins. They knocked on a door to arouse the occupants, then ran like mad so that the hoodwinked resident found an empty doorstep.

In King and Queen Street, he knocked on a door himself. Opposite, an elderly woman at an upstairs window was interesting herself, as many old people did, in the passing scene. After a few moments, Emma opened her front door. A neat eyebrow went up.

'Again?' she said, an immaculate picture in a lacy, high-necked pale grey blouse and a dark grey skirt.

'Once more into the breach,' said Nicholas, making an informal opening.

'Dear friend?' said Emma. 'Or am I the horsed French about to be heavily unhorsed?'

'I'm not too well up with Shakespeare,' said Nicholas. 'I just know a few quotations. They don't include knocking you off your horse.'

'Really?' Emma smiled. 'Never mind. And never mind the curiosity of Mrs Duncalfe over the way, either. Please come in.' Nicholas entered, taking his hat off. She closed the door. 'I'm resigned to being talked about. I don't know what you're here for, but do sit down. You're on duty, of course, but would you like a cup of tea? I excel in making

121

tea. I'd like to excel in painting or music, but my gifts are dull and domestic.'

'You're also entertaining,' said Nicholas.

'Entertaining? What can you mean? I don't dance, you know, or swing on a trapeze, or recite Victorian ghost stories.'

'You're still entertaining, and yes, I fancy a cup of tea, thanks.'

'You're really quite a human policeman, Sergeant Chamberlain. Well, do help yourself to a chair, and throw your hat somewhere while I go and excel in the kitchen. Over the pot of tea, you can tell me why you're here, if I'm under suspicion and when I'm to be handcuffed.'

She disappeared, leaving Nicholas with a grin on his face. He saw an open book, placed face down on the arm of her chair. The lettering on the spine was visible. *The Subjection Of Women* by John Stuart Mill. He had heard of John Stuart Mill, but had never read him. Politicians quoted him when they were talking about the country's economic problems. He sounded like hard going to Nicholas.

He sat down. He thought about Linda Jennings. Only today, Inspector Greaves had been gruffly favourable about her. What could be done for her? Get her a job, said Nicholas. With Laverys, the big bookmakers. Then, if there was a trial, she'd be a witness with a steady job, and could say she'd done that kind of work for years. Might still not save her when defence counsel gets to work on her, said the Inspector, but see to it, it's your chestnut.

Nicholas thought too about the man who had told Mabel Shipman that her golden hair made him feel he had the sun in his eyes. He thought about Steedman Street and Miss Shipman walking home on a drizzly night, a man silently following. A compulsive killer? Or the man she had been with, a man with a queer fixation concerning her hair and a need to get hold of her notebook? Yes, that was the one. And he had to reside in the locality. And did his queer fixation put other women in danger?

'Sergeant Chamberlain?'

He came to. 'Sorry, I almost dropped off.'

'Yes, and it made you look like one of us,' said Emma, placing the tea tray on the small table. She seated herself.

'Who's us?' asked Nicholas.

'Oh, just the ordinary people,' said Emma, filling the cups. 'You've had a long day?' she said, passing him his tea.

'A plodding one. Thanks for the reviver.'

'A biscuit?' She offered the tin. He took two. 'How complimentary. Now, why are you here?'

'I interviewed a friend of Miss Shipman earlier this week.'

'Miss Shipman?'

'Mabel Shipman. The victim. Her friend said one or two things that convinced me the murderer does have a dangerous fondness for women with fair hair like yours.'

'Sergeant Chamberlain, really.' Emma shook her head at him. 'I'm self-educated to some extent, not having had a brilliant education and leaving school at the age of fourteen, but even I can see it's absurd for you to think I'm in any more danger than a thousand other women. Also, you can't possibly know that the man in question is planning a series of similar murders. He may simply have had his own kind of motive for killing poor Mabel Shipman. Isn't it true that many victims are known to their murderers? Did Mabel Shipman know this man? Am I allowed to ask that question, and are you allowed to answer it? There, look at those biscuits, still untouched. You're spoiling my faith in them.'

'I lost track of them,' said Nicholas, and ate them both. 'Are there any more?'

Emma laughed. 'You're bluffing,' she said, but offered the tin. He took another two. 'How kind,' she said. 'Did Mabel Shipman know this man?'

'We think so, but without knowing him ourselves.'

'There you are, then,' said Emma crisply. 'Was he a

friend, I wonder? No, he could hardly have been that, could he?'

'He was a man she visited,' said Nicholas.

'Visited?'

'That's my belief.'

'Visited?' said Emma again. 'Oh, I see. Poor soul. Life takes very unhappy turns for some of us, doesn't it?'

'For women?' said Nicholas, thinking of what had happened to his endearing young wife. 'Yes, it does.'

'Men have a lot to answer for,' said Emma, but not without a smile. 'I really don't know why I'm weak enough to give you tea and biscuits. It's like inviting in the Trojan horse and feeding it. Woe to women who are as weak as that.'

It was Nicholas's turn to smile. 'Don't you know the women of Walworth are all as tough as old boots?'

'Oh, I'm one of them, am I?' said Emma, and Nicholas had a strange little feeling that ground was shifting beneath his feet, and not simply because she had such an engaging sense of humour. 'Incidentally, Sergeant Chamberlain, are you conducting all your enquiries in Walworth?'

'I'm conducting mine here,' he said. 'Inspector Greaves moves farther afield.'

'I see. Have you found out much about Miss Shipman?'

'I've found out life was damned rough on her, so in the end she decided to have fun.'

'Fun?' said Emma.

'Apparently, she called it that,' said Nicholas, 'and apparently it was fun, to her. I'm glad it was.'

'My word, how refreshing you are for a policeman,' said Emma, beginning to like him. 'If I'm ever arrested, I hope it's by you. I might be able to talk you into letting me go.'

'I hope to God that if you misbehave I'll be far away,' said Nicholas.

'It would embarrass you to arrest me?' Emma's smile appeared again. 'But I'm only an old boot.'

'Well,' said Nicholas, 'the advice of a plodding copper

to an old boot is don't get yourself into a situation that calls for your arrest by anyone.'

Emma laughed. 'You're becoming quite entertaining,' she said.

'Entertaining my foot,' said Nicholas severely. 'You're not taking things seriously enough.'

'Well, I like that,' protested Emma. 'I'm not the one who made a comical remark about plodding coppers and old boots.'

'I want you to take care,' said Nicholas. 'Never mind how absurd it sounds, I've a feeling about this man, a feeling that won't go away.'

'Well, I shall take care, of course I will,' said Emma.

'I hope so. Now I think it's time I went.' Nicholas came to his feet and picked up his hat. 'Many thanks for the tea, and the biscuits were first-class.'

'Lucky for you you didn't forget to say so,' said Emma, and Nicholas saw the tease in her smile this time.

'Goodnight, Mrs Carter, and thanks again.'

'Goodnight, Sergeant Chamberlain,' said Emma, opening the door for him. The twilight had been overtaken by night. Farther down the street, a lamp cast its pale glow. Nicholas left, stepping into the shadows.

Dear me, thought Emma, as she closed the door, what excuse will he find for his next call, I wonder?

For Nicholas and the Yard, three matters at least had been resolved that week. The man who had applied to Mrs Buller for lodgings had come forward following newspaper reports. Yes, he had gone to Mrs Carter's house. Receiving no answer to his knock, he had gone elsewhere and finished up getting a room above a shop in Camberwell Road. He had no difficulty in putting himself in the clear. Secondly, Mr Rodney Foster of Dartford had given Mr Jerry Bates a watertight alibi. Nicholas had not thought he would do otherwise. Thirdly, more to satisfy the Rodney Road police than Scotland Yard, a certain Mr Wally Hooper had been found lodging in Page's Walk, off the Old Kent Road.

Constable Harry Bradshaw called on him. He was certainly fat and certainly horrible, but no murderer.

The settling of all three matters was merely in the nature of a tidying-up operation. The primary objective, the apprehension of the Southwark Strangler, as the Press called the murderer, seemed no nearer.

CHAPTER ELEVEN

It was still Friday. Exactly a week had elapsed since the murder. The late-night tram glided to a stop by Manor Place, off the Walworth Road. A woman alighted, then a man. He crossed the road to Browning Street, and she turned into Manor Place. She walked with a healthy swing, her skirts rustling, her right hand keeping them hitched and clear of the ground. She headed towards Crampton Street. It was past eleven o'clock, and the night was dark. The patches of light offered by the street lamps were welcome to the homegoer. Between each lamp, however, there were long stretches of darkness.

The footsteps behind her were silent. Hers clipped the pavement. The chilly April air was sharp, and she was glad of her coat. Lamplight steered her past the steps and doors of Manor Place Public Baths. She left the pale glow behind and entered darkness.

He was on her heels then, noiseless, and far swifter than she was for all her swinging pace. With her handbag dangling from her left arm, she brought both hands up under the collar of her coat. She turned it up to cover her neck against the cold just as a cord, weighted at one end, whipped around her, under her chin. Her reflexes and her turned-up collar played their life-saving part. She screamed on the instant. The cord, encircling her neck, was also around her coat collar, and her hands were still there. As he took fast hold of the weighted end, she kicked backwards with the heel of her shoe. The cord jerked, strangling her new scream. But she struck twice more with the heel of her shoe, and each time his shin took a violent and gouging blow. He hissed, and he fumbled at the cord, giving her a brief second to issue a loud and piercing scream.

The door of a house was pulled open. The cord ran free from her neck, and a fist knocked her savagely to the ground. A window rushed open. The assailant was away, hareing swiftly and silently into the darkness, towards Kennington. At the window, a man shouted. From the open door, another man burst forward, running to the woman lying dazed on the pavement outside. Her hat was off, her hand to her throat, her breathing painful, her hair a pale glimmer of night-subdued gold against the dark pavement.

'The bugger's going to be a pain in my backside,' said Inspector Greaves, as he left a house in Crampton Street with Nicholas. They had had a long interview with the still shaken woman in the presence of her appalled parents.

'He won't like it that he didn't finish her off,' said Nicholas.

'Tell me another,' growled the Inspector. 'You're feeling cocky, are you, that this fits in with your theories? Listen, my lad, when I was your age it was facts, method and commonsense. Somewhere along the line, theories crept in when my back was turned. I'll give you one fact about Miss Morley. There'll be no notebook.'

'Agreed, sir,' said Nicholas, 'she's not on the game. She's engaged to be married. I'm damned relieved she was lucky, she's a sweet girl.'

'Now then, now then, is something up with you, Chamberlain? We've already had your impressions of Mabel Shipman and Linda Jennings. And who else was there? The woman in King and Queen Street, Mrs Carter? Soft in the 'ead, are we?'

'Hope not,' said Nicholas, turning his coat collar up. April was dying, but it had managed to conjure up one of its perversely chilly winds. 'Just a question of human sympathy, inspector.'

'Don't give me that kind of a pain,' said Inspector Greaves, ignoring his own sympathy for Linda Jennings. 'I can get it from peelin' onions. This man who got off the tram with Miss Morley. Find him. He's got to be a prime suspect.'

'A pity she got off first and could give no description of him,' said Nicholas. 'All she could tell us was that she was aware he crossed the road, away from her.'

'Find out which tram it was, and which conductor. Get some information out of him. Stand 'im up against a wall if he has trouble rememberin'. Point is, my son, was the man comin' home from Camberwell, as she was, or is he a Camberwell man who happened to spot her waitin' at the tram stop and decided to go after her?'

'He's a Walworth man,' said Nicholas stubbornly.

'It's not a fact, but all right, I'll go along with it.'

'That'll help, sir.'

'It better had, sergeant. If it doesn't, I'll have your guts for garters.'

The rent collector came on Saturday morning. All the girls had gone to the market to shop for Maggie. Trary was in charge. She was already a shrewd market shopper, and would make the most of the small amount of money her mum had given her. Daisy, Lily and Meg, who loved the market and its boisterous atmosphere, were a sisterly encouragement to Trary's virtuosity. Besides, some nice greengrocer might give them a speckled apple each. Or some overripe bananas. Also, Trary might see Bobby Reeves at Mrs Reeves's second-hand clothes stall now she knew he was that lady's son. At the mention of this from Meg, Trary became scornful and scoffing.

At home, Mr Bates put his head round the kitchen door and asked Maggie if she'd like him to put the kettle on for her. He'd got a bottle of Camp coffee and would like the pleasure of treating her to a cup, and himself as well. His approach was friendly, not loud and brash, and Maggie could not help being responsive. He was, after all, a healthy and invigorating man, and had made the house come alive. In any event, she knew herself perfectly capable of pulling him up if he went too far or took her kitchen for granted. Her kitchen was the family retreat, open to friends and neighbours, but not necessarily to lodgers.

'Yes, come in, Mr Bates, I – ' The rent collector knocked then. Maggie knew his knock, the same as she had known the knock of the moneylender. 'Oh, that's the rent collector, excuse me a minute.' She took her purse from the mantelpiece and went to the front door, leaving Mr Bates in the kitchen, his ears alert, his generous pocket ready to be touched.

'Mornin',' said Mr Dawes, a rent collector used to hard luck stories. His face was gaunt with the strain of listening to them week in, week out.

'I can pay you a full week this week,' said Maggie, 'and a bit off the owings.'

'Much obliged, I'm sure, Mrs Wilson, but a bit off the owings ain't what I'm here for. All off, that's me orders. So with this week's rent and all yer owings, I'm collecting thirty-one bob from you.'

'No, come off it,' said Maggie, 'you can't collect what I don't 'ave.'

'Well now, Mrs Wilson, I begs to inform yer that if you don't cough up, the landlord'll chuck the bailiffs at yer on Monday. Mr Randall's got to live, and so 'ave I. We can't live, can we, nor our fam'lies, if all the owings don't get settled. You can't say you ain't been warned, Mrs Wilson.'

'You can't put the bailiffs in,' said Maggie palely, 'I got four girls who need a roof over their 'eads. Look, I can manage seven an' six against the owings.'

Mr Dawes shook a sad head. 'Don't play about, Mrs Wilson, I ain't got time for games. Listen, you've got a new lodger, I 'eard. Ask 'im to loan yer. Tell him that if he

130

don't, he won't 'ave any lodgings come Monday and you won't 'ave any home. Is he in?'

'Yes, I'm in,' said Mr Bates, putting in a cheerful and manly appearance. 'Rent's rent, I grant yer. I'll be pleased to loan Mrs Wilson the needful, seeing she's 'ardly had the best of luck over the years.'

'Mr Bates,' said Maggie, suffering embarrassment again, 'I really – '

'Let's settle this first, shall we?' said Mr Bates kindly. He took out his wallet, extracted a pound note and a ten-shilling note, and handed them to the collector.

'Much obliged, but I'm due for another bob,' said the gaunt Mr Dawes.

'Right.' Mr Bates produced a shilling, new and shiny. Mr Dawes took it, bit it and put it away.

'Highly pleasin' transaction,' he said. He eyed Mr Bates shrewdly. Mr Bates smiled handsomely. 'The gent's yer new lodger, Mrs Wilson?'

'Yes,' said Maggie shortly, and Mr Dawes noted the faint rings around her eyes had departed, and that her hollows were not so obvious. He filled in her rent book and gave it back to her. 'I'm happy for yer, Mrs Wilson,' he said, and departed.

Maggie closed the door. 'Mr Bates, now you've put me more in your debt,' she said.

'Well, that's how it seems, Mrs Wilson, and I can't say otherwise. Yes, that's how it seems. But it don't quite mean that, not to me. I see it as offering you a mite of 'elp, and enjoyin' the pleasure of 'aving you accept. You've got pride, that's a fact, and pride's something to like in a woman who's had your kind of ups and downs. I know you'll pay me back, because you're that kind of a woman, but like I've said before, just a bit at a time 'ow and when you can afford it will suit me fine.'

'I don't like owin' you so much,' said Maggie. 'It's six pounds, plus thirty-one shillings now, and the laundry cost too. You must take some of it now.' She opened her purse. Mr Bates shook his head.

'Can't take it, Maggie, not yet I can't,' he said.

'Mr Bates – '

'Did I slip up there, callin' you Maggie? Apologies. Look, wait till you're more flush. It's a fact, yer know, that givin' and receivin' is sometimes right. I can't 'elp thinkin' life's still a bit hard on you, specially with four girls, so it's right in my book to make a friendly gesture now an' again. You can put a little bit aside each week, say a bob or two, till it's all there. Then I'll take it, out of respect for you. Right, then, 'ow about that cup of Camp?'

Maggie yielded, feeling she had been gently steamrollered again. But that did not affect her determination to put something aside every week in order to clear her debt.

At the South London tram depot, it did not take Chamberlain and Chapman long to find out which tram had carried Miss Morley from Camberwell Green to Manor Place. The superintendent required only the time the tram stopped at Manor Place to come up with the required information; a number eighteen, its conductor Albert Roach. A look at the duty roster provided the superintendent with his name.

Mr Roach was at home. He lived in Newington Butts with his family, and was on late duty again today. He received the CID men in his shirt, braces, trousers and slippers. A perky cockney in his forties, he was a typically chatty tram conductor. When informed of what had befallen Miss Morley, one of his passengers last night, he looked as if he wanted to spit.

'Bleeder,' he said.

'Do you remember her, do you remember her getting off at Manor Place?' asked Nicholas.

Mr Roach rolled spit around his tongue, swallowed it and did his best to be helpful. Yes, he remembered the young lady. And the man as well. They both got off together at Manor Place. Well, not exactly together. She got off first, and the man followed a couple of seconds later. She looked a nice young lady, the man looked fairly ordinary. Let's see, what was he wearing? Mr Roach said he wasn't an expert on men's or women's clobber. He thought the man wasn't wearing a coat, though.

A mackintosh, perhaps?

No, said Mr Roach, more like a jacket and jersey, like seamen wore. With a cap, yes, he could remember a cap, just an ordinary cap. The young lady went down Manor Place, the man went across the road to Browning Street, and then, said Mr Roach, the tram went on its way again. If he'd known what was to happen to the young lady, he'd have taken a lot more notice of things. But he didn't give her or the man any real thought at all, except as passengers getting off.

Was the man tall and well-built?

No, just average. Well, perhaps just a bit taller than average.

About what age?

Well, said Mr Roach, he couldn't say for sure, but thirty-odd, perhaps.

Could Mr Roach remember what stop the man asked for when he got on? And where he got on?

Camberwell Green was where he got on, and where the young lady got on too. The young lady asked for the Manor Place stop. The man asked for Browning Street. Both the same, actually, being opposite each other.

Could he identify the man if he saw him again?

Mr Roach wasn't sure he could.

Nicholas went through it all again with the tram conductor, but without getting any more out of him.

The Saturday evening papers issued details, and pointed out that the police were asking for the man on the tram to come forward to assist them with their enquiries. They were also asking for the assistance of any person who might have information that was relevant, particularly information from other passengers on the tram at the time.

Nicholas took a needed break from his headaches on Saturday evening.

CHAPTER TWELVE

It was a rainy evening, but that did not discourage the suffragettes. Very little discouraged them. They were women who had the bit between their teeth, and their unrestrained charge towards emancipation had some parliamentarians shaking in their shoes.

The public hall in Chelsea was packed with a thousand of them. A number of supportive men were also present. It was a rallying evening for the Women's Social and Political Union, which was the brainchild of its formidable leader, Mrs Emmeline Pankhurst, a woman of courage and intellectual brilliance. Diehard politicians, of course, thought all her talents and intentions added up to a great nuisance. For her part, Mrs Pankhurst thought all their heads needed cracking. Suffragettes carried brollies in the hope of getting near enough to those heads.

With Mrs Pankhurst on the platform this Saturday evening were a number of her ablest lieutenants, including her daughters Christabel and Sylvia. Christabel, as gifted as her mother, promised to be even more formidable. Cracking the heads of certain politicians was not enough for Christabel. She was in favour of knocking them off.

Emma Carter felt that in some moods, Christabel was more of a liability than an asset to the movement. If Mrs Pankhurst was militant, Christabel was ready to draw a sword or throw a bomb. Nevertheless, Emma was looking forward to the evening's rally. Rallies invigorated and exhilarated her and her sister suffragettes. Sparks flew and lightning flashed.

The men in the audience were firm supporters, although at open-air rallies they became the butt of other men and even of some women.

'Been measured for yer petticoats yet, 'ave yer, Cecil?' That was a frequent sally.

Some newspaper reporters were also present, although the Pankhursts, not without justification, regarded the Press generally as being on the side of the enemy.

The gallery was as crowded as the floor. Seated up there near an exit door and overlooking the platform, was Nicholas Chamberlain, present as an unofficial observer. One knew what the suffragettes were up to, of course, but there was the chance that Mrs Emma Carter might be present. His view of the ladies on the platform was somewhat restricted by the largeness of their hats. His view of the suffragettes in the body of the hall was that of a thousand hats.

The speakers, in turn, addressed the rally from the rostrum. Nicholas grimaced at their warlike outlook, and more especially at the ferocious nature of Christabel Pankhurst, the tigress of the movement. Lloyd George thought her quite mad. Emma, listening with a frown, thought she was heading the WSPU into self-destruction.

Mrs Pankhurst, the last speaker, was herself fiery, but more logical and more believable. She brought the suffragettes and supportive men to their feet. Nicholas had never witnessed such fervent devotion. It was some minutes before the cheering suffragettes resumed their seats, at which point the chairwoman invited questions from the floor. A score of hands went up. The chairwoman singled them out. Questions were put, most of which, Nicholas thought, merely invited a repetition of statements and intentions that had already been mentioned in speeches from the platform. A young man was singled out. He asked his question. Wasn't it possible to storm the Houses of Parliament and occupy the Commons?

'Would you be in the vanguard of our troops?' asked Mrs Pankhurst, who often used military terms.

'I would,' declared the young man.

'You'd be prepared to face arrest and a long term of imprisonment? Perhaps even the gallows?'

'I would.'

'How gratifying,' said Christabel, who plainly did not believe him.

'Thank you for your question,' said Mrs Pankhurst. 'It's the kind that does provide food for thought.'

The chairwoman surveyed the next uprising of hands. With a smile and a gesture, she invited a woman of quiet elegance to come to her feet. Nicholas discovered Emma, then, amid the mushrooming forest of hats. She was wearing a light grey raincoat and a dark grey hat.

'Your name?' asked the chairwoman.

'Carter, Mrs Emma Carter.' Emma then addressed Mrs Pankhurst. 'Ma'am, thank you for the inspiration you always give us, but as I said in a letter I wrote to you last Sunday, I'm increasingly disturbed by the present policy of the union.'

'Your name again, please?' enquired Mrs Pankhurst, fifty years old but still an exceedingly attractive woman.

'Mrs Emma Carter.'

'Thank you, Mrs Carter. I don't think your letter has been passed to me yet. Please put your question.'

Emma, looking quite calm, said, 'I'm afraid it's a pro-test, ma'am, not a question. I beg to suggest accelerating militancy is self-destructive.' That struck a chord with Nicholas. He thought women could get what they wanted merely by a withdrawal of their labour. Only half the women in the country needed to absent themselves from offices, factories and hospital nursing duties for a single day to rock the very foundations of orderly government. Schoolteachers too, and shop assistants. A withdrawal of all they contributed to the family, to society and the country would shake Parliament, particularly if there was a threat of more. Nicholas wondered if Mrs Carter thought on those lines. She was saying, 'Politicians are the enemy, not the people, and we're alienating many

137

people. Militancy is doing us no good.'

'Militancy is the only weapon that will defeat the politicians,' said Mrs Pankhurst. 'Are you a member of the WSPU, Mrs Carter?'

'Yes, since 1905. Ma'am, I firmly believe that the more aggressive we become, the more the Government will hedge. The present Government knows the people are turning against us.'

'Boo,' hissed an angry suffragette.

'It's all very well to boo,' said Emma, 'but is there anyone in this hall who truly believes we're carrying the people with us?'

Brave girl, thought Nicholas. She's on her own down there and facing the prospect of being torn to pieces.

'Mrs Carter,' said Mrs Pankhurst, 'I think the right place for you is among the suffragists of women's rights societies that don't practise militancy.'

'I don't think that's a fair response, ma'am,' said Emma, and Nicholas smiled at her quiet fortitude. 'I'm a member of this union because I believe it to be the strongest and most influential – '

'As a member, Mrs Carter, you are expected to pull with us, not against us. We are at war.'

'Hear, hear!' The suffragettes were uncompromising in their agreement.

'We want war and we'll fight a war,' declared Mrs Pankhurst.

'I believe that to be wrong, ma'am,' said Emma steadfastly, refusing to yield to hissing voices telling her to sit down. 'We want equality with men, we want them as our partners, not our enemies. Mutual respect is our aim, surely, not mutual hatred.'

Christabel positively glared. 'Who can respect men? What have they ever done that women, given the chance, could not do far better? We *shall* make war on them!'

'Are you serious, Miss Pankhurst?' Emma still had the floor, despite opposition. 'We're to make war on husbands, sons and brothers?'

The tigress burst into fire. 'Traitress! How dare you! What idiocy! Sit down!'

'But which men are we to make war against? All of them? Doctors, missionaries and our fathers too?'

Uproar ensued.

'Treason! Impeach her!'

'Resign, resign!'

'Shame on you! Go home!'

'Please sit down, Mrs Carter,' said Mrs Pankhurst, making herself heard. She looked at her watch and glanced at the chairwoman, who nodded and declared the meeting closed. The leaders left the platform, and the suffragettes gave their leader and her lieutenants a tumultuous ovation before they disappeared.

Nicholas was out of his seat quickly. He made his way down to an exit at the side of the hall. From there he walked round to the front doors and waited. Uniformed policemen were on duty, keeping their eyes on a few demonstrators opposed to votes for women. Out came the first of the highly-charged suffragettes. Their exuberant ranks swallowed up the demonstrators.

'Ladies, ladies.' A police sergeant put in his plea for law and order. There were no scuffles, however. The opposition was harmlessly swept away by the tide. Nicholas watched for the emergence of Mrs Carter. It was a little while before she appeared, in a rush of other women. Her hat was askew. The stream broke apart. Nicholas stepped forward. Emma felt a hand take hold of her elbow to draw her gently free of the pavement mêlée.

'Nicely met, Mrs Carter, d'you need any help?'

Emma stared at him in the light of the street lamp. He smiled. She gave him a whimsical look. 'Sergeant Chamberlain, well, it's you again. Is it by accident or design?'

'It's a coincidence,' he said. The night temperature was mild, the pavements wet, the lamps of Chelsea glowing and picturesque. The suffragettes, still emerging, swamped the road. A group marched away, a banner-bearer at their head. Two policemen hurried after them. 'I attended as an observer,' said Nicholas.

'Really? Where were you?'

'Up in the gallery. What a performance. Congratulations. I thought you might get eaten, but here you are, still in one piece, except that your hat's crooked.'

'Is it?' Emma laughed and straightened it. 'I enjoyed myself, and didn't you think Cristabel magnificent in her way?'

'She frightens me to death,' said Nicholas. 'May I see you home now?'

'There's really no need,' said Emma.

'I'd like to.'

'Well, you can at least escort me to the bus stop,' said Emma.

Nicholas, spotting an approaching motor vehicle, stepped into the road and signalled it. Emma watched as the taxi came to a halt. She advanced.

'Will this do?' asked Nicholas.

'I can't afford to ride in a motor taxi,' said Emma.

'Neither can I, usually, but it's my privilege tonight.'

'How kind,' said Emma. A taxi ride was an event in her life. Nicholas opened the door and she stepped in. He gave the cabbie her address in Walworth.

'All that way, guv?' complained the cabbie.

'Yes, enjoy the drive,' said Nicholas, getting in.

'Well, I dunno – '

'Get on with it,' said Nicholas, and closed the glass partition. The taxi pulled away.

'This is really very gracious,' said Emma.

'You deserve it. I thought you very brave.'

'Oh, I was simply trying to make a case for more pacific policies. Did my nerves show?'

'Not a bit.'

'Well, my knees were knocking, I can tell you,' said

Emma. Tucked into a corner of the cab, she was enjoying the relative luxury of the ride as they travelled along the lamp-lit Embankment, the Thames a dark flood on their right. 'But I really can't go along with violence. Christabel, of course, thinks men are our deadly enemies, but there are men and men, aren't there? Rough diamonds are all around me in Walworth. I know navvies and costermongers I wouldn't trade for King Arthur's knights. Of course, some male bastions have to fall, don't they?'

'Good thing too,' said Nicholas. The taxi swished through wetness on its way to Lambeth Bridge, overtaking the occasional hansom cab. Hansom cabs were still plying for hire, but in decreasing numbers.

'If we're going to keep on meeting,' said Emma, 'perhaps I should know your name.' She meant his Christian name.

'Chamberlain, Nicholas Chamberlain.'

'Nicholas?' said Emma, as the taxi crossed Lambeth Bridge. 'Heavens, a policeman called Nicholas when most of them are Toms, Dicks and Harrys?'

'It's not my fault, it's something I found on my birth certificate.'

'Do you have a wife and family?' asked Emma, sure he did not.

'I had a wife,' said Nicholas, 'she died in childbirth. The child was lost too.'

Emma sat up. Her hand lightly touched his arm. 'I'm sorry, truly sorry,' she said, 'that was very hard on you.'

'It was far harder on my wife. She was very young.'

'I was young myself when I lost my husband, but time can be kind, it can heal the hurt. The worst of it, at least.'

'Yes, that's true.' Nicholas sometimes wondered if his marriage had actually happened, it had been so brief. 'All the same.'

'Yes, all the same,' agreed Emma, as the taxi headed for the Elephant and Castle. She glimpsed cockneys walking home through streets shining wet from the evening's rain. One could always pick out cockneys. They had a jaunty walk for the most part, and the women were partial to hats laden with fruit. 'You haven't caught your man yet?'

'No.' Nicholas frowned. 'You read, did you, that a second young woman was attacked last night, in Manor Place, only a few hundred yards from your home?'

'Yes.' Emma was sober, the taxi taking them along the Walworth Road now. 'You're worrying about me again?'

'I should be. The young woman of last night also had very fair hair. Like Miss Shipman's and yours.'

'Oh, dear, the man really is dangerous, isn't he?' said Emma. 'Things aren't too good for you, are they?'

'It's all blank walls, agitated public and critical newspapers,' said Nicholas. 'Watching your performance tonight made a nice change.' He wanted to say a little more than that, but felt it was wiser to take time with a woman like Emma Carter. The taxi pulled up outside her house in King and Queen Street. A young man and a young woman walked by, both eating fish and chips out of newspaper. Nicholas opened the taxi door and got out. Emma followed. 'Here we are,' he said, 'you're all right now.'

'Fuss, fuss,' smiled Emma.

'Three-an'-six, guv,' said the cabbie.

'How much?' asked Emma, shocked.

'Now now, missus, this ain't a donkey-cart, yer know, it's an 'ighly expensive 'Ackney motor carriage, and you've been carried in it all the way from Chelsea. Three-an'-six is a bargain.'

'Fair do's,' said Nicholas, 'but don't rush off, you can drop me in Kennington.'

'I'll be cross if he does,' said Emma. 'You're surely coming in for a little light refreshment, aren't you, after bringing me home?'

'It's not too late for you?' asked Nicholas.

'Don't mind me, guv,' said the cabbie. 'I naturally ain't

got any home to go to meself. Me wife and kids live in a shop doorway, and I kip on the pavement. So take yer time to make up yer mind if yer comin' or goin'.'

'Any more funny stories?' said Nicholas. He handed four shillings and sixpence to the cabbie. 'Keep the change, buy yourself a shop doorway of your own.'

'Ta, guv. Nice to be partin' friends. Good luck, lady.'

'Goodnight,' said Emma. The taxi bowled away and she opened her front door. Nicholas followed her in. He struck a match and applied it to her gas mantle. The room sprang into soft warm light. 'Thanks,' said Emma. 'Now, what would you like?'

'I'll share a pot of tea with you with pleasure.'

'But aren't you a little hungry? I am.' Emma removed her raincoat. 'I'll make some tongue sandwiches.'

'Sounds very welcome,' said Nicholas.

'I cook and press ox tongues myself. I'm very good at it. Isn't it perverse that although I'd like to write music or books, I've only got domestic talents?'

'I think you've got a little more than that.'

'How kind,' said Emma, and Nicholas recognized the teasing note. 'Throw your hat and coat somewhere, and sit down.' She whisked into her kitchen.

Nicholas mused on surroundings now familiar to him. He supposed that as a policeman he naturally liked tidiness, an essential in the matter of any methodical investigation. But there was more to this room than tidiness. Her touch was in everything. She'd created a quiet and cosy little oasis in the heart of Walworth's boisterous cockney world. She liked the cockneys, she lived very serenely among them. She probably also liked the fact that many Walworth women took a pride in keeping their doorsteps scrubbed and their parlours fit to receive the Queen of England, if necessary.

Emma did not take long to bring in a laden tray. She set it down on the table.

'That's quick,' said Nicholas.

143

'Oh, I can sometimes move at the speed of lightning,' said Emma. 'Why are you still standing up? Aren't any of my chairs comfortable?'

'I like them all,' said Nicholas, and sat down. She passed him a plate and offered him sandwiches from a dish. They were quartered. He took a couple. They shared the light repast, the tongue filling palatable and generous, the tea hot and refreshing. He persuaded her to tell him something about her own brief marriage. She spoke easily and affectionately of her late husband, a cheerful cavalryman who had enjoyed conversation and had been a man of very funny Army anecdotes. She said, however, that she would not recommend every woman to marry an Army man. There were too many partings, too many absences, long absences. She thought marriage should most of all be a companionable state. Did Sergeant Chamberlain think that too?

'Well, if you haven't got that, what have you got?' asked Nicholas.

'Silent hours,' said Emma. 'Did your wife like conversation?'

'Don't all wives?'

'I talk to myself sometimes,' said Emma.

'Is that why you always look as if you've just been entertained?'

'Do I look like that?' asked Emma.

'Sometimes,' said Nicholas.

'You said always.'

'Well, yes, always, then, give or take a moment here and there.'

'So how do I look now then?'

'Peaceful,' said Nicholas.

'Peaceful?' Emma laughed. 'Tell me what you really thought of our rally tonight.'

'You'll win.'

'Do you think so?' Emma looked pleased.

'If the suffragettes do things cleverly, in the way you want.'

'Well, I shall work at it,' she said. 'My word, you've flattered my domestic talents this time, you've wolfed the sandwiches, all of them.'

'I thought you ate some, didn't you?'

'I can't remember,' said Emma, 'it's all this talking.'

'Yes, it's late,' said Nicholas, 'time for me to push off.'

Emma did not attempt to detain him, although she silently admitted the time had passed quickly and pleasantly. She rose with him, regarding him with a slight smile as he put his raincoat on and picked up his hat.

'It really was very kind of you to bring me home in a taxi,' she said.

'Pleasure,' said Nicholas. He turned his hat in his hands. 'Do you go out much?'

'Frequently,' said Emma.

'To the music hall, say?'

'Oh, that kind of going out. Yes, occasionally.' Sure of what he was about to come out with next, she added, 'I do have a friend, sergeant.'

'I see,' said Nicholas, disappointment taking immediate hold. He covered it with a philosophical smile. 'Well, it doesn't surprise me. I have to thank you again for being so hospitable. Good luck in your struggle with the Pankhursts. Goodnight, Mrs Carter.'

'Goodnight, Sergeant Chamberlain.'

She wondered, after he had gone, if she hadn't been rather ungracious. His liking for her was obvious. She told herself she did not really want that kind of social commitment. Her life as it was satisfied her, her involvement with women's suffrage a fulfilling one. Her morning job earned her the little extra money necessary for survival, and was a welcome activity. She had many friends among her neighbours and the East Street stallholders, but she did not have a special friend, as she had implied to Sergeant Chamberlain. That had been an excuse to keep him from intruding too intimately. It was a little deflating to feel she had been silly, and even

145

unfair to him. The next time he called, as he would, of course, she must put matters right with her conscience. To be taken out to a music hall might really be quite nice.

Yes, the next time he called she would be a little fairer to him.

CHAPTER THIRTEEN

'Who you looking for, Trary?' asked Jane Atkins. It was just after four o'clock, Monday's classes were over, and the girls were outside the school gate.

'I'm not lookin' for anyone,' said Trary. West Square's two schools, adjacent each other, disgorged boys and girls.

'Not that boy you went home with last week?' said Jane.

'Which one was that?' asked Trary in casual style.

'You know,' said Jane. 'Crikey, is he gone on you? Wasn't he something? Where'd you find him? His name's not really Dick Turpin, is it? Are you standing here waiting for him?'

'Honestly, Jane Atkins, what a question,' said Trary. 'I don't stand anywhere waitin' for boys, I'm just standin' here with you.'

'Watcher, girls, walk you to the Elephant?' Two West Square boys had crept up on them.

'Oh, lor',' said Trary, making a face, 'it's our unlucky day, Jane.'

The boys grinned and started chatting. Jane responded, and Trary, actually a friendly girl, did her best to keep the conversation from getting soppy. But it got soppy, all the same. Well, it did to her way of thinking. It wasn't like talking with . . . Oh, him. He hadn't come to meet her and walk her home, after all. Last week, he'd said he would. Not that she was desperate. Far from it. He was all talk. Yes, so he was. All talk.

'Trary?'

Well, there he was, on the other side of the street, calling to her, a grin on his face. Impulsively, Trary detached herself from Jane and the boys, then checked and just walked casually across.

'Excuse me, I'm sure,' she said, 'but have you come to meet someone?'

'Yes, someone real pretty,' said Bobby. 'Is she here? She's got a pretty nose too, and mostly keeps it up in the air. I think 'er name's Trary something. Anyway, I'll recognize her as soon as her nose turns up.'

'I'll hit you,' said Trary.

'Wait a tick,' said Bobby, peering at her, 'I think she's you. Let's 'ave a proper look at your nose.'

'Just watch your own nose,' said Trary, 'you won't have one at all if you keep this up, I'll hit it with our hammer. Well, come on, don't just stand there, I've got to get home.'

'Why?' asked Bobby, as they began walking.

'Why? Why? Because I live there. You don't think I can go to someone else's home, do you? I hope I'm not goin' to have another daft performance from you, Bobby Reeves, like last week, when I hardly knew how I got home alive. And I hope you're not goin' to talk an' talk, it can deafen a girl if it goes on long enough. I said to mum, I said that boy who came to our 'ouse with a box on his head, I never heard a more deafening boy, he never stops talkin'. I told her I told you you ought to go to a doctor about it, and she said King's College Hospital would be a good place, there's lots of doctors there. Mum's very understandin', she – '

'Crikey, what a crackin' carry-on,' said Bobby, 'you're – '

'There you go again, interruptin' me,' said Trary, her step lively, her satchel swinging. 'Just like last week. You could grow up a desp'rate problem to yourself, you know.'

'Well, I'm as good as grown up now,' said Bobby, 'and I don't reckon I'm problematical yet.'

Problematical? Where did he get that one from, the cheeky beast? But it was easy to tell what it meant, thought Trary. Yes, she could tell Miss Russell that Oliver Cromwell was problematical, which he was when you realized the headaches he gave to people who didn't want to be puritan.

'Well, you soon will be,' she said, and they walked on,

enjoying the kind of conversational set-to already familiar to both of them. Among other things, Bobby said he and his mum had gathered in good business last week, buying loads of second-hand clothes from different places, then sorting through them in the evenings to finish up with a great pile of seconds good as new. Now that was over, he'd have more time to come and walk Trary home from school, which his mum thought he should because young girls ought to be protected. Trary received that remark with scorn, and said a fat lot of good that would be, being protected by a boy as daft as he was.

She seemed to reach home in record time, the minutes seemed to have just flown. Bobby came in to say hello to her mum and her sisters, and the cheeky devil actually told her mum she was getting so handsome he'd take her to the music hall in Camberwell if he was a bit older. Her mum laughed out loud, and her eyes sparkled like they hadn't for years.

And Daisy said, 'Meg, is mum goin' to get kisses from Bobby now, like Trary does?'

'Well, no, not love kisses,' said Meg, 'mums only get love kisses from dads. It's Trary that Bobby gives love kisses to.'

'Some hopes he's got,' said Trary.

'Anyway, that's for when Trary's older,' said Bobby. 'I can see why she's so pretty, Mrs Wilson, she takes after you. Well, I've brought 'er home safe an' sound, and I'll push off now.'

'What a blessin',' said Trary.

'Yes, I've got to 'elp me mum price a load of our new seconds,' said Bobby.

'New seconds?' said Trary. 'Now how can you have new second-hand clothes, you daft lump?'

'Search me,' said Bobby, 'but it sounds all right for the customers. So long, everyone. I'll meet yer tomorrow again, Trary.'

'Oh, help,' said Trary.

149

'I ain't never 'ad no kisses meself,' said Lily, 'except from mum.'

'Well, we ought to put that right,' said Bobby. He picked her up and planted a smacker on her forehead. Lily gave a little yell of delight. 'You just wait,' said Bobby, setting her down, 'when I'm an older man than I am now, and you're a grown up girl, I'll treat yer to a good 'un. Goodbye, Mrs Wilson, you got lovely daughters, and Trary's me dream girl.'

'Oh, I'll fall over, I will,' said Trary. 'What bliss. I don't think.'

Bobby left the younger girls giggling and Maggie smiling.

'That boy's one on 'is own,' said Maggie.

'Well, if there was another one like him,' said Trary, 'the world would get awf'lly problematical.'

'Crikey,' said Meg.

'Crumbs,' said Daisy.

'She's swallered a diction'ry,' said Lily.

At tea, Trary thought it was a relief not to have to put up with the sound of their lodger's hearty voice. He usually put his head in when he got back from his business in the City. He usually said hello to everyone and stayed a bit talking to them, and he usually brought her and her sisters some little treat. But today he was still out.

She went out herself after tea, thinking she'd go and see a friend, Violet Chase, who lived in Elsted Street. She hadn't seen Vi for weeks, she was getting too wrapped up in school friendships, which wasn't fair on Vi. Vi, however, was out, her mum said.

'Larkin' about with boys, I shouldn't wonder,' said Mrs Chase. 'Alfie's in, though. I'm sure 'e'd like to see yer.'

Alfie was Vi's elder brother, all elbows and knees, and a bit of a monster. Trary, after a few quick, well-chosen words, made a rapid escape, going up towards East Street. Much to her delight, she saw Constable Bradshaw turn into

Elsted Street, which led into Rodney Road and to the police station. He was on the opposite side.

'Mr Bradshaw!' Trary, carrying her mum's old but still serviceable umbrella because the weather was showery, waved it and ran impulsively across the street. A baker's van, its horse trotting fast, came straight at her. Harry, trained reflexes impelling him into instant action, leapt from the pavement and rushed at her. The impact was almost bruising, but it did not check his movement. Trary was swept off her feet and carried backwards from the path of the van, Harry's arms tight around her. He rushed her back to the pavement she had sprung from. The baker's van pulled up, its frisky horse rearing.

'Oh, yer young female fiend, yer near cost me all me sleep for a year!' yelled the driver, white and shaken.

'Mind your manners,' called Harry, 'and don't drive so fast in these streets.'

'Bleedin' Amy,' bawled the driver. 'Never mind me manners, what about me 'eart failure?'

'Carry on,' said Harry.

'She all right?'

'She's all right,' said Harry, and the driver, shaking his head, resumed his journey, but at a slower trot. Harry held the quivering Trary. She was shaken too. She lifted her head and looked up at him.

'Oh, crikey,' she breathed, and thought how strong and comforting he felt. His arms gave her a lovely feeling of security.

People were turning the corner. Harry released her. 'Trary, you of all girls,' he said. 'Did you have to do a thing like that?'

'Me of all girls?' she said, recovering.

'Never thought you'd do anything so silly. It's bad enough that careless street kids get themselves knocked down.'

'Oh, I won't do it again, honest,' she said. 'I didn't think, did I? Well, I was so pleased to see you that I just

151

ran across. I was sayin' to Mum what a nice fam'ly friend you've become. Mr Bradshaw, it's really special, you savin' my life. Did you know that in places like China and Arabia – I think it's China and Arabia – well, when you save someone's life there you have to be responsible for them for ever. Miss Russell, our history teacher, told us that. D'you mind being responsible for me all my life? I don't mind a bit myself. Wait till I tell Mum. Mr Bradshaw? Oh, Mr Bradshaw, you're laughin' at me, and after I've nearly been run over too.'

'Sorry,' said Harry, straightening his face.

'The girls do that to me at school,' said Trary, brown eyes alight with pleasure that he was now her hero. 'When I'm being my most serious self, I can hear them giggling.'

'Was I giggling?' asked Harry.

'Oh, no, men don't giggle, thank goodness. Mr Bradshaw, will it be in the papers?'

'Not if I can help it,' said Harry, relief still excessive.

'Not HEROIC POLICEMAN SAVES LIFE OF BEAUTIFUL SCHOOLGIRL?'

'No, my beauty, not if I can help it. But are you all right now?'

'Oh, I'm dizzy with gratitude, Mr Bradshaw, I'll be grateful to my dyin' day. Are you goin' to the police station?'

'Yes, to hand in some reports.'

Trary ignored what she thought that meant.

'Can I walk with you?' she asked.

'Come on, then,' said Harry. 'If my sergeant spots us, I'll tell him I'm takin' you in for frightenin' a horse.'

They walked together, Trary feeling just a little weak around her knees, but blissfully alive.

'When I tell Mum, I expect she'll send you another note of thanks, special thanks, me bein' her first-born, you know.'

'Yes, I suppose we've got to count you her first-born treasure,' said Harry.

'Yes, I'm quite nice on the whole,' said Trary. 'Mr

Bradshaw, that boy Bobby Reeves, he walked me home from school again today. Did I mention what a boy he is for talkin'? I'm only just recoverin' from being deafened. Isn't he a lump?'

'Bobby?'

'Well, perhaps not a lump exactly, but you'd hardly believe some of the daft things he says. I really don't know what I'm goin' to do about him, the way he walks and talks with me, it's like havin' a cross to bear. Mr Bradshaw, Mum said – oh, could you come to tea next Sunday?' In that way, Trary only implied the invitation was from her mum. Her conscience was clear, because she didn't actually say it was from her mum.

'I can't wait,' said Harry.

'Honest?' Trary glowed.

'A pleasure, Trary.'

'Come at four o'clock,' said Trary, 'then we'll be pleasured too.'

'Tell your mother I won't arrive in uniform.'

'Yes, Mr Bradshaw.' They stopped outside the police station. Trary's eyes swam. 'I'm really ever so grateful.'

'So am I, Trary, grateful you're still in one piece. So long now.'

'Till Sunday,' she said, pleased with what she'd accomplished. She hurried home. The rain caught her. She put the umbrella up and ran on dancing feet. The girls were in the kitchen, cutting out shapes from coloured cardboard to build into a country cottage. They were a present from Mr Bates, who had returned from the City and was now up in his room. Maggie was sewing.

'Mum, what d'you think?' Excitedly, Trary recounted the heroic event. Maggie looked as if her eldest daughter was spinning a yarn. Daisy, Lily and Meg gaped.

'Trary, you didn't run out in the road like that, did you?' asked Maggie.

'I wasn't thinkin'. But wasn't it a miracle Mr Bradshaw was there?'

'Oh, crumbs lovaduck, 'e saved our Trary's life,' said Daisy in awe.

'Will 'e get a medal?' asked Lily.

' 'E would if 'e'd saved me,' said Meg.

'Trary, are you 'aving me on?' asked Maggie.

'No, honest, it's true, Mum,' said Trary. 'Oh, he's comin' to tea next Sunday.' She threw that in lightly.

'What's that?' asked Maggie, neglecting her sewing.

'Well, I had to ask him. After all, he did save my life. I couldn't not ask him, it would've been ungracious.'

'And he said yes? He's comin' on Sunday?'

'I told him four o'clock.'

Maggie eyed her eldest daughter shrewdly. 'Trary, what you up to?' she asked.

'Me?' asked Trary.

'Yes, you, lovey.'

'Mum, is the Sunday tablecloth in pawn?'

'Oh, lor', yes,' sighed Maggie. There was any amount of stuff in pawn that she couldn't afford to redeem yet. She gave Trary another look, then got up, put her arm around her and gave her a light kiss. 'You're up to something, love, but you're still a pet.'

'Wasn't it nice that it was Mr Bradshaw who saved me, him bein' a fam'ly friend?' said Trary.

Maggie gave her yet another look, and later, when the younger girls were in bed and Trary was finishing some homework, she said, 'I wonder, does Mr Bradshaw know 'e's a fam'ly friend?'

'He said it was a pleasure, Mum.'

'I see,' said Maggie. 'Well, I know what's on your mind, love, but there's something on mine too. Four growin' girls. That's a lot to expect any man to take on.'

'But I was only thinkin' – '

'Yes, about my future,' said Maggie. 'Well, that's nice of you, but you and your sisters, you're my future. I'll get a job soon, you'll see.'

'Mum – '

'We won't talk about it no more, pet.'

Trary made a little face. But if she'd been pulled up, she wasn't discouraged.

The following morning, after the girls had gone to school, Mr Bates came down and had a word with Maggie.

'I've been thinkin' about your girls,' he said, his expression kind, his voice quite sober.

'What about them?' asked Maggie.

'Well, Maggie, I'm goin' to chance you givin' me a fat ear,' he said.

Maggie smiled. One couldn't help liking him. 'You're goin' to upset me, are you?' she said.

'That I'm not,' said Mr Bates. 'The point is, by the end of this week I reckon I'll have tied up a contract that'll put me into a little office somewhere convenient, and give me all I need to take on two drillers an' set them drillin' in Scotland.'

'What for?' asked Maggie.

'Coal, Maggie. Coal's the king of fuels, yer know.' Mr Bates rubbed his moustache and regarded Maggie like a man who'd come to be seriously admiring of her qualities. 'Now, seeing things look pretty good for me, an' seeing your girls could do . . .' he paused. 'Now don't take offence, but I know you've still got yer back to the wall, and I'd like accordin'ly to make an advance gesture respectin' their birthdays. So would yer mind if I treated them all to a pretty frock each this week, for their birthdays, whenever they're due? Or do I get a fat ear?'

'No, you won't get a fat ear, Mr Bates, I'll just say it's very kind of you but I'd rather you didn't.'

'Understood,' said Mr Bates, looming benevolently large in her kitchen. 'I'm not goin' to argue. But I am goin' to say I admire yer pride, Maggie. Good on yer. Well, it's up to the City again for me. Keep smilin', it'll make yer ship come home one day. I hope I'm there to see it dock.'

★

155

Chamberlain and Chapman spent Monday in the streets immediately west of the Walworth Road. They had the help of the uniformed branch. They suffered the same frustrations the uniformed branch had suffered from the beginning. House calls that were entirely negative because no-one was in, or because none of the occupants could possibly relate to the man they were looking for. They were also the recipients of acerbic comments whenever a housewife realized the questioning was changing and aiming itself at her husband. One such lady threw a saucepan lid at Nicholas.

'Bleedin' cheek! 'Oo d'yer think you are, just because you wear coppers' boots? My old man's upright, let me tell yer, 'e's been upright man an' boy all 'is life. 'E does honest navvyin', mister, and when 'e comes 'ome wore out 'e takes *'is* boots off, 'e don't keep 'em on to go out lookin' for people to murder, so put that in yer pipe an' smoke it!'

Inspector Greaves, meanwhile, was still casting about in the West End.

Bobby didn't turn up at the school that day. It made Trary walk home in an offended way. But he was there on Wednesday, waiting for her. She went by him with her nose in the air. Bobby grinned. What a girl. He went after her, a parcel under his arm.

'Hello, Trary, you're lookin' friendly,' he said.

'Well, bless me, it's you,' she said, 'have you rose up from the dead?'

'Well, no, not from the dead, just from me mum's stall. Sorry I couldn't walk you home yesterday, but I had to go to Norwood. That's the kind of work I do for me mum, I go out collectin' stuff while she stays at the stall. Of course, me dad ought to . . . well, never mind that. Did you get home safe yesterday? It worried me a bit, not bein' able – '

'Here we go round the mulberry bush,' said Trary, hiding

156

her delight at the prospect of another talking fight with him all the way home. He never talked soppy like other boys, even if he did say daft things.

Bobby took a look at her and saw a peach of a girl, her boater saucily tipped, her school frock swinging to her lively walk. 'I told me mum I could manage to walk you 'ome today, and she said I'd grown up to be a thoughtful man.'

'Man? Man?'

'Well, nearly,' said Bobby. 'At my age, I'm only a few years short. I'm glad to say I've never seen you lookin' prettier, except up the park in yer Sunday frock that time. Incidental, I've – '

'What?' demanded Trary. He'd done it again, used a word she never had.

'Incidental, I've – '

'You don't know what that means.'

'Yes, I do. It means by the way. Well, by the way, Trary, I've brought you something.' Bobby showed her the parcel.

'What is it?' asked Trary, thinking she liked him being taller than other boys.

'It's for you.'

Trary stopped. Boys and girls from the schools passed them by, the girls with a look and a giggle, of which Trary took no notice.

'I bet it's a dead mouse,' she said.

'Dead mouse?'

'That's what a boy gave me once, in a wrapped-up box. Bobby Reeves, you open that parcel yourself.'

'Here? Now?' said Bobby.

'Yes. Go on.'

'All right,' said Bobby, and untied the string and unwrapped the brown paper. Trary saw a royal blue frock with a scalloped hem and puffed sleeves. She stared. 'Good as new, honest,' said Bobby, 'it's only been worn once or twice, and I know it'll fit you, I can size up girls. Me mum let me have it specially for you. I told her I don't know any girl I'll want to marry more than you. Would you like to have it, Trary?'

For once Trary didn't know what to say. The frock was lovely.

'Oh, you Bobby,' she said. That was all she could manage. Trams went by. Horses and carts went by. People went by. The sunshine of early May dappled the Elephant and Castle junction with light and shade.

'I don't want you to be offended,' said Bobby.

'I'm not,' she said, 'but I can't take it.' She was actually longing to take it.

'Why not?'

'Girls can't take frocks from boys.'

Bobby thought, frowning about it. He looked at Trary, into her brown eyes, wistful with longing. His frown cleared.

'It's not from me, Trary. Me mum's givin' it to yer. Trary, you don't want to be proud, yer know, we're all poor together, but we've all got kind 'earts to each other, we all do give an' take together. That's what it's all about in Walworth. If someone high an' lordly from Mayfair came an' doled out treats to us, I expect someone like me Uncle Joe would stuff 'im up a chimney, 'is treats as well, but we wouldn't do that to each other.'

'Oh, you Bobby,' said Trary again. She touched the frock, feeling the material. It was silky crepe-de-chine. 'Oh, it's lovely, I don't mind so much now that you're a talkin' boy. Is it really from your mum?'

'She'll be pleased if you 'ave it.'

'Oh, wrap it up again, I wouldn't want to offend your mum by not havin' it. You Bobby, I could nearly kiss you.'

'Not here,' said Bobby, wrapping the dress up again, 'the kid's'll throw things at us.'

'Of course not here, what d'you think I am?' said Trary, as they resumed their walk, she on feet of dancing delight. 'And I only said nearly. We're still not kissin' friends, you know. Still, you can walk me home, I can't not let you,

158

now you've been unexpected nice. I'll tell Mum you've got some good points, she'll be relieved about that. Oh, what d'you think, Mr Bradshaw saved me life the other day.' Trary recounted the deed in detail. Bobby said anyone could trust Constable Bradshaw to be heroic, him being a straight-up copper with a kind jam tart. But he hoped Trary wasn't going to make a habit of trying to get herself run over. 'Well, I might, I just might,' said Trary. 'You can't tell what a girl might do when she gets talk poured into her ears all the way home. Mr Bradshaw's comin' to tea on Sunday – oh, blow it, we don't have our Sunday tablecloth out of pawn, we've got nearly everything at "Uncle's".'

'You ought to 'ave a best tablecloth if you've got a visitor comin',' said Bobby.

'Mum's only best tea service, that's in pawn too,' said Trary in despair.

'Here,' said Bobby, 'you get hold of the pawn tickets and we'll go to "Uncle's" an' get the tablecloth an' service.'

'I can't, I don't have any money,' said Trary, as they entered the subway. 'And Mum don't have much, either.'

'Look,' said Bobby, 'I've got savings in a tin box under me wardrobe, which me dad don't – well, never mind that. I don't mind loanin' you, Trary, you can pay me back when you leave school and get a job.'

'But Mum don't want me to leave school till I'm sixteen.'

'Bless the girl,' said Bobby, 'that's a good thing, that is, Trary. I know it's a long time waitin' till you're sixteen before you can pay me back, but you ought to get those things out of pawn. I've got savings because me mum pays me a few bob wages, and there's me apprentice pay when I start workin' for Lord Northcliffe. So you get hold of the pawn tickets.'

'Oh, thanks ever so,' said Trary. They came up into the light of Walworth Road. 'I will pay you back, honest. I know where Mum keeps the tickets.'

'I'll meet yer tomorrow,' said Bobby, 'and we'll go to "Uncle's" from your school.'

'It's awf'lly good of you, really,' said Trary. 'You can do talkin', if you want, I can suffer it more gladly now.'

Bobby grinned. What a girl. They got on with their talking, Trary's feet dancing over the pavements. When they reached Charleston Street they met Mr Bates coming out of the house. His smile of greeting was warm and fatherly.

'Well, hello, Trary, good to see yer,' he said. 'I'm back early from doin' business, I'm just steppin' out to buy a packet of Gold Flake. How'd yer do, Bobby.' Mr Bates put out a hand. Bobby shook it. Mr Bates's grip was firm and manly.

'Come on, Bobby,' said Trary.

'See you again sometime, Bobby,' said Mr Bates, and went whistling on his way.

'Don't you like yer lodger, Trary?' asked Bobby.

'Well, I don't actu'lly dislike him,' said Trary, 'he's been kind really, and he don't drink. That's something.' The previous lodger had often smelled of drink. 'You can come in.'

'Honoured,' said Bobby. They went through to the kitchen. There was a bottle of R. White's kola water on the table, and Daisy, Lily and Meg had a glassful each, which they were drinking with delight. Maggie was slicing bread for tea.

'I didn't know we could afford kola water, Mum,' said Trary.

'Mr Bates brought it 'ome for you girls,' said Maggie. 'Hello, Bobby, you're lookin' nice.'

Bobby, placing the parcel on the sewing-machine, said, 'Same to you, Mrs Wilson, I'm pleasured you're Trary's mum, yer know.'

'She's my mum too,' said Daisy.

'An' mine,' said Lily.

'Well, lucky you,' said Bobby. 'Anyway, I've brought Trary 'ome safe again, Mrs Wilson. Look after 'er.'

'I'll do my best,' said Maggie.

160

'I'd be very appreciative. Well, I'd better get goin' now.'

'See Bobby to the door, Trary,' said Maggie.

'Yes, all right, Mum,' said Trary, 'we don't want him losin' his way.'

The girls giggled. Bobby grinned. Trary saw him to the front door.

'So long, Trary.'

Trary fingered her school frock. 'Bobby, thanks ever so much,' she said.

'Well, I like you,' he said, and went.

Trary, who could hardly contain her eagerness to try on the blue frock, returned to the kitchen and picked up the parcel.

'What' s that?' asked Meg.

'It's a frock,' said Trary, 'a present from Bobby's mum.'

'His mum?' said Maggie in surprise.

'I'll go an' try it on,' said Trary, and dashed upstairs with it. She came down after some while. She was faintly pink. Her mum and sisters stared. Trary was a picture in silky royal blue, the pretty hem floating around her calves. She looked so enchanting that Maggie was bothered by a lump in her throat. Meg's mouth fell open.

'Crikey,' she said.

'Trary, it looks new,' said Maggie.

'Bobby said it was nearly new, Mum. Is it all right, does it do me proud?'

'It's a princess frock,' said Maggie. 'Now you're the one that'll 'ave to write a note. Bobby's mother could get shillings for that on her stall. Imagine her givin' you a frock as lovely as that.'

'I thought it was from Bobby at first,' said Trary, 'I told 'im I couldn't take a present like that from a boy.'

'I see,' said Maggie.

'I'll wear it Sunday,' said Trary.

'For Bobby?' asked Maggie.

'Bobby?' said Trary.

'You surely invited 'im to tea too, didn't you, love, after

161

bringing you a frock like that? I've given our old tablecloth a good wash, I think it'll just about do.'

'Oh,' said Trary, and Maggie saw confusion.

'You mean you didn't invite him?' she said. 'I'm sure he 'ad something to do with his mother givin' you the frock.'

'Oh, lor',' said Trary. 'Well, I was all overcome, and he was talkin'. It's not easy for a girl to think straight when she's overcome and bein' talked to as well. I'll ask him tomorrow.'

Maggie picked her purse off the mantelpiece. She opened it and took out a sixpence, which she handed to Trary. 'There, you could buy a nice hankie with that, love,' she said.

'Mum, you can't afford givin' out sixpences,' protested Trary, 'and I don't need a new hankie.'

'A boy's hankie,' said Maggie. 'Bobby's a nice boy.'

'Can't she just give 'im a kiss?' asked Meg.

'Mum, 'is muvver give Trary the frock,' said Lily.

'She didn't give me one,' said Daisy.

'Mum, a whole sixpence,' said Trary.

'Well, we've got a bit of money still,' said Maggie, sure that the frock had been Bobby's gift to her daughter.

'All right,' said Trary, 'I'll buy a hankie in me dinner-time tomorrow.'

Mr Bates, having come home early from his business calls, was invited by Maggie to have tea with them again. It was a simple mid-week repast of poached eggs (cracked ones) on thick slices of toast. Mr Bates said he'd ate like a lord in the City, that he'd just like to share the pot of tea with them. As usual, he brought himself like a fresh, healthy breeze to the table, and took only a little time to arouse giggles in the younger girls. And Maggie kept smiling at some of his remarks, which didn't please Trary a bit. Nor did the fact that their lodger was now very much at home with the family. Trary regarded that as interfering with

162

Mr Bradshaw's place in the family affections. That was how she saw it.

Mr Bates, having told a joke, brought laughter from the girls and from Maggie too. Trary remained aloof. Oh, blow him, she thought.

'You ain't 'alf comic, mister,' said Meg.

It had been a soppy joke to Trary. She was sure Mr Bradshaw wouldn't tell soppy jokes. Nor would her talking boy. Thank goodness. She'd have to tell him to depart from her life if he ever got soppy.

CHAPTER FOURTEEN

Emma thought the girl utterly sweet, despite the shabby look of her boater and her obvious need of a new school frock. It was twelve-fifteen, she wasn't due to finish till one o'clock, and as there were no other customers at her counter for the moment, she was willing to let the girl take her time.

'I've never bought a hankie for a boy before,' Trary was saying. The superior look of this department in Hurlocks the drapers did not intimidate her. She liked shops with a superior look. 'My mum thought I should because – well, it's – '

'It's his birthday?' smiled Emma.

'Birthday? Oh, lor', I hope not,' said Trary, 'he's already had sixteen, and if he has another one, he'll start orderin' people about. I mean, even at sixteen he talks to me as if I'm still in my cradle. Still, he's quite kind, so I'm buying 'im a hankie.' She frowned at dropping an aitch in the superior atmosphere of Hurlocks. 'I can pay sixpence.'

'We can sell you a lovely hankie for sixpence,' said Emma. 'Fivepence-three-farthings, actually.'

'Oh, what sort of a one could you sell for fourpence, please?'

'At threepence-three-farthings, quite a nice one,' said Emma.

'Could you really?' Trary's bright eyes grew brighter. She could take tuppence-farthing change back to her mum. 'Oh, it's not that I want to be mingy, only – '

'I'll show you,' said Emma. She reached under the counter and brought out a drawer containing pristine-white men's handkerchieves, with finely stitched hems.

164

'Oh, he could blow his nose quite good on one of those,' said Trary. 'Not that he blows his nose much, but he might if he caught a cold. Would one of those be all right as a present for a boy?'

'I'm sure it would,' said Emma. 'I'm sure it would fit any boy's nose. They're men's hankies.'

'Help,' said Trary, 'if I give him a man's hankie, he'll think more of himself than he does already. He'll get so problematical he'll have to see a doctor.'

'Pardon?' said Emma, enchanted.

'Yes, it could be awf'lly worrying,' said Trary. 'Still, could you please wrap the hankie up for me?'

'I've a little flat box that's going spare,' said Emma. 'Shall I put it in that, and then in one of our little striped paper bags?'

'That's ever so kind of you,' said Trary. When her purchase was placed in her hand and she had received tuppence-farthing change from her sixpence, she said, 'Thanks ever so much.'

'It's been a pleasure,' said Emma, 'do come again.'

'Oh, I will,' said Trary, 'when I've got a job. I'll come an' do lots of shoppin' here. Goodbye.'

'Goodbye,' said Emma, sorry to see her go.

When she got home after one o'clock, she scanned her daily paper for news of what progress the police were making in the murder investigation. She thought the content of the report rather suggested they were making no progress at all. But at least Sergeant Chamberlain, that quite dry Scotland Yard man, had found no further excuse to call on her. He would, of course, in time. One simply knew he would. Oh, dear.

Trary came out through the school gate and looked around for Bobby. He wasn't there. There were groups of chattering girls and boys, but no Bobby. Jane Atkins was nearby, and giving her a sly smile, of course.

'Hasn't he come, Trary?'

165

'Who?'

'That cheeky-looking boy with the long legs.'

'Blessed if I know who you mean,' said Trary, and escaped not only Jane but advancing boys as well. Hurrying round the corner into St George's Road, she came face to face with Bobby. 'Well, thank goodness,' she said, 'I thought you'd gone to your doom. And your cap's nearly fallin' off.'

Bobby pulled his cap forward from the back of his head, his grin showing.

'Glad to hear you're in form, Trary,' he said.

'Well, come on,' she said, 'or we'll get drowned by the mob.' She began to walk in her quick, bobbing way, with Bobby striding beside her. The afternoon was cloudy, the traffic smelling of labouring horses. Noisy, clanging trams demanded the right of way down the centre of the road. 'Bobby, the frock's awf'lly nice, honest it is, and it fits perfect. I've written a note to your mum, it's to thank her for bein' so kind. Oh, and look, this is for you.' She drew the note and the boxed hankie out of her satchel, and gave them to him. Bobby slipped the note into his pocket. He peered into the little striped drapery bag. He saw a flat white box.

'What's this?' he asked.

'I told you, it's for you,' said Trary.

Bobby discovered what the little box contained. 'Well, blow me,' he said, 'this is for me?'

'Mum said you're nice.'

'I like her too,' said Bobby, 'but I don't know I deserve a new 'ankie.' He was touched, of course, especially as he knew how poor Trary and her family were. 'And I don't know I ever 'ad any hankie as good-lookin' as this one. Trary, yer a lovely girl, I'm goin' to take really good care of you, I'm goin' to 'elp your mum see you grow up the best girl ever. It's chronic 'ard luck you haven't got a dad, but I'll be around.'

'Here we go,' said Trary, exhilarated, 'now he's goin' to

166

be a talkin' father to me. Anyone would think he was forty, not just sixteen.'

An approaching woman stopped, 'You talkin' to me, young lady?' she asked.

'Oh, no, really I'm not,' said Trary earnestly, 'I was sort of addressin' the multitude at large.'

The woman peered at her from under her large hat, then spoke to Bobby, ' 'Ere, Sonny Jim, you better keep an eye on this girl, she's orf her rocker, poor thing.'

'I'll do that, missus,' said Bobby, 'I'll keep an eye on her, I promise.'

'That's a good boy,' said the woman, and went on.

'What a funny woman,' said Trary. 'Well, come on, Dad, don't let's stand about.' She and Bobby walked on, Bobby's grin huge. 'I mean, if you want to be a father to me, how can I stop you? I don't know that anyone could stop you when your mind's made up, I'm sure you could talk them all to death.'

'Yes, when me mind's made up, I'm remorseless,' said Bobby, and Trary gave a tight little yell of disgust. He'd done it again. Again. Remorseless. 'Trary, have you got a pain?' he asked.

'Yes, a shockin' one,' said Trary. 'Remorseless, ugh, what a conceited word. I wish you wouldn't keep showin' off, Bobby Reeves. Oh, I brought the pawn tickets.'

'That's the stuff,' said Bobby, 'and I've brought some dibs. What'll you tell yer mum?'

'Oh, she won't like me borrowin' from you, so I'll say the money came out of some savings. I won't say your savings, just savings. Well, I don't like tellin' her actual fibs. Bobby, thanks ever so. As soon as Mum can afford it, she's goin' to buy me some nice stockings to go with the frock.'

'I'll bring you some stockings,' said Bobby.

'You'd better not.' They were approaching the familiar subway. 'Only fast boys give girls stockings, and only fast girls take them.'

167

'A pair of old stockings is fast?' said Bobby.

'Cheek, I don't want old stockings.'

'I didn't mean old-lookin'. My mum'll sort you out a nice pair now she calls you special.'

'I've been to her stall with mum,' said Trary, 'but I don't suppose she really knows me, so why does she call me special?'

'Because I told 'er you were.' They descended the subway steps. 'We'll go to the pawnshop first, Trary, then I'll take you 'ome and have a look at your legs.'

Trary nearly fell over. In this day and age, it was obvious that young girls had legs. Calf-length frocks showed they had. But when they became young women, their legs at once disappeared beneath long skirts and petticoats, never to be seen again.

'You'll do what, Bobby Reeves?'

'It's only to make sure about the stockings. I'm good at sizin' up regardin' clothes and things.'

Trary was sure she shouldn't ask, but did. 'What things?' she demanded.

'You know,' said Bobby, 'stockings and lacy stuff.'

'I'll die if I keep listening to you, Bobby Reeves.'

'I hope yer won't, Trary, I'd miss you something rotten.' They ascended steps. 'It's just that I'd want the stockings to fit you decent.'

'You cheeky beast,' said Trary, 'show you my legs? You've got a hope.'

'It's only legs,' said Bobby, keeping his face straight.

'Only, only?' Trary was springing along in the cloudy May light, her pigtails darting about to keep up with her. 'My legs aren't only, they're mine and they're private. D'you go round askin' other girls to show you their legs?'

'Well, no, not often I don't, you can get a cripplin' answer. I've learned some painful lessons, I can tell you.'

'You'll learn another one if you're not careful,' said Trary. They dodged round oncoming people.

'All right, I'll just guess about stocking size for you,' said

Bobby. 'I'm not a bad guesser, and it'll 'elp me mum sort you out a nice pair that'll fit.'

'Bobby, your mum can't keep givin' me things.'

'She wouldn't if you weren't special,' said Bobby.

'Oh, I just remembered,' said Trary, 'would you like to come to tea on Sunday?'

'You bet,' said Bobby, 'only I can't, not Sunday, we're goin' to see Aunt Ada and Uncle Joe. Aunt Ada come round this mornin' to invite us.'

Oh, blow, thought Trary. She should have asked him yesterday.

Mr Amos, the pawnbroker, had wrinkles all over his face, and he had a hundred more when he broke into a smile, which he did when he handed Trary the Sunday tablecloth and Maggie's best tea service in exchange for the sum of three shillings and ninepence, which included the due interest.

'Thanks, Mr Amos,' said Trary.

'Thank you, my pretty.' Mr Amos peered at Bobby. 'At your age, you have a young man?' he asked Trary.

'Oh, he's just a talkin' friend,' she said.

'That is a new fashion, to have a talking friend?'

'Well, he can carry boxes on his head as well, Mr Amos,' said Trary, and Bobby walked her home with a stout cardboard box containing the tea service on his head. Trary had fits, but Bobby kept one hand on his burden. She said he looked daft, walking through the streets like that. Bobby said the only daft thing about it was that it was flattening his head.

Maggie was astonished when the young couple arrived with the redeemed items. Trary said she'd used money out of savings. Maggie looked at her, then at Bobby. Bobby smiled and said, 'Nice to see you again, Mrs Wilson.'

'Bobby,' she said, 'what've you an' Trary been up to?'

'I just went with her to the pawn, Mrs Wilson, that's all.'

'Trary,' she said, 'you sure that money came out of savings?'

'Honest, Mum, it did.'

'I didn't know you had savings.'

'I fink I've got savings,' said Daisy. 'I fink I've got two farvings in a shoe.'

'I ain't even got one,' said Lily.

'I don't know what money looks like meself, not even farthings,' said Meg.

'I've been like that more times than I like to think about,' said Bobby, 'but there's a silver linin' somewhere around for some of us. Look, 'ere's a bit of a silver linin', even if it is only a tiddler.' He produced a threepenny bit from his pocket. 'That's a penny each. Who's oldest?'

'Me,' said Meg.

'Well, you take it, Meg, and get it changed for a penny each,' said Bobby. 'I've 'ad a lucky day meself, a new hankie from yer sister Trary.'

Maggie thought what a nice natural boy he was, so much so that it made her forget she wanted to ask him just how the tablecloth and tea service came to be redeemed.

And Trary felt cross with herself that she hadn't invited him to Sunday tea when she should have.

The gas ran out that evening, just after the younger girls had gone to bed. The kitchen and passage gas mantles failed, plunging the house into darkness. Maggie groped for the candle and matches on the mantelpiece. She lit the candle in its holder. There were pennies in a cocoa tin on the dresser. Trary took one out and went to the gas meter in the passage, her mum lighting the way for her with the candle. Trary reached up and slipped the penny in. It stuck. She pushed. The penny jammed. At which precise moment, the front door opened from a pull on the latch-cord, and Mr Bates, back from a long day out, entered.

'Hello, hello,' he said, seeing candlelight. 'In the dark, are we, Maggie?'

Trary felt she didn't like that familiarity. Maggie said, 'The gas ran out, and the penny's got stuck.'

170

'Let's 'ave a look,' said Mr Bates with masculine cheer and self-confidence. Trary moved out of his way, Maggie lifted the candle higher, and he inspected the meter. Only a little of the jammed penny was showing. He tried to ease it out. It remained obdurate. 'A thin knife, that'll shift it,' he said.

'I don't know we've got a thin one, just kitchen knives,' said Maggie.

'Don't you worry,' he said, 'this'll do.' He took a pen-knife from his pocket, a handsome one. He pulled open the main blade. In the light of the candle the thin steel gleamed sharply. He inserted it down beside the penny and gently probed. The coin came free. He took it out, slipped it in again and it dropped.

'Oh, thanks,' said Maggie, and lit the passage mantle with the flame of the candle, then hurried to light the kitchen one.

'That's more like it,' smiled Mr Bates, following Trary into the kitchen. 'That's more like home from home, eh, Trary?'

'Would you like a cup of tea?' asked Maggie.

'I won't say no,' said Mr Bates, 'I've been talkin' meself hoarse with certain business coves all day and evenin', yer know. Never been out of the country, most of 'em. They don't see things the way I do, you 'ave to talk 'em into it. Yes, a cup of tea would be revivin', Maggie.'

Trary inwardly groaned, and not without justification, because Mr Bates sat at the kitchen table with them for the rest of the evening, and not sounding at all as if his voice had been under strain all day. His warm, friendly cheer-fulness brought smiles from her mum. Trary felt Mr Bradshaw was being undermined. She wasn't a bit pleased. For all that Mr Bates was helpful and entertaining, she just liked Mr Bradshaw more, a lot more.

Saturday morning.

Emma was at work, Nicholas was in a state of frustration,

171

Inspector Greaves had the Assistant Commissioner, the Press and the public on his back, and Trary and her sisters were in East Street market.

The second-hand clothes stall was piled high. The stall-holder was a woman in her late-thirties. The May day was fine, so she wore a light straw hat, a white blouse and only one petticoat beneath her navy blue skirt. Her face was round and rosy, and her hatpin had a round and rosy knob to it. Her eyes were sharp and quick, but her expression was good-natured. Her sharpness of eye was necessary on account of women who sometimes managed in a miraculous way to tuck an unpaid-for garment under their skirts and walk off stiff-legged with it. Her good nature was inherent. She had two cheeky young daughters whom she fussed and spoiled, but the true apple of her eye was her son Bobby, lately doing his best to keep her erring husband from landing himself in a pack of trouble.

'Good morning, Mrs Reeves,' said Trary, with Daisy, Lily and Meg agog with interest behind her.

'Oh, 'ello, ducks.' Mrs Reeves showed an interest of her own as she eyed the pretty girl. 'I know you, don't I? Ain't I seen you 'ere with yer mum Mrs Wilson?'

'Yes, only we've never properly met,' said Trary, 'and as I was passin' by, I thought I'd stop and say thanks ever so much for the frock. I never had a more expensive-lookin' frock.'

'The frock? Oh, yes.' Mrs Reeves beamed a smile. 'You're Bobby's new friend. My, I can see that lad of mine 'as got good taste. 'E's got a good eye for clothes too.'

'He can talk as well,' said Trary.

'Talks me dizzy sometimes,' said Mrs Reeves, and swivelled an eye in the direction of a large woman who had begun to turn over garments. 'Nice, that frock was, it come from a lot we got from a lady in Norwood that was sellin' up. I got yer little note, ducky, but it was more Bobby's doin' than mine. 'E said 'e wanted it for Lady 'Ortense.'

'Beg your pardon, Mrs Reeves?' said Trary.

'That's what Bobby calls yer, 'is Lady 'Ortense,' smiled Mrs Reeves, and Trary's sisters giggled.

'I'm goin' to have to speak to him,' said Trary. 'You don't mind if I do, Mrs Reeves?'

'Not a bit.' Mrs Reeves laughed. 'Won't do you much good, though. I been speakin' to 'im all 'is life. 'E just comes back with things like, "How's yer grandma, Mum?" 'E's been lookin' at stockings this mornin'. We sell good seconds in stockings sometimes.' Mrs Reeves took her eye off the large woman to peer over the stall at Trary. ' 'E'll find yer a nice pair, love. Says 'e reckons you got pretty legs.'

Trary went pink. Her sisters' giggles became hysterical. 'Mrs Reeves, I'm happy you don't mind me speakin' to Bobby. Will you mind if I hit him as well, with me mum's umbrella?'

Mrs Reeves laughed. 'I'd like to be there,' she said. Another customer arrived.

'I won't keep you, Mrs Reeves,' said Trary, 'thanks ever so much again.'

'Pleasure, I'm sure,' said Bobby's mother.

Inspector Greaves slid a list across his desk to Nicholas.

'Bring those men in for questioning,' he said. Nicholas picked up the list and ran an eye over it.

'Bring them in, all five of them?' he asked.

'Here, to the Yard. We're getting nowhere on doorsteps. They're all Walworth men, and the only possibles I've found on your reports this week. They all live close enough to Steedman Street. Never mind the alibis their wives have given 'em. There's a common factor about all of 'em. They were all out on the two Friday evenings in question. Let's have 'em in.'

'No luck in the West End?' asked Nicholas.

'Needles in haystacks,' said Inspector Greaves, 'and Linda Jennings is worn out. What about that job for her, by the way?'

'She starts on Monday, at Laverys' head office in Wardour Street. It'll give her a chance to live a – '

'Don't tell me any more,' said Inspector Greaves.

Nicholas looked at the list of five names again. The Inspector, he thought, was snatching at straws in the wind.

Trary thought Sunday tea was turning out lovely. To begin with, her mum had done up the parlour. She'd given the furniture a good shine and everything else a good dusting. The Sunday tablecloth had been washed and ironed, and she'd laid the table with the redeemed tea service. She'd also baked a fruit cake, and bought twopennyworth of Kennedy's salmon and shrimp paste to make nice sandwiches, using sliced cucumber as well for the filling.

And Mr Bradshaw had arrived looking quite posh in a Norfolk jacket and brown trousers. Most Walworth men who had Sunday suits looked very stiff in them. Mr Bradshaw proved ever such good company, without drowning anyone with hearty laughter like Mr Bates did. Mum had said she thought they ought to invite their lodger to join them, but much to Trary's relief she finally said no, perhaps not. In any case, Mr Bates had put his head into the kitchen while they were having dinner to tell them he was going out to see an old friend, and wouldn't be back till evening.

Trary felt the tea was a happy occasion. Her sisters had already taken to the man they called their nice policeman, and he kept them very amused with stories of his days as a street kid, a Walworth ragamuffin. He didn't say things to ingratiate himself with their mum, he just spoke nicely to her. But he did ask if he could have another slice of her fruit cake, which was a compliment to her.

'Pleasure, I'm sure,' said Maggie. 'We couldn't not give another slice of cake to someone who saved our Trary's life and tells stories to little girls, could we, pets?'

'I'm gettin' on a bit meself,' said eleven-year-old Meg, and saw the smile on the policeman's face as her mum gave

174

him his second slice of cake. Crikey, he likes our mum, she thought. Mr Bates likes her too. Fancy our mum being popular like that.

After tea, Harry played Snap at the table with them. Maggie took his presence nicely in her stride. She thought him a worthy man, really. Glancing at Trary once, she saw that her eldest daughter was giving him a fond look. Maggie sighed a little, and put down a card.

'Snap,' said Harry.

Trary laughed.

CHAPTER FIFTEEN

Nicholas and Chapman were back in the neighbourhood west of the Walworth Road again on Monday. On Saturday, during the afternoon and evening, they had managed to bring five men and their wives to Scotland Yard at different times, where Inspector Greaves had conducted exhaustive interviews with them. In each case alibis could not be broken, and cockney umbrage was loud and blistering. Helping the police with their enquiries was all right for some, it wasn't for people who were as bleeding innocent as babes in cradles.

They were straws in the wind all right, thought Nicholas. But Inspector Greaves had his back to the wall and had to clutch at something. Nicholas accepted that.

Today, he and Chapman were asking residents if they had noticed Mabel Shipman on the night she was murdered. They produced a photograph of her. Had she been seen either coming from or going towards Steedman Street during the hours of darkness up to eleven o'clock? Nicholas hoped for answers that would help him pinpoint the street in which the suspect lived. The cockneys were a close-knit community, not given to being too informative to outsiders or the police, except where murder was concerned, especially the murder of a woman. No-one, however, claimed to have seen Mabel Shipman. And by eleven o'clock, anyway, most respectable people were in their beds.

Did anyone know of a lodger in the area who had recently moved out? Oh, he was the bugger, was he, someone's lodger? He could be. Residents said they'd ask around, and let Nicholas know.

Nicholas thought again about a rather nice woman in

Charleston Street, a Mrs Maggie Wilson, who had taken in a new lodger on the Sunday after the murder. A Mr Bates, whose friend Rodney Foster of Dartford had given him an alibi. Mr Bates was almost too good to be true. A breezy, hearty innocence shone out from all over him. A mining engineer lodging in Walworth? That was a point to debate.

'Frank, let's go to Charleston Street and see what Mrs Wilson's lodger has been up to.'

'Bloody barmy,' said Chapman.

'It's just occurred to me that he might be too good to be true, so might his alibi.'

'Bleedin' blind alley,' said Chapman.

'All the same, let's find out what he was doing on the night Miss Morley was attacked.'

Mr Bates was in, taking the day off. He was enjoying an early afternoon cup of tea with Maggie, who was coming to think him progressively more acceptable. Answering a knock on her front door, she recognized the two CID men.

'Or, lor', not again,' she said.

'Sorry, Mrs Wilson,' said Nicholas, 'but was your lodger Mr Bates with you on the Friday evening before last?'

'With me?' Maggie grew a little frosty. 'What d'you mean, with me?'

'Yes, I could have put that better, couldn't I?' Nicholas's smile was apologetic. 'I meant was he in?'

'No, he was out. Most of the day and all evening.'

'Is that a fact? Is he in now?'

'Yes, but I don't know he's goin' to like you askin' him more questions. And what was special about last Friday week?'

'There was an incident in Manor Place.'

'Oh!' Maggie remembered hearing about a young woman being attacked. 'If you're suspectin' Mr Bates, I never heard anything more silly. But I'll call 'im.'

Nicholas and Chapman interviewed the cheerful lodger in the parlour again, with Maggie present. Mr Bates, not at all put out by this second inquisition, informed Nicholas that he had spent Friday evening with his old cully, Rodney Foster, and that they'd been to the Holborn Empire.

'What time did you get back here, sir?' asked Nicholas.

'Call me Jerry,' said the gregarious Mr Bates. 'I feel out of place when anyone calls me sir. What time did I get back? No idea. Late, of course. Mrs Wilson was in bed, I know that.'

'What time did you go to bed, Mrs Wilson?' asked Nicholas.

'You an' your questions,' said Maggie, put out by all the implications. 'About half-ten.'

'If you don't mind me askin',' said Mr Bates, 'what's it all about this time?'

'A young lady was attacked in Manor Place just after eleven o'clock,' said Nicholas, going along with the feeling that Jerry Bates was too good to be true. 'A man attempted to strangle her.'

'Nasty,' said Mr Bates, 'I read about it. I can see what yer after, sergeant. I'm new here. You could say my arrival practically coincided with that murder.' Maggie winced. 'Well, me friend Roddy told me he confirmed he 'ad the pleasure of me company that partic'lar night. And he'll tell yer another thing, that the last turn at the 'Olborn Empire last Friday week was Nellie Wallace. Brought the 'ouse down. That was ten-thirty. You ask Roddy.'

'Ten-thirty,' said Nicholas thoughtfully. He was clutching at straws himself, and knew it.

'Like to search me room, would yer?' suggested Mr Bates amiably.

'What for?' asked Chapman.

'Clues?' grinned Mr Bates. 'Like a lock of hair? I can read newspapers, yer know.'

'You're very helpful, Mr Bates,' said Nicholas, 'but we don't have a search warrant and – '

'You're still welcome,' said Mr Bates.

'I don't think we could justify a search.'

'I should think you couldn't,' said Maggie, 'and I'm goin' to get cross any minute.' Mr Bates, she thought, was a man you couldn't miss about the house, not with his boisterousness. A man like that never hid anything. All his thoughts and his feelings came out through his cheerful mouth. He liked to be friends with everyone. He wasn't the kind of man who'd lay violent hands on young women. The girls liked him, which was a lot in his favour. Well, Trary was a bit reserved, but Trary always took her time with new faces. It was surprising she'd become thick with Bobby in just a few days.

'They've got their job to do, Maggie,' said Mr Bates.

'You said that before.'

'What time did you leave the Holborn Empire, Mr Bates?' asked Nicholas.

'A bit after half-ten,' said the lodger. 'Ask me friend Roddy.'

He could still have got to Manor Place by eleven o'clock, thought Nicholas. Physically, he fitted. And curiously, for a mining engineer, he lodged in Walworth. But he still represented a shot in the dark. Unless he also had other lodgings, the use of another upstairs back room, one that he left empty most of the time, but which might hold the raincoat, the length of cord, a lock of hair and a notebook.

'Well, thanks for putting up with us again, sir. Sorry to keep troubling you. And apologies, Mrs Wilson, for troubling you too.'

'It's all right,' said Maggie, going into the passage with both men. She couldn't help liking the detective-sergeant. 'You've got your duty to do, like Mr Bates said.'

'Fact, that is,' said Chapman.

After they'd gone, Maggie remarked to Mr Bates that it was all very upsetting.

'Not to me, Maggie,' he said. 'If you're guilty, every

179

minute's a worry. But if you're innocent you can smile at the devil 'imself.'

Trary, with Jane Atkins on her heels, came out through the school gate and saw Bobby at once, waiting on the opposite side of the street. He had something in his hand, something long and wrapped in white paper.

'He's there again,' said Jane, 'you can introduce him properly to me now.'

'Oh, you fancy him, do you?' asked Trary.

'Golly, is he free then, don't you want him for walking out with?'

'I'm usually busy at walkin'-out times,' said Trary, and crossed the street, Jane with her.

'Hello,' said Bobby.

'Would you like to meet a friend of mine?' asked Trary. She didn't at all mind facing up to the challenge of a possible rival. Bobby had that effect on her, of making everything an exciting little challenge. 'Her name's Jane Atkins.'

'We met before, actually,' said Jane, fluttering her lashes.

'Oh, so you did,' said Trary. 'Then you don't have to meet again, do you? Come on, Dick Turpin, we'd better go an' find Black Bess. See you tomorrow, Jane.' Bobby smiled at Jane, and Jane sighed as he and Trary walked towards St George's Road. 'Excuse me,' said Trary, 'but what's that you're carryin', Mr Turpin, is it carrots for Black Bess?'

'No, it's flowers for your mum,' said Bobby. 'I happen to 'ave a friend in the police force. He stopped me and asked if I'd take 'em to her. I was just leavin' me mum's stall to come an' meet you.'

'Flowers for mum from Mr Bradshaw?' breathed Trary in gladness. 'Oh, I think that's nice, don't you think it's nice? I can't remember when someone last gave mum flowers. I wonder what it means?'

'Mr Bradshaw said in appreciation of Sunday tea. He couldn't get round to your 'ouse himself, he was on duty something chronic, he said.'

'Of course he didn't say chronic, policemen don't use words like that. I'm surprised you do.' Trary was up in the air with pleasure. 'Oh, I do like Mr Bradshaw. Wait a minute, I want to speak to you, Bobby Reeves.'

'Don't see why you can't,' said Bobby, 'you're natural at speakin'. Most girls are, they're born speakin'. I suppose it makes up for not bein' born with much common. Still, I'm not sayin' they don't have their good points, and they're not bad to kiss, either. Not that I've kissed 'em all, you'd 'ave to spend every day at it if you contracted to do that.'

'Oh, can't you just show off?' said Trary.

'I was only sayin' – '

'Yes, you're always only sayin', I don't know any time when talkin' hasn't been comin' out of your mouth, Bobby Reeves. I could do contractin' myself, you know, I could contract not to let you walk me home any more so as to save myself bein' sent deaf an' dumb. Excuse me, I'm sure, but are you grinnin' again?'

'Me? Course not,' said Bobby, 'I'm just thinkin' that later on, when you're older, I'll ask yer mum if we can walk out official.'

'That's a laugh,' said Trary. 'When I am old enough, I'll be walkin' out with a tall, kind and handsome man.'

'Yes, me,' said Bobby, 'I'm nearly that now.'

Trary's shriek of laughter pealed, and the horse of a passing van pricked up its ears.

'What a joke. I never met a barmier boy. And just you listen, what d'you mean by tellin' your mum I was Lady Hortense?'

'Well, you're special,' said Bobby, 'partic'larly when you've got yer nose up in the air. Mind, I like you for it, Trary, I never knew any girl who could put her nose up in the air as pretty as you do.'

'I don't know what you're talkin' about,' said Trary loftily, 'you sound incurable to me. Oh, and there's something else, what d'you mean by discussin' my private legs with your mum?'

'I had to,' said Bobby, 'you can't talk about suitable stockings without mentioning whose legs they're for.'

'Oh, cheeky devil. Bobby Reeves, I'm just not speakin' to you any more.'

'I bet that won't last long,' said Bobby, 'but while it does I don't mind doin' the speakin' for both of us. Well, I'm better at it, I make more sense.'

'D'you want both your legs broken?' asked Trary.

'Said it wouldn't last long,' remarked Bobby. 'I said to Mr Bradshaw when he asked me to take these flowers to yer mum, I said I'd give 'em to me Lady 'Ortense when I met her from school.'

'I bet Mr Bradshaw said you were daft.'

'No, he didn't, he said, "Give me kind regards to 'Er Ladyship".'

Trary smothered another shriek of laughter. 'I don't believe you,' she said.

'By the way, I brought the stockings,' said Bobby.

'Honest? No, I couldn't take them. What colour are they?'

'Black.'

'Black cotton?'

'Silk,' said Bobby.

Trary gasped. 'Black silk stockings? Silk? Oh, me mum wouldn't let me wear black silk, not when I'm only nearly fourteen.'

'Well, would yer mum like them? They're good as new, and they're in me pocket, careful wrapped. I kind of favour yer mum. Has she got legs as good as yours?'

'I'll scream,' said Trary, but held it back while they went through the subway. Emerging, she said, 'I'll probably collapse an' pass away if you get any saucier, Bobby Reeves. Fancy talkin' about legs, and even my mum's.'

'Well, I've never actu'lly seen them, of course,' said Bobby. 'I suppose she's got some or she wouldn't be able to walk about. I think all women should 'ave legs to walk about on.'

'Here we go,' said Trary, quivering with the joy of being alive. 'It was bosoms before.'

'Well, I happen to be well-versed in matters – '

'Well-versed? Well-versed? Oh, I never met such a show-off. Just don't say one word more, you Bobby, not about anything. Oh, d'you think mum might just let me wear black silk? Only on Sundays, of course, and only with my new frock. It looked ever so lovely on me yesterday, and Mr Bradshaw was overcome with manly pleasure. Bobby, you're quite kind really.'

'I'm tall and handsome too,' said Bobby, and Trary laughed and laughed, her boater quivering. People looked as if the bright, vivacious schoolgirl was making their day. Trary wondered how long it would take to properly grow up and always have silk stockings for Sundays.

It was sheer bliss when her mum, having received Mr Bradshaw's bouquet from Bobby, inspected the stockings and said all right, just with the new frock on Sundays, then.

'Oh, thanks, Mum,' said Trary, and gave her a hug.

'They're from Bobby's mother?' asked Maggie.

'Well, I couldn't give them to Trary meself, Mrs Wilson,' said Bobby, 'it's too private, as I expect you know. A feller can't even mention legs to a girl, she stops speakin' to him when he does. Only for about five secs, though.'

'Mum, would you hit him for me?' begged Trary.

'Not now, lovey,' said Maggie. 'Bobby, would you like a cup of tea and a slice of cake?'

'I'd like it a lot better than a punch in the eye, Mrs Wilson. I keep gettin' 'orrifying threats, they make me feel it's goin' to 'appen one day, and in front of horses, carts and tram-drivers. But don't be alarmed, I'll still do me best to 'elp you make something of Trary. I mean, she's got promise, don't you think so, Mrs Wilson?'

The girls shrieked. Maggie laughed.

Trary threw her boater at Bobby.

A letter arrived the following morning for Maggie.

Dear Mrs Wilson,

I did tell you how much I enjoyed Sunday tea with
you and your girls, it took me back to the days when
we had Sunday tea at home. There was always Sunday
tea, even when my parents were really hard-up. Could
I give you and your girls a little treat in return? Would
you all like to come to the Zoo next Sunday? I believe
your girls have never been to the Zoo. By the way, I've
been talking to shopkeepers, and if you still really
need a job would you like a morning one with the newsagents opposite the Albany pub? They don't pay much,
but it's something. The proprietor, George Gardner, said
he does need help in the mornings. I gave you a good
recommendation.

Sincerely, Harry Bradshaw.

Oh, the dear man, thought Maggie. The family had found
a new and very good friend. The girls would love a trip to
the Zoo.

There were eyes covertly watching Emma, who was quietly
attired as a counter assistant in a dark grey dress, the
sleeves cuffed with white. The morning had not been too
bad at all, mainly because customers had not been too fussy
or demanding. Some often were. Women with a little more
money to spend than most people in Walworth required
good value, and they took time to be satisfied with their
purchases. Amid the little whirrs and rings of the travelling cash canisters, a man and his wife came to Emma's
counter. The woman was nice-looking but fluttery, her
hat, blouse and skirt of inexpensive origin, but worn quite

184

attractively.

'Can I help you?' smiled Emma, her braided hair neat and compact.

'Oh, I'm lookin' for a lace-fronted blouse,' said the woman. 'It's me husband's birthday present to me. He's got the mornin' off from his work, so he's come with me, although he's got a bit of a bad back.'

'That's what I call making a noble effort for a good cause,' said Emma.

'It's not too painful,' smiled the husband, a man with a square chin, mild blue eyes and a friendly look. 'It's the beige colour blouse she wants.'

'Yes, beige,' said his wife.

'Like the one on the dummy, Maudie.'

'Yes, like that one, Herby.'

'It'll suit you.'

'Well, I hope so, it'll be a nice birthday present.'

Emma smiled at the marital cross-talk, and pulled open a drawer. 'Size, madam?' she asked.

'Oh, what's me blouse size now? I'm always forgettin'.'

'Forget your own head next, you will,' said the husband, and winked at Emma. Emma made a guess and lifted out a blouse.

'Would you like to try this one on, madam?'

'Oh, it looks nice, I'm sure it'll fit.'

'Best to try it on, Maudie,' said the man, shaking his head affectionately at her flutters.

'Yes, p'raps I'd better, Herby.' The woman carried the blouse to the fitting room.

'I mostly have to make her mind up for her,' confided the husband.

'Yes, some of us do like others to make the decisions,' said Emma. He nodded, and since he seemed a sensible man, she asked him a question. 'Do you believe women should have the vote?'

'I can't see why they shouldn't, though I expect Maudie would forget she'd got one as soon as she had it.'

185

Emma laughed. The woman reappeared, wearing the blouse. Emma had got the size right. The blouse, decoratively lacy, fitted perfectly.

'Champion, Maudie,' said the husband.

'Yes, it's ever so nice. I'll have it, shall I?'

'My treat, Maudie, my pleasure,' he said, and she fluttered happily back to the fitting room. He turned to Emma. 'When you're putting the blouse in a bag, slip in a nice pair of silk stockings and blow the expense. She deserves the blouse, and she deserves the stockings as extra. I'll make them a surprise to her.'

'They'll be a very nice surprise,' said Emma. 'White or black or grey?'

'Black, yes, that sounds good. Here's a pound to cover.' He handed Emma the banknote. Emma extracted a packeted pair of black silk stockings and wrapped them. The woman returned, carrying the new blouse. Emma took it from her.

'Oh, I forgot what the price was, Herby,' she said.

'Told you,' said the husband to Emma. 'She'll leave her own head on a counter one day. Never mind, Maudie, the blouse is settled for, and I'll have to be on me way to work once we get back home.'

Emma made the bill out, put it in a canister, with the pound note, and pulled on the wire. The canister shot across the ceiling to the cashier ensconced in her windowed cubby-hole. When it returned with the change, the blouse had been put into a stiff white paper bag by Emma. The stockings were already in the bag. The man took it, his fluttery but happy wife thanked Emma, and they departed.

When Emma left for home at one o'clock, the watching eyes were at her back and at a distance.

Inspector Greaves was tersely dismissive of Mr Jerry Bates as a suspect. What had made Nicholas have a second go at the man? Just a feeling, said Nicholas.

'Again? What comes next, your own crystal ball?' Inspector Greaves was growling. 'Or perhaps you'll get your landlady to read your tea leaves for you.'

Nicholas was now poring over reports, hoping to find a pertinent something that had escaped him.

Mr Bates, returning from a day in the City on Wednesday evening, presented the girls with a toffee-apple each. They were all delighted, except Trary, who said thank you but she didn't lick toffee-apples at her age.

Trary was putting her hopes in Mr Bradshaw, who had invited the family to the Zoo on Sunday. She thought there was promise in that, even though Mr Bates was making himself more at home. Still, her mum was taking that in her stride. She was ever such a cool one sometimes, when you couldn't tell what she was thinking. Actually, Maggie was beginning to suspect that after several years as a widow, she suddenly had two men interested in her, both very pleasant. Not that she thought either of them had serious intentions regarding a widow with four girls. But it was nice to feel men could still be interested, as long as they didn't have the wrong ideas about her.

She went to see Mr George Gardner, who ran the newsagents situated a little way past East Street. Mr Gardner, thin and harassed, told her he'd decided he'd got to have help in the mornings or he'd get run off his feet and die an early death. Maggie said she was willing to save him from that. Mr Gardner said that was kind of her, but she'd have to start at eight o'clock and work through to twelve, Mondays to Fridays. His daughter, still at school, helped at weekends. Maggie knew she could rely on Trary to see that her sisters had their porridge before they went to school. She'd take the job, she said. How much would Mr Gardner pay her? Five bob, a shilling for each morning. He couldn't offer more. Maggie couldn't turn down five bob. She accepted the job.

Mr Gardner said he was pleased, specially as she'd been highly recommended by Constable Bradshaw. She'd got to watch kids who came in for a ha'porth of suckers, as some of them were little . . . well, no, he couldn't repeat that in front of a lady. Maggie promised to watch them, and to start on Monday.

Emma was quite surprised when the weekend arrived and Sergeant Chamberlain had not, after all, found an excuse to call on her again. Dear me, she thought, am I really to be left alone to enjoy my life in the way I've become accustomed to? How kind of you, Sergeant Chamberlain.

Her neighbours said the police were still out and about, still asking questions all over Walworth, they were. You could always spot their flat feet. Emma couldn't recall Sergeant Chamberlain having flat feet.

By Saturday morning, Trary was feeling miffed. That Bobby Reeves, he'd just disappeared from her life. She hadn't seen anything of him since Monday, when he'd brought Mr Bradshaw's flowers for her mum and a pair of nearly-new black silk stockings for her. Mum had washed them, of course. You had to do that with second-hand things. Trary was going to wear them to the Zoo.

She had looked for her talking boy every afternoon when leaving school, but he hadn't been there. She got haughtier about it every day. On Saturday morning, her mum said, 'I 'aven't seen much of Bobby since Monday, love.'

'Who?' asked Trary distantly.

'Bobby.'

'Oh, him. Well, I can't talk now, Mum, I'm goin' out to meet a school friend.'

Mr Bates presented his companionable self to Maggie on

her return from market shopping. All the girls were out.

'Just the lady I'm lookin' for,' he said.

'I'm a bit busy,' said Maggie, unloading shopping on which she'd spent money carefully. She was never going to get into debt any more. It irked her, of course, that she owed so much money to her lodger, good-hearted though he was.

'I won't keep you, Maggie. Look.' Mr Bates produced some tickets. 'I didn't forget that yer girls said they'd never been to the Zoo. I'm goin' to take all of you tomorrow, and with these tickets we walk straight in, we don't have to join the Sunday queue.'

Maggie stared at them, hardly able to believe what a coincidence they represented. She lifted her gaze to her lodger. His smile was warm and affectionate. 'It don't make sense,' she said. 'You're not 'aving me on, are you?'

'I'm straight as a die with you, Maggie.'

'Well, I'm sorry,' she said, 'but we all happen to be goin' with Mr Bradshaw.'

'Eh?' Mr Bates looked very taken aback. 'The local copper that 'ad tea with you last Sunday?'

'He's a kind man, and a friend,' said Maggie. 'I must say, I've never been more surprised, 'aving you offering to take us after we've already been invited by him.'

'Well, can't be helped, it's just my 'ard luck.' Mr Bates smiled ruefully. 'I'll hand the tickets to some of the street kids. No, I'll keep one, it's been years since I was at the Zoo meself. Might see you there, eh? Not that I'll intrude, I don't 'old with bein' a pushin' friend. Have a good time.'

Lord, thought Maggie, I do have two men interested in me all of a sudden.

Sunday turned out lovely and sunny. The Zoo had the girls agog and capering about. Meg darted off. Maggie called after her.

'Mum, it's the way to the lions over 'ere!'

'We'll all go there together later, so come back 'ere.'

'She'll get ate up,' said Daisy. 'Lions eat people, don't they, mister?'

'Only little fat shockers,' said Harry, 'not little girls like you, Daisy, or bigger little girls like Lily, or growing-up ones like Trary and Meg.'

'Nor mum?' asked Lily, in awe at the wonders of the Zoo.

'I shouldn't think so,' said Harry. 'Every lion knows that mums are far too valuable to be eaten.' Lily looked pleased and relieved about that. Meg came back. Maggie told her she wasn't to go off by herself, not in these crowds.

'I know,' said Trary, 'you hold on to Lily and Meg, Mr Bradshaw, and I'll hold on to Daisy. Then mum can have a day off worryin'. Come on, Daisy.' She took Daisy's hand. And she was very pleased when Lily and Meg happily placed themselves in Mr Bradshaw's charge. Their fingers clung around his. Maggie did not miss their willingness. Girls liked a father figure. She caught Trary's eye. Trary smiled.

'I'm onto you, my girl,' she whispered, 'but it won't make no difference.'

'Don't know what you mean, Mum,' said Trary, who thought her mum had made herself look really nice for the outing in her one and only decent Sunday dress of light grey, even if her hat was a widow's black one. Maggie always felt a nice grey was becoming to a widow.

An elephant lumbered into view, the crowds parting to get out of its way. Daisy and Lily were both awe-struck. The elephant, guided by its keeper, was giving rides to children in a large basket on its back.

Lily, tightening her hold on Harry's left hand, gulped, 'Is it a real one, mister?'

'I should think so, Lily, it's plodding about and its trunk's movin'.'

'No, is it really real?' asked Daisy.

190

'Oh, yer soppy thing,' said Meg, 'course it is, it wouldn't be movin' if it wasn't real.'

'Yes, I s'pose if it wasn't real, it 'ud fall over,' said Lily. The girls gazed up at the laughing children.

'Yes, so it would,' said Harry. 'Elephants that aren't real don't have any bones in their legs.'

The searching trunk hovered above Lily's boater as the elephant approached. Lily squealed.

'Oh, crikey,' breathed Daisy.

'March on, Napoleon,' said Harry to the placid beast, and it moved on, trunk wandering.

'Oh, it 'eard yer, mister,' said Lily. 'Yer saved me 'at bein' ate up.'

'Mr Bradshaw's Trary's 'ero,' said Meg.

'To me dyin' day,' said Trary, a picture in her blue frock, Sunday boater and black silk stockings. The stockings gleamed around her calves and ankles, and felt utter bliss to her, and excitingly posh. A boy stopped to give her the eye. Her nose went up in the air immediately.

They gazed at lanky, strutting ostriches. One was parading about free, but under the eye of a keeper.

'What's it called?' asked Daisy.

'Could be something like Lulu,' said Harry. Meg laughed and squeezed his hand. It affected him.

'Daisy means what is it,' said Maggie.

'Well, I bet it's not a canary,' said Lily.

'It's an ostrich,' said Maggie, 'they're all ostriches.'

'I seen 'em in books,' said Daisy, 'only I forgot the name. I'm always forgettin',' she said darkly to herself. 'Oh, look,' she cried as they went on amid the crowds. 'Mum, look. Monkeys!'

The monkey house was a fascination to the girls. Harry bought a bag of nuts and shared them out. Daisy and Lily yelped with delight at being able to feed the chimps. Lily asked to be lifted a bit. Harry lifted her. She stretched out a tentative hand and offered a nut. A quick paw took it from her, and the chimp's bright-eyed expression became a smile to Lily as its lips parted.

'Look, it's smilin' at me. Trary, look, it's givin' me a smile. Mister, look, can you see?'

'That's a smile all right,' said Harry, 'and you know what it means, Lily, don't you? Love at first sight, that's what I reckon.'

'Crikey,' said nine-year-old Lily, and offered another nut. Her new friend snatched it and made short work of it. Again its bright eyes gleamed and its teeth showed happily.

'Ask 'im 'is name,' said Meg, 'you want to know what to call 'im when he starts walkin' out with you.'

'Soppy,' said Lily. The chimp leapt about. Lily, laughing, turned in Harry's arms and gave him a hug. 'Oh, ain't it fun, mister?' she said.

'Me, give me a lift,' begged Daisy, hand clutching nuts. Harry set Lily down and took the youngest girl up. Two chimps darted to perch themselves close.

'Ain't our Daisy popular?' said Meg. 'She's got two after 'er, an' before she's given them any nuts.'

Daisy offered one. It was grabbed. She offered another. The chimps chattered and gobbled. Meg threw a nut. A chimp leapt and caught it in the air. Daisy was laughing, giggling and quivering. They stayed a while, all the monkeys fascinating. Then they moved on. Meg slipped her hand back into Harry's, and Lily clung to his other. Maggie bit her lip. Girls liked a dad. Boys liked a mum.

They moved around the Zoo. They watched penguins, polar bears and two huge hippos. Then they found a seat to accommodate all of them and ate the sandwiches Maggie had made. Harry went and bought two bottles of lemonade, and they drank it out of a mug, passing it round and refilling it. The sun shone, the girls chattered. Trary thought it was just like a family outing, a full family outing, with Lily and Meg showing a nice fondness for Mr Bradshaw.

192

A strong and cheerful voice broke through the noise of the crowds. 'Well, hello, hello, thought I might run across yer.'

They all looked up into the hugely benevolent smile of Mr Bates.

'Oh, you've come too,' said Meg.

'Picture postcard, that's what all you girlies make. How'd'yer do, Maggie. How'd'yer do, old man?' Mr Bates smiled at Harry. 'So we meet, eh?'

'So it seems,' said Harry, who knew Detective-Sergeant Chamberlain had had his doubts about Maggie's lodger. That was something that had disturbed Harry, but the man was in the clear now. And his air of genuine pleasure at seeing the family he lodged with couldn't be faulted. 'Like some lemonade?'

'Not goin' to rob you, wouldn't dream of it,' said Mr Bates handsomely. Oh, go away, thought Trary. Their lodger was larger than life sometimes. 'No, yours truly don't intend to barge in. Maggie, you all look as if yer local constab'lary is takin' good care of you, which is the name of the game, as they say about a sudden strike of gold in Australia. I'll leave yer to yer Sunday out. Seen the kangaroos, 'ave yer, Daisy me pet?'

'Oh, could we see some kangaroos, mister?' Daisy asked of Harry.

'If they haven't all jumped out of sight,' said Harry.

Mr Bates laughed. 'Good point, that, constable,' he said. 'So long now, girlies, see yer later.' He went bouncily off, laughing.

They did some more strolling and looking, Lily and Meg again hand in hand with Harry, and Trary hanging on to Daisy, leaving Maggie as free as the air. They saw the lions and tigers, strongly caged. The lions lay crouched for the most part, tails lazily flapping, eyes gazing incuriously and with the undemanding mildness of animals that had just been fed. But they were in time to see the tigers receiving their ration of meat. There was growling,

193

snarling and hissing as the big striped cats competed for the large red chunks.

'Cor, I bet they'd eat anybody,' said Daisy, as huge teeth grated on bone.

'Well, who they eatin' now?' asked Lily.

'Where's Trary?' asked Harry. 'Mother O'Riley, where is she?'

'Oh, you silly, she's 'ere,' giggled Lily.

'Oh, yes, so I am,' said Trary, hand in Daisy's. 'What a relief.'

'Yer 'aving us on, mister,' said Lily.

'Still, I s'pose they're eatin' somebody,' said Meg.

'Might be the Prime Minister,' said Harry.

'Oh, we don't mind 'im bein' gobbled up,' said Meg. 'And don't they gobble up ferocious, mister?'

'Only way to eat a Prime Minister, I reckon,' said Harry.

'Oh, yer fun,' said Meg, which was the prime compliment from an eleven-year-old girl to a grown-up. Trary's eyes danced. Maggie smiled wryly.

'Would you like a pot of tea, Mrs Wilson?' asked Harry.

'That sounds like a bit of 'eaven,' said Maggie.

'A pot of tea for six, girls, with cakes?' said Harry.

'We'll just love you for it, Mr Bradshaw,' said Trary.

'Give you kisses,' laughed Meg.

'I don't mind,' announced Daisy.

'Specially if the cakes is nice,' said Lily.

'What a palaver,' said Maggie.

Harry took them to the Zoo refreshment rooms, where they sat down to two pots of tea and fruit buns with butter. Trary thought he simply must be fond of her mum, he was spending money in such a romantic way, on flowers, on tickets to the Zoo and fruit buns with butter. Butter. Trary had a feeling Mr Bates would have been just as generous, but in a loud show-off way, with his laughs rolling about all over the Zoo. Oh, crikey, if mum did go and marry him, those same laughs would roll about all over the house, drowning everyone. That reminded her of Bobby Reeves and how he could talk. She supposed some other girl was having to listen to him now. Not that she cared.

'All right, Trary?' Mr Bradshaw was looking at her from the other side of the table. Her partly eaten fruit bun lay neglected on her plate. She felt very touched by his affectionate smile.

'Yes, thank you, Mr Bradshaw, I was only thinkin' what a lovely day mum and me and the girls are havin'.'

'It's mutual, Trary, I'm havin' a lovely time myself,' said Harry.

'Can we go an' find the kangaroos in a minute?' asked Daisy.

'An' some parrots,' said Lily. 'I like parrots.'

'Well, you're one yerself,' said Meg, and Lily giggled.

'You're on,' said Harry. 'We'll take a look at the kangaroos and then go and meet some of Lily's brothers and sisters.'

Maggie laughed out loud. It made the girls smile, and it made Trary think that her mum was happy. Meg said again that Harry was fun, and Trary said yes, really nice fun.

When they left the refreshment rooms, Maggie took charge of Daisy and Lily. Meg attached herself to Harry again. Trary walked on his other side. He took her hand too. Her fingers curled contentedly around his, and a little unbreakable bond established itself between the Walworth constable and Maggie's eldest daughter.

On their way to find the kangaroos, Maggie saw Mr Bates again. He was talking to a man in a natty striped suit and a boater, whom she thought looked a bit flash. Mr Bates lifted his hat to her. His companion lifted his boater, and eyed her with keen interest.

'Nice to see you again, Maggie,' called Mr Bates.

' 'Ow'd'yer do, lady,' said Mr Rodney Foster, 'good day to yer.'

Maggie thought his cockney accent quite unlike anything she'd ever heard, it was so broad and nasal.

'Good day,' she said, and went on with her daughters and Harry.

The Zoo trip was memorable for all of them, even if the kangaroos made no attempt to jump as high as a house.

CHAPTER SIXTEEN

Mr Bates put his head round the kitchen door on Monday morning. The girls had just finished their porridge, and Trary was running a tidying comb through Daisy's hair before going off to West Square. She had to leave by half-past eight at the latest, as she always walked, unless it was raining, when Maggie gave her a penny for a tram fare. The younger girls did not need to leave until five-to-nine, as St John's School was only a minute away.

'Hello, hello, where's you ma?' asked Mr Bates.

'Gone to work,' said Trary briefly.

'What?'

'What fell off a ladder an' broke 'is leg, yer know,' said Meg reprovingly.

'What work?' asked Mr Bates.

'She's got a morning job at a newsagents,' said Trary.

'That's the most shockin' bit of news I ever heard,' said Mr Bates, looking quite upset. 'Your mum goin' out to work? It's a sad day, girlies.'

'She wasn't cryin',' said Meg, now instinctively favouring Constable Bradshaw as her mum's best gentleman friend.

'Well, I am,' said Mr Bates, 'I'm cryin' me eyes out. Can't be right, Meg, your mum havin' to go out to work.'

'Mum needs the money to buy our daily bread,' said Trary, putting the comb on the mantelpiece.

'I'm hurt I wasn't told', said Mr Bates sadly.

'Oh, dear me, fancy that,' said Trary. 'Well, I'm goin' now, Meg, you see you all get to school on time. Excuse me, Mr Bates.'

'Pleasure,' said Mr Bates, standing aside, 'I'll see yer sisters leave for school on time.'

'Thanks, but they don't need you to,' said Trary, and left.

Maggie quite enjoyed her first morning at the newsagents, needing only a little guidance and advice from Mr Gardner in the matter of relating to customers. The shop was quite busy, selling tobacco, confectionery and other little items in addition to newspapers and magazines. Housewives liked to have a chat while purchasing magazines like *Home Chat* and *Peg's Paper*, or an ounce of shag for a husband's clay pipe. Maggie's inherent friendliness came through, and Mr Gardner told her at the end of her four hours stint that he was downright pleasured by her nice ways.

On her way home she stopped at Mrs Reeves's second-hand clothing stall to inspect what was on offer. The girls were badly in need of some decent seconds, and she could now afford to spend a couple of shillings on frocks they could wear to school. Mrs Reeves was often able to supply very wearable frocks for sixpence or even less.

Beaming, Mrs Reeves said, 'Well, it's that nice to see yer again, Mrs Wilson. Your eldest girl stopped by for a little chat a week or so ago. Ain't she growed a lovely gel? That Bobby of mine says 'e's fair been laid out. At 'is age, would yer believe. I told 'im, no good buildin' castles till 'e's a man and knows what 'is prospects is. I just hope your Trary's not embarrassed by 'is 'igh-falutin' tongue, her bein' only thirteen. Mind, when she was talkin' to me, I said to meself, I said there's a gel who can 'old her own.'

Maggie laughed. 'She can do that all right, Mrs Reeves. It's more like can any boy hold 'is own with her, and if he can it won't be no embarrassment to her, more like a challenge. But I don't think she's seen much of Bobby this last week.'

'No, well, he's been down with tonsillitis,' said Mrs Reeves. 'Shock to 'im that he couldn't use 'is tongue like he usually can. Today's 'is first time up and about. 'E's busy upstairs sortin' through a stock we had come in this mornin'. Reg'lar sharp eye that lad's got for sortin' an' pricin'.'

'I like Bobby,' said Maggie, 'I'm sorry about his tonsillitis.'

'I'll give 'im your regards, Mrs Wilson, he's got a soft spot for you and yer fam'ly,' said Mrs Reeves. 'Would yer be after anything off me stall?'

'Well, something for the girls to wear for school?'

Mrs Reeves beamed again. 'Tell you what, Mrs Wilson, I'll get Bobby to bring yer round a bargain box of stuff this evenin'. 'E knows yer girls. There's a few nice frocks 'anging there, and more in the stock that come this mornin'. Bobby and me'll see he brings you a nice selection, an' yer girls can try them on. Bobby'll price anything you want to buy. Is yer 'ard luck times a bit better?'

'Much better,' said Maggie. 'Mrs Reeves, that's really nice of you.'

'Well, we all got to pull together,' said Mrs Reeves, a motherly body. 'No good relyin' on no Government to 'elp us out, I don't know what we 'ave Governments for. Chuck 'em all out, Mr Reeves says. Can I 'elp you, lady?' She addressed the question to a shabby-looking woman who had been hovering and who had advanced to tentatively finger one of the hanging frocks. Maggie smiled, said goodbye and left Mrs Reeves to make a sale.

Bobby appeared at the stall ten minutes later. Monday morning business in the market was desultory, and his mum had time to chat to him. He was a little peaky from his illness, but as alert as ever, and he wanted to know what had happened to a prime fox fur and a winter coat with a fur collar that had been among the stock that had arrived during the morning.

'Upstairs,' said Mrs Reeves. She and her family lived in the flat above the shop that was behind the stall. 'We put them aside for that special customer I told yer about.'

'Well, they've gone missin',' said Bobby.

'Where's yer father?' asked Mrs Reeves quickly.

'Blimey,' said Bobby, and gave his mum a wry look. 'He's nicked 'em, he went off with a parcel ten minutes ago.'

'He's goin' to flog 'em,' said Mrs Reeves. 'Jewels, they are, Bobby, that fox fur an' coat. 'Ardly been wore. We could of got near to thirty bob for 'em.'

'I'm off,' said Bobby.

'Where?'

'To Dad's second home. The pub,' said Bobby, and was off at speed to the Sir William Walworth public house, his dad's favourite haunt. He was under age, but he went into the public bar all the same, and made straight for his dad, sitting at a table in the corner, with a crony. The proprietor turned a blind eye. He knew Bobby, and he knew Bobby's dad.

Mr Reeves was a thin, wiry man of forty-five, with bright beady eyes that looked everywhere at once from beneath his ever-present bowler hat.

' 'Ere, what you after, Bobby?'' he asked. 'Yer can't come in 'ere, not at your age, son, you'll get Gus nicked, an' me as well.' Gus was the proprietor, temporarily blind of eye.

'D'you mind if I speak to me dad private?' asked Bobby of the crony, a burly man.

'Yer welcome, son,' said the man, and moved to another table, taking his half of old and mild with him. Bobby sat down next to his father.

'You perisher,' he said, having spotted the parcel under the table.

' 'Ere, 'old 'ard,' said Mr Reeves, 'yer talkin' to yer lovin' dad, yer know, yer young rip.'

'I'll give you lovin',' said Bobby. 'What's lovin' about nickin' the fam'ly's bread an' butter for a whole bleedin' week?'

' 'Swelp me,' said the pained Mr Reeves, 'was yer brought up to use that kind of language to yer 'ard-workin' dad?

No, yer wasn't, and I got a good mind to clip yer one.'

'Well, Dad,' said Bobby, 'you can clip me a packet, if yer like, but it won't 'elp. It grieves me to use unkind language to you, but it's time you mended yer ways. It also grieves me to tell yer you're not hard-workin', yer bone idle and shifty as well.'

'Gawd bleedin' blimey,' said Mr Reeves, 'is me ear'oles 'earing right?'

'I reckon,' said Bobby. 'You're livin' off mum an' Lucy.' Lucy was his fourteen-year-old sister who had a job in a factory for seven bob a week. 'It's not to your credit, yer know.'

'Them's uncharitable words to use to yer father,' said Mr Reeves, shaking his head in gloom that he could be so misjudged by his own son. 'Is it my fault I ain't bin able to get a job?'

'Yes,' said Bobby.

'Eh?'

'Yes, it's your own fault. You're a shirker, Dad, and dead crafty as well. You pinched that fox fur an' the coat with a fur collar, good as brand new, and yer waitin' here for some bloke you're goin' to flog them to. Is that nice, is it fam'ly-minded? We're all fond of yer, you got some good points, but we're not proud of yer.'

'Well, sod me if I ever 'eard the like of this,' said Mr Reeves, even more pained. ' 'Ow would yer like it if I took me belt to yer backside?'

'You'd have a job,' said Bobby.

Mr Reeves took a huge draught of his old and mild and gazed forlornly at the empty glass mug.

'You ain't well, son,' he said, 'it's yer tonsillitis that's done it. It's give yer brains a nasty tannin', so I don't bear no 'ard feelings.'

'I got sore feelings myself,' said Bobby, 'all on account of havin' a dad that nicks from 'is own fam'ly. It's honest-to-God grievin', yer know, me and me sisters not able to hold our heads up. I met a really nice girl just recent,

201

with a nice fam'ly, and I don't want to have to tell them that the father of me own fam'ly pinches our bread and butter. I'm not goin' to meet a nicer girl, not even if I live to be a 'undred, so I'm askin' you very reasonable, Dad, to mend your unhappy ways, because they're very grievin'.'

'Now look, son – '

'What's that?' asked Bobby, looking over the top of his father's bowler hat. With a guilty start, Mr Reeves took a hasty look over his shoulder. Bobby swooped, came up with the parcel and walked away with it, the publican grinning as the boy disappeared fast through the public bar door.

'Bleedin' hell,' said Mr Reeves.

'Done it on yer, 'Enry,' said Gus. 'Time you got learned a thing or two, and I'll have that glass back if you've finished with it.'

'Done me,' gloomed Mr Reeves. 'Me own flesh an' blood.'

'You got a good 'un there, 'Enry.'

Mr Reeves, an eternal optimist, perked up, 'Don't I know it,' he said proudly.

'Blank walls?' said Inspector Greaves tersely, his moustache itself stiff and bristling.

'It happens in cases like this one,' said Nicholas, 'where there's no motive like revenge or jealousy or blackmail.'

'Do I need that kind of information?' asked the Inspector. A bombardment of sarcasm from the Press was being aimed at Scotland Yard and scoring hits that were damaging him. 'Come with me. We're going to see a Mrs Stubbs of Walworth. She's been to Rodney Road. She wants to talk to someone about her lodger. She can talk to us.'

Mrs Doris Stubbs lived in Crampton Street, not far, Nicholas realized, from Steedman Street. She was a stout woman, busy and bustling, her husband a costermonger. Her children were all married, her lodger's contribution to the rent a welcome thing.

202

'Yes, and 'e gets on well with me old man. Men don't like other men in their 'omes unless they get on with 'em. Well, what I want to tell yer is that when one of yer constables first come and asked if we 'ad a lodger an' was 'e out that Friday night of the murder, I've been wondering if I give 'im the right answer.'

Nicholas, who had checked the notes of that particular constable, along with all others, said, 'You answered that he never went out, Mrs Stubbs.'

'Well, I wasn't meself, I don't like coppers knockin' on me door when I'm busy and askin' questions that's not very nice.' Mrs Stubbs busied herself then, by bustling about and putting cushions to rights, a sign, thought Nicholas of a worried woman. She went on to say that she told the constable her husband and lodger played crib every night, going at it hammer and tongs, as if it had got into their bloodstreams, like drink. But she'd started to think a bit more about it, and she'd asked her husband if he did play crib with Mr Cox, the lodger, on that horrible Friday night. Her husband thought about it and said only for about an hour, then Mr Cox went out. That made her think some more, it made her remember that he had a visitor before he went out. It was a woman. She heard her on the stairs, she must have used the latchcord to let herself in. She heard her call up, 'I'm here.' And Mr Cox called down, 'That's nice, come up.' Mrs Stubbs remembered thinking perhaps he'd got a lady friend all of a sudden.

'Then he went out?' asked Inspector Greaves.

Mrs Stubbs said yes, after about five minutes. Nicholas grimaced. He'd have liked it better if the answer had fitted his theories. Mrs Stubbs said her lodger also went out on the Friday evening when the young woman was attacked in Manor Place. Her husband, when she asked him last night, had said so.

'Can you remember what time he got back on those two nights?' asked Nicholas.

'It must've been late because he 'adn't come in before me 'usband and me went to bed, which we usually do a bit after half-past ten. But 'e's never been the sort to come in noisy an' drunk, 'e's a quiet man, yer know.'

'Would you allow us to examine his room?' asked the Inspector.

Mrs Stubbs was glad to. She didn't want it all hanging over her, she said. Mr Cox rented two rooms, bedroom and living. Inspector Greaves and Nicholas searched both under the landlady's worried eye. They found a flat cap, a dark mackintosh, and boots with rubber soles. But no lock of hair, length of cord or little notebook came to light. They persevered, but without success.

'Mrs Stubbs,' said the Inspector, 'if the young woman let herself in by the latchcord, would you know if that meant she'd visited Mr Cox on other occasions?'

'I don't remember 'im 'aving no lady visitors before, I never 'eard none. But 'e did 'ave one that evenin', me memory come back very clear once I'd spoke to me 'usband and me worried thinkin' started. When yer constable first called, I only thought about all that crib reg'lar as clockwork, except on Saturdays. Me an' me old man like to go to the pub Saturday evenings, an' Mr Cox liked to go up West.'

'Is that a fact?' asked Nicholas.

'Yes, I got to 'oping 'e'd find a nice young woman for hisself, 'im bein' a deservin' gentleman, I thought. Not that we wanted to lose 'im as a lodger, but yer can't 'elp wishin' kindly for some people. I can't 'ardly believe I might 'ave a lodger that might be the man you're lookin' for, and I just won't rest till it's settled one way or other.'

'We'll see, Mrs Stubbs,' said the Inspector.

' 'E does clerkin' work at the coal merchants offices in the Walworth Road, yer know,' said Mrs Stubbs.

'We'll give him a call,' said Inspector Greaves.

* * *

A young woman looked up as the CID men entered the offices of the coal merchants. In her white blouse and black skirt, the blouse adorned with a black neck ribbon tied in a bow, she was a typically neat lady clerk. Coming to her feet, she advanced to the counter.

'Can I help you?' she asked.

'Yes, we'd like to see Mr Cox,' said the Inspector. 'Is he here?'

'I'm sure he is,' she said, her manner bright and extrovert. She pointed to a door. 'That's his office. Just knock and go in. It's business, is it?'

'Yes, it's business,' said Nicholas.

'Well, as long as you haven't come to rob the safe,' she said.

Nicholas smiled, the Inspector knocked on the door and a man's voice called, 'Come in.'

They went in, Nicholas closing the door. At a desk and facing them sat a broad-shouldered, pleasant-faced man. He was about thirty, and wearing a workaday grey suit, with a stiff white collar to his shirt, and a grey tie. On the desk were account books, an open ledger in front of him and a pen in his hand. He looked as if he could have been a competent woodsman or wheelwright, except that his steel-rimmed spectacles placed him in a more sedentary mould. He took them off to inspect the callers, and Nicholas guessed they were only for reading.

'Mr Cox?' enquired the gravel-voiced Inspector.

'Yes?' Puzzled grey eyes regarded the CID men. 'Are you from head office?'

'No. Scotland Yard. I'm Detective-Inspector Greaves, this is Detective-Sergeant Chamberlain. We're makin' certain enquiries. We think you can 'elp us, Mr Cox. Sorry to interrupt you at your work, but I'd be obliged if you could answer a few questions.'

Mr Cox flinched. 'What about?' he asked.

'Our enquiries concern the murder of a Miss Mabel Shipman.'

'Oh, good God,' said Mr Cox, and looked stunned. Then he shook his head as if to clear his mind of shock. 'You'd better sit down, I suppose.' The Inspector and Nicholas drew up chairs and sat down. 'Are you investigating me?'

'Askin' for your co-operation, sir,' said the Inspector.

'We understand you're keen on cribbage,' said Nicholas.

'What?' Mr Cox looked utterly perplexed.

'The card game.'

'Oh, that. Yes. Good game for two.' Mr Cox was flat-voiced, his fingers twisting his spectacles about. 'I think you must have been talking to my landlady.'

'An 'elpful woman,' said the Inspector. 'Now, sir, let me put it to you, what were you doing the evening of the murder, last Friday fortnight?'

'Doing? Last Friday fortnight?' It seemed to pain Mr Cox, the effort of casting his mind back.

'It wasn't an evening when nothing 'appened, Mr Cox. You can remember, can't you?'

'My God, yes.' Mr Cox's nervous fingers became still. His forehead showed a slight film of perspiration. 'Steedman Street.'

'You got it, Mr Cox, at one go,' said the Inspector.

Mr Cox exhaled breath, leaned back in his chair and laughed, a man hugely relieved. It was a laugh totally unexpected in the face of his nervous twitches.

'Can we share the joke?' asked Nicholas drily.

'God, it's no joke,' said Mr Cox, 'you had me on the rack for a bit. D'you mind if I call Kitty in?'

'Is that the young female clerk?' asked the Inspector.

'Yes. Miss Kitty Lane. D'you mind?'

'Not if it's goin' to 'elp us.'

'It will,' said Mr Cox. He got up, walked to the door and opened it. Kitty Lane was at the counter, attending to a customer. He waited until the customer departed, then called her in.

'What d'you want?' she asked with a smile.

'Kitty,' said Mr Cox, 'we've been out together lately.'

'Yes, so we have, but why d'you ask?' She looked in curiosity at the CID men.

'When was the last time we went out?' asked Mr Cox.

'Saturday night.'

'And before then?'

'Last Friday week,' she said. The Inspector's grizzled look darkened. That was the Friday when Miss Morley had been attacked. 'What d'you want to know for?' asked Kitty.

'I'll tell you in a moment,' said Mr Cox. 'Can you remember the other time before last Friday week.'

'Yes, the Friday before that. Percy, what's it all about?'

'The police are asking me to help them with their enquiries,' said Mr Cox.

Kitty's eyes flashed. 'What enquiries?'

'The murder,' said Mr Cox.

'Oh, that's wicked!' Kitty looked furious. 'Or it's a sickening joke.'

'Murder's no joke, neither is an investigation into murder,' said Nicholas, 'it means questioning the innocent as well as the guilty. Miss Lane, can you remember what time you reached your home on each of those two Fridays?'

'About eleven both times,' she said.

'You're quite sure?'

'Of course I am.'

'And Mr Cox was with you on each occasion?' asked the Inspector.

'Of course he was. Mr Cox wouldn't let a young lady go home on her own. It would come to something, wouldn't it, if a man did that?' Kitty put a question to Nicholas who was that much younger than the Inspector. 'Wouldn't you take a young lady home if you went out with her?'

'Yes, I would,' said Nicholas.

'I don't know how you can come asking Mr Cox questions

207

about murder. He wouldn't hurt a fly. He's gentle, he is. He was out with me those nights, and when he brought me home he came in and my mother made a pot of tea for us, so she can tell you too where he was.'

Inspector Greaves uttered a low, growling murmur of frustration.

'Yes, thank you, Miss Lane,' said Nicholas. 'What was the arrangement last Friday fortnight?'

'Arrangement?'

'Yes, where did you meet each other?'

'I went to his lodgings,' said Kitty. 'I had a little framed water colour for him. It was his birthday. I jolly well hope that satisfies you.'

'Could you oblige me with your address, miss?' asked the Inspector.

'Yes, Merrow Street.'

That was close to Camberwell Road. It put Mr Cox definitely in the clear.

'Thank you, Miss Lane,' said the Inspector and came abruptly to his feet. 'Thank you, Mr Cox.'

Nicholas rising, smiled ruefully and said, 'Sorry we had to trouble you.'

'Exactly why did you?' asked Mr Cox.

'Because you were out on the two evenings in question,' said Nicholas. 'That alone made it necessary for us to interview you.'

'Yes, of course, I understand,' said Mr Cox. He saw them out and shook hands with them.

Outside, the Inspector said, 'First-class lead, bloody useless result.'

'I thought we were on to something when he started to sweat,' said Nicholas.

'Never count your chickens,' said Inspector Greaves sourly.

Trary came out of school in company with friends, and at a moment when Bobby turned into West Square from St George's Road. Trary's boater went up and so did her nose.

'I'm in a hurry,' she said, and detached herself from her friends to walk fast. Bobby came across to meet her. She went straight past him in her haughtiest fashion. She entered St George's Road, going at a quick, springy pace. Bobby went after her.

'What's up, your house on fire, Trary?' he said.

'Kindly don't speak to me, whoever you are,' said Trary.

'Now what've I done?' asked Bobby.

'I'm sure I don't know,' she said. 'I've never hardly seen you before, and you can stop followin' me or I'll call a policeman.'

'Well, blow me hat off,' said Bobby. 'I come all this way with a kind 'eart, and what do I get? A carry-on.'

'I'm just not speakin' to you, that's all,' said Trary, her nose higher.

'That's not much of a change,' said Bobby.

'Oh, you cheeky beast. Go away.'

'Well, I'd better walk you 'ome first, seein' you've had to do it by yourself for nearly a week. I've had a worryin' time about that, I can tell you.'

'Oh dear, what a cryin' shame,' said Trary.

'Hello, something gone wrong at home, Trary?' Bobby was cheerfully impervious to her aloofness, if still a little peaky. 'Is yer mum up against it again? I've suffered a chronic week meself, laid up with tonsillitis. Couldn't eat, couldn't hardly talk. Me mum said she didn't mind me not talkin' – '

'Tonsillitis?' said Trary, and cast him a look. She saw his peakiness. A guilty feeling assailed her. 'Oh, you Bobby Reeves, why didn't you say?'

'Say? I've just told you, I couldn't hardly talk, let alone say.'

'You could've sent a note. I don't know, you boys, you just can't take care of yourselves. Fancy gettin' tonsillitis when it's summer. That's just the sort of thing you would do, Bobby Reeves, and I don't suppose you should be out of bed yet, either. I'll just have to take you straight home. D'you want to lean on me?'

Bobby shouted with laughter. People looked. Trary went haughty again.

'I think I can manage to keep standin' up,' said Bobby, 'in fact, I feel miles better for seein' you, Trary. You get prettier all the time. Did you wear the silk stockings with yer Sunday frock. I bet your legs looked swish in them, I'd like to 'ave seen 'em.'

'Oh, you blessed cheeky devil,' said Trary, hiding every ounce of delight she felt that her talking boy was in such good form. 'You're talkin' about my legs again.'

'Yes, it's nice you've got legs, Trary. I've seen some at the music hall, but I bet yours are better. Of course, I wouldn't look unless you insisted. I mean, I wouldn't mind you insistin'.'

'You'll be lucky,' said Trary. 'Of all the nerve. Me insistin'? Well, I don't know, you've got the sauciest talkin' mouth I ever heard. I don't show my legs to any boys, let alone hooligans like you, what d'you think I am?'

'Grand, that's what you are, Trary,' said Bobby. 'I was fair racked last week, thinkin' about what might be 'appening to you with all the West Square boys chasin' after you, and me not there to knock 'em silly. I had a real grievin' week, what with bein' laid low and worryin' about you, besides not bein' able to swallow or say much. You're 'ardly livin' when you can't talk, yer know.'

'Oh, bless my soul, poor boy,' said Trary, hugely enjoying herself, 'but you're doin' all right now, you're pleased to say.'

'Yes, I'm better when I don't feel ill,' said Bobby. 'Don't you worry, I'm set on lookin' after you for always. Mind, I'm not sayin' you're not lucky you met me – '

'Lucky? Lucky?' Trary's spirits were high, her adrenalin flowing, her step springier than ever. 'I'd like you to know, Bobby Reeves, that you're just someone I met accidental on our front doorstep wearin' a box on your head. I never heard it was lucky to do that, meetin' a boy with a box on his head, specially a talkin' one.'

'Talkin' box?' said Bobby.

'Talkin' mouth,' said Trary.

'Good on yer, Trary, you're better than any medicine, you are.'

They walked on and talked on, their tongues fighting each other. When they reached the baker's on the corner of Heygate Street in the Walworth Road, Bobby stopped.

'Now what?' asked Trary.

'I won't be a tick,' said Bobby. 'I left something in 'ere which they're lookin' after for me.' He popped into the shop. When he came out again, there was a large cardboard box on his capped head, and a bland look on his face. Trary stared at him.

'I don't believe it,' she said, 'you're doin' it again.'

'I did'nt want to bring it all the way to yer school,' said Bobby. 'It's for yer mum. I'll carry it to her like this.'

'Oh, no, you won't,' said Trary. 'I'm not walkin' home with any boy who's got another box on his soppy 'ead. D'you think I want all the street kids laughin' at me. Take it off.'

'All right,' said Bobby, and shifted the box to his arms. It had a lid to it.

'What's in it?' asked Trary, as they resumed their walk.

'It's for me favourite lady's inspection. Your mum.'

'What's in it, you aggravatin' boy?'

'You'll see.'

When the box arrived on the kitchen table and Maggie took the lid off, a selection of the very best seconds in the way of frocks was revealed. Bobby had done an excellent sorting job with the help of his mother, and there were sizes to fit all four girls. Meg yelled with joy when Maggie said they could choose one each. Daisy and Lily goggled. Trary stared and swallowed. Oh, that Bobby, standing there all innocent-looking to hide how kind he was.

211

She felt ever so pleased then that he hadn't spent last week walking and talking with other girls.

Every frock was of good quality, some looking as if they'd hardly been worn. The kitchen became bright with colour as the box was emptied and there were frocks everywhere. The girls went through them all.

'How much are they, Bobby?' asked Maggie. 'Or are they different prices?'

'All the same, Mrs Wilson,' said Bobby, 'but mum said don't buy what you can't afford. I'm afraid they're pretty pricey. Fourpence each.'

'Fourpence?' Maggie gave him a direct look. He took his cap off and dusted it against his trousers. 'Fourpence, Bobby?'

'Sorry, Mrs Wilson, I know it's a lot.'

'You're 'aving me on,' said Maggie. 'Your mum wouldn't put any of these on her stall for less than ninepence.'

'Well, we thought fourpence each if you buy four, one each for yer girls, and one for my young lady.'

'Bobby, you got a young lady?' asked Meg, holding a blue frock against herself. 'Who is she?'

'Trary,' said Bobby.

'Bless us, it's just not believable what comes out of that boy's mouth,' said Trary, eyes on a lovely peach-coloured frock that looked as if it might fit her.

'Bobby, be sensible,' said Maggie. 'Fourpence each can't be fair to your mum.'

'It's a special price if you buy four,' said Bobby. 'Mum says you've been a good customer for years, Mrs Wilson. You can keep them till tomorrow, you can take your time. I'll leave you to it. I've 'ad tonsillitis, by the way, but I was pleased I was recovered enough to start walkin' Trary home from school again. You don't mind I've decided she's me young lady, Mrs Wilson? When she's older, I mean.'

'No, I don't mind a bit,' smiled Maggie.

'Some hopes he's got,' said Trary. She saw him to the front door, her eyes very bright. 'Thanks ever so much, Bobby, all the frocks look lovely.'

'Well, I like you, Trary, and yer fam'ly,' said Bobby.

CHAPTER SEVENTEEN

Maggie accepted the price that had been offered out of friendship. She bought two frocks for each of her girls for the sum total of two shillings and eightpence. She was buoyed up by the fact that her little job would add five shillings a week to her income.

Mr Bates, arriving back from the City in the evening, asked her if she'd kindly talk with him in the parlour.

'Yes, what is it, Mr Bates?' she asked, and her lodger regarded her with an unusually diffident smile.

'Now I don't want you to think I'm interferin',' he said, 'it's always been a rule of mine not to poke me nose into other people's affairs. But you're different, and so's yer fam'ly, and I've got to say it depresses me to know you've had to start goin' out to work. I said to meself, Jerry, I said, something's got to be done about it. What's my good lady most in need of, I asked meself. Security, I said. No financial worries, a decent roof over 'er head and no obstreperous landlord to come knockin'. Also, a bit of a garden with roses, and her precious girls sufferin' no want. Maggie's had a rough time, I said to meself, and 'ere she is havin' to go out to work when she's still got this house and 'er four girls to look after. Jerry, I said, it's up to you to speak your piece.'

Maggie stared at him. His breeziness was muted, his smile very kind. 'Mr Bates, what you talkin' about exactly?'

He coughed, and he fiddled with his tie. 'To be candid, Maggie, I'm talkin' about me feelings. Deep feelings. I've been around, as I've said, but you're the first woman I've met that I've 'ad deep feelings for. Now I'm not supposin' it's mutual, but it might be in time, it might well be, so

214

what I'm proposin', Maggie, is that you take me for better or worse, and as a willin' father to yer girls.'

'Lord save us,' gasped Maggie. 'Mr Bates –'

'It's floored you?' Mr Bates's smile was understanding. 'Well, you don't have to decide right now, I wouldn't ask you to or expect you to. Just take your time thinkin' about it.'

Maggie's breath was taken. She put a hand to her throat. This healthy and vigorous man was actually willing to marry her and become a father to her four girls? He had lifted her worries concerning her debts in a generous way, and been no trouble at all as a lodger. His presence was always a cheerful one. Now he wanted to marry her?

'Mr Bates –'

'Jerry.'

'Yes. Oh, lor', I still don't know what to say.'

'Will this 'elp Maggie?' He put his hands lightly on her shoulders and bent his head. Maggie was so defenceless in her confusion that she let the kiss happen. His lips pressed hers firmly and affectionately. She had not been kissed by a man for years, and the sensations were a natural pleasure to her. They did not, however, make her feel she was in love with him, but they were a reminder of what a woman could be to a man whom she did love. His lips withdrew, he lifted his head and smiled at her. 'That wasn't too bad, Maggie?'

'No, it was kindly given, but I just can't think straight at the moment.'

'Understood,' said Mr Bates. 'Look 'ere, though, when I've finished gettin' contracts, I won't be wantin' in finances, I'll be able to provide very comfortable for you an' the girls, and in a decent house with a bit of a garden. But you take yer time gettin' your thinkin' straight, I'm not goin' to rush you. Take a couple of days, say, then if it's yes I'll marry you come June.'

'June? That's next month,' said Maggie in new confusion.

'Best month for a weddin', yer know,' smiled Mr Bates.

215

'Best month to fit the girls up as yer bridesmaids.'

'Lord, I just don't know,' breathed Maggie. A father for her girls, that had to be thought about, that and a decent home for them. 'But I will think about it, and serious.'

'All me own thinkin' is very serious,' said Mr Bates, 'but I'm not goin' to say any more just now, Maggie, I know when a woman needs to be by herself, and you're a woman and a half. You give yerself a couple of days.' He smiled again, gave her shoulder a gentle pat and went upstairs to his room.

Later, when the younger girls were in bed, Maggie thought about telling Trary of Mr Bates and his proposal. Trary, she knew, was a bit cool towards their lodger.

'Trary love?'

'I was just thinkin', Mum, is Mr Bradshaw comin' to see you again?'

Oh, lor', thought Maggie, I forgot Harry Bradshaw is Trary's hero. 'Well, yes, he did say he might come an' knock this week.'

'Well, he's nice, don't you think he's nice, Mum?'

'Yes, of course,' said Maggie, and made no mention of Mr Bates, after all. Instead, her thoughts turned to the local constable and the trip to the Zoo. He'd behaved very natural with her girls, and her girls had been very responsive. Harry Bradshaw was a quieter man than Mr Bates, but he knew how to talk to young girls.

All the same, the plain fact was her four girls did need a dad.

Emma spent the evening making notes for proposals to submit to the suffragette hierarchy. She intended to have the proposals signed by those members in favour of tactics more subtle than militancy. She had enjoyed a very animated discussion with a dozen supporters that afternoon, at a friend's house in the Edgware Road.

Preposterously, thoughts of Sergeant Chamberlain periodically interrupted her scribbling. She really had expected him to find an excuse to call again. It was not all that difficult for a woman to detect a man's interest in her. One had to admit Sergeant Chamberlain was far from being a stolid and regimented policeman. His concern for her had been genuine, even if exaggerated. She really ought to make up for the little white lie she had told. She was quite willing to accept a companionable friendship. Not that she had decided never to marry again. Simply, she would need to be in love. Marriage for the sake of it was out.

If the man didn't call, bother him, she need not worry about her little white lie. She frowned. Now why should she say bother him?

Harry walked into the newsagents on Tuesday morning. Maggie, serving a customer, saw him. He smiled and touched his helmet. She felt a quick little rush of pleasure.

'Morning, Harry,' called Mr Gardner from the tobacco counter, where he was selling a cigarette mixture and Rizla cigarette papers to an elderly man. 'Be with you in a minute.'

'I'm not buyin', ' said Harry, 'I'm callin'.' Maggie's customer departing, he said, 'How's the boss treatin' you, Mrs Wilson?'

'What a question,' said Maggie.

'Just thought I'd step in and see if George had his whip out.'

'Soul of marshmaller, that's George,' said the elderly gent, 'except when 'e's weighin' out me baccy. 'Ard as old iron 'e is then. Look at that, call that an ounce?'

'It's what my scales call it,' said Mr Gardner.

'I seen them scales goin' up an' down man and boy,' said the old one. 'I dunno I ever seen 'em in me favour.'

Harry leaned across the counter to Maggie. 'You finish at twelve?' he said.

'That's right,' said Maggie, still burdened by confused thoughts concerning Mr Bates's proposal.

'Mind if I come knockin' at about one-fifteen?' said

Harry. 'I've something to show you. I'll be on my midday break.'

'I'll put the kettle on,' said Maggie, her facial hollows all gone.

'I like the sound of that,' said Harry.

'My pleasure, I'm sure,' smiled Maggie.

Daisy, Lily and Meg, having eaten their midday dinner, had gone back to school before Harry knocked at twenty-past one. Mr Bates was up in town and on Maggie's mind. However, she received Harry with a smile and put the kettle on. When the tea was made she sat down with him at the kitchen table.

'It's business or social?' she asked, filling the cups.

'Come again?' said Harry, thinking her more attractive each time he saw her. He knew many Walworth mothers with large families. He didn't know any mother of four who looked as attractive as Maggie.

'You said you had something to show me,' she said.

'Yes, I did, Mrs Wilson, and so I have.'

'I don't know you should still call me Mrs Wilson after spending all day Sunday at the Zoo with me an' the girls,' said Maggie. 'It's a bit stick-in-the-mud, Harry.'

'You don't mind if I call you Maggie, then?' he said, and she found herself liking his smile and his stalwart looks. What a problem she had now, with a proposal from her lodger and a growing liking for this Walworth constable.

'I'm Maggie to all me friends,' she said.

'Maggie's a favourite name with me,' said Harry, sipping the hot tea.

'It's Margaret, really, only no-one's ever called me anything but Maggie.'

'Yes, I like it,' said Harry. 'You don't buy newspapers, do you?'

'Am I missin' much?' she asked.

'You've missed this, I think,' he said, and took a folded page from his pocket. 'The *Daily News*, Maggie. Well, a page of it from today's edition. Read what it says there.'

It was a little notice in the *Personal* column, circled by Harry in ink. Maggie read it. It said that if Mrs Margaret Annie Wilson, niece of the late Henry Albert Rushton, who was last known to be residing in South London, would get in touch with Eden, Pendlebury and Rouse, solicitors of Gracechurch Street, she would hear of something to her advantage.

Wide-eyed, Maggie read the notice again, then lifted her head and said, 'Lord above, that's my uncle, Uncle Henry, who's been in South Africa for years. Oh, I didn't know 'e was dead, I used to write to him, he was a lovely man and always sayin' he was goin' to make his fortune one day.'

'Well, perhaps he's made it,' said Harry, 'and left some of it to you and the rest of his family.'

'He didn't have no fam'ly,' said Maggie. 'He was a larky old bachelor.'

'Then I think you should go and see these solicitors as soon as possible.'

'Oh, 'elp,' breathed Maggie, a little flushed, 'shall I go quick?'

'You could put your hat on and go now,' said Harry, 'but keep your feet on the ground in case it isn't a fortune.'

'Oh, he'd 'ave wrote me if he'd made his fortune, I'm sure he would,' said Maggie. 'But poor Uncle Henry, I wondered why I 'adn't heard from him recent, not for months. Mum didn't mention him when she last wrote. Uncle Henry was 'er brother. Did I tell you my parents and sister went to Australia the year I got married? My dad thought he'd go and make 'is fortune too, but he's still hard-up after fourteen years out there. Harry, d'you really think I should go up to Gracechurch Street now?'

'I'd take you myself, but I've got to get back on duty at two o'clock. More plod-plod.'

'You're still tryin' to catch that murderer?'

'Scotland Yard is,' said Harry. 'Maggie, you put your hat

219

on and go and find out what something to your advantage means.'

'You're a dear for comin' to show me that notice,' said Maggie, 'and you're Trary's hero as well.'

Harry, rising, said, 'I'm partial to Trary.'

'She's a bit young for you, isn't she?' smiled Maggie.

'I didn't mean that kind of partial,' he said. 'If I did, I think I'd have Bobby on my tail.' He laughed. 'Good luck at the solicitors, Maggie.'

CHAPTER EIGHTEEN

Maggie had had her moments of despair but had never thought of giving up. Nor was she a woman to get into a flutter. However, she was in a flutter now, and for the first time in her life. She had put on her best dress and hat, such as they were, and she had her birth and wedding certificates with her, as Harry had advised. She did her very best not to quake nervously on arrival at the solicitors' offices in Gracechurch Street, just across from London Bridge. Since she hadn't made an appointment, she was told by a prim-looking woman with severely dressed black hair that it might be a little while before Mr Rouse could see her. It was Mr Rouse who had had the Press notice inserted, and he kept her waiting hardly at all. He entered the waiting-room himself, greeted her courteously and with a very charming smile, and ushered her into his office. It was all brown to Maggie. Brown furniture, brown walls and brown curtains. And Mr Rouse had brown hair. But he wore what looked like a morning suit, with a stiff collar and grey tie. He expressed pleasure at meeting her, and seemed indeed to regard her with approval. Her hat and dress wouldn't have done for Ascot, but Maggie did have a wholly pleasant appearance, and the largeness of her hazel eyes enhanced her looks. Harry always felt he was falling into them.

'Please sit down, Mrs Wilson,' said Mr Rouse, and Maggie sat down on the far side of his desk. He seated himself, then asked her if she had the means of identifying herself. Maggie produced not only her birth and wedding certificates, but also the last letter Uncle Henry had written to her from Johannesburg. Mr Rouse expressed himself happy, then referred to the matter in hand.

His firm had received a communication from Messrs Williams and Horst, solicitors in Johannesburg, requesting assistance in the matter of locating the niece of their late client, Mr Henry Albert Rushton. They had in their possession a document legally identifiable as his last will and testament, in which he left the whole of his estate to his beloved niece Mrs Margaret Annie Wilson.

'Estate?' said Maggie, eyelashes quivering. 'Mr Rouse, what's that? Does it mean a house an' garden in South Africa?'

Mr Rouse smiled. He saw an extremely nice-looking woman with a refreshing lack of artifice. He looked at a letter on his desk. It was a letter of some length, from the Johannesburg solicitors.

'Not much of a house,' he said. 'No more than what South Africans would call a shack.'

'Oh,' said Maggie. 'Oh, well, never mind, I expect it was quite comf'table, he was a one for comfy things like rockin'-chairs an' sofas. Is that what he's left me, a bit of a house and furniture and stuff? Imagine him thinkin' of me like that, bless him. He was in the Army, you know, and the Boer War. I wrote to him a lot over the years. Of course, I wouldn't be able to do anything with what he left. Is something to my advantage what I could get if they were sold? And 'ow much would I owe you if you arranged for everything to be sold?'

'Mrs Wilson, would you like some tea?'

'Tea?' Maggie thought that being offered tea by a solicitor in his City office, where he must have rich clients, was very gracious. 'Oh, I would, thank you, Mr Rouse.'

Mr Rouse pressed a bell button. The prim-looking woman entered. 'Miss Wetherby, would you please ask Leonard to deliver to my desk a pot of tea for two? Hot tea. Immediately, if not sooner.'

'Immediately, if not sooner? Really, Mr Rouse.' Miss Wetherby sniffed and departed. Mr Rouse smiled.

'I think hot tea's just the thing,' he said. 'You're a widow, you said. With children?'

'Yes, four girls.' Maggie, all nervousness gone because Mr Rouse was so kind, opened up to add, 'Daisy, Lily, Meg an' Trary, and they're all pets. I just wish I was a bit better off for their sakes.'

'You look remarkably young to be the mother of four,' said Mr Rouse.

'Oh, aren't you nice?' said Maggie impulsively.

'I'll tell Mrs Rouse that.'

'I don't know much about solicitors, I never met one before,' said Maggie. 'I always thought they'd be ever so grave and solemn. Uncle Henry stayed in South Africa after he come out of the Army, that was when 'e wrote to tell me he was goin' to make his fortune before he came home for good. Still, even if he didn't, I expect he 'ad a rare old time tryin', he was full of adventure. It's sad he died, he was only in his forties, but bless 'im for thinkin' of me.' Maggie smiled reminiscently, and tried to imagine what his shack and his furniture and other things were like. Leonard, the office boy, a young lad with a quiff, brought the tea in, placing the tray on the desk.

'It's 'ot, Mr Rouse, like you ordered,' he said.

'You'll get the sack if it isn't, my boy,' said Mr Rouse.

Leonard grinned and disappeared. Mr Rouse poured the golden, steaming tea and placed a full cup, with its saucer, in front of Maggie. He offered her the sugar bowl. Maggie helped herself to a little. 'Thanks ever so much,' she said. Mr Rouse smiled, noting there was no suggestion of avid interest about her. She simply seemed intrigued. She sipped her tea. It was piping hot, as she liked it. 'But I really can't 'elp feelin' sad about Uncle Henry, he enjoyed life, even if he never had much. What did he die of, does it say in the letter?'

'A fever, apparently,' said Mr Rouse. 'Mrs Wilson, you said you wished you were a little better off for the sake of your daughters. I think you will be. Well, you'll at least be richer than you are now. Five and a half thousand pounds richer. Approximately. That is, give or take a pound or two.'

Maggie put her cup back in its saucer before her shaking hand dropped it. She stared in huge-eyed incredulity at Mr Rouse, a paternal man. 'How much?' she gasped. Something to her advantage had made her think in terms of, say, a hundred pounds. 'How much?'

'Five and a half thousand pounds.'

'You're jokin'. Mr Rouse, you're jokin'.'

'I don't think so, Mrs Wilson.'

'Mr Rouse, it's a terrifyin' lot of money. I wouldn't mind five hundred pounds, but five and a 'alf thousand. Oh, 'eaven preserve me.'

'Your uncle has done his best in that respect, Mrs Wilson.'

'It's a fortune,' breathed Maggie. 'Oh, he did it, after all, he did make 'is fortune, only 'e didn't live to enjoy it. Mr Rouse, I honestly don't know if I'm comin' or goin'. You sure you said the right amount?'

'Quite sure,' smiled Mr Rouse, delighted for this pleasant and wholly unaffected widow with four children. He glanced at the letter. 'Actually, I think your uncle expected it to be far more. He opened up a diamond mine, you see, not long before he died. After his death, his Johannesburg solicitors had this new mine investigated by experts. The vein, apparently, was brief. Nevertheless, it means five and a half thousand pounds for you. Messrs Williams and Horst contacted us because they were concerned at not hearing from you or about you. The will was handed to them for execution by a friend of your uncle's, a man who was with him when he died.' Again Mr Rouse referred to the letter. 'Your address wasn't known, and couldn't be found among your uncle's effects, and his friend, a Mr Jeremy Bates, offered—'

'Who?' Maggie stared. 'Who?'

'Mr Jeremy Bates. He offered to come to England to find you. That was over four months ago. He's a mining engineer, but he seems to have dropped out of sight or given up, without advising Williams and Horst. Certainly, they've heard nothing from him. That was why they contacted us. They knew only that you lived in South London. That information they received from Mr Bates.'

Mr Bates knew more than that, thought Maggie. He knew exactly where she'd been living. 'Well, I never,' she said calmly, 'a Mr Jeremy Bates.'

'Yes. I imagine he lost interest. We'd have put a special investigator onto the task of finding you if our notice in the Press hadn't been answered. I'm delighted you saw it and came to us at once. I'll be cabling Johannesburg. You can, of course, arrange for a solicitor of your own choice to handle all necessary matters for you, perhaps a solicitor near your home.'

'Mr Rouse, could you please 'andle everything?'

'With great pleasure, Mrs Wilson. Are you perhaps—' Mr Rouse stopped. 'H'm,' he said.

'Am I what, Mr Rouse?' asked Maggie, thinking of Mr Bates, and thinking too of Harry, and how glad she was that she could give Mr Bates his answer.

'If, perhaps, you are in need of a small advance – you have four children – a widow's circumstances can be very strained – expenses and so on—'

'Mr Rouse, you're a very kind gentleman,' said Maggie. 'I've been blessed lately, meetin' kind gentlemen.'

'We shall be very happy to advance you fifty pounds – a hundred?'

'Lovely,' said Maggie, 'I can buy whole new outfits for the girls. Thank you, Mr Rouse, fifty pounds would be like magic. Bless you.'

Mr Rouse smiled. She was a cockney, of course, and quite charming. 'You're very welcome, Mrs Wilson. Now, there are a few formalities.' He outlined them. Maggie, head in the clouds, hardly took them in. She signed two papers, one concerning herself as the sole beneficiary and another in respect of the advance of fifty pounds. That done, she talked to Mr Rouse for a little while longer.

* * *

Nicholas and Chapman were getting no joy from a hopeful interview with Mr Rodney Foster, who was renting rooms on the top floor of a three-storeyed house in Dartford. The man had been cocky and insolent by turn, laughing at the very idea that his old friend, Jerry Bates, could be a possible suspect in a murder case.

'Yer off yer chump, sergeant. I got to say that. No dis-respect intended. He was here all that day and all that night. You see me, don't yer, standin' here livin' and breathin'? You hear me sayin' it, don't yer?' He had a twangy accent and a weasel look, his nose pointed, his eyes beady and his grin a mile wide. It was a grin to ensnare the rabbits of the world.

'What's your job, Mr Foster?'

'Don't have one, not right now. Just come back from Down Under, and I'm not on me uppers. I've got a few quid.'

He had a tanned faced. So did Mr Jerry Bates.

'Did you and Mr Bates come home from Australia together?' asked Nicholas.

'What's that to do with you?'

'It's just a question,' said Nicholas, wholly distrusting the man, and still sure that his friend, Mr Bates, was too good to be true. All the same, how did that relate to perverted murder? It didn't relate at all, and Nicholas felt himself to be chasing shadows out of sheer hope. And against the Inspector's strict instructions.

'Listen, sergeant,' said Mr Rodney Foster, 'I know me legal rights, I know what's legal and what ain't. Still, you're still wonderin' why I don't have a job, and as I daresay you're lookin' for promotion, I'll tell yer. I'm livin' on me savings, for the time being. I haven't chucked me acquired oof away on wine, women an' song, yer know. I'm careful, I am. You got to be if you don't want to end up in a flamin' workhouse. Me in a workhouse at my tender age? No wonder you're laughin'.'

'I'm not. Actually, Mr Foster, I'm a bit fed-up.'

'That's your hard luck', said Mr Foster. 'Listen, you're wastin' your time. Jerry's a minin' engineer and a good 'un. I've given him a hand on some of his jobs out there.'

'Out there?'

'What did I say?'

'Out there.'

'Australia. I'm what yer might call a freelance, and a Jack of all trades. Willin' to turn me hand to anything.'

'Anything?' said Chapman.

'Give over, sunshine,' said Mr Foster, 'do I look like a bloke that's aided and abetted? I got mitts that are as clean as yours. You'll want to know about me medical afflictions next, which I don't have, bein' healthy and undiseased. Turn it up, gents, you've got me sworn testimony that Jerry Bates was here with me that Friday night. Don't wear me out, or I might call a solicitor.'

It was a hopeless exercise, another shot in the dark gone wide of the mark. 'Sorry you've come near to being worn out, Mr Foster,' said Nicholas, 'but thanks for your co-operation.'

He and Chapman left, Chapman muttering about more wasted time. Nicholas turned his mind on better things. Lately, better things all ended up as Mrs Emma Carter. Lovely woman, really. No wonder she had a special friend. Bound to be a man who supported the suffragettes. Time the Government gave women the vote. Better that than having them burn down the Houses of Parliament. Or Scotland Yard. Scotland Yard in flames. Inspector Greaves wouldn't like that.

'What's funny?' asked Chapman.

'Funny?'

'You're smilin'. Buggered if I can see why.'

'You're right, Frank. We've got a sod of a case.'

Resumed house-to-house enquires were taking time. Walworth was to be covered from its main road west to Kennington Park Road, and from the Elephant and Castle south to Ruskin Street, Camberwell. It meant second calls on most of the houses in this area, and a more thorough detailing of adult male residents.

In Amelia Street, a woman opened her front door in answer to a knock and found two CID men wanting to talk to her. They were both detective-constables.

'Sorry to bother you, Mrs Stephens,' said one. 'You are Mrs Stephens?'

'Yes, but what d'you want?' she asked.

He consulted a notebook. 'It's just you and your husband who live here, Mrs Stephens?'

'Yes, just him and me.' Mrs Stephens looked worried. 'Why?'

'We're continuing enquiries concerning –'

'But I had a policeman call ages ago, about if we had a lodger, which I told him we don't.'

'Yes, I see you don't,' said the CID man, tapping the notebook. 'Is your husband in?'

'Now why would he be in this time of day, when he's at work?' asked Mrs Stephens, hands fluttering over her apron.

'How old is he?'

'Old?'

'Yes, what's his age?'

'Thirty-eight, but I don't see as how –'

'Thirty-eight. Fine.' The constable was friendly. He consulted the notebook again. 'He's fairly tall, isn't he?'

'Yes, fairly.'

'Good build too?'

'Yes, but what you askin' for? I told the policeman all about him before, my husband said I did right.'

'Yes, but this time we want to be absolutely sure about men we can cross off our list, if you see what I mean.'

'Well, I suppose so.' Mrs Stephens still looked worried. 'But anyway, there's his bad back.'

'Oh, yes.' Another look at the notes. 'He doesn't go out much in the evenings.'

228

'No, he likes a rest of an evening, and so would anyone with his back.'

'It's pretty bad?'

'Well, he's had to go to the doctor with it. Dr Fuller in Walworth Road.'

'He's not much of a runner, then, eh?'

'Runner?' Fluttery hands vied with indignant voice. 'Well, he can walk, he does walkin' day in day out at his job, but if he did any runnin', he'd cripple himself. He puts up with it very courageous, and cheerful too, considering it's hard for him to do things like other men —' Mrs Stephens stopped and fluttered into faint colour.

'What's his job?' asked the CID man tactfully.

'He works for the gas company, readin' meters and collectin' the pennies. His bag gets weighty, I don't know how he manages, but he hardly ever grumbles. I wish they'd give him a sittin'-down job.'

'Don't wish that, Mrs Stephens, sitting down all day's not the best cure for a bad back. Anyway, it keeps him indoors, does it?'

'He don't go out in the evenings, but he comes for a walk with me to the shops sometimes, and to the market Saturday afternoons. I go out once a week myself, to see my mother. I like havin' him home in the evenings, he's good company, I just wish he didn't have a sufferin' back. He's had medicine from the doctor, which eases the ache a bit, but —'

'Thanks, Mrs Stephens, that's all. It's just been routine. Not to worry. Goodbye now.'

When she told her husband about the CID men that evening, he was hardly surprised. 'Yes, they're still going the rounds, Maudie, they're still after the geezer they call the Strangler.'

'Yes, but fancy askin' questions about you, Herby, when I told the police constable before all he wanted to know.'

'No good looking at it like that, y'know, Maudie. If they don't do their job properly, if they don't keep askin' questions, they'll never find the man.'

'Herby, when I told them about your back, they said a sittin'-down job wouldn't do it much good.'

'Wouldn't it? That's not what the doctor said. Anyway, if they call again, tell them to come back when I'm at home.'

'I don't think they're goin' to call again. Still, I worried a bit.'

'You worry too much, Maudie. What's for supper?'

'Time you got it settled,' said Mr Rodney Foster that evening. He was in a West End pub with Mr Bates.

'Listen, it's only been a few weeks,' said Mr Bates. 'How many times have I told yer you've got to lay the ground first, and walk careful on it?'

'All the time you're walkin' careful, you're spendin' my money. I financed you all the way. So get it over with, church the lady, an' quick. I've got a signed piece of paper, Jerry, and it'll hang yer if you don't come up with the goods.'

'I don't fancy gettin' hanged, so stop sweatin'. You'll get yer dues.'

'I better 'ad. Two-fifty expenses and ten grand on me investment. You owe me, mate, so inform me on the church date, as soon as you got it fixed,' said Mr Foster. 'Also, me lovin' friend, don't forget that if the worth of that mine tops a quarter of a million, I'm due for another twenty thousand.'

'Your round,' said Mr Bates cheerfully.

'They're all my rounds,' said Mr Foster acidly. 'But I'll say this much, I'm doin' it with a good heart and with confidence in yer, Jerry. You're a ladies' man right up to yer handsome eyebrows.'

'It ain't goin' to waste, Roddy, not this time,' said Mr Bates.

'Well, after you've pushed the next pint down, get yourself back to Walworth and find out if yer good-lookin' diamond mine has made up her mind. I'd like to collect me earned dues and go for a cruise. I'm buggered if I'm in favour of havin' any more pie-eyed coppers knockin' me up on account of not likin' the look of you.'

'I'm not responsible for them 'aving all their brains in their flat feet,' said Mr Bates, and grinned hugely.

Maggie played her cards with a cool flourish when her lodger came into the house late that evening. So far she had said nothing to anybody, not even to her girls. She wanted first to settle the issue with Mr Bates, and then open her heart to her family.

Trary had just gone up to her bed when Mr Bates put his head into the kitchen. 'Maggie? There you are,' he said, smiling.

'Come in,' said Maggie. He came in, virile, cheerful and healthy. 'Sit down.'

'Pleasure,' he said, and seated himself at the table. 'You're lookin' lively, Maggie. Suits you. You're a handsome woman, yer know.'

'You're a handsome man. What d'you think 'appened today?'

'Well, what I've been thinkin' all day is do I get to be a happy man?'

'Oh, you're always happy,' said Maggie, 'I never met no-one more cheerful or more pleased with 'imself. Look.' She pushed the *Daily News* page across the table to him. 'Read that, where it's been circled round.'

Mr Bates's first reading was a casual skimming. His second seemed to be accomplished with difficulty. Gallantly, however, he said, 'What's it mean?'

'I'm rich,' said Maggie.

'You're what?' Mr Bates engineered surprise and a smile of disbelief. 'Tell us another,' he said.

'My Uncle Henry left me a diamond mine in South Africa, would you believe it?'

'No, is that a fact?' Mr Bates tried to sound as if he was humouring her.

'Would yer like a rich wife, Jerry?'

'Now, Maggie, come off it, what's yer uncle really left yer, a few old iron bedsteads?'

'No, a diamond mine,' said Maggie, as cool as sliced cucumber. 'I've just told you. You didn't know about my Uncle Henry, did you?'

'Well, I can't recall you mentionin' him, but it's all one to me, Maggie.' Mr Bates was making a very gallant effort indeed to maintain a cheerful innocence. 'It's you I've got deep feelings for, you and yer girls, not a few bits an' pieces that might net yer a couple of 'undred quid.'

'But you'd 'ave me as your wife, Jerry, wouldn't you, rich or poor?'

'Rich sounds embarrassin' to yours truly, Maggie.' Mr Bates tried earnestness. 'But I'd have you even if you were in the work'ouse. A diamond mine? That's all gammon, yer teasin' girl.'

Maggie smiled, and Mr Bates wondered if he'd been found out. She'd been to that firm of solicitors, of course, the firm mentioned in the notice.

He had spent several years in South Africa, trying his hand at various things in a country burgeoning with promise after the end of the Boer War. He met Henry Rushton early on, and partnered him in prospecting for diamonds or gold. They split up after a fruitless year and went their separate ways. While old Henry stuck to prospecting, he himself drifted from one project to another. He fell in with Rodney Foster, who made money by his wits, not by bending his back. They made money together in the booming mining towns of South Africa, mostly by confidence tricks or gambling. What he made always seemed to drain from his pockets. But then he liked good company, good drinking company and the classier and more expensive type of woman. Rodney Foster banked what he made. He ran into Henry Rushton again, and at a time when he was broke and too many men knew him for what he was, a confidence trickster. Also, he had some woman and her father on his tail, the woman swearing he was the father of her child, that he'd promised to marry her. He would have married her if she'd had any money, but her father was only a piffling railway official. Old Henry, an optimistic character, took him on again as a companion and friend. Henry had a feeling about a new area, as well as a bit of money. He lent Jerry some to equip himself for a fresh go at prospecting. They talked at night of England and home, and old Henry spoke often of his favourite niece Maggie, married for several years to a man called Wilson, but now widowed. Old Henry, if he struck it rich, meant to ask his niece to come out and join him, with her four girls.

They were companions, not partners, prospecting individually. Henry always went about it as if a strike was just round the corner, and eventually he did strike. A rich vein of blue, he said, a blinder. Jerry accompanied him to Johannesburg, where he had the mine legally documented. They stayed several days in Johannesburg, celebrating. They met Rodney Foster on their last day, and he joined the celebrations. Never having got close to prospecting himself, and never having seen a strike, Roddy rode back with them the next day, by which time good old Henry wasn't too well. He dosed himself with quinine, while Roddy made uncomplimentary remarks about the shack. The following day, it was obvious Henry needed a doctor, he was in high fever. He had lucid moments, however, during one of them he managed to write out his will and to get Roddy and himself, Jerry, to witness it. He asked him to see that it got to his solicitors in Johannesburg, if that was how things were going to work out.

Mr Bates remembered how he'd had a go at bringing an old Zulu witch doctor. It was only a thirty-minute ride. He felt if he could keep Henry alive, he'd get far more out of him than a dying handshake. But by the time he returned with the old Zulu, Henry had gone, and Roddy was cursing at being in charge of a corpse on a day fierce with heat. He and Roddy buried him, and left for Johannesburg the next day. On the way, Roddy referred to the will and the fact that old Henry's niece Maggie was going to be a rich woman. A rich widow woman. An idea was born and took root. Any rich widow was worth marrying, even one with four children.

They turned about, rode back to the shack and found a letter, just one. It was from old Henry's niece, and bore her address in Walworth, South London. Mr Bates handed the will to the Johannesburg solicitors, but kept the letter. He was going back to England immediately, he said, and would be only too pleased to find Mrs Wilson. It was what his old friend, Henry Rushton, would have wanted him to do. Roddy financed the venture. The idea, of course, was to marry the widow before she came to know about the legacy. Just use your natural charm, said Roddy, and she'll jump at you. In return, Roddy was to receive ten thousand pounds, plus a further twenty thousand if the value of the mine turned out to be sky-high.

They were held up on the voyage, the ship's engines giving trouble. They had to put in to Sierra Leone for repairs. They got to England a lot later than envisaged, which made them worry about the possibility of the widow receiving the glad tidings in advance of Jerry Bates. That didn't happen.

But she had had the news now. And what else did she know? Nothing that was upsetting her, judging from her friendly smile. Well, she had a lot to feel friendly about. He'd feel friendly to Lucifer himself if he'd just been left a diamond mine.

'It was lovely and kind of you, Jerry, to offer to be a father to my girls,' she said. 'Not many men would take on as much as that.'

'A privilege, Maggie, not a liability. Soon as I met you all, I said to myself, Jerry, I said, 'ere's a house that's as good as a treasure chest. I'm not sayin' bein' comfortably off don't count, but in the long run, what's money? It buys yer bread and pays yer rent, but it don't give a man something priceless. An' what's the top note

234

in pricelessness? As far as yours truly's concerned, it's a ready-made fam'ly, it's a fine wife and four girls. I'd swap any diamond mine for that.'

'You're such a good man, Jerry, honest you are,' said Maggie, 'you've never minded me bein' poor, and you've done me lovely kindnesses, like settling with that Mr Monks and my rent owings. I don't 'ardly know I could live up to you if we married. But if we did, you wouldn't be embarrassed about my riches because I'm not really rich, after all, not after what I did about what Uncle Henry went and left me. I told the solicitors that my mum an' dad, an' my sister, were to 'ave everything except two and a half thousand pounds. Well, Uncle Henry was my mum's brother, and she an' dad's havin' a terrible time in Australia, and so's my sister. Her Australian husband's out of work, and my dad only gets to do bits of jobbin' carpentry. I couldn't take all that money, I signed a document at the solicitors.' She had. She had made over part of the legacy to her parents and her sister. They were to have three thousand pounds between them, leaving her with two and a half thousand pounds, less solicitors' expenses. 'So no, I'm not really rich, y'see, I'll just have about two and a half thousand pounds. That won't embarrass you, will it?'

Mr Bates's healthy face was a study. It had turned a mottled red. 'I've got to believe this?' he said hoarsely.

'Yes, the document's been signed, like I said.'

'You're crazy,' said Mr Bates, having trouble with his breathing.

'I like to be good an' kind too,' said Maggie sweetly.

'That ain't bein' good an' kind,' panted Mr Bates, 'that's bein' off yer flamin' rocker. What d'yer mean by doin' a thing like that, yer silly cow?'

'Oh, dear,' said Maggie, 'that's not nice, Jerry.'

'You get left a diamond mine and you give away all it's worth except two and a 'alf thousand nicker?' Mr Bates was now nearly purple.

'I wouldn't want more than that, specially not if I 'ad

Mr Bates looked at his watch. It was just turned nine-thirty. The Walworth pubs were still open. 'What I need is a drink, yer brainless female,' he said, and got to his feet, his face still mottled.

'Yes, go and 'ave a nice pint,' said Maggie. 'Oh, you best take this money.' She rose from her chair and took an envelope from the mantelpiece. 'It's all there, everything you lent me. I wouldn't like you to think I wasn't in proper appreciation of your kindness.'

'Yer'll excuse me bein' speechless,' said Mr Bates. He took the envelope and left the house with a rattling slam of the front door.

Maggie smiled. Two men in her life. One had fallen flat on his face. One remained. 'I'm goin' to buy meself a new hat an' new clothes Saturday, and invite Harry to Sunday tea again,' she said to her sewing-machine. 'And Bobby can come too.'

Her sewing-machine voiced no objections.

CHAPTER NINETEEN

The trail, so promisingly marked by the statement from Linda Jennings, had petered out. The newspapers, much to Inspector Greaves's growling disgust, had got their teeth into the failure of the police to make an arrest. They made much of the fact that the murder of Mabel Shipman followed by the attempted murder of another young woman was not something the public would accept lightly in the event of total failure.

Nicholas, walking along Walworth Road, was deep in depressing thought. He was due to meet Frank Chapman in the Rockingham public house by the Elephant and Castle, for a ham sandwich and a beer. They were then to go to Manor Place Baths to interview an employee whose wife had let slip to CID men that he was out most nights, including the two nights that mattered most. She hadn't said so before. This morning questions put casually to her had drawn the information from her. Nicholas, however, held out no great hopes. For a start, the husband was nearly sixty years old and did not own a mackintosh. In his introspective mood, Nicholas bumped into a woman coming out of Hurlocks.

'Sorry – so sorry –'

'So you should be, Sergeant Chamberlain, I had no idea you could be so bruising,' said Mrs Emma Carter.

'Oh, hell,' said Nicholas, looking rueful.

'Pardon?'

'Not my day. Well, it was bad luck nearly knocking you over of all people.'

'Why, am I special, then, or exceptionally fragile and delicate?' Her expression was solemn, but her eyes were teasing.

'I was thinking of how hospitable you've been,' said Nicholas. 'Sorry about my clumsiness. How are you?'

'Recovering,' she said. Nicholas grimaced. 'No, no, I'm teasing you. I'm very well, thank you, and pleased to see you. I presume, as you haven't found it necessary to call on me lately, that you've stopped worrying about me.'

'I'm not so worried now I know you've a close friend to keep an eye on you,' said Nicholas, envying the man, whoever he was. Emma wrinkled her nose. 'What are you doing at the moment?'

'This is where I work in the mornings,' said Emma. 'Hurlocks. I've just finished, and am on my way home.'

'I'm on my way to meet my colleague,' said Nicholas. 'Sorry again about bumping you, but —'

'You've still got problems?' asked Emma.

'Yes, still going round in circles, Mrs Carter. Take care now. Good luck.' Lifting his hat to her, Nicholas went on his way. He knew it would do him no good to linger. It would only stoke the fires. She was a remarkably appealing woman.

Emma stood for a moment, looking after his striding figure. She felt almost cross that he had departed so abruptly. She turned and made her way home.

Oh, bother it.

The interview with the man who worked at Manor Place Baths produced nothing but an explosion of cockney indignation. And why shouldn't he take umbrage when all he did on his nights out was to play darts around the pubs with his mates? Sod off, go and ask them.

We'll have to.

You do that.

Sorry you've been troubled.

So am I.

Walworth brooded by day on the murderer lurking in its midst, and kept its young women indoors at night.

'So there you are, my pets,' said Maggie. All the girls were home from school, and Maggie had told them of yesterday's happenings, although that did not include what had taken place between her and the lodger. The girls were spellbound.

'Oh, Mum, oh, crikey,' breathed Meg.

'Mum, it's a miracle,' said Trary, utterly blissed for her mother.

'Uncle 'Enry's like Jesus,' said Lily. 'Jesus did miracles.'

'I never met Uncle 'Enry,' said Daisy. 'Mum, d'you fink 'e'd let you buy me some new boots that don't let water?'

'You're goin' to have expensive shoes, love, not boots,' said Maggie. 'You're all goin' to have shoes, not boots, and lots of new clothes. Lots. Trary can have lots of new stockings because she's nearly fourteen and because she likes to feel proud when Bobby's walkin' her 'ome from school – now don't break up the happy 'ome.'

The girls were all joyously dancing. 'We're rich, we're rich!' Girlish exuberance produced a riot of noise.

'I'd like to hear meself speak, if you don't mind,' said Maggie. 'Daisy, stop jumpin'. Meg, and you too, Trary, stop wavin' your clothes in the air, just look at you. Listen, is that Bobby comin' back, is that him I can hear comin' down the passage?'

Trary, whose clothes were high and her legs kicking, hastily pushed everything back into place. Maggie laughed. 'That caught you, my girl,' she said. 'Still, it's nice to know you've got modest ways, love. Boys can be cheeky enough, without givin' them any encouragement.'

'Oh, I don't care,' said Trary, eyes alight with the joy of being alive. She gave her mum a hug. They all gave her a hug. Maggie's eyes turned a little misty. 'Mum, you're the best ever.'

Maggie coughed. 'Well, we've got money for all the rainy days now,' she said. 'I'll take you all out on Saturday, we'll all go shoppin' for new clothes and things. We'll go to Hurlocks, they're the best drapers.'

239

'Oh, yes, I met an awf'lly nice lady who served me when I bought that hankie for Bobby,' said Trary.

'We'll see if she'll serve us,' said Maggie. 'And I thought, oh, yes,' she added casually, 'p'raps we'd better invite Constable Bradshaw to tea again on Sunday, seein' 'ow kind he was to come an' show me that notice in the newspaper. Yes, we ought to show our gratefulness.'

'We can't not,' said Trary, 'gratefulness is special.'

'Well, yes, all right,' said Maggie, 'if that's what all you girls would like. I'll send 'im a note invitin' him. If you're sure.'

'What's mum askin' us for?' enquired Lily of Meg.

'Oh, I expect it's something to do with a widow's secrets,' said Meg. 'Mum's a widow.'

'Is she really rich?' asked Daisy, still awe-struck by thousands of pounds.

'No, I'm not,' said Maggie crisply, 'and don't any of you go puttin' it about that I am. We've just got something to spend on clothes and things, and for rainy days.' But she knew they had a little more than that. They could actually buy a house, they could buy a nice one with a garden for three hundred pounds, and never have to pay rent again. That prospect made her feel giddy. 'Well, then, p'raps Trary could take a note round to Mr Bradshaw this evenin'.'

'I'd love to,' said Trary, already in love with the idea of having a policeman as a father.

'I'll go with her,' said Meg.

'Me too,' said Lily.

'I'm only little,' said Daisy.

'Oh, you can come too, little girl,' said Meg graciously.

'I likes 'Arry,' said Daisy.

'Daisy, don't you call him that,' said Maggie, 'it's disrespectful.'

'Crikey,' said Daisy, 'I didn't know I was old enough to be dis'pectful.'

'I'm not sure what Mr Bradshaw's goin' to say if you all

turn up on 'is doorstep,' said Maggie. 'It might be carryin' gratefulness a bit far.'

'Oh, I'm sure he'd like to see all of us, Mum,' said Trary. 'Well, he lives all alone, and visitors must be awf'lly welcome to him. His disappointment might be bitter if only one of us turned up. I can't think why some nice comely woman doesn't go and marry him.'

'A what one?' asked Maggie, having not unusual difficulty in keeping her face straight.

'Comely,' said Trary. 'That's attractive with a nice figure.'

'Crumbs, our Trary, don't she fink of funny fings to say?' said Daisy.

'I see,' said Maggie, 'attractive with a nice figure. That sounds like Mavis Smith.' Mavis Smith was the unmarried daughter of neighbours. 'Yes, I suppose she's what you'd call comely. Shall I invite 'er to tea as well, so's she can be company for Mr Bradshaw at the table?'

'Oh, Mum, 'eaven forgive you if you do,' said Trary in horror. 'She's a lump, she's all soft and lumpy.'

'But Mr Bradshaw might like her,' said Maggie.

'Mum, you can't ask her,' said Trary, aghast, 'we'd all fall down dead, an' Mr Bradshaw as well, I shouldn't wonder.'

'Well, all right,' said Maggie.

'You shouldn't give us nasty turns like that,' said Trary, 'not at our ages.'

'You give me all kinds of turns, lovey, with the way your mind works,' smiled Maggie. 'Oh, and when you next see Bobby, you could at least invite 'im. You forgot last time.'

'Yes, Mum. I suppose we could put up with a talkin' machine comin' to Sunday tea, especially now Uncle Henry's taken kind care of our rainy days. We can count our blessings, can't we? Mum, what's happened to Mr Bates?'

'He 'ad to leave,' said Maggie, 'he's done all his City business, he was gone by the time I got home from me morning's work.'

'Ain't 'e comin' back?' asked Lily.

'Don't we 'ave a lodger no more?' asked Meg.

'Well, pets, we don't really need one now, do we?' said Maggie.

Gladness put warm light in Trary's eyes. Now there was only Mr Bradshaw. Oh, he'd just got to marry her mum. Her mum deserved what Uncle Henry had left her, and she deserved a nice husband too.

Harry, opening his front door, was greeted by Trary, spokesman for the party of four.

'Good evening, Mr Bradshaw, hasn't it been a lovely day?'

'Good evening, Miss Trary Wilson, yes, it's been lovely apart from the wind and the showers. Is that Daisy and Lily and Meg behind you?'

'Yes, they've all come,' said Trary, 'you know what young children are.'

'I'm not young, not now I'm growin',' said Meg. 'Mister, we brought a note from our mum. Trary's got it. Well, she's the oldest an' bossiest.'

'Come in,' said Harry. They surged in happily, eager and curious to see what his house was like. He sat them down in his living-room, which was as his mother had kept it before she began her decline. The brown leather armchairs and the matching sofa had known years of wear, but had comfortably endured. Trary looked around, instinctively seeking signs that he was in need of a wife. Yes, he was. A picture on the wall hung a little crookedly, ornaments on the mantelpiece needed proper arranging, and books and newspapers on a table were all higgledy-piggledy. And perhaps there was washing-up not done in the scullery.

The girls were chatting away to him. Trary produced her mother's note and handed it to him. He broke open the envelope, took out the note and read it.

Dear Harry, I had an interesting time at the solicitors, it was so kind you letting me know. The girls would like you to come to tea again on Sunday, and I would too, we all hope we can expect you about four o'clock. Then

242

after tea I'll tell you what the solicitors said. Yours sincerely, Maggie.

Trary, watching him, saw a smile appear, 'Oh, can you come on Sunday?' she asked impulsively.

'I'm on duty, but I finish at three,' said Harry. 'Tell your mum I can't wait to get there, especially if there's goin' to be another fruit cake. Are all of you invited too?'

'Us?' said Lily.

'What's 'e mean?' whispered Daisy.

'Oh, you silly, Mr Bradshaw,' said Meg, 'mum don't have to invite us, we're 'er fam'ly.'

'I just wanted to make sure,' said Harry, 'seein' it wouldn't be as much fun if you weren't there.'

'All of us?' said Meg.

'All of you,' said Harry.

'I likes 'Arry,' said Daisy in an aside to Lily.

Trary laughed. Harry gave her a wink.

Bobby wasn't outside the school the following afternoon. Oh, that boy again, thought Trary. If he couldn't be reliable, she'd have to dress him down a bit. Most boys needed dressing down, anyway, and at least once a week. She'd read that in a girls' story book, the heroine had said it to her father, and it had sounded right to Trary. And you could tell that that Bobby Reeves was a boy you had to dress down regularly, for his own good. Otherwise, he'd get above himself, like all cheeky boys did. A girl could live a terrible downtrodden life if she let herself walk out regular with a boy who'd been allowed to get above himself.

Walking along St George's Road with Jane Atkins, Trary thought that if that Bobby Reeves didn't turn up at all, she'd think about giving him the kind of talking-to that would take the grin off his face for ever. Jane, of course, was smirking because she knew she was miffed. She parted company with her as they reached the Elephant and Castle. Then, going towards the subway steps, she saw Bobby emerge.

'Oh, there you are,' she said.

'Hello, is that you, Trary?'

'What d'you mean, is it me?'

'Thought it was,' said Bobby, peaked cap on the back of his head as usual, his grin as cheerful as usual. 'Best girl in London, you are. I don't know what it is that does it, and I don't even know if it's fair, but each time I see you you're more of a treat to me peepers. I hope I don't get to 'ave problems. I mean, by the time you're sixteen and we're kissin' friends, you might be the best looker in England and I might 'ave to fight duels with lords an' dukes. I hope I don't 'ave to duel with Lord Northcliffe, though, it might damage me future. I know I'm a bit late, but —'

'D'you mind if I get a word in edgeways?' asked Trary haughtily. 'I don't know, standin' there grinnin' and talkin', and bein' late as well —'

'I was only goin' to say I'm a bit late because I had to go to Peckham with me mum's handcart. I picked up —'

'You're interruptin' me,' said Trary.

'Me?'

'Yes, you. You need a good talkin'-to, you do, Bobby Reeves. Oh, can you come to tea Sunday?'

'Me?'

'Stop sayin' me, you blessed boy. Yes, you. Mum says she'd like the pleasure of your company. Well, come on, don't keep standin' there, you don't want Mr Bradshaw arrestin' us for bein' obstructions, do you? I don't suppose he'd mind arrestin' you, but it would break his fond heart to have to take me to the police station. I happen to be his favourite young lady. You Bobby, don't you be late again, or I'll get another boy to walk me home in the afternoons.'

'Crikey,' said Bobby, admiration total, 'that's the best carry-on you've ever done, Trary.' They descended the steps. 'Is there any more?'

'Yes, there is,' said Trary, 'and it's for your own good. You don't want to get above yourself, do you? Turnin' up late and then grinnin' about it is gettin' above yourself. All

244

boys get above themselves if they're not given a good talkin'-to. Girls don't need to be. They're nicer. Anyone can tell I'm much nicer than you are.'

'Well, you've got a nicer figure, Trary. I'm just straight all the way up an' down. You're –'

'Oh, you cheeky monkey! D'you want to be my death?' Trary ran up the stone steps into the light, where the noise of tangled traffic and bawling drivers helped to drown her laughter. By the time Bobby was beside her again, her nose was in the air. 'You wait till I see your mum again,' she said, 'I'll tell her about your disrespectful talk.'

'I'll tell her meself,' said Bobby, 'I'll tell her I mentioned you've got a nicer figure than I 'ave. I don't think she'll say it's disrespectful.'

'Of course it is, you're supposed to be respectful to girls. I just hope you grow out of it, all my friends at school are already sorry for me the way I have to walk home with you. I can't think why mum doesn't order you never to darken our door again. Can you come to tea Sunday? You haven't said.'

'Would you acquaint your gen'rous mum with me glad confirmation?' said Bobby.

'Oh, you blessed show-off, Bobby Reeves,' said Trary, gritting her teeth with envy again. 'I'm sure I don't know why mum thinks your company would be a pleasure, but of course she's ever so considerate, she thinks there's good in everybody, she'd invite Bill Sykes to Sunday tea in the hope of even findin' a bit of good in him. I suppose she hopes there's a bit of good in you. Oh, you Bobby!'

Bobby was shouting with laughter, just as he had once before. And people were looking, men grinning and women smiling. Trary went hoity-toity.

'I'm fallin' about, I am,' said Bobby. 'Tell you what, I'll try and bring me good side with me on Sunday. Also, would you like to come roller-skatin' at Brixton on Saturday afternoon? Mum says I can take the time off. She's gettin' dad to help 'er Saturday, if he don't — well, never mind that.'

'I've never met your dad,' said Trary. 'Is he nice, is he like Mr Bradshaw? You are lucky, Bobby, that you've got a dad. But I don't know about roller-skatin', I've never done any.'

'Like me to help you learn?'

'Oh, would you?'

'Pleasure, Trary.'

'You're sometimes awf'lly kind,' said Trary, feet dancing and boater bobbing.

Friday night. The man was waiting in the shadows at the side of Ashford's sweet shop, which was on a corner where a narrow street met Browning Street. The former led to the stables for Southwark's work-horses. The night was well on, the air mild and benign, and Walworth might have known the blossoms of early summer if it had not been sootily arid with bricks, mortar and paving-stones.

The woman had gone out. Not many were venturing abroad in the evenings unless in company. This one had left her house in King and Queen Street by herself. Nicely dressed, with a small toque hat crowning her fair hair, she looked a cut above her neighbours. She looked ladylike. She had entered Browning Street, and gone on to catch a tram at the Manor Place stop in the Walworth Road. It was odds-on she would return the same way. He didn't mind waiting. He was as good as invisible in this kind of darkness. It hadn't been dark when she'd left her house, when he'd only been a part of the evening pattern, just one more person out and about. He had strolled along the Walworth Road while it was still light, keeping the Browning Street tram stop in sight in case she returned early from her outing. When darkness arrived, he took up his wait, his jacket collar turned up, the brim of his bowler hat low on his forehead. He kept himself flat against the brick wall.

He was still waiting. Most people were now in their beds, the pubs closed, the workers of Walworth at their well-earned rest. A bobby on his slow, measured beat approached and passed by, going towards King and Queen Street without so much as a brief sideways glance. A tram stopped in the Walworth Road. The waiting man heard it. He had heard others, but she had been on none of them. Or if she had, she had not come this way. She had to be on this one. If not, he would have to give up. He tensed, calculating how far away the bobby would be by the time his possible quarry reached this corner. She would be on this side, because it was on this side that King and Queen Street lay. He waited, not moving a muscle, even though the inner excitement, erotically galvanizing, was almost unbearable. It was well past eleven o'clock. The woman would not be later, surely.

He heard quick footsteps. A little way up, on the other side of the street, a lamp glowed on the corner of Colworth Grove. He saw her in its light. Damnation, she was on the wrong side. But she crossed then, stepping from the pavement to traverse the street diagonally, heading straight for Ashford's sweet shop, which was blanketed by darkness. His hands tightened around that which would become a noose. Then he sickened with rage, for a man appeared. He too was seen in the light of that street lamp, and he too crossed there, coming on in the wake of the woman, who passed Ashford's.

The waiting man gritted his teeth as the following man passed by. The acute frustration brought bile, acid and bitter, into his throat, and he almost vomited. His heated body shuddered, and his perspiration became clammy. He turned his jacket collar down, adjusted his bowler, put his hands into his trouser pockets and walked away.

A fluttery wife, arriving home at midnight with her husband, went straight up to bed leaving him to see to things, like laying the kitchen fire for the morning. He was a good husband. When he came up, she was asleep. But he woke her up when he joined her in bed.

'Oh,' she breathed a minute later, 'oh, Herby.'

'Makes a nice change, Maudie.'

'Yes, but – oh, my word – but your back –'

'I'm putting up with it.'

'Oh, you'll bruise me. Herby – oh!'

She had never known him so urgent, and him with his back and all. If she'd been a girl again, she'd have blushed. Still, like he'd said, it did make a nice change.

CHAPTER TWENTY

Saturday morning.

'Hello.'

Emma, putting a selection of gloves away after making a sale, looked up. Trary smiled at her.

'Well, hello again,' said Emma, returning the smile. The girl looked more appealing than ever in a peach-coloured frock. Beside her was a small girl.

'We're all here this mornin',' said Trary, 'my mother, my three sisters and me. This is my youngest sister, Daisy. Daisy, say hello.'

' 'Ello,' said Daisy. None of the girls were shy.

'Hello,' smiled Emma.

'Mum and Lily and Meg are buyin' shoes at the moment,' said Trary, 'Daisy and me have got ours. We all want to buy frocks and things, so Daisy and me came to make sure you could serve us, you were ever so nice last time. Mum and my other sisters won't be long, so if you could start with Daisy and me, that would save time, wouldn't it?'

'How nice, I'm delighted,' said Emma. 'Could I ask your name?'

'Trary – Trary Wilson.'

'I'm Mrs Carter, Mrs Emma Carter. Yes, let's get busy, shall we? What colour and style of frocks do you have in mind?'

'Oh, I'd like one in crepe, in a fawn shade, but not with a sash or anything fussy,' said Trary. 'Daisy wants pink, with a big sash. Oh, and would you have a skirt and a petticoat a bit short for roller-skatin'? I'm goin' to the Brixton rink this afternoon.'

'She's goin' wiv Bobby,' said Daisy, offering the infor-

249

mation readily. She offered more. ' 'E kisses 'er sometimes.'

'Lucky Bobby,' smiled Emma.

'Oh, you Daisy, you're a little 'orror,' said Trary. Daisy giggled. Emma thought both girls delicious. She got busy.

Trary and Daisy had a rapturous time. So did Meg and Lily when they arrived. So did Maggie, who was buying for herself as well as the girls. Emma's counter became alive with excited chatter. She found it utterly enchanting to involve herself in the wants, wishes and decisions of the pleasant-looking mother and her four girls. In and out of the fitting room they all went, Maggie at her happiest in being able to provide so well for her daughters. Having paid Mr Bates what she owed him, she still had over forty pounds in her purse. Over forty pounds. Lovely Uncle Henry, the Lord rest his wandering soul, had turned her purse into a little goldmine. If really nice frocks were as much as half a guinea, what did it matter?

The assistant serving them was a charming woman, and so helpful. Emma, indeed, was not in the least worried about the length of time it took to serve all of them. She was almost sorry when the prolonged transaction was finally concluded, with everyone very happy. Trary could hardly contain her bliss at the acquisition of her roller-skating outfit, which consisted of a lovely white lawn blouse with pearl buttons, a dark green skirt with a wide flared hem and a dazzling white petticoat fringed with layers of lace. Maggie's own purchases included two handsome brocade dresses, like tea gowns, and two fashionable toque hats, so favoured by Princess Mary of Wales.

Emma, adding up the bill, had to acquaint Maggie with the dire news that it came to twelve pounds, eleven shillings and sevenpence-three-farthings.

'Oh, heavens,' said Maggie, and Emma wondered for a moment if Mrs Wilson could meet such a bill. Her clothes hardly spoke of affluence, although her girls were all wearing very nice frocks. 'I never spent so much money in all me life. Well, never mind, we're all happy, an' you've been such a 'elp.' Maggie opened her purse and handed three white five-pound notes to Emma.

'Thanks so much, Mrs Wilson,' said Emma, 'it really has been a great pleasure to serve you all.' The sale meant welcome commission for her on top of all the enjoyment. The cash canister whirred on its way.

'It's been lovely,' said Trary.

'I'm all dizzy,' said Meg.

'I'm giddy,' said Lily.

'I'm little,' said Daisy.

'Oh, little girls are nice girls, aren't they?' smiled Emma.

'Yes, I fink I am,' said Daisy.

The canister came back with the bill and the change. The family said goodbye and departed, leaving Emma feeling a flat dull quiet had taken their place. Laden with parcels, the family went home, enriched by the ownership of new dresses, skirts, blouses, shoes, socks, stockings, hats and oceans of new underwear.

The Brixton roller-skating rink was crowded with enthusiastic young people. Exuberant cockney boys and girls from places like Camberwell, Walworth and Kennington, mingled with the lively sons and daughters of the lower middle-classes from Brixton Hill, Herne Hill and Norwood. The latter received their entrance fee from their parents, the cockney boys and girls scraped it together somehow. It was fun for all, integrating fun.

Bobby thought Trary looked stunning. Trary herself felt almost grown-up in her outfit. Well, she felt fifteen at least, especially as she also wore white silk stockings and white button-up shoes. The stockings represented an extravagant but affectionate gesture on Maggie's part. Her eldest daughter was so funny in all she said about Bobby, but Maggie knew she considered him the only boy worthwhile. It sent her dotty that he could out-talk her sometimes, and being sent dotty meant laughter to a girl like Trary. Maggie, quite aware she wanted her roller-skating outfit to knock

Bobby flat, had accordingly splashed out on the white silk stockings.

Trary and her talking boy had come all the way to Brixton on a tram. He'd brought two pairs of roller skates with box-wood wheels with him, the skates strapped and clipped to boots. Seated on a bench beyond the rink itself, Trary gazed in fascination at the scene. The polished rink floor was solid beneath the humming of boxwood wheels and the rasping of metal wheels. Some of the boys and girls were fluent and expert, some halfway to proficiency, and some making the tentative movements of beginners. Show-off boys sped round, weaving their way through groups of slower skaters. Tomboy girls sped after them. Proud-looking girls glided around in upright and stately fashion, ignoring the young show-off males who, of course, meant to impress them and get off with them. Trary badly wanted to become one of them, to skate in a proud, superior style, while Bobby fell about all over the rink. But she had a feeling it was going to be the reverse. At the moment, he was down on one knee in front of her. Her new shoes were off, and he was slipping a boot, with its fixed skate, onto her stockinged right foot.

'How d'you know it'll fit?' she asked.

'How do I know? It's me that brought the boots an' skates, Trary, not Simple Simon. I've seen your feet, I know about sizes.' The boot went smoothly on, and Trary asked if he had lots of boots and skates. 'A few,' said Bobby, 'we get them in sometimes with a load of footwear. Well, 'ow's that, me young sweetheart?'

Trary wriggled her foot inside the boot, 'Crikey, it really does fit,' she said, her excitement charged with nervousness. 'But it feels ever so heavy.'

'There's a skate on it, that's why,' said Bobby, and tied the boot. 'Now give us your other foot, me precious.'

'You Bobby, stop usin' romantic talk. We're not kissin' friends, we're not even holdin' hands yet. Kindly don't call me sweetheart an' precious.'

'All right,' said Bobby amiably, slipping the left boot on

her foot, 'we'll keep it all for later on, when you're gettin' to be grown up. We'll wait till you're fourteen before we hold 'ands, and I'll give you yer first kiss when you're fifteen. I can't say fairer than that, can I?' He tied the boot.

'Well, of all the nerve,' said Trary, 'you're not gettin' to kiss me till I say so, which I might never do if you don't stop all your grinnin'.'

'Can't help meself, Trary, you're fun, you are, and don't you look prettier than a bunch of roses this afternoon in yer new clothes and that fancy petticoat an' silk stockings? You come into a fortune?'

Since her mum had strictly forbidden any talk of Uncle Henry and the will, Trary said lightly, 'Oh, mum's a bit better off now, and don't even have to go to her job at the newsagents any more. Bobby, oh, help, have I got to stand up now?'

The rink was buzzing with movement, a three-piece band playing above the refreshment alcoves that ran along one side of the hall. And Trary knew she'd got to enter the fray.

'Well, it's best if you do stand up,' said Bobby, 'you can't skate on yer bottom. You can fall on it, you can't skate on it. Come on.' With his own boots and skates on, he took hold of her hands. Drawing a deep breath, Trary gazed up at him. He looked ever so tall and confident, and ever so nice-looking too in his skating jersey and trousers. She felt quite proud at being with him. But she also felt doom-laden. She was sure she was going to fall as soon as she stepped onto the rink. 'Come on, Trary,' he said again, and brought her to her feet. She stood on the carpeted strip adjacent the rink, Bobby still holding her hands.

'Don't you let go,' she said.

Bobby saw the light of nervous excitement in her eyes, and the little flutters of uncertainty. He couldn't see there was ever going to be any girl for him except this one.

'I'll hold you like this,' he said, retaining his clasp of her left hand, putting himself beside her and placing his right arm around her waist.

'Wait a minute,' said Trary, 'are you takin' a liberty?'

253

'Not likely,' said Bobby, 'I don't want a punch in the eye, not while the band's playin'. I'm just holdin' you politely, for learning. Come on.' He brought her onto the rink through the opening in the low surround, Trary moving with quivering caution. Once on the rink, her left foot immediately ran away from her. She gave a little yell. Bobby righted her. A boy and girl, bumping each other, tumbled and went down. The girl's skirts scattered around her limbs, and her legs showed to her knees. Boys shouted in glee. The girl sat up, laughed and climbed to her feet.

'Do us an encore, darlin',' whooped a boy as he sped by.

'Bobby Reeves,' said Trary, right hand gripping the smooth top of the surround, 'I hope you 'aven't brought me to a den of hooligans.'

'Don't worry,' said Bobby, 'hooligans get chucked out. Right, let's make a start, shall we?'

Trary drew another breath and pushed forward into the unknown, Bobby's arm around her waist. He began to teach her the basics, to lean, to push forward, one foot after the other, and to let her skates glide. Trary said her problem was not to let her skates leave her behind. Bobby said don't let 'em do that or you'll fall on your Jamaica Rum. Not if you hold me properly, I won't, said Trary, and kindly don't be rude. The band kept playing, the lively music a challenge to the show-offs and an encouragement to the beginners. Trary slowly circled the rink, keeping close to the surround. Not a girl who lacked belief in herself, she nevertheless felt she'd never be able to go round on her own. Her skates were wayward.

'Bobby, you sure these skates have got straight wheels?'

'Hope not, they're supposed to be round,' said Bobby, 'I expect it's yer legs that feel a bit wonky. I mean, it's yer first time. But don't worry, you're doin' fine.'

Trary gritted her teeth and persevered. It helped just a little to see that other beginners were having problems. Even so, she didn't want to stay a beginner all afternoon. Her left hand clung to Bobby's, and her right hand stayed close to the top of the surround. Then her skates began to behave, to feel smoother and not so awkward, and it was suddenly exhilarating to find herself moving forward quite well. Confidence surged and she pushed with enthusiasm. Bobby let go of her to give her her head. Away she went, and disaster struck. Her skates left her behind and she fell on her bottom. Her new skirt and petticoat took umbrage and finished up any old how. Her shapely young legs, gleaming in white silk, caught a score of eyes and brought forth admiring whistles.

A boy called, 'Cor, you got a lovely pair of clo'es pegs there, gel.'

Bobby arrived and brought the pink-faced Trary to her feet, 'What's the idea, showin' your legs like that?' he asked. 'I thought you were partic'lar at keepin' them private.'

'Blessed cheek, I didn't show them on purpose,' declared Trary with feeling. 'You made me do it by lettin' go of me.'

'What a life,' said Bobby, ' 'ow did I know you were goin' to try skatin' on yer bottom? I told you you couldn't.'

'I'll hit you,' said Trary, 'and if you let go again, I'll box your ears as well.'

'All right, Lady 'Ortense, I'll hold you unconditional, 'ow about that?'

'Stop showing off,' said Trary, 'just hold me proper.'

'Yes, Yer Ladyship, very good, Yer Ladyship,' said Bobby, and his arm encircled her waist very firmly this time. She saw boys and girls going round and round so easily, crossing one leg over the other as they turned corners, the girls' skirts roomy, petticoats light and short, ankles and calves showing. The band music was infectious, the atmosphere almost like a carnival.

'Oh, it's fun,' she said. 'Come on, I'm ready again now, and you'd better take good care of me this time, or else.'

'Yes, Yer Ladyship,' said Bobby, and she gave him a look. She saw the grin on his face. Oh, that boy, what a handful he was. His arm squeezed her waist. Her look became haughty. He winked at her. Trary couldn't hold laughter back any longer. It burst from her.

Then they began to move again. It had been all pitfalls so far, and it was all pitfalls for another hour. The session was for three hours, from three till six. Bobby encouraged her, held her and guided her. She just wished her skates would stop being contrary. Bobby was so accomplished, and being really nice, doing all he could to pass his skill on to her. And eventually she achieved balance and then rhythm. Suddenly, she put it all together and without any feeling of alarm. She was upright and gliding, her head a little forward. From then on, happy excitement prevailed. Everything was fun, the band, the speeding boys, the graceful girls, the laughter, the shrieks, the squeals, and the running boxwood wheels of her skates. She had never had such a lively, lovely afternoon of action and fun. At ten past five, Bobby treated her to tea and a fruit bun in the long covered refreshment arcade that was divided into alcoves in true Edwardian style. A waitress served them, a young waitress who exchanged jokes with Bobby, and of course that talking boy had to show her what kind of a tongue he had. The waitress giggled coming and going.

When they were drinking their tea and eating their bun, Trary said cuttingly, 'Excuse me, you boy, but when you're with me, kindly don't talk all the time to other girls. It's not good manners.'

'Oh, you've got to be nice to people, Trary, specially waitresses, or you get stewed tea and stale buns. It's best to say 'ow's yer father to them. I was sayin' to me mum only yesterday – '

'Here we go again,' said Trary.

'Yes, I was only sayin' to her – now what was I sayin'?'

'Something daft, I bet,' said Trary. 'It's a shame, I think, that your mum's only son can't help drivin' her dotty.'

'Oh, most mums are dotty naturally,' said Bobby, 'so are most girls. That's why we like 'em.'

'Are you includin' me, Bobby Reeves?'

I'm specially includin' you, Trary, you're pretty *and* dotty.'

'Oh, I am, am I?'

'I also like you when yer proud and haughty,' said Bobby. 'You're me one and only best girl, Trary.'

'You'll be lucky. After all those things you just said about me, we're partin' for ever, Bobby Reeves.'

'Right now, Trary?'

'Well, no, not right now, perhaps. We'll do some more skatin' first. Come along, you boy.'

They went back onto the rink for the last thirty minutes of the session, Trary in renewed enthusiasm. Bobby made complimentary remarks about her progress, and told her she was a natural, as well as the best-looking girl skater there. Trary said that as his manners had improved, he could see her home and she wouldn't say goodbye for ever to him until they reached her doorstep. When the end of the session came at six o'clock, she could hardly bring herself to put all the fun behind her.

On the tram going home, she said, 'Bobby, could we go again?'

'You really liked it, Trary?'

'Oh, I never had such fun.'

'You were goin' like a champ at the end.'

'You're awf'lly good yourself,' she said.

'Agreed unanimous,' said Bobby.

'Crikey,' said Trary, 'no wonder your cap don't fit you, no wonder it's always on the back of your head, your head's too big for it. And you're showin' off again. Now what you doin'?'

'Givin' you a squeeze,' said Bobby.

'Blessed sauce. We don't do squeezin' yet, so stop takin' liberties, specially not on a tram with people lookin'. Bobby, could we go again?'

'I'll see how well me dad did at 'elping mum out at the stall. She's busy Saturday afternoons, she's got to have either me or dad there, and if dad – well, never mind that.' Bobby could imagine his dad skiving off well before the

257

afternoon was over, and while his mum's back was turned. And his mum was far too easy with his dad. Other women went for skiving husbands with a rolling-pin or saucepan.

'Well, let's hope for next Saturday, Trary.'

'Sometimes,' said Trary, 'you're quite a nice boy.'

'Sure?'

'Yes, sometimes, so we won't part for ever until after next Saturday,' said Trary, who was never going to admit how much she enjoyed being with her laughing, talking hooligan.

CHAPTER TWENTY-ONE

Sunday was fine. Little white clouds sailed serenely across the blue sky that sat high above smoky London. Summer had decided to stop shilly-shallying and to be more positive. Street kids were making crickets bats out of slats of wood, and cricket balls out of rolled-up rags tied with string. Girls were chalking hopscotch designs on pavements or tuning up for 'Oranges and Lemons'. Last year's conkers had either died a brave death in winter battles or been put away to hibernate until next winter.

The desk sergeant on duty in the police station in Rodney Road looked up at the entry of a neatly dressed woman wearing a wide-brimmed hat.

'Good morning, sergeant.'

'Mornin', ma'am, what can I do for you?'

'Do you know Detective-Sergeant Chamberlain of Scotland Yard?' asked Emma.

'That I do, he's been almost livin' here these last weeks. Well, on and off, you might say.'

'We all might say,' smiled Emma. 'He's interviewed me several times concerning the murder enquiry. Could you let him know I'd like to see him?'

'Concerning same case, ma'am?' enquired the sergeant.

'Yes.'

'He might just be on duty today.'

'Oh, I wouldn't want to drag him out on a Sunday if he's not. Tomorrow would do. I'm Mrs Carter of fifteen King and Queen Street.'

'Right. Mrs Carter.' The sergeant scribbled. 'Any partic'lar message, Mrs Carter?'

'Just say I hope to be of help.'

'Right. That makes it urgent in my book. I'll take details, if you like.'

'I'd prefer to give them to Sergeant Chamberlain.'

'Very good, Mrs Carter. I'll see if someone can get hold of him.'

'How kind. Thank you,' said Emma. She turned on her way to the door. 'Incidentally, sergeant, do you support votes for women?'

'Ah,' said the sergeant.

'Ah yes or ah no?' smiled Emma.

Stolidly, the sergeant said, 'I'm not permitted as a police officer to disclose me political views.'

'Coward,' said Emma, and left.

The sergeant lifted the phone off its hook and made a call to Scotland Yard.

At ten minutes to three that afternoon, Nicholas arrived at Emma's house. King and Queen Street again had an air of Sunday quiet. He knocked. Emma answered. He noted the crispness of the lace on her light-brown blouse.

'Afternoon, Mrs Carter.'

'Why, it's you,' said Emma.

'Weren't you expecting me?'

'Was I? Oh, yes, I suppose I was. But I thought to-morrow, perhaps, I didn't want to disturb your Sunday.'

'You're not.' Nicholas was businesslike.

'Then do come in,' she said. He could never fault her composure. She always gave him the impression she was in control of herself and events. He stepped in. She closed the door, took his hat and hung it on the door peg.

'How are you, Mrs Carter?'

'Perfectly healthy, I'm happy to say. Do sit down. Would you like some tea?'

'I'd really like to know why you wanted to see me.'

'Oh, dear,' murmured Emma, 'are we a little bit grumpy today?'

'Do I sound as if I am?' he asked.

'Yes,' said Emma.

'Sorry.'

'No, no, I didn't mean it,' she said. 'I've met very grumpy policemen. You're not one of them. Let me see – oh, yes, of course you want to know why I asked to see you.' She smoothed her skirt. 'I was followed home on Friday night.'

'What?' He shot the word at her.

'Yes. I went to a friend's flat in Southampton Street, off the Strand, to meet her and other suffragettes, and we had a rousing discussion on how best to get our views across to our leaders. I suggested we presented these views in the form I'd written down, addressing them to the general committee, not to Mrs Pankhurst, and that copies should reach every committee member. We –'

'Yes, very interesting, Mrs Carter, but could you come to the point?'

'Oh, dear,' said Emma.

'Never mind oh dear,' said Nicholas, 'I want to hear about the person who followed you home.'

'Yes, of course,' said Emma. 'I keep forgetting you're a policeman, you have so many nice ways. Well, I got back to Browning Street on a tram at about five past eleven.'

'Five past eleven? By yourself?'

'Yes. It's not an offence, is it?'

'My God, women,' said Nicholas.

'I hope you're not going to be old-fashioned,' said Emma. 'When I got off the tram, I noticed there were two or three couples in Walworth Road, but Browning Street was empty of people. However, I think I was followed all the way down it, and all the way home.'

'You think?' Nicholas was slightly exasperated by her calmness. 'You mean you're not sure?'

'I mean there was a man behind me, definitely, but there's the possibility he may not have been following me, just walking in the same direction, on the way to his own home. But I began to hurry, of course.'

'Didn't you turn your head and look?'

'Yes. I saw him, about twenty yards behind me.'

'What was he like?'

'I couldn't say precisely. It was very dark.'

'Mrs Carter, there are street lamps in Browning Street.'

'Yes, but far apart. I can say he was fairly tall, and I had the impression he was muffled up.'

'Was he in a cap and raincoat?'

'A cap, yes. I'm not sure about a raincoat. There had been some rain during the day, but it was a mild night and dry. Still, I think he had some kind of coat on. I turned into King and Queen Street, and thought for a few moments that he'd continued on. Then I knew he was still behind me, still about twenty yards away. I walked as fast as I could, I was worrying by then, of course, thinking he might be the man you're after. I dug out my doorkey while I was still walking, and I was ready to scream the place down if I didn't get my door open in time. I managed to open it very quickly. I glanced. He was closer, much closer. I threw myself indoors and shut the door fast.'

'I'm appalled,' said Nicholas.

'But aren't you pleased I acted so quickly?'

'I could say a few things to you, Mrs Carter.'

'Pardon?' said Emma.

'Out by yourself at that time of night, d'you think that was sensible?'

'I wasn't by myself until I got off the tram at Browning Street, I was among the public. Stop scowling at me.'

Nicholas muttered. Emma remained calm.

'Mrs Carter, when you took your last look and found he was much closer, didn't you see him clearly?'

'He just seemed like a dark, moving shadow, muffled up. Heavens, I didn't stand and stare, sergeant, I took only a lightning glance before throwing myself indoors. I'm not a six-foot Billingsgate porter, you know.'

'No, you're a vulnerable woman,' said Nicholas, stern-faced and reproving. 'Don't come home again in the dark, not when you're by yourself, and not until we've caught this man.'

'Oh dear,' said Emma, 'that sounds like an order.'

'Officially, it's necessary advice. From a personal point of view, yes, it is an order. Damn it, woman –'

'Pardon?' said Emma again.

'Sorry. That was out of order. But don't you realize the risks of being out so late? You're probably a marked woman now.'

'But the man might be completely innocent, he really might have been on his way to his own home. I admit I felt I should tell you –'

'I'm much obliged,' said Nicholas, 'but I'd have thought a woman of your intelligence would have arranged for your friend to have gone with you and seen you home. I'd also have thought you'd have reported the incident before today.'

'Heavens,' said Emma, 'I'm doing my very best to help you with your enquiries, and here you are bullying me.'

'Stop playing games,' said Nicholas.

'Well, really. Sergeant Chamberlain, you're ruining my Sunday.'

'Mrs Carter, you're ruining my peace of mind. Just make sure that if you do go out at night, you have your friend with you.'

Emma made a little face. That was the trouble with white lies, they rebounded.

'I'm used to being independent,' she said.

'Look,' said Nicholas, 'most women are basically nice. A number of men are basically unpleasant. But there are the better kind. Having one as an escort doesn't mean you lose your independence, it means you're not putting yourself at the mercy of the unpleasant. The unpleasant in this case is a maniac. I'm sure your friend would be only too pleased to keep you safe. Under the circumstances, you've been a naughty girl, haven't you?'

'Oh, my word,' said Emma, a little taken aback, 'you *are*

bullying me. It's the policeman coming out in you.'

'Was this man on the tram with you? Did he follow you off it?'

'I really don't know. I mean, if anyone did, I wasn't aware of it.'

'You said you saw two or three couples about. Did you notice any solitary person?'

'No, I can't honestly say I did.'

'Well, we'll trace the tram, and the conductor, and talk to him.'

'Oh, good,' said Emma. 'Is my ordeal over now? I suppose it's your duty to be stern and hectoring, and I shan't harbour any hard feelings. Will you stay and have some tea?'

'That's kind of you,' said Nicholas, 'but it's a working day for me. I've got to get back to the Yard, I'm reexamining all reports from the uniformed branch and the CID in the hope of alighting on something I've missed or someone else has missed.'

'I see,' said Emma.

'I'll call again in a few days.'

'Will you? Why?'

Nicholas knew why, even if she didn't. He supposed he liked punishing himself. 'Just to check up,' he said.

'To make sure I'm behaving myself and not wandering about in the dark?'

'That's as good a reason as any,' said Nicholas, 'and perhaps I should have a word with your friend sometime.'

'Certainly not,' said Emma in some haste, 'but thank you, all the same.'

'Take special care, just in case you are a marked woman,' said Nicholas, opening her front door.

'Yes, of course.'

'You'd better,' said Nicholas by way of a heavy parting shot.

With his going, her living-room returned to peace and quiet. Since this didn't please her too much, Emma frowned.

None of the girls wore their new frocks for Sunday tea.

Maggie had had a little chat with them, pointing out that Bobby would be there, and that if new frocks were worn it would look as if they didn't think much of those his mother had let them have so cheaply, and which were as good as new. It would be nice to let Bobby see they appreciated them. The girls, very happy about the way good fortune had arrived at their door, made no fuss.

Maggie herself, however, did put on one of her new dresses from Hurlocks, a handsome brocade creation in rich brown silk. Harry found it difficult to keep his eyes off her. Putting two and two together, he guessed her visit to the solicitors had resulted in something to her advantage.

Trary sparkled in the blue frock originally presented to her by Bobby as a gift from his mum. Her sisters all looked very appealing. Meg asked Harry if he liked her in her apple-green frock.

'You're good enough to eat,' said Harry.

'Specially with custard,' said Bobby. 'I'll finish her up if there's any leftovers, Mr Bradshaw. And I'll 'ave Daisy for afters, with jelly.'

'I'll have Lily,' said Harry, 'with blancmange.'

Giggles arrived, and then chatter. Maggie thought Harry fitted in just right, he had a nice easy way of bringing the girls out. No-one mentioned Mr Bates, and she felt very buoyant that she no longer needed any kind of lodger.

When she was cutting the sultana cake she'd baked that morning, Bobby asked if he might say something about her.

'You'll have to let him, Mum,' said Trary, 'he'll say it, anyway.'

'I'm not goin' to make a speech,' said Bobby.

'Not much,' said Trary.

'I just wanted to say I've never seen your mum look more queenly,' said Bobby. 'I don't get to see a lot of queenly women in the market, nor on trams, either. And I've never seen any comin' out of a pawnshop, have you, Mr Bradshaw? No, I thought you 'adn't. I bet both of us don't often have Sunday tea with one.'

265

'This is the first time for me,' said Harry, making himself acquainted with a slice of the cake.

'Well, now you mention it, I think it's the first time for me too,' said Bobby. 'I can't recollect ever 'aving the privilege before.'

'I said he'd make a speech,' declared Trary. 'Now he's showin' off as well.'

'Is Bobby sayin' fings about our mum?' asked Daisy.

'Yes, 'e's callin' 'er a queen,' said Meg.

'Mrs Wilson,' said Bobby, 'you don't mind me sayin' it's an honour to see you lookin' as good as Queen Mary?'

'I'm overcome,' said Maggie.

'I'll fall off my chair in a minute,' said Trary, 'can't someone stop him?'

'I think he's finished for the moment,' said Harry.

'Thank goodness,' said Trary, 'I was just about to start prayin'. Honest, Mr Bradshaw, when that boy gets started, it's only 'eaven that can help you.'

'Have you tried cake?' asked Harry.

Daisy giggled. 'I likes 'Arry,' she said.

'Daisy's said it again, Mum,' remarked Lily.

'Little imp, I heard her,' said Maggie.'Bobby, don't you like sultana cake? You haven't had any yet.'

'Well, thanks, Mrs Wilson,' said Bobby, 'I was just doin' some thinkin'.' He helped himself to a slice. 'I was –'

'Oh, lor',' said Trary, 'he's off again.'

Maggie saw her eldest daughter watching Bobby, a threat showing warm and bright in her eyes.

'Yes, I was thinkin', Mrs Wilson,' he said.

'What about?' asked Maggie.

'I forget.'

'He's daft,' said Trary.

'No, it's a good idea to forget sometimes,' said Harry, 'it keeps you out of trouble.'

'Actu'lly,' said Bobby, 'I'm always forgettin' lately, Mrs Wilson, I've been like it ever since I met Trary. I just hope that later on, when she's decided to be me future wife, I

266

don't forget to turn up for the weddin'. I'll have to — what's up with her, Mrs Wilson?'

Trary was having hysterics.

'Time for the cake cure, Trary,' said Harry.'

Trary swooped, not for Bobby's slice of cake, but one of two jam tarts left on a plate. Bobby read the warning signs. He leapt from his chair and made a dash for safety. Amid shrieks of excitement from Daisy and Lily, Trary went after him, with the jam tart. She caught him in the passage. They heard him shout with laughter. Then, 'Trary, I don't know why you're upset — oh, crikey!'

Trary came back, wiping her hand on her hankie.

'Trary, where's that jam tart?' asked Maggie.

'All over Bobby's face,' said Trary.

The girls shrieked. Harry roared with laughter. Maggie shook her head and hid a smile. They could afford for Trary to use one jam tart to get her own back on her talking boy, even though it was a waste of good food.

The girls and Bobby did the washing-up afterwards, allowing Maggie to be alone with Harry in the parlour.

'I didn't mention anything over the tea table,' said Maggie.

'Anything about what?' asked Harry, filling his pipe.

'About what 'appened at the solicitors.'

'Well, you didn't have to, Maggie, it's your own affair.'

'Yes, but if you hadn't come round an' shown me that notice in the paper, I wouldn't be all dressed up in silk, and I wouldn't 'ave bought new things for the girls. I just want you to know you've helped to make me a bit better off, that My Uncle Henry left me something in 'is will.'

'Well, good for you,' said Harry.

'I've got enough to buy a little house, with a garden. That would be real nice for the girls, don't you think so, Harry? I wondered, well, I wondered if you could give me a bit of help, if you'd advise me, I don't know much about buyin' houses.'

'I think you've got enough sense to get yourself just the place you need, Maggie, but if you do need any

267

help, just ask. Your lodger's gone?'

'Yes,' said Maggie, and smiled. 'He took off a bit urgent. I think 'e's gone to South Africa.' Not Australia, she thought. It had never been Australia, she was sure. Mr Bates had had obvious reasons for not mentioning South Africa. She dismissed the man permanently from her mind. 'You don't mind bein' a help to me, Harry?'

'It'll be a pleasure,' said Harry, lighting his pipe. Maggie smiled again. He looked at home, and that made him seem a comforting man as well.

'Would you come an' look at houses with me, an' give me advice, like tellin' me if I'm gettin' value for my money? I can afford three hundred pounds for one.'

'Can you? Well, good old Uncle Henry. It'll be a sound investment.'

'D'you think so? I like to feel I do 'ave some sense, but men know a bit more about – about –'

'Bricks and mortar?' said Harry.

'Yes, I wouldn't want to buy something and not know if it was goin' to fall down.'

'I get regular Sundays off,' said Harry. 'We could take the girls with us.'

'They'd like that,' said Maggie, 'but wouldn't they be a bother?'

'Not to me.'

'Four girls can be a lot.'

'Yes, a lot of fun if they're like yours,' said Harry.

'Not all the time,' said Maggie. His pipe had gone out. She rose from her chair and handed him a box of matches from the mantelpiece. The slanting evening sun, too powerful to be subdued by the dusty air of Walworth, beamed light through the window and tinted her hair with gold. Harry thought her entirely irresistible then.

'Yes, I suppose it's easier for me to see them as fun,' he said. He struck a match and applied the flame to his pipe while wondering if all of them, Maggie and her four girls, would take him on. He knew himself in love with the mother. It was a lot to ask, since all the girls would have to be agreeable to it. Step-fathers weren't acceptable to every child. Resentment on the part of one could mean permanent trouble. 'Tell you what I'll do, Maggie, I'll bring some local papers carrying house advertisements.'

'Somewhere nice, like Herne Hill,' said Maggie.

'There's Trary's schoolin', of course. You'd need to get her into a similar school, she ought to have the benefit of stayin' till she's sixteen.'

'There, that's what I want,' said Maggie, 'good advice. I don't know I'd manage without someone givin' me some.'

'You'd manage, Maggie, the same as you managed to get through your hard times.'

'The Salvation Army was a great help one time,' said Maggie with a smile.

'The Salvation Army?' enquired Harry.

'Yes, don't you remember? It was you that collected their big box of food an' sent it round with Bobby. I don't think Trary's ever goin' to forget openin' that door an' seeing him with the box on 'is head.'

'Oh, yes,' said Harry, 'I remember.'

'I never knew anything more kind, Harry. I suppose I 'ave managed to manage, but you won't mind if I lean on you a bit about buyin' the house and everything?'

'That's what friends are for, Maggie.'

'Yes, some friends,' she said. She looked at him. Little trails of smoke ran upwards from his pipe. She felt a surge of warm affection. A man about the place. She knew the girls would like it, providing he was the right kind of man. Trary could hardly wait for him to become her new dad, and Meg thought him fun, which oddly enough was something she hadn't said about Mr Bates. As for Lily and Daisy, all they'd ask for was someone to tease them, tickle them and make them giggle. 'You're a kind friend yourself, Harry.'

'It's me duty as your local copper,' said Harry. 'You're a fine woman, Maggie, with four fine girls.'

'That's promising, thought Maggie. But I think he's going to make haste slowly. He hasn't asked a single question about just how much money I'm going to get, he's acted like it isn't his business. I'd better make it his business. It might be a lot for him to take on, me and the girls, but I'd better get him to marry me. I wouldn't like a man like him to go to waste. My girls could do with having him around. So could I. Then would be the time to tell him we've got a nice little nest egg. I wonder if he's got a weakness for a lady's new petticoat?

'Oh, Lord,' she said aloud, and laughed.

'What's the joke?' smiled Harry.

'Oh, I was just 'aving some thoughts.'

'Penny for 'em,' said Harry.

'No, I couldn't,' she said, 'you'd fall about laughin'.'

There were sudden girlish shrieks from the kitchen.

Bobby was making himself at home too.

CHAPTER TWENTY-TWO

'You want to get something done about that back of yours,' said the gas company superintendent, 'or you'll end up bent over permanent, like a cousin of mine. Lumbago's cripplin'.'

'Who said it was lumbago, I didn't,' observed Herbert Stephens, one of the company's collectors. 'It's just a weak back.'

'It's all lumbago, back trouble, ask anybody,' said the superintendent. 'Ask your doctor, for a start.'

'I've asked him, more than once, super,' said Stephens. 'Well, I've asked him what my weakness is, and I can't recall he's ever said lumbago.'

'It's all lumbago,' said the superintendent again. 'Get it properly treated before it gets incurable. Have you tried a Thermogene pack? I've heard they're a help.'

'Thermogene's for women's backs,' said Stephens, inspecting his collecting bag and his new book.

'Anyone's backs. Ask your doctor. Buy yourself one and wear it. You don't want to get yourself into a condition where you can't do your job.'

'Here, steady on, super, I can't afford to turn myself into an invalid. I can manage, I can live with it. I'm not saying I like it, but I can still put up with it, and I don't ask for time off.'

'Well, we wouldn't want to lose you,' said the superintendent, 'you've always done a good job.'

'And I'll still do a good job, for the sake of my wife. All right, perhaps I'll pick up some Thermogene from the chemist's, but Maudie won't like the look of it. She worries enough, as it is. She'll worry more when she sees me wrapped up in Thermogene. On the other hand, I don't know, though, it might make her laugh her head off for a change.'

'Well, you do that,' said the superintendent, 'you try a Thermogene pack. Can't do any harm. Anyway, you've got what you wanted, a transfer to the Walworth round, startin' from today. It's an easier round, and closer to your home.'

'Well, I've thanked you for that, super, and I'll thank you again,' said Stephens, and went out to begin his new round.

Maggie was working the morning away at the newsagents. She felt it only fair to see a second week through, so that Mr Gardner would have time to find someone to take her place. He shouldn't have any trouble. Any amount of women would gladly help him out for five bob a week. Yes, said Mr Gardner, but in a shop like this he didn't want a woman who'd got light fingers. That would cost him money he couldn't afford.

'Now,' said Miss Russell, 'who can tell me why the Restoration came about?' Several hands went up. 'Yes, Jane?'

Jane Atkins stood up. You always had to stand up to address a teacher. It was good manners and showed respect.

'Well, it was either that or being governed by the Army, Miss Russell.'

'Or?' said Miss Russell encouragingly.

'Or what, Miss Russell?'

'What was the other alternative?'

'Oh, I'm stumped there, Miss Russell,' said Jane, and sat down.

'Edna?' said Miss Russell, choosing to ignore Trary's raised hand for the moment.

Edna Cook stood up, 'It was riots, Miss Russell.'

'Yes, the possibility of riots, Edna. What would we call that?'

'Larky,' said Agnes Moore.

'Hardly,' said Miss Russell. 'Do you know, Edna?'

'I forget the word,' said Edna.

'Does anyone know?'

'Could I say, Miss Russell?' asked Trary, who had been rolling the word around her tongue.

'Yes, enlighten the class,' said Miss Russell, and Trary came to her feet in a new school frock, her glossy pigtails dancing at her back. The class quivered in anticipation.

'It's anarchy, Miss Russell,' said Trary, 'which is rule by mobs. Of course, if you don't mind me sayin' so, there was something else besides that and Army rule. Actu'lly, Miss Russell, the people were sickeningly fed-up, they'd lived problematical lives for years an' years because of Oliver Cromwell and what came after him. I think people can put up with an awful lot, don't you, Miss Russell, but not if there's no dancing or singing. I think General Monk could see that, and I think he had a long talk with himself. Talking's important, well, I think it is. I happen to have a friend –'

'Dick Turpin,' said Jane with a giggle.

'Who?' asked Miss Russell.

'That's his name,' said Jane.

'Pardon?' said Miss Russell.

'I shouldn't take any notice of Jane if I were you, Miss Russell,' said Trary, rising above all giggles. 'I'm surprised how uneducated she is. I mean, fancy anyone not knowin' Dick Turpin's been dead for nearly two hundred years. He was hanged at York, you know, in 1739, so he must be dead. Miss Russell, I was goin' to say this friend of mine does so much talkin' that I'm sure he talks to himself when he's not with me, and I think that's what General Monk did, I think he – ' Trary stopped to search for the right word.

'Conferred with himself?' suggested Miss Russell.

'Yes, that sounds just right,' said Trary, 'yes, I think that's what he did, he conferred with 'imself about what was best for the people.'

'And then?' said Miss Russell.

'He decided to side with them and put King Charles II on the throne, he knew King Charles would bring back dancing and singing, and do away with puritan miseries.'

The class of girls whooped in exuberant agreement.

'Thank you, Trary.' Miss Russell smiled. 'If the school ever puts on Shakespeare's *Prince of Denmark*, I'll ask for you to play Hamlet.'

'Oh, yes, I like 'To be or not to be,' don't you, Miss Russell? I don't know – '

'You may sit down now, Trary,' said the captivated history teacher.

Trary wanted to tell Bobby that her mum was thinking of buying a house in Herne Hill, but her mum didn't want anyone to know about it yet. However, she did tell him she'd mentioned him to her history teacher.

'I'm honoured,' said Bobby, walking her home.

'Yes, I said you were so talkative that you probably talked to yourself when you weren't with me. Do you do that?'

'Not much, an' not out loud,' said Bobby.

'I bet you confer with yourself all the time,' said Trary. 'I mean, I've never known you when you weren't talkin'.'

'You can't 'ave a proper conference on your own, Trary.'

Conference? Conference? Oh, the rotten beast, he was always doing that, getting one up on her. 'I never met such a show-off as you, Bobby Reeves.'

'Yes, me mum says I'm pretty good, she says I can leave me dad standin', and he's a lot older than me.'

'Of course he's a lot older, what a daft thing to say. Does your cap feel smaller?'

'No, why should it?'

'Because your head's gettin' bigger,' said Trary.

Bobby laughed. They both laughed. And Bobby thought that Trary's new school frock and her mother's new silk

274

dress had to mean the Wilson family weren't as poor as they had been.

On Tuesday, Inspector Greaves was studying reports. He came across one from Detective-Sergeant Chamberlain, concerning a woman who had been followed home by a man on Friday night. The name of the woman was all too familiar. Mrs Emma Carter. He read the report carefully, then called Nicholas in.

'What the 'ell's up with you?' he asked.

'Frustration, mainly,' said Nicholas.

'Don't get clever, my son. You interviewed Mrs Emma Carter again on Sunday. This is your report. Sunday, eh? I put it to you, what's today?'

'Tuesday, Inspector,' said Nicholas, 'but the report's been on your desk since yesterday.'

'Don't stand there 'anding me baloney. Why wasn't I told first thing?'

'I haven't seen you since Friday, sir, you've been – '

'You'll get trodden on if you keep answerin' me back. I've seen some incompetent reports in my time, this is the pansy of 'em all. Listen, my son, you've made a cock-up of it. Vague description, eh? That's all she could give you? My eye. Treated 'er gentle, did you? You forgot, did you, that witnesses can remember a lot more than they think they can if you help them shake their brains about? A state of shock is only temp'rary. You're goin' soft, my lad.'

'Far from it,' said Nicholas. 'Mrs Carter accused me of bullying her.'

'Well, well, well. Gave you a nasty turn, did it, the said witness goin' for you while being sound of mind? So you went soft on her. Wasn't there someone else? Yes, Linda Jennings. That makes two of 'em.'

'I'd like to point out – '

'Don't, my son. I'll interview Mrs Carter myself this afternoon. This here footnote about the tram conductor, it's all you got out of 'im?'

'He remembered Mrs Carter getting off his tram, but couldn't remember anyone else doing so. Nor did he spot anyone who might have been the suspect. He wasn't looking. He'd rung the bell and the tram was away before Mrs Carter reached the pavement. We've hit another blank wall, sir.'

'Oh, we have, have we?' growled the Inspector. 'Well, they're no problem to our man, the bugger's out and about, and jumpin' over all of 'em.'

'With any luck, he'll break his neck one night,' said Nicholas.

'Bloody 'ell,' said Inspector Greaves, 'is that supposed to be funny? It's not makin' me laugh.'

Emma opened her door to a knock that afternoon. A middle-aged man confronted her. His bushy eyebrows and thick moustache were peppered with grey. He wore a dark blue suit and a black Homburg hat, and had a look of authority. There was another man with him, younger but of the same ilk, except that he wore a bowler.

'Mrs Carter?' said Inspector Greaves.

'Yes?'

'I'm Inspector Greaves of Scotland Yard. This is Detective-Sergeant Arnold.' The Inspector produced his card. 'Have you got five minutes to spare?'

'Yes, if you like,' said Emma wryly. Sergeant Chamberlain, the silly man, had persuaded his superior to come round and buttonhole her. That hadn't been the idea at all. 'Please come in.'

The men from the Yard entered. The Inspector got down to business at once. Emma found him quite different from Nicholas. His gravelly voice went with his burliness. He was a rough diamond of a policeman. He referred her to her experience on Friday night, reminding her she had not been able to describe the man in any real detail. Was that because she had been in shock?

276

'I wasn't in shock, Inspector, I remembered everything very clearly.'

He pointed out there were several street lamps between the top of Browning Street and her house midway down King and Queen Street.

'Several?' said Emma. 'One on the corner of Colworth Grove, and one on the corner of King and Queen Street. One and one are two, aren't they?'

'Two, then,' said the Inspector, a no-nonsense arm of the law. 'I'm accordingly suggestin' you had two chances to get a good look at him.'

'Oh, but when one suspects one is being followed by a very questionable character, one is too alarmed to act logically, especially when one is only a weak woman.' Knowing much of Emma by now, Nicholas would have recognized this for what it was, a dart of feminine whimsy. The Inspector merely regarded her as if he was still making up his mind about her. 'On the occasions I did look back he was very indistinct.'

The Inspector nevertheless put it to her that she might have collected a clearer picture than she realized. Might he be bold enough to suggest her memory could be jogged now she was out of a state of shock? According to Sergeant Chamberlain the man was quite close to her when she opened her front door.

'True,' said Emma.

'Well, then, can you put your thinkin' cap on, Mrs Carter?'

'It's on,' said Emma, 'and I can tell you what I told Sergeant Chamberlain, that the man was fairly tall, that he wore a cap and was muffled up.'

'Scarf?' enquired the Inspector.

'Could have been.'

'Scarf, scarf.' The Inspector mused like a well-fed bulldog over a bone. 'Woollen?'

'I really can't say.'

'Costermongers wear woollen scarves,' said Detective-Sergeant Arnold.

'His cap,' said the Inspector. 'Cloth cap? Tweed cap? Peaked cap?'

'Flat cap,' said Emma.

'Costermongers wear flat caps,' said Detective-Sergeant Arnold.

'I put it to you, Mrs Carter,' said the Inspector, 'there's a street lamp not far from your door. Near enough, you might say, to give you a bit of light.'

'How near is forty yards?' asked Emma, showing nothing of her exasperation.

Inspector Greaves persisted, taking her through the incident from the beginning. Emma repeated all she had said to Nicholas, including the fact that she had suggested the man was not following her in a strict sense, but simply going to his own home.

'Said suggestion was in Sergeant Chamberlain's report, Mrs Carter.'

'And I've just thought of something else,' she said. 'If the man was following me with foul intent on his mind, he'd have had plenty of time to catch me up well before I reached home, especially as there was no-one about. But as he didn't, that could mean he really was simply going to his own home.'

'Can't be sure, can we?' said the Inspector. 'I'm partial to facts, and the fact was he had nearly caught you up by the time you opened your door.' But there was a glint of approval in his eyes. He was beginning to respect Emma's intelligence, as well as her demeanour. 'I'll accordingly get the newspapers to print an account of said incident. We want that man to come forward and clear 'imself.'

'Oh, bother that,' said Emma, vexed, 'I really don't want my name in any papers, Inspector.'

'I can inform you it won't be,' he said.

'I'd rather you gave the man the benefit of the doubt,' said Emma.

'Can't be done, Mrs Carter.'

'Bother,' said Emma again, and made a mental note to

give Sergeant Chamberlain a piece of her mind.

The account appeared in the following day's papers, with
a request for the man in question to come forward and help
the police with their enquiries. It created a buzz of alarm
among the residents of King and Queen Street, and a heated
curiosity as to which woman it was who had been followed.

Emma felt very cross.

'So you're back,' said Bobby to his father, who had been
out when he should have been in. That was often the way.

'Yes, it's me, son,' said the wiry, wily Mr Reeves.

'Lofty Short's just been an' gone,' said Bobby sternly.

'Lofty?' Mr Reeves looked alarmed. 'What for, to give
me an 'eart attack?'

'He said you were expectin' him.'

'Me?' said Mr Reeves in protest. 'I've given up expectin'
Lofty, and it ain't safe to invite 'im to call, neither. 'E's
bad for me 'ealth Bobby, 'e's just done a Norwood job.'

'He'll get nicked,' said Bobby, 'and when the coppers
can't find the swag, they'll be round here to look for it an'
to nick you. He's dumped it on you, Dad. He said you owed
'im a favour.'

'Me? I don't owe Lofty nothing except the wrong end
of a barge pole.'

'He said you did. That's why he left the swag.'

'Bleedin' O'Reilly,' said Mr Reeves. His eyes, like bright
buttons, swivelled about. ' 'E'll get me jugged, me that ain't
injured the law since I dunno when, an' then it was 'ighly
circumstantial. Bobby, yer dozy 'a'porth, why'd yer let him
plonk the stuff?'

'Best thing, that's why,' said Bobby. 'Now you've got
a chance to do yerself and your fam'ly a good turn.
Otherwise, we'll all disown yer.'

' 'Ere, 'ere, you startin' to run my life for me?' demanded
Mr Reeves. 'And what d'you mean, disown me?'

'Bolt the door on you,' said Bobby. 'Listen, the swag's

on the larder floor. Get it an' take it to the police station. They know you've done receivin', Dad, even if they've never nabbed you, except that time when Mr Bradshaw 'elped to get you off light. Go on, take that stuff to the police station, tell 'em you found it dumped at the door of the flat, that someone expected you to take care of it, but that you're turnin' it in on account of goin' straight.'

'Eh?' said Mr Reeves.

'You 'eard,' said Bobby. 'They can't nick you if you turn the stuff in, and you don't have to name names.'

'Don't 'ave to? Course I don't. Nor won't, son. I ain't goin' to be sent to me grave as a coppers' nark. That won't get me to 'eaven. I got some rights as a Christian, yer know. Look, you ain't old enough yet to take these kind of liberties – '

'I'm old enough, and an inch taller than you,' said Bobby, 'so that's what you're goin' to do, deliver the swag to the police station. There's a reward, anyway. Said so in the paper this mornin'.'

'Eh?' Mr Reeves perked up. 'Reward? No, I couldn't do that, Bobby, it's dead against me principles. 'Ow much reward?'

'Fifty quid,' said Bobby.

'Fifty quid?' said Mr Reeves. 'That's arm-twistin', if yer like. It's bleedin' unscrupulous.'

'I'm writin' Lofty Short a letter,' said Bobby, 'I'm tellin' him I turned the loot in myself on account of fam'ly principles, that I did it before you got 'ome. So that's it, Dad, off you go. Put the swag bag in one of mum's shoppin' bags, and while you're about it just remember I don't want to 'ave to do all the thinkin' for this fam'ly. Time you took a turn. Still, mum said you didn't do too bad on the stall last Saturday. That's something.'

'Well, blind old Mother 'Awkins, if I ain't a pie-eyed marine,' said Mr Reeves.

'Better than the Scrubs,' said Bobby. 'I've got to remind you, Dad, that I'm dead against you disgracin' this fam'ly, that I want to be able to hold me 'ead up in Mrs Wilson's house. So go on, off you go with that swag.'

'Well, if that don't beat Fred Karno's Army,' said Mr Reeves, 'who's 'ead of this fam'ly, might I ask?'

'Right now?' said Bobby. 'Me. Still, as soon as you're really goin' straight, Mum and me'll hand you back the trousers.'

Mr Reeves thought hard. His brow creased as if his thoughts hurt. Then he chuckled, 'Dunno 'ow I come to 'ave one like you, Bobby,' he said.

He was on his way to the police station a few minutes later, carrying the swag in a shopping bag. It took the police a long time to believe that the man they knew as Shifty Reeves really was handing in stolen goods. The bugger was even enquiring after the reward.

Bobby had won one more round.

The meter man from the gas company knocked on Maggie's door on Wednesday afternoon. His face was new to her.

'Where's George?' she asked, the May sunlight gilding her hair.

'We've changed rounds,' said Herbert Stephens, 'it's more convenient. Well, it's more convenient to me. You're Mrs Wilson,' he added, looking at his book.

'Yes, and the meter's down the passage,' said Maggie. 'If there's any overs, they're for my girls' money-boxes.' There were often overs when a collector found there were too many pennies against the registered amount of gas used, and the Walworth housewives gladly received such surplus.

'You'll get them, Mrs Wilson, and welcome,' said Stephens, stepping in. Maggie left him to it. He emptied the meter, counted the coppers, checked the output and called her. 'There we are, Mrs Wilson.' He handed her three pennies with a smile.

'Thanks,' said Maggie. It was money she didn't need these days, but it could be put away for the girls in a communal money-box. As the new meter man was a nice improvement on George, a slightly morose character, she saw him out. 'Pleased to 'ave met you,' she said.

'Mutual, Mrs Wilson,' said Herbert Stephens, and departed for the next house.

Emma had a different caller herself. She had been out during the afternoon, visiting a number of sister suffragettes in order to get their signatures to *Ten Proposals For Alternative Action*. She could not go out in the evenings, it seemed. Sergeant Chamberlain had forbidden it, unless she was back before dark or had an escort. The escort he had in mind was a chicken come home to roost.

The knock on her door came just before seven o'clock. Heavens, she had been inundated with knocks lately. Who was it this time? Sergeant Chamberlain? He had said he would look in on her. Well, she had a few things to say to that gentleman.

It wasn't him, however. It was a young man from the East Street market, the twenty-year-old son of a stallholder. She bought much of her greengrocery from the stall.

'Hello, Alf,' she said.

'I dunno about 'ello, missus,' said Alf Barker, 'I just come from the police station. Me old man said I'd best go and get it sorted out.'

'Oh, dear,' said Emma.

'You know what I'm talkin' about, don't yer, Mrs Carter?'

'I can guess,' said Emma. 'Come in for a moment.' He came in. She closed the door. 'Alf, was it you, then, last Friday night?'

'Blimey, didn't yer know it was?' said Alf, a well-built young man. 'When I read about it this mornin', I didn't give it too much thought. Well, it didn't give yer name, it only said a woman 'ad been follered 'ome by some geezer considered suspicious, an' the police was askin' 'im to clear hisself. I knew it wasn't me. Well, I thought it wasn't. I never been suspicious in me life. But me old man started thinkin' about it this afternoon, 'e thought

282

about what time I'd got 'ome, an' which way I'd come. I'd been to see me girl friend in Amelia Street, I walked 'ome from there to Brownin' Street, then up King an' Queen Street. That made me old man think some more. 'E asked did I see a woman. I said I'd seen you. Mind, I didn't know it was you at first, it was dark most of the way. Then comin' up King an' Queen Street, I said to meself, that's Mrs Carter, she's out a bit late, considerin' what's been goin' on. I started to catch you up an' said goodnight to you just as you was closin' yer front door. Didn't you 'ear me? I suppose you couldn't 'ave, seein' you didn't say so to the police, which put me in shoes that didn't fit an' was uncomfortable as well. I did speak, yer know, I said, ' 'Ello, Mrs Carter, goodnight to yer.'

'I'm dreadfully sorry, Alf, I really wish the police had accepted my suggestion that it was just someone going innocently home,' said Emma, 'but they're so pernickety.'

'Well, they can't leave stones unturned, yer see,' said Alf. 'You bein' a good customer, me old man said I'd best go to the station an' get it sorted out, which I just did. Mind, I said to me old man I dunno 'ow it was yer didn't know it was me, not when I'd said goodnight out loud. The police said I couldn't 'ave been loud enough.'

Had Nicholas been present he might, at this point, have suspected Emma of actually looking guilty.

'I'm so sorry, Alf, I really am. I suppose I was just so glad to get indoors that my hearing failed me. Oh, well, we women are silly, aren't we?'

'You ain't, Mrs Carter,' said Alf. 'Me old man noticed yer name in the paper a while ago, when you made yerself 'eard at some suffragettes' meetin'. Sensible gel, he said you was.'

'What happened at the police station?' asked Emma.

'Blimey, they didn't 'alf make a meal of me partic'lars,' said Alf, 'me that's been straight up and all square since me bornin' day. I told 'em what I 'ad to tell 'em about

Friday night, an' then all about me life's work an' me comings an' goings. Then they said I could go, that I was in the clear.'

'That's good,' said Emma, 'I'm glad you had the courage to go and sort it out with them.'

'Well all right, Mrs Carter, no 'ard feelings, I can understand why you was dead scared.'

'Many thanks, Alf, for letting me know.'

'The rozzers said I'd better come an' see yer.'

'Yes, thanks very much,' said Emma, her smile rueful as she let him out. 'Oh, I hope you won't mention my name to people, or everyone will be gaping and gawping at me.'

'Don't worry,' said Alf, 'the police told me I'd got to treat it 'ighly confidential.'

'That's a relief, thanks again, Alf,' said Emma, and he went on his way.

Twenty minutes later, there was yet another knock. This time it was the gentleman to whom she had a few things to say.

'Good evening,' said Nicholas.

'I'll give you good evening,' said Emma.

'That sounds as if I'm in hot water.'

'You are. But come in, so that I can boil you in private and not on the step.' Nicholas stepped in. She closed the door and addressed him. 'You wretch,' she said. 'Having done my duty by reporting the incident on Friday night, my reward is to have van loads of Scotland Yard men descend on me. Aren't you ashamed of yourself? What do you mean by sending your po-faced Inspector Greaves and his assistant to bully me in my peaceful little home?'

'Sergeants don't send inspectors, Mrs Carter, they run about for them.'

'Serve you right,' said Emma. 'Look what it led to, total embarrassment for a young acquaintance of mine, Alf Barker.'

'Yes, I've been informed Mr Barker was able to clear

284

himself,' said Nicholas. 'That's why I'm here, to let you know officially that that particular matter has been settled.'

'Really, Sergeant Chamberlain, must you talk like a police notebook?'

'I frequently have to.'

'You've a lot to answer for,' said Emma, 'poor Alf was most upset.'

Nicholas eyed her severely, 'Are you playing games with me, Mrs Carter?'

Emma looked astonished, 'I don't play games,' she said, 'I'm far too serious a person.'

'A likely story,' said Nicholas. She wrinkled her nose at him like a girl. He wanted to laugh, but managed to keep a straight face. 'You reported being followed home. That meant we had to make enquiries. So what's this little Miss Madam act all about?'

'Little Miss Madam? Heavens,' exclaimed Emma, 'what an abusive question. I shan't answer it. I'll put it down to the strain you're under. Perhaps you could force yourself to sit down while I make a pot of tea. Would you like some tea and a slice of home-made cake? It's cherry cake.'

'Cherry cake? I can't say no to that.'

'How kind.' Emma wondered exactly what was happening to her, and why she had been lately thinking there had to be other things in her life besides women's suffrage. 'Well, please sit down while I go and make the tea.'

In the kitchen she found herself humming a song.

Over tea and cake, Nicholas forgot some of his frustrations. He said all the right things about her cake. Emma asked what his interests were outside of his duties. He could have said his prevailing interest right now was herself. He frankly found her utterly engaging.

'I like watching county cricket at the Oval,' he said. 'How about you, how are you getting on in your campaign against militancy?'

Emma said she had high hopes, but that so much of her

spare time was taken up by her pursuit of women's emancipation that she was afraid she was turning into a very dull person.

'You've probably noticed that,' she said.

He laughed, and it made her think that he was really a very nice man.

'If you're dull, I'm the king of cabbages,' he said.

'No, but I really must find time to enjoy some social pleasures,' said Emma. Pointedly, she thought.

'Good for all of us,' said Nicholas.

'I'm quite fond of the music hall, you know.'

'Who isn't?'

Bother him, thought Emma, I'm trying to make up for cold-shouldering him and he isn't taking the bait.

'It's ages since I've been,' she said.

'Well, Marie Lloyd is on at the Alhambra this week,' said Nicholas.

'Really?' said Emma. 'I've never seen Marie Lloyd.'

'Someone ought to help you put that right. Can't you get your friend to take you?'

'My friend's away all this week.' The little white lie slipped out all too easily.

'All week? With Marie Lloyd in the West End? I call that very inconsiderate.'

'I can't go on my own,' said Emma, 'you won't allow me to.'

'Could I do the next best thing?' asked Nicholas. 'Could I stand in for your friend?'

'Why, Sergeant Chamberlain, how kind of you, I can freely forgive you now for landing Inspector Greaves on my doorstep.'

'I'm not falling for that,' smiled Nicholas, 'especially as I've excused you for not hearing Alf Barker when he said goodnight to you.'

'Oh dear, yes,' said Emma, 'it would have saved so much bother if I had heard him. But in my agitation – I'm sorry.'

'Let's be relieved that you aren't a marked woman, after

all,' said Nicholas, then noted again the brightness of her hair. 'At least, I hope you're not.'

'Oh, I feel you're taking quite good care of me,' said Emma, tongue in cheek.

'Do you like living alone?' asked Nicholas.

'It hasn't worried me up till now, and I've never felt alone, not pathetically alone. One doesn't, not in Walworth. Walworth hums with life and people. It's like a beehive.'

'Who's the queen?' asked Nicholas.

'Mrs Ruby Mason,' said Emma.

'Who's she?'

'Walworth's Pearly Queen,' said Emma, and laughed.

They parted on very friendly terms later, having arranged the visit to the Alhambra for Saturday evening. Emma wondered, however, if in making up for being ungracious, she wasn't digging a pit for herself. His interest in her was so obvious. To encourage him was to ask to be pursued. A pursuing policeman would probably be difficult to shake off. Oh, dear. A little laugh escaped her. Saturday evening suddenly seemed very appealing.

CHAPTER TWENTY-THREE

The professionalism of Inspector Greaves was under strain. He always used tried and proven method in his approach to detection and solution, in the justified belief that in most cases things eventually fell into place. But nothing was falling into place in the case of the Southwark Strangler. Every lead had led nowhere. He and his team had ended up in blind alleys. The stack of reports grew higher daily until it began to look like the proverbial haystack.

Somewhere in that haystack, thought Nicholas, was the proverbial needle, the vital clue whose importance had been overlooked. He had a feeling about that just as much as he had a feeling the man was going to strike again. He suggested to the Inspector that if the man was single, his parents must either be unimaginative or mistakenly protective. And if married, the same applied to his wife.

'I put it to you, my lad,' said the Inspector heavily, 'that he's clever enough to keep 'is better half ignorant of his excursions.'

'That's a point,' said Nicholas.

'Bloody obvious, I'd have thought.'

The gas collector called at Emma's house on Thursday afternoon, fifteen minutes before she was due to go out.

'Afternoon, madam, read your meter?' said Herbert Stephens.

'You're new,' said Emma.

He smiled beneath his smart peaked cap. She felt she had seen him before.

'They're all saying that, Mrs Carter. That right, you

are Mrs Carter?' He referred to his book.

'Yes,' said Emma, 'come in.'

'I've just taken over this round, and I've been meeting my new customers this week.'

'I hope you're finding we're all satisfactory. The meter's here.' She led the way. The meter was mounted above her kitchen door. 'Have we met before?'

He looked enquiringly at her. He saw a nicely-dressed charming woman, with bright braided hair. He smiled broadly, 'I've got you now, Mrs Carter. Hurlocks. Right?'

'A beige blouse for your wife, and a pair of silk stockings as an extra, a birthday surprise,' said Emma.

'You should have seen her face,' said Stephens. 'She nearly fell over herself, she was that tickled.'

'How nice,' said Emma. 'Well, I'll let you get on with emptying the meter.' She went into her kitchen. The man took longer than the previous collector usually did.

Calling her eventually, he said, 'You've only got tuppence comin' back to you Mrs Carter, and it took me a while to empty it. There's something wrong with the works. It's registering the output all right, but the input system needs seeing to. Have you had trouble getting the pennies to drop?'

'Only when I've tried to hurry it,' said Emma.

'I'll get someone to look at it. I'd like to look myself, but I don't have the tools. Anyway, a fitter'll call, or I might just come back and fix it myself if it means keeping you waiting, otherwise.'

'As long as it's working, I shan't fuss,' said Emma.

'Nice to meet you, Mrs Carter. See you again in three months, if I don't see you before.'

'Goodbye,' said Emma. She saw him out and went back to her kitchen to finish clearing-up after biscuit-making. Through the help of a suffragette friend, she had just secured a little contract to supply three pounds of biscuits a week to the teashop near Camberwell Green. Wait till she told Sergeant Chamberlain.

Now why should she want to tell that particular gentleman?

'We're all goin' out Sunday afternoon,' said Trary, walking home with Bobby.

'You and your fam'ly?' said Bobby, matching his stride to her springy walk. Trary kind of bobbed and danced along, as if she was bursting with health. She looked that way too. Bobby didn't know any other Walworth girl with such a creamy complexion as Trary. She made him think about Devonshire cream. He'd never had any, but he'd heard it was a real treat. When he was earning enough, he meant to go to Devon and try that cream. He'd take Trary, of course. It wouldn't do to leave her behind. She'd get surrounded if he did. 'Well, I'm not sure you can go,' he said. 'I don't mind your fam'ly, but I don't know about you. I was thinkin' that on Sunday afternoon – '

'Here we go,' said Trary, rolling her eyes.

An approaching woman, noticing this, said, 'What's that Sunny Jim doin' to yer, love, tryin' to lead yer up the garden path, is 'e?'

'Yes, and round the mulberry bush as well,' said Trary.

'What a life for a gel,' said the woman, 'in for a penny, in for a pound, that's what I say. Wish I was you, love.' Laughing, she went on.

'Funny old girl,' said Bobby. 'What was I saying?'

'I'm sure I don't know,' said Trary, 'I'm just waitin' to suffer long speeches.'

'Oh, I know,' said Bobby, 'I was thinkin' that on Sunday afternoon you and me could wheel mum's handcart to the workhouse off the Old Kent Road. She's goin' to fill it with unrequired seconds that we don't want, and givin' them to the poor people in the workhouse.'

'Oh, that's ever so charitable, Bobby, I hope your mum gets blessed by the vicar, but can't you take them to the workhouse in the mornin'? Then you could come with us in the afternoon. Mr Bradshaw's comin' too.'

'Well, Sunday morning's busy down the market,' said Bobby. 'Tell you what, Trary, I'll get me dad to wheel the handcart. Yes, 'e can take the stuff to the workhouse. I'll tell him he won't get any Sunday dinner if he says no.'

'Oh, you are funny about your dad sometimes,' said Trary.

'I'm doin' my best,' said Bobby. 'Where you goin' to on Sunday afternoon, then?'

'It's a special outin',' said Trary. Her mum had said Bobby could be let into the secret if he wanted to come with them. 'I'll be in my Sunday best, I'm expectin' to look ravishin', so perhaps you'd better not walk with me, in case people wonder why a lovely girl like me has to put up with a talkin' hooligan like you. But you could walk with Lily, if you like, Lily never minds who she's with.'

'Well, I can't resist that,' said Bobby, 'I'll walk with Lily. I like Lily, we've had kisses. We could 'ave some more.'

'Cheeky beast,' said Trary, quivering with bliss because she'd found a boy utterly entertaining. 'I don't want you draggin' my little sister Lily into the bushes, thank you. I've heard about boys like you. Still, notwithstandin', you can – '

'Notwithstandin'?' said Bobby, showing his usual grin of admiration.

'Yes, you can come with us,' said Trary, 'we're leavin' after dinner, we're goin' to look at houses in Herne Hill.'

'What for?' asked Bobby.

'Mum's thinkin' she'd like us to move there.'

'Herne Hill?' said Bobby. 'She's goin' to rent a place in Herne Hill? It'll cost 'er a quid and more a week. That's disastrous, that is Trary. It's all over before we've 'ardly started.'

'What d'you mean?' asked Trary in alarm.

'Well, me here in Walworth, you miles away in Herne

291

Hill. You'll get a Herne Hill boy, I'll 'ave to look for a Walworth girl. That's grievin' news, Trary.'

More alarmed, Trary made the Elephant and Castle subway ring with indignation as she cried, 'Don't talk silly. I'm surprised at you, a boy your age talkin' as silly as that.'

'It's not silly, it's – '

'I'm not listening!' Trary mounted the exit steps with her nose high in the air.

Out in the sunshine, Bobby said, 'I'm only pointin' out – '

'If you go with other girls, Bobby Reeves, I'll never speak to you again! Oh, you blessed miserable boy, what about your dyin' promise never to let me walk home from school by meself? When I go to a new school, you've got to keep your promise, you've still got to come an' walk me home, so there!'

'At Herne Hill? 'Ave a heart, Trary. And I wouldn't be able to come once I started me apprenticeship, in any case.'

'Oh, you rotten squiffer,' said Trary, totally upset, 'you might as well say goodbye to me now, then. You're just talk, you are, like I've always said. Anyone would think Herne Hill was in Australia. I never thought you couldn't be faithful to your friends, I wonder you've got any. Don't you talk about not comin' to see me when it's only Herne Hill, or you can just go and – you Bobby, look at me when I'm talkin' to you, d'you hear?'

The schoolgirl was flushed, and Bobby had his cap pulled down to hide most of his face. People looked. Trary and Bobby were both oblivious.

'Well, Trary – '

Trary gave a tight, muffled little scream, 'Oh, you rotten 'ooligan, you're grinnin'!'

'Not much,' said Bobby, shifting his cap to the back of his head. 'The fact is – '

'I am not speakin' to you, and I'm not listening, either.'

'Your boater's nearly fallin' off, Trary. The fact is, nothing's goin' to – '

'You've been grinnin' all the time, I know you,' declared Trary, 'you're the most aggravatin' grinnin' boy I ever met.'

'Still, nothing's goin' to stop me comin' to see you, Trary.'

'What?' she said.

'Well, a man's got to stand up to fate's blows an' wallops. Herne Hill's a wallop, but I'll get over it somehow. A man's got to when his future wife counts as 'is life's work, yer know. He can't let himself be put off, or he wouldn't be worth a light.'

'Oh, you daft thing,' said Trary in a spasm of delight, 'walkin' me home from school don't make me your future wife.'

'Was that something I mentioned before?' asked Bobby.

'Yes, it was, you barmy boy. Bobby, are we goin' roller-skatin' again on Saturday, and can you definitely come with us on Sunday?'

'I can say I'd be honoured in both cases,' said Bobby. 'And I'll walk with Lily on Sunday, then you won't get looked at.'

'You're grinnin' again,' said Trary.

'Mrs Pankhurst has passionate convictions, yes, but I think Christabel's our real problem,' said Emma. It was Friday evening, and she had a visitor, a suffragette friend, Amy Wagstaff. 'Christabel sees herself as a modern Boadicea.'

'No, Mrs Pankhurst has to be our Boadicea,' said Amy.

'She won't be, not if Christabel gets to the chariot first,' said Emma. 'Then she'll mow down every man in sight.'

'Might do 'em good,' said Amy.

'Well, I suppose men generally aren't as nice as we are,' said Emma.

'No, they're jolly well not,' said Amy, clerk to a solicitor, 'they're far too aggressive. And there's a very nasty specimen lurking about in Southwark, isn't there?'

'I'm afraid there is,' said Emma, 'but my friends at Scotland Yard are preparing a noose for him, the monster.'

'You've friends at Scotland Yard? Policemen? Those wretched harassers of the suffragettes?' Amy looked a little disappointed in Emma.

'I do have an acquaintance, he's not quite – ' Emma was interrupted by a knock on her door. Another one? She thought immediately of Sergeant Chamberlain. A little smile arrived at a further thought, that of introducing him to Amy, given to dressing down policemen whenever she had the chance. 'Excuse me.' She got up and crossed the room. Opening the door she found not Sergeant Chamberlain, but the new meter man from the gas company, in a brown suit and Homburg.

'Evening, Mrs Carter, is it convenient to put your meter right? I've brought tools.' He had a tool bag in his hand. The street was in the first stage of darkness. 'Oh, sorry, you've got company,' he said, as he saw Amy.

'Never mind, you're here now,' said Emma.

'No, I'll come back some other time,' said Herbert Stephens, 'I don't want to disturb you. I know it's a bit late, but I thought – '

'It's all right, my friend won't mind. Just go through.' Emma stepped aside and he came in.

'Evening,' he said to Amy, 'nice night outside.'

'Cosy in here,' said Amy, and his mild blue eyes twinkled. He went through the room and to the meter outside the kitchen. Emma closed the dividing door and resumed her conversation with Amy.

'We really need more signatures,' she said, 'fifteen simply aren't enough.'

'I don't think we'll get more than two dozen,' said Amy, 'Mrs Pankhurst commands overwhelming loyalty. Oh, and I've heard, by the way, that Christabel is going to propose a motion calling for your eviction from the WSPU.'

'Oh, bother,' said Emma. 'Well, I shall fight it. How are things with you and Donald?'

'Going backwards,' said Amy. 'What a swine. He won't budge till I've given up votes for women, and I won't talk to him until he swears eternal support. Suffragettes shouldn't fall in love, it mucks everything up.'

The dividing door opened following a knock, and the meter man appeared, a triumphant smile on his face.

'Found the trouble, Mrs Carter. A little spring's got to be changed. I can get one from the store. But I've left the old one in for the time being, it'll last out. You can still put your pennies in. I'll get a fitter to bring a new spring, or again I don't mind popping in myself if I'm passing. I'll see what's quickest. Sorry I disturbed your evening. Goodnight.'

Emma opened the front door for him, 'Thanks, anyway,' she said.

'No bother, Mrs Carter.' He glanced at Amy. 'I don't like mentioning it, but your friend shouldn't leave it too late if she's got some walking to do. Well, you know what I mean.'

'It's all right, she's staying the night,' said Emma.

'Good idea,' said Stephens, and went on his way, whistling. In Browning Street, a man passed him. 'Nice night,' said Stephens cheerfully.

'Seen worse,' grunted the man, going on.

Charleston Street was quiet, the younger children in bed. Harry passed through the street on an overtime beat, from nine o'clock until midnight. Extra policing during these hours was taking place in Walworth.

A man slipped into the shadows of a doorway. He put his ear to the door and listened. He put his hand on the latchcord. If he could open the door silently, close it silently, and slip into the parlour, he could bide his time.

In the kitchen, Maggie said, 'Is the front door bolted, Trary?'

'I'll see,' said Trary.

'Harry – Mr Bradshaw – said we ought to keep it bolted at night.'

'Oh, did Harry say that, Mum?' said Trary with overdone innocence.

'Go on with you,' said Maggie, 'an' don't be familiar about your elders.'

Trary smiled and went along the passage to the front door. By the light of the gas lamp she thought she saw the latchcord move.

'Who's there, is that you, Mrs Phillips?' Their nosy neighbour was apt to pop in, whatever the hour, and cadge a bit of sugar or tea.

The latchcord was still. Trary opened the door. There was no-one there. She went to the gate and looked up and down the street. She saw no-one. Satisfied that her imagination had played tricks, she went back in and bolted the door.

She had no idea that her little intervention had saved her mother from being strangled in her bed.

A thirty-year-old woman of Wooler Street, not far from East Street, was not so lucky. She left a Walworth Road pub just before ten-thirty, when a little too much stout had made her quarrelsome enough to thump her husband and to stalk out, her hat askew on her tumbled mass of yellow hair. Her husband, bruised, and with everyone roaring with laughter, had a mind to let her do the walk home alone. But several minutes later, someone said, ' 'Ere, yer best get after 'er, Sid, she's a fine-lookin' gel, even if she did land yer a fourp'ny one.' He thought about it, finished his beer and went after her.

He made his way along the Walworth Road, went up through East Street, turned right into Portland Street, passed Trafalgar Street and reached the corner of Wooler Street, where he and his wife lived. He peered. Way down the street, at a spot opposite a lamp-post, a woman lay face down and inert. A man was down on one knee beside her, his hands at the back of her neck. Sid Hoskins stood paralysed for a moment. Then, shouting his lungs out, he pounded down Wooler Street. The man was up in a flash, haring away towards the maze of streets that crowded the neighbourhood. Sid Hoskins might have gone after him had it not been for the fact that when he reached the prone woman he found himself, as he had fearfully suspected he might, staring down at his wife, strangled to death outside their own house. Her hat was off, a strand of her yellow hair missing, and a stocking that had been gruesomely tight around her neck was partly loosened. A slipknot had made a noose of it, a noose the murderer had had to leave.

'Mrs Carter?'

Emma, at her counter, looked up. The floor-walker was addressing her.

'Yes, Mr Springer?'

'You can leave the counter for a moment. The gentleman over there would like a word with you.'

Emma glanced. She saw Nicholas, hat in hand. She went across to him.

'Good morning,' she said soberly.

'It's not too good,' he said.

'I know. I saw the *Stop Press* in my morning paper, and a customer showed me the early edition of the *Evening News*. I'm dreadfully down about it, dreadfully sorry. And you must be utterly sick.'

'We had extra uniformed men on the beat, but you can't station them in every street, or even every other street.' Nicholas was brooding. 'It's hell at the Yard, and it's hell in the home of the husband. He's blaming himself for not going after her as soon as she left the pub.'

'Then I'm terribly sorry for him, he has to live with that.'

'He can't even give us a decent description, except that

297

the size of the man tallies with the first description. About tonight – '

'I understand,' said Emma, 'the Alhambra's off.'

'This is going to be a twenty-four-hour day for me,' said Nicholas. 'I'm sorry.'

'Nicholas, I'm sorry too.' It was the first time she had used his Christian name. 'But I'm far sorrier for that poor woman and her husband than for missing the music hall. Please don't worry about that, it's trivial under the circumstances.'

'Yes. I can't stop. Must go. Take care.'

She saw that his collar had a crumpled look, and that his face was a little drained. He had probably been up all night. He and Inspector Greaves, and the whole of Scotland Yard, had the entire country on their backs now.

'Yes, I'll take care,' she said.

He left in an abstracted way, and Emma realized then just how much she had been looking forward to seeing Marie Lloyd, the queen of the music halls and the darling of the cockneys.

CHAPTER TWENTY-FOUR

Sunday afternoon was fine, if a little breezy. Fluffy white clouds sailed in from the east, and the winds of heaven blew them westwards, leaving huge patches of blue.

Harry led the way out of Herne Hill station. He had had a long week of duty. In six days, from Monday to Saturday, he had put in nearly sixty hours. Yesterday, Saturday, his stint had been ten hours. The latest murder had again meant the uniformed branch doing all it could to help the CID. The people of Walworth were rattled and complaining, and the local police as edgy as Scotland Yard. Friday's murder had been committed only a third of a mile from the Rodney Road police station.

Disastrous.

But today, Sunday, Harry was off duty. He walked between Daisy and Meg along Railton Road. Bobby followed with Lily. Behind them came Maggie and Trary, Maggie in her new silk dress and a new toque hat. She felt proud of her girls in their new frocks and new boaters. Bobby was right about Trary, she thought. Her eldest daughter did seem to be getting prettier all the time. She was watching Bobby, who had charge of Lily. Lily had beamed when he said he was going to walk with her. She was chattering nineteen to the dozen now. Maggie saw the little smile on Trary's face, and knew she was thinking that Lily's tongue had the beating of Bobby's at the moment.

'That boy, Mum,' said Trary out of the blue, 'he gave me the 'orrors when he walked me home on Thursday.'

'That's 'is latest, is it, givin' you the 'orrors on top of everything else?' said Maggie, eyeing houses with approval.

'There's no tellin' what that boy's capable of, Mum. When I told him we were thinkin' of moving, he said it was all over with us.'

'What was all over?' asked Maggie, trying, as usual, not to smile.

'Beg your pardon?' said Trary.

'What did he say was all over with you?'

'Oh, I'm sure I don't know,' said Trary casually, 'I hardly ever know what he's talkin' about.'

'What give you the 'orrors, then?'

'I can't remember now,' said Trary, trying to get out of the pit she had impulsively dug for herself. Not even to her mother would she admit that Bobby was her one and only. 'Still, he made up for it, takin' me roller-skatin' again yesterday. Oh, it really is fun. Anyway, Herne Hill's not all that far from Walworth, is it? We've got here easy on the train from the Elephant an' Castle.'

'Oh, I see,' said Maggie.

'What?' asked Trary.

'You're a bit young to be in love at thirteen, pet.'

'I'm fourteen, Mum. Well, nearly.'

'Yes, but it's still a bit young to – '

'Look, there are front gardens,' said Trary.

'Still, I suppose it's a nice feelin', even at fourteen, said Maggie, 'and you won't find a nicer boy. And he's got 'is head screwed on the right way.'

'Some head,' said Trary. 'Look, his cap's nearly fallin' off, it's always nearly fallin' off. I've spoken to him, but you know what he is, he just goes on talkin'. Now if his tongue fell off, I could deal with 'im a lot better.'

'You're so funny, pet,' said Maggie, 'you're a pair, you are, you an' Bobby.'

Harry, still leading the way with Daisy and Meg, stopped on the corner of a street. Sunday afternoon in Herne Hill seemed even quieter than in Walworth. There was just the little metallic sound of a hand-mower being used in someone's back garden. Harry turned, 'Here we

300

are, Maggie,' he said.

They all congregated on the corner, and Harry consulted a local paper he'd brought with him.

'Crikey, it's called Regent Road,' said Lily, 'ain't that posh, Bobby?'

'Well, nice,' said Bobby.

'Yes, nice, not posh,' said Meg, 'we can't live nowhere posh, we'd 'ave to 'ave servants.'

'Number ten,' said Harry, and they all walked to number ten. It was empty, its front garden a little overgrown. Maggie regarded the house, and thought its central door made it look quite grand. It was two storeys, not three, like most in the road. But the advertisement had said four bedrooms. Its blank windows shone in the sunlight. It looked much larger than their little house in Charleston Street. There was a bathroom too. Imagine that. They wouldn't have to go to the public baths any more, or use a scullery bath. Of course, they'd only come to look at it from the outside, to see if they liked its appearance.

Harry was making no comment. He knew it was up to Maggie and her girls. It was their choice, yes or no, not his.

But Maggie said, 'What d'you think, Harry?'

He didn't hesitate then, he said, 'Looks a good family house, Maggie, and two storeys would mean less work than any of these three-storeyed ones.'

'And what do you think, Bobby?'

'Well, Mrs Wilson, I'm glad you asked, I thought you wouldn't – '

'Here we go,' said Trary joyfully.

'I can't say I've got much experience about the best kind of 'ouses to buy,' said Bobby, 'so I can't say – '

'Not much,' said Trary.

'Yes, I can't say anything, Mrs Wilson, except I'd like a house just like this when we're married.'

'When who's married?' asked Lily.

'Me and me future wife,' said Bobby.

'Can you believe that boy, Mr Bradshaw?' said Trary. 'Can you believe what comes out of his mouth sometimes?'

'Trary's gone all pink,' said Daisy.

'She keeps doin' that,' said Lily.

'I suppose all future wives are a little shy,' said Harry.

'Mr Bradshaw, don't say things like that,' begged Trary, 'it'll only encourage him, he's daft enough, as it is. Mum, I like the house, don't you? I mean, I like the look of it, it looks as if it's got two parlours and lovely windows. And there's trees about. It's nice, Meg, don't you think it's nice?'

'Oh, crikey, fancy us livin' 'ere,' said Meg breathlessly.

'It's my opinion you've got a winner here, Mrs Wilson,' said Bobby, 'as long as it's all right inside.'

'Oh, I couldn't do without your opinion, Bobby,' smiled Maggie.

'My pleasure,' said Bobby. Trary rolled her eyes.

'Look, the side gate's open,' said Harry, 'let's see what the back garden's like.'

'I likes 'Arry,' said Daisy, taking hold of his hand.

'Will you stop callin' 'im that, you pickle?' said Maggie.

They all walked up the side path to the back garden. Everyone gazed at a long rectangular lawn of long uncut grass, a velvet green to their eyes. There were flower beds down each side, perennials sprouting amid burgeoning weeds.

'Mum, it's a real garden,' said Meg, 'it's got flowers and everything.'

'You could play cricket,' said Bobby.

'Could you come an' play wiv us?' asked Lily.

'Could you play wiv us too?' asked Daisy of Harry.

'They can come to Sunday tea,' said Maggie, eyeing the back of the house. Everything looked just right. 'What d'you think now, Harry?' The price of the house, according to the advertisement, was two hundred and ninety-five pounds. And the furniture could be offered for.

'I think you'd like to be shown round,' said Harry.

'You could come up during the week and get the agents to let you in.'

'Yes, I suppose so,' said Maggie.

'But, Mr Bradshaw, Mum couldn't come by herself,' protested Trary, 'she's only a woman – '

'Well, thanks very much, I don't think,' said Maggie.

'Oh, I don't mean you're not as good as a man, Mum, you can do lots of things men can't.' Trary's clear young voice sent echoes rippling around the garden. 'And I'm easy as good as Bobby. Well, I'm better, in fact, I'm more useful and I'm not barmy. But a woman ought to have a man with her if she's lookin' inside an empty house. There might be mice or spiders. Spiders give mum the 'orrors, Mr Bradshaw, and I wouldn't wish the 'orrors on anybody, I've had them myself just recent.'

'You didn't tell me,' said Lily.

'Nor me,' said Daisy.

'What 'orrors?' asked Meg.

'I'm over it now,' said Trary. She glanced at Bobby. He was looking up at chimney pots. He had a grin on his face. 'That boy,' she said.

'If all goes well, Maggie, I'll be off duty at three o'clock on Tuesday afternoon,' said Harry. 'Would that do?'

'I'd be ever so grateful,' said Maggie.

'I'll look after the spiders.'

'I'll look after Trary,' said Bobby.

'I won't be comin',' said Trary, 'I'll be at school.'

'I meant I'll look after you gen'rally,' said Bobby. 'I promised her I would, Mrs Wilson, an' she's relyin' on it. Well, she's still young yet, yer know. Can't believe it sometimes, can you, the looks she's got at her age. Fortunately, I've got manly vigour meself – '

Trary shrieked and clapped a hand to her mouth.

'Thank you, Bobby,' said Maggie, 'I need a bit of help with Trary sometimes. Well, we can all go 'ome now. Mr Bradshaw's stayin' to tea. Would you like to stay too, Bobby?'

'I'm honoured, Mrs Wilson.'

'I likes Bobby,' said Lily, taking his hand for the walk back to the station.

'Two talkin' parrots together, that's what you are,' said Trary.

Bobby grinned. Maggie smiled. She caught Harry's eye. He winked.

They were alone again in the parlour, after tea. Bobby and the girls were doing the washing-up once more. Trary had insisted. It was all part of her campaign.

'Maggie, if you buy the house, you'll have rates to pay,' said Harry.

'Will I?' said Maggie, as if she hadn't been aware of that. 'How much would they be?'

'A few shillings a week.'

'I think I could manage that, I won't be payin' no rent.'

'And there'd be a water bill, and any repairs or decoratin'. It'll be a bit of a financial responsibility, and you've only got your pension, haven't you?'

'I'll have a bit over from Uncle Henry's will.'

'Not much, I imagine.' Harry lit his pipe and mused over it. 'I did say buyin' a house is a sound investment, but not if you get into debt. You need to have money comin' in, Maggie. I was wondering.'

'About what?' smiled Maggie.

'Well, if you had a lodger, would his bit help?'

'What lodger?'

'I was thinkin', I've got my own house, I've paid off the mortgage, and I don't really need a house all to myself.'

'You're offerin' to be my lodger?' asked Maggie.

'If there's a room to spare and my rent would help, and if − '

'Is that the only way you'd live with me an' the girls, as our lodger?'

'I'd miss you all otherwise,' said Harry.

'What kind of a miss would it be?' asked Maggie.

'Like a ruddy great hole in my life,' said Harry.

'Bless the man,' murmured Maggie, 'he loves Trary, that's what it is.'

'I love all your girls, Maggie.'

'And what about me?' Her faint smile showed. 'Or don't I count?'

'I love you too, Maggie, don't you know that?'

'Well, then?' Her smile became affectionate. 'You're not just goin' to sit there, are you?' Harry put his pipe aside and stood up. Maggie made her comparison. Yes, Harry was a far nicer man than Mr Jerry Bates. He was quieter, but he wasn't dull, and the girls thought him fun. 'Harry, why don't you try givin' me a kiss? I'm not an old woman yet, I've still got feelings.'

'So have I,' said Harry fervently, and kissed her with great feeling. Maggie knew then that here was a man she could be a lover to. When Mr Bates kissed her, she'd felt natural pleasure. But not excitement, not need. With Harry, her healthy body came alive, and she pressed herself close to him. There had been too many years of having no-one to make love to her.

Harry lifted his head and said, 'I want you Maggie.'

'You'll do, Harry love,' she said, 'you'll do for all of us.'

'The girls won't mind.'

'Oh, go on with you, you know they can't wait for you to be their new dad.'

Trary danced in delight at the news. Daisy and Lily looked awe-struck at the prospect of having a policeman for a dad. Meg asked him for a kiss and got one. Bobby said, 'I hardly know what to say, Mrs Wilson, not on an 'istorical day like this.'

'Well, go on, make it hysterical,' said Trary.

'If I could try an' say something?' said Bobby.

'Oh, our pleasure,' said Trary, blissful for her mum.

'Well, I'll just say you've picked a real 'andsome future wife, Mr Bradshaw. Mind, I'm not surprised, you're a thinkin' man, an' with good sense as well as good taste. I couldn't be more short of breath about you an' Mrs Wilson – '

'Not much,' said Trary.

'Which reminds me, Mrs Wilson,' said Bobby, 'could I ask you about me own future wife? I mean, would you mind tellin' me if she puts curlers in her 'air at nights?'

Trary shrieked at him. Bobby ran for his life. Trary caught him before he could get through the door. She dealt with him.

Daisy, agog, asked, 'What's Trary 'itting Bobby for?'

'Girls always 'ave to 'it boys they're in love with,' said Meg. 'Well, you do 'ave to or they get cheeky. I expect when mum gets married, she'll 'ave to 'it our new dad with a rollin'-pin.'

'Oh, you 'orror,' said Maggie.

'Only now and again,' said Meg.

'Like Mrs 'Arper does wiv Mr 'Arper,' said Lily.

'I likes 'Arry for our new dad,' said Daisy. 'I don't want 'im 'it wiv no rollin'-pin.'

'Bless you, Daisy,' said Harry.

Friday, thought Nicholas, as he walked down Browning Street, always on a Friday. Something nagged at his mind. What was it? Damn it, what was it?

Scotland Yard was beginning to believe that the man wasn't local, after all, that he was coming in from distant fields. The Assistant Commissioner, concerned with the public's worry and dissatisfaction, had now authorized the police to offer a reward of five hundred pounds for information that would lead to the apprehension of the killer, wherever he lived.

Emma appeared, turning into Browning Street from King and Queen Street. It gave Nicholas a lift to see her. The skirt of her light grey dress swirled gently around her ankles. Her neat matching hat had a single white feather. She had been a shop assistant in Reading, she was a shop assistant now. But how elegant.

She stopped and smiled as they met.

'Hello, you're going out?' asked Nicholas.

'I am out,' said Emma. 'Were you coming to call on me?'

'No, to talk to a couple of uniformed men at the police station.'

'Yes, I see,' she said, feeling a little rebuffed. A breeze picked up dust from the middle of the street and redistributed it. 'I'm just on my way to visit a friend in Denmark Hill.'

'How long for?' asked Nicholas.

'Pardon?'

'What time will you be back?'

'Dear me,' she said, 'am I being interviewed again?'

'Mrs Carter – '

'My name's Emma, as you well know. Please don't be so stuffy, Nicholas. It isn't the thing around here.'

'It's a habit with every copper to be formal with the public,' said Nicholas.

'Heavens,' said Emma, 'I thought I'd become a friend, I'd no idea I was still the public.'

'D'you mind if I ask you what time you'll be back from your outing?'

'Really, I – ' Emma pulled herself up. He looked tired out. Two murders and one attempted murder, and there was still no arrest. 'I'm sorry, I know how you must be feeling. I'll be back about nine, just before dark.'

'I'll be at the tram stop, waiting for you,' said Nicholas. 'If you're late, if it is dark when you get back, I'll run you in for failing to co-operate with the police.'

'You're not serious,' said Emma. A passing neighbour said hello to her and gave Nicholas an interested look. Emma knew she was being talked about. Cockneys, in and out of each other's houses, always liked to know what their neighbours were getting up to. 'You're not keeping a watch on every woman in Walworth, are you?'

'No, only you,' said Nicholas, 'you don't happen to be every woman, just yourself. Why isn't your fiancé going with you to Denmark Hill?'

'Oh, you've given me a fiancé now, have you?'

'I've assumed he's your fiancé, or close to the privilege.'

Oh, bother, thought Emma, this is getting ridiculous. 'He's not my fiancé, or about to be,' she said.

'Well, be back at nine, Emma,' he said firmly.

'You're really going to be waiting at the tram stop?'

'Yes.'

She smiled. 'I'll be a good girl,' she said, and they parted.

She felt guilty on her way back. She was late, after all. But the discussion with her friend had been so stimulating that she'd overstayed. It was well after nine when the tram reached Manor Place, and dusk had arrived. Nicholas was there, waiting. She smiled brightly as she alighted.

'Thank goodness I'm not late,' she said, seeing his grim look.

'You're late all right, and you know it,' he said. He had spent the evening at the police station, going through all the latest reports from the uniformed branch.

'What's the time, then?' she asked, as she crossed the Walworth Road with him.

'Nine-thirty.'

'Oh, dear.'

'Never mind oh dear, Emma, you're under arrest.'

They entered Browning Street.

'I'm what?' said Emma.

'Just a case of locking you up until we've caught this man.'

'Locking me up? You're joking.'

'It's no joke,' he said, 'I ought to lock you up.'

'But we were talking about our next rally,' said Emma, 'and about the suffragettes who broke windows in Whitehall yesterday. Of course, although broken windows aren't terribly militant – '

'Don't let me catch you at it,' said Nicholas, 'the women concerned were arrested.'

'Yes, poor things. You're very hard on them.'

'They wanted to be arrested.'

'Yes, it's necessary publicity. Nicholas, I'm really very sorry I was later than I promised, but when two suffragettes get together to solve the problems caused by envious men – '

'Envious?'

'Well, yes,' said Emma sweetly, 'we don't have hairy legs or bald heads, but we do have many virtues. We don't bully old ladies or weak widows, and – '

'What weak widows?'

'Me, for one,' said Emma, and Nicholas was hard put not to pick her up and run off with her. 'And you know very well our home-made biscuits and fruit cakes are the products of kitchen genius. Oh, did I tell you I've a little contract for supplying biscuits to the teashop near Camberwell Green? What do you think of that?'

'Triumph of kitchen genius.'

'Yes, I'm glad you believe in women.' They turned into King and Queen Street. A house curtain fluttered. Emma smiled. *Who was that gent I saw yer walkin' 'ome with last night, Emma?* A policeman. *Lord 'elp yer, love, you don't go out with a policeman, do yer?* I wouldn't mind occasionally. *Gawd save yer, ducks, watch out for 'is 'ands, every copper's got 'eavy ones.* 'Nicholas, you must come to our next rally and speak your mind to Christabel.'

'And get eaten alive?' said Nicholas. 'Is that what you'd like?'

'Actually, I think you could surprise her. You're quite a nice policeman, and a quite reasonable man. And you don't have horns.' They reached her door. 'Thank you for meeting me, I do understand your concern.'

'Take care,' he said. 'Goodnight.'

'Goodnight? Shame on you. Come in, and I'll make a pot of tea. And you can talk to me about this awful murder case. Well, as much as you're allowed to. I can be a good listener, really.'

What he told her over the pot of tea was not of any great account, since the whole case had become enveloped in fog. Not a single person in South London had been able to point a finger at the right man. Inspector Greaves was beginning to believe he came from north of the river. Nicholas still stuck to his conviction that the answer lay in Walworth, that Mabel Shipman had visited the man there. There was one difference about the second murder. The maniac had strangled his victim with a stocking, not a length of cord.

'Why would he have done that?' asked Emma.

'He used a length of cord on the young woman he attacked in Manor Place. She was positive about that. The cord failed him on that occasion. I can imagine him brooding on that failure.'

'So he used a stocking instead?' said Emma. 'Then he's probably a married man, isn't he? He probably used one of his wife's stockings.'

'Emma, you're a clever girl,' said Nicholas.

'Oh, you're not so bad yourself, you know.'

'I'm not a clever girl.'

'Yes, how very nice that you happen to be a man,' said Emma.

'Nice for whom?' asked Nicholas.

'Oh, for all women who don't think every man is a

gorilla,' said Emma.

She awoke at midnight. She sat up with a start. What had woken her? Either a noise or a bad dream? What had she been dreaming about? A gallows, a noose and a hanging body. A woman's body. And the noose had been a stocking.

No, there was a noise, a faint metallic noise travelling through the silent house. It sounded like a key being repeatedly turned in the lock of her front door. And the front door was bolted. She had taken to doing that, because a certain sergeant from Scotland Yard would bully her if she didn't.

She slipped from her bed, the linoleum cool to her bare feet as she crossed to her window. Her heart beating a little too fast for her liking, she silently eased the bottom frame up and put her head out. A distant street lamp cast its pool of light, but it did not reach her house, which lay in darkness. But with eyes adjusted to the night, she was able to see there was no-one below, no-one at her door, no-one within vision. Old and dilapidated Walworth was asleep, its resilient men and women, and their boisterous children, wrapped up in their beds.

She closed the window, walked to her bedroom door and opened it. She stood listening. There was complete quiet. Her dreams had played tricks with her ears. She went back to her bed and back to sleep. Emma Carter was not a woman who frightened easily.

The fluttery wife woke up.

'Herby, where you been?'

'Downstairs. It's all right.'

'Haven't you been to bed yet?'

'For a bit, but I couldn't sleep. I made myself some tea

and did some reading. That's a good book of yours, *The Mayor of Casterbridge*.'

'Was it your back again?'

'I'm putting up with it.' He settled into the bed. 'Go to sleep, Maudie.'

'Yes, all right, Herby.'

CHAPTER TWENTY-FIVE

'You're gettin' quite reliable,' said Trary, as she walked away from the school gate with Bobby. Other girls were watching. Some were giggling. Bobby was a familiar figure now, and she knew that more than one girl had an eye for him. 'Not many boys are reliable.'

'Yes, I'm pretty good,' said Bobby.

'You've said that before.'

'It's self-confidence,' said Bobby, 'you need to 'ave a fair bit of that, or you don't get on.'

'Bless the boy,' said Trary, 'he's showin' off again.'

'I've been thinkin' lately about our destiny,' said Bobby.

'Our what?'

'Well, you an' me, Trary, we met our destiny, yer know, when I had that Salvation Army box on me loaf of bread.'

'Our destiny? Oh, you daft thing, destiny's just something that you read about in books.'

'That's printed in books, Trary. I'm talkin' about the book of life.'

'You're potty,' said Trary.

'Well, I've got to admit it,' said Bobby, 'I'm potty about you. I don't know it's believable, the way a feller can go off 'is chump when he meets a destiny like you. I 'ardly know what I'm eatin' sometimes, and sometimes I don't know if I've eaten or not. D'you feel like that about our destiny?'

'Oh, you barmy boy, girls don't meet their destiny when they're only fourteen, and I will be fourteen next month. It's June twelve.'

'I'll make a note,' said Bobby, 'I'll try an' get a card with words about destiny comin' but once in a lifetime. Incidental, I saw your mum down the market this mornin'. She said she's goin' to buy that house, she an' Mr Bradshaw looked it over yesterday afternoon. She told me she'd been left a bit of money. I told 'er I was downright rapturous for her. Well, I'm fond of your mum, if I'd been older an' she'd been younger – '

'You've said that before too. I was goin' to tell you about the house, but all this talkin' you keep doin', I know it's goin' to send me deaf and dumb one day.'

'Well, don't worry, you'll still be my girl. I'm goin' to miss you when you move.'

'But you're goin' to come and see me, aren't you? Bobby, you promised.'

'Every day,' he said.

'Every day?'

'Well, every week.'

'Yes, every week sounds more sensible,' said Trary, 'specially when you start workin' at the *Daily Mail*. I suppose I could get to like you one day, some girls do get to like daft boys.'

'Yes, I'm fairly likeable,' said Bobby. 'On Satudays, of course, we'll go roller-skatin'.'

'Oh, Bobby, yes,' she said. Every time roller-skating was mentioned, Trary fell over her tongue. 'But you keep payin' for me, and you can't have much money.'

'I've got what mum pays me, and it's me pleasure to treat you. On Sunday afternoons, we'll go walkin' out round Herne Hill.'

'Bobby, you cuckoo, people our age don't walk out. We just do walkin', not walkin' out.'

'It's our destiny,' said Bobby.

'Well, just don't get any more tonsillitis,' said Trary, 'or our destiny might finish up under the doctor. Well, yours will.'

Two women, coming up from the subway, encountered

a boy and girl going down who were laughing their heads off.

Emma opened the door to Nicholas.

'That's quick,' she said, 'I only left the police station half an hour ago.'

'And I left Detective-Constable Chapman there only five minutes ago,' said Nicholas. 'We had to call in, and I was given your message.'

'Come in,' said Emma.

Nicholas, entering, said, 'Why did you ask to see me again, Emma? Don't tell me you're actually going to give me a lead.'

'A clue, you mean? I wish I could. It's just that I'm wondering if I shouldn't have treated your concern about me more seriously. I think someone tried to get into the house on Monday night.'

'Monday night? It's Wednesday afternoon now.'

'Yes, I know.'

'Well, damn it all,' said Nicholas in exasperation.

'Oh, dear,' said Emma.

'Emma, for God's sake, you should have reported it immediately, you know that.'

'But it was after midnight, and at the time I felt it was my imagination.' Emma recounted the incident. 'I felt then that I must have imagined it, but it kept coming back into my mind, and now I feel it wasn't my imagination, I feel sure someone was trying to open the door and getting impatient.'

'It's taken you two whole days to reach that conclusion?' said Nicholas.

'You're bullying me again,' said Emma, 'what am I going to do with you?'

'More to the point, what am I going to do with you? Oh, hell, he's changed the pattern again. First a stocking instead of a cord, now Monday night instead of Friday night, and an attempted entry instead of keeping to the streets.'

'Nicholas, you don't know it was him.'

'I'd be a fool if I thought otherwise. Emma, you're absolutely sure you heard the sound of a key in your lock?'

'The more I think about that sound, the surer I am,' said Emma. 'Oh, wait!' she exclaimed on a sudden thought. She dashed into her kitchen. She searched a shelf of her dresser. Then all the other shelves. She went back to Nicholas. 'I think, I only think, that I might be able to point you at the man you want.'

'What?' Nicholas put his hands on her arms, just below her shoulders. She winced a little at the tightness of his grip. 'Emma, what did you say?'

'If you'd stop trying to pull my arms off?' she said. He released her. 'Look, I keep my spare doorkey on a shelf of my kitchen dresser. I rarely have any need of it, I rarely even notice it. One doesn't, one takes it for granted. But it's not there now, I've searched all the shelves, and it's missing. I know I haven't moved it, but I think I know who did, I think I know who has it. I should have thought about it each time the incident returned to my mind, each time I became surer that someone was using a key. I should have thought about whether or not it was my key, my spare key.'

'Not necessarily. You might have thought of a bunch of keys, and a man trying them one at a time.' Nicholas was tense. 'Emma, who is the man?'

Emma sat down, eyes wide and large, the electricity of little shocks attacking her body. The man, the one the police desperately wanted, had he actually been in her house?

She spoke slowly, telling Nicholas of the gas company meter man, a man new to the round, whom she recognized as the husband of a woman customer at Hurlocks. The woman wanted a beige blouse, and while she was in the fitting room, her husband, who was buying it for her as a birthday present, also purchased a pair

316

of silk stockings for her as a surprise extra. When he was emptying her meter, he found something wrong with it.

'I wonder,' said Nicholas.

Emma wondered too. Anyway, the man promised to get a fitter to call, or to come and do it himself. He did come himself, on Friday evening, just as darkness fell.

'Friday,' said Nicholas.

'Yes,' said Emma. 'I had a friend with me. Amy Wagstaff. I thought it kind of him to come in his own time, that he was doing me a favour because I'd served him that day at Hurlocks.'

'Emma, didn't you realize it was highly suspicious, calling to fix your meter at that time of night? No gas company would approve that, nor would they except as an emergency, and even then they'd send a fitter, not a collector.'

'I simply thought he was doing me a good turn,' said Emma. 'I left him to it. After a little while he said he'd found that a little spring needed replacing. He said he'd get one from the store and call back again, or get a fitter sent. I haven't seen him since. But I'm sure he's the one who's got my spare key, that he saw it and took it while I was talking to Amy. Nicholas, there's another thing I've just thought of. On his way out he said it would be a good thing if Amy didn't leave it too late if she had to walk to the tram stop. "You know what I mean," he said.'

'That was to find out when he could count on you being alone,' said Nicholas.

'I told him Amy was staying the night, which she did.'

'Emma, that saved you. He had your key, undoubtedly. He'd have come back. But knowing your friend was still with you, he didn't. He waited until Monday night. My guess is that you'll see him again on Friday evening, when he'll tell you he's brought the new spring.'

317

'Yes, he did say the meter was all right for the time being. That, I suppose, was to keep me from reporting it to the gas company.'

Nicholas regarded her soberly. She was a marked woman, after all, probably from the time when he'd been at her counter in Hurlocks. Her hair, her bright shining hair. He must have followed her home when she left Hurlocks. He was new to the round? There was something to think about in that.

'Emma, you precious woman, you've blown the fog away.'

'My word, you're letting yourself go, aren't you, Sergeant Chamberlain?' said Emma.

'I daresay I am. I'm charged up. Suddenly, Emma, we're on top of him. You said he bought his wife a pair of silk stockings as a surprise present. Can you remember the colour?'

'Black,' said Emma.

'It was a black silk stocking that was found around the neck of Mrs Blanche Hoskins,' said Nicholas. Frustrated by the presence of Amy Wagstaff, the meter man had been denied his planned target. Mrs Hoskins was the victim of that frustration. Nicholas felt positive about that.

'Oh, my heavens,' breathed Emma, visibly shaken at last.

'Inspector Greaves has it. Our maniac made a noose of it, and pulled it so tight he left a deep weal and the mark of the slipknot. But after he'd cut off a strand of her hair, he couldn't get the noose off in time, he had to leave it. The Inspector's had men doing the rounds of shops all over South London to try to trace the sale of the stocking.'

'Most good shops stock that brand,' said Emma, 'but as far as I know the men haven't reached Hurlocks yet. Nicholas, there's another thing I remember. It's something that doesn't quite fit. The man's wife said he had a bad

318

back. Oh, and she called him Herby. That would be Herbert, wouldn't it?'

'Emma, you're worth your weight in gold. A bad back?' Another little light clicked on. He had seen that mentioned in some report, a husband with a bad back. And something else. What was it? Something that had been nagging at his mind? 'Emma, I'm going to the police station to telephone the Yard, and then I'm going to call on the man's wife.'

'Aren't you going to the gas company's office, to find out who he is, and where he is now? They'll know who's on this round, and he'll be emptying meters somewhere in Walworth.'

'I'd rather call on his wife first. I think I can find out her name and address, from a report I've seen. Let's leave our suspect in blissful ignorance for the moment. I want a search made of his house, I want enough evidence to make an arrest on more than suspicion alone. I want that bugger, Emma – '

'Pardon?' said Emma.

'Yes, excuse my French. I wonder, did his wife receive those silk stockings? And did he enjoy buying them from a counter assistant he intended to strangle? God, what an escape you've had. Never mind. Put your hat on.'

'I'm to come with you?'

'You're safer with me, and you'll be able to tell me if the woman I'm going to interview is the one who called her husband Herby and said he had a bad back.'

'Very well, Nicholas,' said Emma, 'the chase is hotting up, isn't it?'

'Yes, and you lit the fire, Emma.'

From Rodney Road police station, Nicholas telephoned the Yard. He remembered one thing about the report concerning a husband who had a bad back, that the address was Amelia Street, not far, by Christ, from Steedman Street, where Mabel Shipman had been murdered.

Through to the Yard, he asked for Inspector Greaves. The Inspector was out, interviewing a shop manageress in Kennington, who recalled selling black silk stockings to a man a few weeks ago. Nicholas spoke to a detective-constable, referred him to reports covering Amelia Street, and asked him to dig out the one in which a housewife had said her husband hardly ever went out because of his bad back. The report was found, the constable rang back and gave Nicholas its details. The woman's name was Mrs Maud Stephens, her husband was Herbert Stephens, and the address was number twenty-two. Yes, she had referred to his bad back, and said he never went out in the evenings, but sometimes went with er to the market on Saturday afternoons. She didn't o out much herself, except to see her mother once week.

That was it, that was what had been the nagging something. Which day of the week was it, and was it during the evening? The report didn't say. But it did mention that Mr Stephens worked for the gas company as a collector.

'Right,' said Nicholas, 'the moment Inspector Greaves is in touch, let him know I'm going to twenty-two Amelia Street to interview Mrs Stephens on the grounds that her husband's our prime suspect.'

'Prime? I'll inform 'im accordin'.'

'Chapman's arranging a search warrant.'

'Good luck, sarge.'

On the way to Amelia Street with Emma, Nicholas said, 'With just a little luck, we've got him.'

'You need luck now?'

'You've pointed us at him, but nothing you've said is real evidence.' They entered the Walworth Road. 'Keep your fingers crossed that we'll find some.'

'What are you going to look for?' asked Emma. 'A stocking that matches the one you found around that poor woman's neck?'

'That and other things,' said Nicholas, thinking of a cord, a notebook, a mackintosh and locks of fair hair. They crossed the road amid slow-moving horse traffic. When they reached Amelia Street, he stopped.

'What now?' asked Emma, her heart beating a little fast.

'We're waiting for Frank Chapman and a search warrant.'

Amelia Street had its quota of Victorian terraced houses. A few women were gossiping at open doors. Another woman, carrying a straw shopping bag, turned into the street from the corner opposite Nicholas and Emma. Emma glanced at her and recognized immediately the fluttery woman who had come to her counter to ask for a beige blouse. She even walked in a fluttery way.

'Nicholas, that's Mrs Stephens. At least, it's the woman I served.'

'Good on yer, Mrs Carter, you're a born help to the law.'

'You know, I like talking to you,' said Emma.

'You like taking me to pieces, you mean,' said Nicholas, his eyes following the woman.

'That's not true.'

'No, not all the time. Sometimes you give me tea and cake.' He watched Mrs Stephens turn in to her door and pull on a latchcord. Latchcords proliferated in Walworth. She disappeared into her house. 'Good,' he said, 'now we know she's in.'

They waited. It was a little while before Chapman arrived, another plain-clothes man with him. The search warrant had been secured. Emma walked with the three men to number twenty-two, doorstep women watching them.

Mrs Stephens, opening her door to a knock, stared at the three men and a lady attired in a grey hat and a dark grey white-cuffed dress.

'Mrs Stephens?' said Nicholas.

321

'Yes?' A worried look appeared.

'Police, Mrs Stephens. CID.' Nicholas showed her his card.

'What d'you want?' she asked in a rush of anxiety.

'May we come in?'

'What for?'

'We've a warrant to search your house, Mrs Stephens.'

She sagged in shock. Emma at once came to her help, putting an arm around her and assisting her into the parlour. Nicholas followed, gave the unfortunate lady a few moments to recover, then began to ask questions as kindly as he could.

'Mrs Stephens, I believe you visit your mother once a week. Which day do you go?'

'Fridays,' she said palely.

'Friday evenings?'

'Yes.' Her mouth twitched. 'I stay until my husband collects me.'

'What time would that be, Mrs Stephens?' asked Nicholas, thinking of an absent wife and a husband free to do as he wished.

Mrs Stephens swallowed, her throat working convulsively. 'He lets me stay late. My mother likes a long chat, and don't like going early to bed.'

'So your husband calls for you at about what time usually?'

'Between half-eleven and quarter to twelve, and never lets me down. Why d'you want to search our house?' Her anxiety was acute, her apprehension visible.

'We've reason to believe we need to,' said Nicholas. Emma, seated on a sofa beside the woman, felt distressed for her. Nicholas, for all his experience, felt his lot was a bitter one now, for he knew that there was no way to save the peace of mind of a woman whose husband was going to be accused of murder. 'Mrs Stephens, do you wear silk stockings?'

'Silk stockings? Me?' She stared up at him, her body trembling, her face very pale. Then, looking as if she suddenly believed her answer would put everything right, she said, 'I've never had any silk stockings, except at my weddin' fourteen years ago, when I wore a lovely white pair.'

Noting her hair, a mousy brown, Nicholas asked, 'Hasn't your husband ever given you a pair as a birthday present, say?'

'Herby couldn't afford silk stockings, not on his wages. No, he's never been able to buy me any, so I don't wear any. What's all these questions about? You've got to tell me.'

'I'm not able to tell you yet, Mrs Stephens, only that we do have to search your house.' Nicholas was as gentle as he could be. Emma thought him compassionate, and liked him the more for it.

'Shall I sit and talk with her?' she asked.

Chapman and the other man looked at Nicholas. Mrs Carter was not a policewoman and she might say something she shouldn't to Mrs Stephens. Their glance cut no ice with Nicholas. He knew Emma.

'Yes, look after her, Mrs Carter,' he said. 'Oh, by the way, Mrs Stephens, was your husband out on Monday night?'

She looked pathetically relieved to be able to say, 'No, he wasn't, he was here with me all evening till we went to bed about eleven o'clock. He had to get up after a while, though, his back was bad. He's had a chronic back this last year and more. He didn't wake me, he's considerate like that, he went downstairs and made himself some tea and did some reading in the kitchen. I did wake when he come back to bed, though.'

'What time was that?'

'Just gone one o'clock, it was, I looked at the alarm clock, its figures glow in the dark. Anyway, he didn't go out, not at anytime that evening.'

'Thanks, Mrs Stephens,' said Nicholas, thinking of Emma's declaration that she was sure someone tried to get into her house just after midnight. King and Queen Street was less than a quarter of a mile from Amelia Street. 'We'll carry out the search now, we'll try not to take too long.'

The search began. They quickly brought to light a dark mackintosh, two flat caps, a Homburg hat, and boots and shoes with rubber soles. Some of these items were relevant, but no real evidence by themselves, they were common to many men. The search became exhaustive in every room, including the parlour, where Emma was doing her best to comfort the now petrified Mrs Stephens. It wasn't possible for any Walworth woman at this time not to associate the questions and the search with a murder investigation.

A frustration, not uncommon to the case, began to show in the CID men. No black silk stocking, no length of cord, no notebook and no locks of hair. Nicholas, in the kitchen for a second time, said in a suppressed voice to Chapman, 'Climb up that damned chimney.'

'Don't be funny,' said Chapman sourly.

'Take a look,' said Nicholas, and prowled around restlessly. He stopped at the window. It was covered by a wooden-slatted Venetian blind. He opened up the half-closed slats and saw a small wooden shed in a corner of the yard. He went out fast through the back door, Chapman following. The shed door was padlocked. Nicholas returned to the parlour.

'Mrs Stephens, where's the key to your shed padlock?'

Mrs Stephens, shaking, whispered faintly, 'It's my husband's shed, it's only where he keeps his tools and does bits of carpentry.'

'Yes, but where's the key?'

'Herby keeps all his keys on his key ring.'

'I see.' Nicholas went back to the yard, where Chapman was trying to pick the padlock. The other detective-constable came down from upstairs and joined them. Nicholas said get the damned door open. The padlocked holding bar was levered free by use of the kitchen poker. Wood splintered. Chapman pulled the door open and Nicholas went in. The shed was a little workshop. He searched but found nothing of any consequence. In the confined space, Chapman was in his way. He elbowed him aside and went down on his hands and knees. He fished about under the bench's low shelf. Nothing except dust. But then his fingers touched something. He scrabbled at it, moving it. He drew it out, a biscuit tin that had lain against the shed wall. He placed it on the bench, Chapman and his colleague squeezing in and looking on as he took the lid off. The white tin interior shone. One by one, he extracted the items it contained. A long length of cord, weighted at one end with a small disc of lead. Two tresses of fair hair, each wrapped in tissue paper. A little notebook with a red leather cover. Nicholas thumbed through it. Names and addresses were neatly inscribed. Nicknames. Mabel Shipman's code words for her clients. *Ginger, Four-Eyes, Napoleon, Larky, Saucebox, Bigfeet, Smiffy.* He came across the one he was looking for, *Samson. 22 A. Street, Walworth.*

'Got him, Frank.'

'Ruddy good,' said Chapman, 'my bleedin' feet are killin' me.'

Nicholas put some final questions to the sick and suffering Mrs Stephens.

'Is your husband at work?'

'Yes. Oh, me gawd, it's not about the murders, is it? This lady won't say. It's not about them poor women, is it?'

'I'm afraid it is, Mrs Stephens. What time are you expecting your husband home?'

Mrs Stephens, close to fainting, sagged on the sofa, her mouth working. Emma, an arm around her, said, 'She told me Mr Stephens said he'd be a bit late this evening, he has overtime to do.'

'Oh, Herby didn't do it, he didn't, did he?' gasped the anguished woman.

'We'll be talking to him, Mrs Stephens,' said Nicholas. 'Don't you think it would be a good idea to go to your mother's? Mrs Carter and I will take you. Where does she live?'

Her mouth worked again without finding speech.

'Penrose Street,' said Emma, into whose ears Mrs Stephens had poured a jumbled mass of desperate words.

'That's not too much out of our way,' said Nicholas. There was plenty of time to get to the gas company and to wait until Stephens reported in with his day's collection. 'Mrs Stephens, we'll wait while you get yourself ready. I don't think you should stay here. I'll be leaving one man in the house, and sending another to join him, just in case your husband should arrive home early. Better for you to go to your mother's.'

Emma wanted to weep for the suffering woman.

CHAPTER TWENTY-SIX

He stopped at the door of fifteen King and Queen Street.
He knocked, then opened up his works book, took a pencil
out from under the side of his peaked cap, and made a
note while resting the book against the door. He turned
to glance casually up and down the street. There were
people at the far end, the market end. And there were
two little kids walking towards Browning Street with their
backs to him. He stood there, his right hand behind him,
book in his left hand. His right hand moved. He turned
to the door again, and knocked a second time. Again he
turned his back to it, whistling. The door opened. He
wheeled round.

'Afternoon, Mrs Carter.'

He stepped into the empty house.

The door closed.

Nicholas and Chapman were on their way to the offices
of the gas company. Emma was still with them. There were
two CID men lying in wait in the Stephens' house. Mrs
Stephens was with her mother in Penrose Street, both
women in a state of shock.

'I'm so sad for her,' said Emma.

'Yes,' said Nicholas, 'some people get worked up about
what the law does to crooks and thugs and murderers.
Not too many think about the victims or about the suffering
a murderer inflicts on his womenfolk. Frank, would you
take Mrs Carter home now? I'll pick up a uniformed man
on my way to the gas company.'

'I'm dismissed?' said Emma in relief.

'Frank will look after you,' said Nicholas.

'Yes, very well.'

'I want to be sure of picking Stephens up. He told his wife he's on overtime this evening. But is he? We didn't find a second stocking.'

'So what's on his mind?' asked Chapman.

'Something unpleasant if he's not doing overtime,' said Nicholas. 'Many thanks, Mrs Carter, for all your help. You deserve a medal. Take care of her, Frank.'

'Right,' said Chapman, 'and I'll see you later.'

Emma did not argue for feminine independence.

'Stephens, you said?' queried the gas company superintendent.

'Yes, what's he like?' asked Nicholas, a police constable at his side. He had managed to pick up Harry, a reliable man.

'He's a muscular man with a bad back,' said the superintendent. 'He thinks he could have been a Samson at weightliftin' if it hadn't been for that.'

Samson. The little notebook. The nicknames.

'When's he due in with his collecting bag?'

'He's been in, he's finished his round for the day.'

'What?'

'At half-three, thirty minutes ago. I let him go, his back was playing up, and he's a good worker – '

'Christ,' said Nicholas.

'What's the problem?' asked the superintendent.

'This is a murder enquiry. We need to take Stephens in for questioning.'

'Eh?'

'Can't talk to you now,' said Nicholas. He left at speed, Harry with him. 'Step on it, Harry. To Mrs Carter's. The bugger's slipped us, and she's his current target. Thank God Chapman's with her. If he got into her house while she was out, then she and Chapman walked in on him.'

'You think he was goin' to go for Mrs Carter in her own house, in the middle of the afternoon?' said Harry. They were striding fast. Street kids watched them out of cheeky, curious or furtive eyes.

'God knows what he had in mind, he told his wife he'd be late home because of overtime. He'll have reached Mrs Carter's house in front of her and Chapman if he went straight there after finishing his round. He's got her spare key. I've a feeling he didn't go home. If he did, then he's done for.'

'I don't think he'd have gone for Mrs Carter in the middle of the afternoon, sarge,' said Harry. 'He'd have left himself wide open, someone's bound to have seen him comin' or goin'.'

'Keep moving,' said Nicholas.

They made quick time to King and Queen Street. Kids were about, home from school. Women, home from the market, were dragging some kids indoors with them. Coming to a halt at Emma's front door, Nicholas heard a woman call. He turned. From the open window of her upstairs bedroom, old Mrs Duncalfe, habitual observer of the passing scene, let herself go.

' 'Ere, what's goin' on? More of you gents, a copper as well? It ain't respectable. I seen the first one come an' go. The second one's still there. Your turn now, is it? I never thought Emma Carter – '

'It's nothing like that,' said Nicholas. 'What was the first man like?'

'Gas collector. Dunno 'ow she managed to let 'im in, seein' she was out an' didn't get back till after 'e'd gone. I've seen you before, an' the bloke that was with 'er, the one that's in there now. It ain't respectable.'

'Nothing to worry about, Mrs Duncalfe,' said Nicholas. Emma appeared then, she had heard his voice.

'Nicholas? What's happened?'

'We'll come in,' said Nicholas, and he and Harry went in. Emma closed the door.

'Has something gone wrong?' she asked.

'Looks like it,' said Chapman, rising from a chair.

'He's been here,' said Nicholas, 'he finished his round

329

at three-thirty and his superintendent gave him the rest of the afternoon off. He let himself in – '

'Who said?' asked Chapman.

'Mrs Carter's neighbour, Mrs Duncalfe,' said Nicholas. 'He came and went before you both arrived. He used the spare key, of course.'

'He's been in here?' breathed Emma.

'Yes, but for what reason? What was the point? Finding you weren't at home, why did he come in?' Nicholas's mind raced, trying to work out what the man's intentions had been. To call on Emma and tell her he could put her meter right? To gain entry in that way and then strangle her? No, Harry Bradshaw was right, it would have left him wide open. Finding Emma not at home, he had let himself in. For a purpose. What purpose? He could only have been in the place for a few minutes. He'd been lucky that Emma and Chapman hadn't walked in on him.

'Once he was in,' said Chapman, 'why didn't he simply wait for Mrs Carter? He wasn't to know I'd be with her.'

'Well,' ventured Harry, 'as I said to Sergeant Chamberlain, I don't think – ' He checked. Emma managed a weak smile.

'That he'd have murdered me at this time of day?'

'Ruddy hell,' said Chapman.

'If he's gone home, he'll have walked into our arms,' said Nicholas, 'but I don't think he has. He had a reason for telling his wife he'd be late because of overtime. How late, I wonder? After dark? Jesus, that's it, he's going to come back.'

'Won't work,' said Chapman. 'Mrs Carter keeps her door bolted after dark. The spare key's no good to him. He knows it. He's tried it.'

'Wait,' said Emma, and hastened to her kitchen. She came back with a strange expression on her face. 'It's there,' she said, 'on the dresser shelf, where I normally keep it.'

'He's put it back?' said Nicholas.

'He's put it back,' said Emma.

'Mind if I butt in?' asked Harry.

'Go ahead,' said Nicholas, 'help us with our enquiries. You've got some standing as a local arm of the law.'

'I think you've got a point, about him comin' back,' said Harry. 'He could have had a new key cut, of course, but from what you told me and what's just been mentioned, he knows Mrs Carter bolts her door at night. So if he is comin' back, he's worked out his own way of gettin' in. He can't get into her yard and to her back door without climbing her wall from someone else's yard. Even if he could, he knows her back door is bound to be bolted. Is that right, Mrs Carter?'

'Yes,' said Emma, quite aware the talk was all about how Herbert Stephens might be planning to murder her. It had its effect on her nerves, but she remained calm. She had only to look at Nicholas to feel she was in good hands.

'So if he's up against bolted doors front and back,' said Harry, 'there's only one way he could get in.'

'I'm following you,' said Nicholas, 'it's his obvious choice.'

'Window,' said Chapman, 'either front or back.'

'Front,' said Nicholas, 'he'll never get into the yard, not without first entering someone else's house behind this one to get into their yard. Let's see.' He moved to the living-room window that looked out onto the street. The strong catch securing top and bottom frames had been released. 'So that's why he came in. If Mrs Carter had been here, he'd have made her meter his reason for calling, and he'd have fiddled about with it until he found an opportunity to release this catch, in the hope, of course, that she wouldn't notice it when she drew her curtains. That settles it as far as I'm concerned, it's convinced me he'll be back tonight.'

'Right,' said Chapman, 'but until then? What's he goin' to do, walk the streets?'

'Tuck himself away?' suggested Emma.

'I can't see him walking the streets or tucking himself

away, not for that amount of time,' said Nicholas, 'but I can see him losing himself in surroundings where he could thoroughly enjoy his mood of anticipation. There was Mabel Shipman, Frank.'

'Poor tart,' said Chapman.

'Yes,' said Nicholas, 'and what's more reasonable than to suggest he knows others like her, that he'll spend hours with one of them, one with a back room of her own somewhere around Soho or the East End? That would take him right out of South London, and give him thoughts about the kind of prostitute who'd give him an alibi. I'd say he could easily confuse his wife about the time he finally arrived home. We know that that can't happen now, but he doesn't, not unless he has gone home.'

'Dear me, your imagination, Sergeant Chamberlain,' murmured Emma.

'It's assumptions, Mrs Carter,' said Harry, 'you have to start somewhere, and you start with assumptions and keep workin' on them till you hit the bulls-eye.'

'I like imaginative assumptions,' said Emma. 'What about my window catch?'

'Leave it as it is,' said Nicholas. 'I'm going to Amelia Street with Frank, to see if Stephens did walk into our arms. Inspector Greaves may be there now, in any case. I'm going to ask Constable Bradshaw to stay with you.' He would have liked to stay with Emma himself, to talk to her, to enjoy her remarkable air of calmness and her total lack of fear or hysteria. 'But leave the catch as it is, Mrs Carter.'

Emma made a little face because he was being so much the formal policeman. He was going to let Herbert Stephens finally and conclusively trap himself, and in that there was a reason for a small smile, wasn't there? Now, why should a small smile be important to her at a moment when a decision to trap a murderer made everything else so trivial by comparison?

'Very well,' she said.

'I'll be back,' said Nicholas.

'Thank you.'

'Stay with her until then, will you, Harry?' said Nicholas.

'Rely on it,' said Harry, liking Emma and her composure.

'Come on, Frank, let's be on our way,' said Nicholas. But the weakness of a man in love surfaced then, although a woman would not have seen it as a weakness. 'No, you stay too, I'll feel happier if both of you are here. We can't trust all our assumptions.'

Inspector Greaves was pacing about like a growling grizzly bear with toothache. He had Detective-Sergeant Arnold with him. Also present were the two CID men who had been lying in wait. The Inspector pounced on Nicholas, who gave him a coherent and detailed account of events. Since Stephens had put in no appearance, and since his intentions could only be a matter of guesswork, the Inspector was in favour of immediate action while agreeing on precautions relating to the released window catch. Nevertheless, he could not neglect what was fact, that a maniac was at large and quite capable of murderous mayhem before making a further attempt to get at Mrs Carter. He went back to the Yard, taking Nicholas with him, and leaving Arnold in charge of the other two men. At the Yard, he took steps to alert police stations north and south of the river, and he gave them a comprehensive description of the wanted man.

'It doesn't look like he's comin', Mum,' said Trary. It was getting dark.

'Well, he only said he might pop in,' murmured Maggie, applying the final touches to Daisy's hair with a brush. 'He didn't say definite.'

' 'Ave I got to go to bed wivout seein' 'Arry?' asked Daisy.

'Yes, it seems like it,' said Maggie, 'and if you call him Harry once more, you little mischief, you'll 'ave to have a smack.'

'Crikey, when I'm only little?' said Daisy.

'You'll soon be able to call 'im dad,' said Meg.

'That's when Mum marries 'im,' said Lily informatively.

'I expect it's nice marryin' 'Arry,' said Daisy, and received a little thump on her bottom from the hairbrush. She giggled.

'You'll feel it next time,' said Maggie, but she was in no mood to be stern. The Lord had been good to her and her girls. They didn't look hungry any more, nor shabby. Only weeks ago she had been almost as far down as a mother could go in providing for her children. The workhouse had loomed. Some mothers sold themselves to avoid that. Wasn't it strange how the worry and hardship of poverty had disappeared in just a few weeks, to turn girls with hungry eyes into girls alive with mischief and giggles? And look at Trary, always the brightest and bravest of them even when things were at their worst, and now brighter than ever. Those eyes of hers always told a story. No wonder Bobby had said only yesterday, 'I'm done for, I am, Mrs Wilson. I don't mind Trary havin' one eye like hers, but two together, well, is it fair on a bloke? I don't know I'm ever goin' to be able to say no to 'er. What a life for a man like me that's got a kind jam tart. I'll just 'ave to give in to it, I suppose it could be a happy death.'

Luck had changed for the better on a particular day, the day Harry had called for the first time, and Bobby had later arrived with a box of food on his head. Trary would never forget that moment.

Maggie smiled.

'Penny for 'em, Mum,' said Meg.

'That Bobby,' said Maggie.

'I likes Bobby,' said Daisy.

'He's so funny,' said Maggie.

'I don't know any boy more daft,' said Trary.

'Oh, don't you want 'im, Trary, could I marry 'im when I'm grown up?' asked Lily.

'I'll ask him,' said Trary.

'Could Lily an' me both marry 'im?' asked Daisy.

334

'No, you couldn't,' said Maggie, 'now up to bed with you.' She ushered her younger girls up to bed.

Harry didn't appear at all. Trary knew her mum was a little disappointed. She was making herself look very nice these days. Trary wondered what had stopped her future step-father from popping in.

The house lay in darkness. It was a little after ten. The night was warm, the night sky heavy, with cloud blanketing the new moon and far-off stars. King and Queen Street awaited the turn-out from the pub in Browning Street. A shadow blotted out the best part of a downstairs window. Fingernails made a fractional insertion into the crack between the lower window frame and the sill. Strong fingers pressed and dragged. The window slid slowly up with the tiniest of creaks. When it was fully open, the man stood listening. He looked left, and then right. He did not hurry. It was thirty seconds before he began to climb in, at which point he heard footsteps. He completed his climb over the sill, straightened up, turned, and without haste he quietly closed the window. He stood in the darkness, waiting and listening. A man passed by the house.

Inside Emma's living-room, his eyes adjusted themselves to its darkness, and Herbert Stephens moved slowly and silently forward. They came at him then, Nicholas, Chapman and Harry. A fourth man, Detective-Sergeant Arnold, applied a struck match to the gas lamp. The room sprang into light. Stephens was a raging bull, his blue eyes no longer mild, but hard, glassy and bulging. Nicholas, Chapman and Harry could scarcely hold him. With a muted roar he broke free, hurled himself across the room and snatched the brass-handled poker from the fireside companion set. He launched himself at Nichclas, the poker flailing murderously. Nicholas, keyed-up, had only a fraction of a second in which to save himself from being brained. His reflexes sent him forward to meet maniacal force, and his head and shoulders ducked low. The poker whistled above him and his head thudded into the man's stomach. There was another muted roar and the bull staggered. Nicholas pitched downwards. Chapman leapt, his head low too, and wound his arms around Stephens' ribs. The poker whirled back for a killing blow. Harry smashed downwards with drawn truncheon and caught the poker in mid-air. Chapman held on, head buried in the man's chest, his shoulders pushing. The wavering poker straightened and was aimed point down at Chapman's bent back. Harry smashed again with his truncheon. Nicholas was up, and Arnold joined the mêlée. The raging bull was smothered, but they could not bring him down, or check his strange muted roars. Harry struck again, and his truncheon took Stephens full in the back of his knees. He fell like a pole-axed gladiator, but he raged about over the floor with the CID men trying to smother him. Furniture crashed. Harry had no option but to smite the bull senseless. It took more than one blow of his truncheon.

Upstairs, Inspector Greaves and Emma were listening. They heard the sounds of the frenzied struggle subside to a momentary silence. Then they heard Nicholas's voice.

'That's Samson? Thank God I'm not Delilah.'

The Inspector's moustache moved to a twitch of his lips.

'I'll give him Delilah.'

'No, no, Inspector, I like to think there's a very nice sense of humour inhabiting Scotland Yard. And thank you for being with me up here, thank you for your company and comfort.'

Emma, of course, was working on behalf of Nicholas.

In Stephens' pockets they found a black silk stocking and a five-inch penknife of the finest Sheffield steel, its long primary blade honed to razor-like sharpness. From Stephens himself they got nothing at all, not a single word, only a vacant stare from blue eyes as mild as a September sky. Manacled, he was taken to Rodney Road police station, and from there to Scotland Yard.

'Goodnight, Emma, can't thank you enough,' said Nicholas on leaving her house.

'Goodnight, Nicholas.'

'You'll be required to make a statement, a long one.'

'I'll endure that, the worst is over. When am I to make the statement?'

'I'll call on you.'

'Call on me. How kind. Goodnight Nicholas.'

'Take care,' he said automatically, and left.

CHAPTER TWENTY-SEVEN

Much to Emma's embarrassment and disgust, the following day's papers made her the heroine of the hour. Inspector Greaves and Detective-Sergeant Chamberlain of Scotland Yard were quoted as being unstinting in their praise of her. Sergeant Chamberlain, responsible for the arrest, paid her particular tribute, all in respect of the apprehension of an unnamed man who was to help the police with their enquiries. One reporter had found out she was a suffragette, and he had obtained a tribute from Mrs Pankhurst herself.

'Mrs Emma Carter,' Mrs Pankhurst was quoted as saying, 'is one of our most valiant members. We are proud of her.'

Emma fixed her mind on the perfidy of Nicholas. He was responsible for all this, she was sure. You wait, she said to herself, I'll make your life not worth living.

She was appalled by the sight of reporters outside her front door when she was about to leave for work. She fled them. But Hurlocks provided no respite from embarrassment. Staff and management converged on her from all directions, expressing fulsome admiration.

'But I didn't do anything, except to identify him as the man who bought stockings from us.'

'That's not what the papers say, Mrs Carter,' said the managing director, 'nor what the police say. Well done.'

'But the man hasn't been charged yet.'

'I'm sure he will be. Yes, very well done, Mrs Carter.'

Emma could hardly wait to get her own back on Nicholas. She would have the opportunity for that when she made her statement. But his perfidy continued, for it was Detective-Sergeant Arnold who called about this, not Nicholas. For her convenience, would she like to make her statement at Rodney Road police station in the presence of Inspector Greaves on Monday afternoon.

'Certainly not,' said Emma.

'Beg your pardon, Mrs Carter?'

'I said certainly not.'

'Sorry, Mrs Carter, but – '

'I was told by Detective-Sergeant Chamberlain that he would take my statement.'

'Were you?'

Emma thought. She frowned. No, he had not actually told her that, he had simply said he would call on her about it.

'Where is Sergeant Chamberlain?'

'He's a bit busy with the suspect.'

'I see. Very well, Monday afternoon at the police station, then.'

'Two-thirty, Mrs Carter.'

'Very well,' said Emma.

Harry received a pat on the back from the police superintendent, which meant that in two months time he would receive his promotion to sergeant. Maggie was utterly happy for him, her affection for him growing each day. Trary, whose affections had been stirred from the beginning, was utterly proud of him. Meg kissed him, while Daisy and Lily were awe-struck. Bobby, meeting him on his beat, stopped him and asked to shake his hand.

'A man's got to shake 'ands with another man, Mr Bradshaw.'

'Man to man, is it, Bobby?'

'A bit more than that,' said Bobby. 'Well, the way I'm planning things, you're goin' to be me future dad-in-law.'

'Does Trary know?' smiled Harry.

'What a girl,' said Bobby. 'She's playin' Nelson now, she

339

keeps turnin' a blind eye to her destiny. I've told 'er it's no good fightin' it, but you know Trary, Mr Bradshaw, she's goin' to fight it all the way till it 'appens. It's her pride. I've never seen any girl put her nose up in the air more than Trary. You ever seen 'er do that?'

'Yes, I've seen her, Bobby.'

'Trouble is, that when she does it she looks prettier than ever. Man to man, Mr Bradshaw, I'm done for. Still, Mrs Wilson agrees with me, it could be a happy death. Well, so long, Mr Bradshaw, glad about yer promotion, an' you've got friends down the market that's pleased for you. Oh, and me dad's goin' straight permanent.'

'Permanent?' enquired Harry.

'It'd better be permanent, or it'll be my duty, as his only son, to nail 'is feet to me mum's kitchen floor.'

'Good luck, Bobby.'

At the Brixton roller-skating rink on Saturday afternoon, Trary and Bobby took a breather to allow Trary to treat her talking boy to tea and a fruit bun.

'You don't have to do that, Trary, I'm earnin' a bit from me mum, remember, and you're still a girl that's poor.'

'Mum said – well, she's treatin' us both, she's given me a shilling.' Trary hid the fun of the game by adding solemnly, 'She says you're a dear boy – '

'She says what?'

'Yes, she said "What a dear boy young Bobby is, bless 'is cotton socks, treat him to a nice currant bun."'

'I'll have to talk to your mum,' said Bobby, and gave the order to the larky waitress, who did a bit of cheeky give-and-take with him before departing, much to Trary's disdain. Up in the air went her nose. 'Yes, I'll have to talk to your mum,' repeated Bobby. 'Something's gone to her head, and it's made her mix me up with some Sunday School kid in a sailor suit. It's probably bein' in love. I know how she feels, I don't know what I'm doin' meself sometimes.'

'Are you speakin' to me, Bobby Reeves, or that common girl?'

'Well, you have to say how's yer father to her, Trary, or – '

'You've said all that before. Oh, I just remembered,' Trary perked up, 'the wedding's goin' to be the first Saturday of our school holidays.'

'You sure?' said Bobby.

'Of course I'm sure.'

'Well, I'm glad you've let me know,' said Bobby, 'or I might not 'ave turned up. To be candid – '

'What?'

'Yes, to be candid,' said Bobby, 'I didn't even know we were engaged. I know we've talked about our destiny, but – hold on, you sure we can get married at our ages? And can we afford it?'

'Well, if you don't take the cake,' said Trary.

'It's buns,' said the waitress, reappearing with the order, and Trary went aloof while the tea and buns were set out on the table amid a rendering of the *Skaters' Waltz* by the band. 'Don't get fat,' said the waitress, and winked at Bobby before departing again.

'Ugh to her,' said Trary.

'Still, she don't give us stale buns,' said Bobby. 'Anyway, Trary, about our weddin', are you sure – '

'Bobby Reeves, you get dafter all the time. And more grinnin'. Don't think I can't see you're grinnin'. Is what you said supposed to be funny?'

'Gettin' married's not funny, Trary, it's our life's work. But I think we ought to wait a bit, say until I'm – '

'D'you want me to fill your face with my currant bun?' asked Trary.

'Don't you want to wait, then?' asked Bobby.

Trary, not for the first time since she'd known him, clapped a hand to her mouth and smothered shrieks.

341

Oh, that boy, look at him, he'll be my death. She cleared her throat, 'One day, Bobby Reeves, you'll be carted off to a loony bin, you will. Boys your age don't talk to girls my age about gettin' married, you blessed lump. If you must know, I 'appened to be speakin' of my mother and Mr Harry Bradshaw, and of their weddin'. Afterwards, they're goin' to Eastbourne on honeymoon, while I look after Daisy, Lily an' Meg. Then when they come back, we're all movin' to our new house in Herne Hill. My new dad's selling his house in Westmoreland Road, and he and mum are buyin' the new one between them. Mum's ever so pleased about that. Oh, and you're gettin' a special invite to the weddin'. I don't know why, but mum seems to like you.'

'It's mutual,' said Bobby. 'What's special about the invite?'

'Well,' said Trary, consuming her bun, 'me an' my sisters are goin' to be bridesmaids, and you're goin' to be a pageboy, like they have in posh weddings. Have you got a blue velvet suit with a lace collar and knickerbockers, and can you get your hair curled? Mum wants you to look pretty. Oh, and Daisy an' Lily asked if they could both marry you when they're older, poor things.'

'Could you say all that again, and more slowly?' asked Bobby.

'Mum said you'd be lovely as a pageboy, specially in blue velvet.'

'No, she didn't,' said Bobby.

'Yes, she did. She said, "Oh, that Bobby, he'll make a lovely pageboy." But she did ask me to ask you not to wear a box on your head. I could curl your hair for you at home one evenin', if you like.'

Bobby finished his bun and looked at the girl who had inspired him to put his foot down with his work-shy dad. Her brown eyes were bright with glee. What a performer.

'Trary Wilson, you're makin' an Aunt Sally of me.

I'll get me own back.'

'You'll be lucky.'

'All right, quits,' said Bobby. 'Tell you what, last one round the rink pays the tram fares 'ome.'

Challenges excited Trary, especially challenges from Bobby. They got up and clumped their way over the carpet to the rink. With the band playing a gallop, off they went, weaving their way around other skaters, Bobby quickly in the lead, the much improved Trary on his heels, laughing and exhilarated. The rink, the rendezvous of the young, was a sea of movement. Bobby went at speed, and Trary's skirt whipped as she raced after him. Skate crossing over skate, they executed fast turns, Bobby making a dash for the finish. There he described a swishing circle and came to a full stop. Trary skated straight into his arms, and Bobby kissed her, right on her mouth. Girls yelled in delight at them, and boys whistled.

'Oh, you cheeky devil!' cried Trary.

'I'll give you pageboy,' said Bobby.

'Take that,' said Trary, and handed out a push. Bobby wobbled backwards, grabbed at her, and they fell together. Boys and girls swerved around them, shouting with laughter.

'Give 'im another, Trary!'

Trary sat up, face flushed, eyes dancing, 'Oh, you 'ooligan, wait till I tell mum!' she gasped.

'Tell her what?' said Bobby. 'Are we engaged, then? I still think we ought to wait a bit. Still, I suppose it's our destiny.'

'Oh, you daft lump,' said Trary, and sat there, helpless with laughter, a young girl full of the joys of living.

At the local police station on Monday afternoon, Emma had her long statement read out to her by Detective-Sergeant Arnold, with Inspector Greaves present and Nicholas still an absentee. The latter fact quite vexed her. Something had to be done about that gentleman.

Finding the statement in order, she signed it. 'That's all for the time being?' she asked.

'Until the court proceedings,' said Inspector Greaves. 'It's my pleasure to inform you, Mrs Carter, that we owe you considerably.'

Emma shook her head, 'May I ask if the prisoner's confessed?'

'Not yet,' said the Inspector, and advised her in ponderous fashion that Stephens was trying to climb into the heavyweight division by declaring he couldn't remember a thing about what he had done to seriously offend the law. His recollections of said capital crimes were nil. By which forgetfulness he was hoping to be committed to a criminal asylum.

'Doesn't he remember why he chose fair-haired women, why he cut a strand of their hair off?' asked Emma.

'He shakes his head. In all my experience, Mrs Carter, I've never seen any prisoner do a better job of shakin' his head. But we're persistin' patient and methodical, you might say. We're in helpful possession of the silk stocking and sharp-bladed penknife duly found on him, which can be presented as items relatin' to premeditation. Which could to a jury accordingly dispose of his suggestions that he must 'ave suffered brainstorms. That's 'eavyweight division, Mrs Carter, brainstorms.'

'Yes, I suppose so,' said Emma. 'Inspector, I'm relieved your men weren't badly hurt. Where's Sergeant Chamberlain at the moment?'

'Doin' most of the work on the prisoner,' said Inspector Greaves.

'I see,' said Emma, and made up her mind that what must be done to the absent gentleman, she must do herself.

An hour after she arrived home, a messenger boy called with a presentation bouquet of red roses and an accompanying letter. From Nicholas.

Dear Emma,

I think you deserve something more than thanks for all your help. If anything pleasant came out of this case, it was getting to know you. I thought about letting you get on with your private life, but if your friend is only a friend, I think I'll give him some competition. I have to see you, in any case. Will you let me know when it's convenient to call? Best wishes and affectionate regards, Nicholas.

Affectionate? That was all? We'll see about that, said Emma to herself, and replied briefly but graciously.

Dear Nicholas,

I was touched by your gift of roses, they're lovely. How kind of you. Please come to tea on Sunday. Four-thirty. Yours sincerely, Emma. PS. You wait.

Wait? What for? That was the first question Nicholas, newly promoted to Detective-Inspector, asked when he arrived on Sunday afternoon. So Emma, of course, took him to task for talking to newspapers about her and accordingly being responsible for reporters besieging her door. Nothing to do with me, said Nicholas, blame someone else at the Yard. And by the way, he said, you're up for the reward. What reward? For help and information leading directly to the capture of Herbert Stephens. Five hundred pounds. Who says so? I do, said Nicholas, I've put your name forward and you'll get it. Oh, you dear man, said Emma. But remembering something had to be done about him, she asked if he truly believed women should have the same rights as men. Nicholas said yes, as long as they didn't sneak in a few extra, of which they were perfectly capable. Well, we're smarter, of course, said Emma, but do you truly believe? Yes, said Nicholas. Good, said Emma, then may I have the right of asking you to marry me? Nicholas tottered. Emma said she didn't have much to offer a Detective-Inspector except herself, although she might shortly come into a fortune of five hundred pounds. Were herself and five hundred pounds enough for him?

Nicholas, hardly able to believe she was his, fell over. Well, almost.

Emma laughed.

But she still kept one thing to herself. She didn't want him to be cross with her, not now. The fact was she had known it was Alf Barker who followed her home that night. She'd recognized his voice when he said goodnight to her, but if she'd admitted it she'd have had no reason to ask Nicholas to call on her at a time when she was feeling stupidly fretful about his absence from her life.

Herbert Stephens was committed at a magistrates' court for trial at the Old Bailey. There he pleaded guilty. His counsel pleaded guilty but insane. The judge, guided by medical reports, accepted the plea. It saved Linda Jennings going into the witness box, and more importantly for her, it saved all the darker details of Mabel Shipman's life being served up to the world.

Coming out of school with Jane Atkins, Trary saw Bobby turning the corner into West Square. He gave her a cheerful wave.

'Oh, come on, Trary,' said Jane, 'his name's not really Dick Turpin, I bet it's not. Who is he really?'

Trary saw Bobby's smile, his long walking legs, and how he looked as if the world was made for fun and laughter. Her young heart did a little flip.

346

'He's mine,' she said, and ran across to meet him. Bobby put out his hand and she took it.

He walked her home. She was fourteen, and at fourteen it was her destiny to be holding hands with him.

THE END

TWO FOR THREE FARTHINGS

BY MARY JANE STAPLES

Horace was ten, Ethel seven, when Jim Cooper, home from the trenches, minus an arm and just about managing on his own, found them huddled in a doorway on a wet night in Walworth. Slightly against his better judgement he took them in, fed them cocoa, and put them to sleep in his bed. A few days later he found that – somehow – he had become the unofficial guardian of Horace and Ethel. It was him, the orphanage, or separation for the gutsy little pair who would have to be farmed out to anyone who would take them, and Jim felt a sudden affinity for the two cheeky cockney kids. The first thing he had to do was find fresh lodgings for them all.

Miss Rebecca Pilgrim was a woman of strict Victorian principles, eminently respectable, and determined to keep her privacy intact. She had reckoned without her new lodgers – Horace, Ethel and, above all, the irrepressible Jim Cooper. And thus began the humanising of Miss Pilgrim, who turned out to be younger, prettier, and far gentler than any of them had suspected.

0 552 13635 2

OUR EMILY

BY MARY JANE STAPLES

Emily had been a quite horrible child. Pushy, rough, and none too clean (for it must have been Emily who passed on her head-lice to the Adams family), she had been the bane of Mrs Adams and her children who lived next door, and especially she had been a trial to Boots, who had avoided her whenever he could.

But Emily grown-up was a different matter. She was still a cockney girl, but now she had a certain elegance, a style. The fighting toughness was still there – and she needed it. For Boots, back from the trenches, was blind, and Emily was to prove the mainstay, the breadwinner, and the love of his life.

Here again is the Adams family from DOWN LAMBETH WAY – Chinese Lady determined more than ever to be respectable, Tommy facing unemployment, and Sammy well on the way to becoming a street market tycoon. And above all here is our Emily.

0 552 13444 9

RUTH APPLEBY

BY ELVI RHODES

At twelve she stood by her mother's grave on a bleak Yorkshire moor. Life, as the daughter of a Victorian millhand, had never been easy, but now she was mother and housekeeper both to the little family left behind.

As one tribulation after another beset her life, so a longing, a determination, grew – to venture out into a new world of independence and adventure, and when the chance came she seized it. America, even on the brink of civil war, was to offer a challenge that Ruth was ready to accept, and a love, not easy, but glorious and triumphant.

A giant of a book – about a woman who gave herself unstintingly – in love, in war, in the embracing of a new life in a vibrant land.

0 552 12803 1

THE MOSES CHILD

BY AUDREY REIMANN

Oliver Wainwright was sixteen when he first set eyes on Florence Mawdesley. He was hiding in the water of the lake on Sir Philip Oldfield's land – taking refuge after stealing a mallard duck.

She was standing at the water's edge, silk-gowned, sheltered by her parasol, the privileged, aristocratic granddaughter of Sir Philip Oldfield. Oliver thought he had never seen anyone so lovely.

That same day he ran away – left the estate and the life of servitude that had killed his father – and took the first steps towards his future – as a self-made cotton king, a mill owner, a man of property. It was in the mill that he met Rosie, dark, warm, beautiful, who began to cast her spell over him, even though she was a married woman.

But even as he rose to power – fighting Sir Philip Oldfield's vicious and vindictive revenge every inch of the way – he never forgot the vision of the beautiful girl at the water's edge.

0 552 13521 6

A SELECTED LIST OF FINE TITLES
AVAILABLE FROM CORGI BOOKS

THE PRICES SHOWN BELOW WERE CORRECT AT THE TIME OF
GOING TO PRESS. HOWEVER TRANSWORLD PUBLISHERS RESERVE
THE RIGHT TO SHOW NEW RETAIL PRICES ON COVERS WHICH MAY
DIFFER FROM THOSE PREVIOUSLY ADVERTISED IN THE TEXT OR
ELSEWHERE.

☐	13600 X	The Sisters O'Donnell	*Lyn Andrews*	£3.99
☐	13482 1	The White Empress	*Lyn Andrews*	£3.99
☐	13230 6	An Equal Chance	*Brenda Clarke*	£3.99
☐	12887 2	Shake Down The Stars	*Frances Donnelly*	£3.99
☐	13384 1	A Whisper to the Living	*Ruth Hamilton*	£3.50
☐	13616 6	With Love from Ma Maguire	*Ruth Hamilton*	£3.99
☐	12607 1	Doctor Rose	*Elvi Rhodes*	£2.99
☐	13185 7	The Golden Girls	*Elvi Rhodes*	£3.99
☐	13481 3	The House of Bonneau	*Elvi Rhodes*	£3.99
☐	13309 4	Madeleine	*Elvi Rhodes*	£3.99
☐	12367 6	Opal	*Elvi Rhodes*	£2.99
☐	12803 1	Ruth Appleby	*Elvi Rhodes*	£4.99
☐	13521 6	The Moses Child	*Audrey Reimann*	£3.50
☐	13413 9	The Quiet War of Rebecca Sheldon	*Kathleen Rowntree*	£3.99
☐	13557 7	Brief Shining	*Kathleen Rowntree*	£3.99
☐	12375 7	A Scattering of Daisies	*Susan Sallis*	£3.99
☐	12579 2	The Daffodils of Newent	*Susan Sallis*	£3.99
☐	12880 5	Bluebell Windows	*Susan Sallis*	£3.99
☐	13136 9	Rosemary For Remembrance	*Susan Sallis*	£3.99
☐	13346 2	Summer Visitors	*Susan Sallis*	£3.99
☐	13545 3	By Sun and Candlelight	*Susan Sallis*	£3.99
☐	13299 3	Down Lambeth Way	*Mary Jane Staples*	£3.99
☐	13573 9	King of Camberwell	*Mary Jane Staples*	£3.99
☐	13444 9	Our Emily	*Mary Jane Staples*	£3.99
☐	13635 2	Two For Three Farthings	*Mary Jane Staples*	£3.99

All Corgi/Bantam Books are available at your bookshop or newsagent, or can be
ordered from the following address:
Corgi/Bantam Books,
Cash Sales Department,
P.O. Box 11, Falmouth, Cornwall TR10 9EN

Please send a cheque or postal order (no currency) and allow 80p for postage and
packing for the first book plus 20p for each additional book ordered up to a maximum
charge of £2.00 in UK.

B.F.P.O. customers please allow 80p for the first book and 20p for each additional
book.

Overseas customers, including Eire, please allow £1.50 for postage and packing for
the first book, £1.00 for the second book, and 30p for each subsequent title ordered.

NAME (Block Letters) ....

ADDRESS ....

....